"*Triumff* is a witch's brew of alternate history, hocus pocus, cracking action and cheesy gags. Reads like *Blackadder* crossed with Neal Stephenson. It's a Kind of Magick – don't miss it."

Stephen Baxter

"Endlessly inventive, joyously irreverent, drenched with adrenaline and wicked humour, Dan Abnett's *Triumff* is a brilliant occult-comedy-historical adventure that's true to the best traditions of the genres it so eagerly devours."

Mike Carey

"If there's one thing Abnett does well, it's write a kick-butt action sequence."

JP Frantz, SF Signal

"The cinematic scope and dizzying vision we're shown puts most of the recent SF movie epics into deep shade… Dan Abnett entertains from the ground up."

Nathan Brazil, SF Site

"Dan Abnett is brilliant."

SFX

DAN ABNETT

Triumff

HER MAJESTY'S HERO

**ANGRY
ROBOT**

ANGRY ROBOT

A division of HarperCollins*Publishers*
77-85 Fulham Palace Road,
London W6 8JB
UK

www.angryrobotbooks.com
00VII

First published by Angry Robot 2009
1

A catalogue record for this book is available
from the British Library

ISBN-13: 978 0 00 732769 0

Set in Meridian by Argh! Nottingham

Class Ltd, St Ives plc

For Nik,
first and only
(again)

TRIUMFF
Her Majesty's Hero

Being the true and AUTHENTICK account of the expl'ts
and
incid'nts following the RE-TURN to London
of
Sir Rupert Triumff, adventurer,
from his CELEBRATED Voyage of Discovery
to the Meridional Climes.
Never before made publick.

Given in this, my hand, this XXIIIrd day of APRILE,
XX hundred and X Anno Domini,
in the splendid reign of the thirtieth Gloriana.

VIVAT REGINA!

Wllm Beaver, esq.

EDITOR'S NOTICE.
To the Great Variety of Readers.

FOR THOSE READERS unfamiliar with the affairs and nature of the Anglo-Hispanic Unity, care has been taken to furnish Master Beaver's manuscript with footnotes and commentary to make all such matters comprehensible.

However, this editor has been charged with making the following basic facts known from the outset. The Anglo-Hispanic Unity, the longest-lasting and most powerful Empire ever to arise upon this terrestrial stage, was founded in the year Fifteen Hundred and Seventy-Five, following the marriage of Queen Elizabeth the First of England to King Philip the Second of Spain. Said union of power and lands, including as it did the virginal tracts of the New World, soon eclipsed all other nations of the globe, and has persisted since, through a worthy line of potent female monarchs, all styled "Elizabeth Gloriana".

The other matter that helped to preserve the preeminence of the Unity was, of course, the Renaissance, which thoroughly reawakened the Sublime Lore of Magick, dormant since Antiquity. The schools and employment of the Esoteric Arte of Magick were monopolised by the

Church and Church-Guilds of England, and ensured the Unity's absolute command and superiority over all the World, especially the British bits of the Unity.

This didn't please the Spanish bits very much at all. But that's another story.

Part of this one, in fact.

THE PERSONS OF THIS STORY.

SIR RUPERT TRIUMFF, gentleman adventurer and lately come discoverer of The Vast Southerly Continent

AGNEW, his man

LORD CALLUM GULL, Laird of Ben Phie, Captain of the Royal Guard

CARDINAL THOMAS WOOLLY, first minister of Her Majesty's United Church

SIR JOHN HOCKRAKE, Duke of Salisbury, a scoundrel

ROUSTAM ALLASANDRO DE LA VEGA, Regent of Castile, Governor of Toledo, and victor of Lille

ROBERT SLEE, of the Queen's Privy Council

THE DIVINE ALEISTER JASPERS, a junior officer of the United Church

UPTIL, a noble autochthon from foreign climes

DOLL TARESHEET, a notable actress of the Wooden Oh and these parts

NEVILLE DE QUINCEY, a police surgeon and examiner

MOTHER GRUNDY, of the countryside

GIUSEPPE GIUSEPPO, an Italian gentleman of ingenuity

TANTAMOUNT O'BOW, a villain

CATHEAD

& in addition ~

Divers servants, ladies and lords, as well as some personages I might have forgotten in this compilation, along with copious hautboys and tapers, and fanfares on all entrances and exits.

The setting is the present day.

Staged in the modern style.

Vivat Regina!

THE FIRST CHAPTER.
Which is set upon St Dunstan's Day.

It had rained, furiously, for all of the six days leading up to St Dunstan's Day.

Water rattled off slopes of broken slates, streamed like horse-piss from split gutters, cascaded from the points of eaves, boiled like oxtail soup in leaf-choked drains, coursed in foamy breakers across flagged walks, and thumped down drainpipes in biblical quantities. For the same measure of time that it had taken the Good Lord God to manufacture Everything In Creation, the entire city was comprehensively rinsed. There was water, as the Poet had it (the Poet, admittedly, was wont to have it mixed with brandy), everywhere, and every drop of it was obeying Newton's First Law of Apples.

In the rents of Beehive Lane, near Boddy's Bridge, unpotted chimneys guzzled in the rain and doused more than a score of ailing grates. The steep cobbled rise of Garlick Hill became a new tributary to the Thames, and the run-off that washed down it from the foundations of the spice importers' hilltop barns had loose cloves floating in it and tasted like consomme. At Leadenhalle, the rapping of the rain upon the metal roof drove several market traders temporarily psychotic, and deprived many more of their usual cheery dispositions, and so the cheap was suspended until the inclement weather subsided ("if sodden London don't subside first" remarked more than one tired and emotional stall-holder). Many worried that, if the fantastically grim weather persisted, the Great Masque that coming Saturday might itself have to be abandoned. And that didn't bear thinking about.

The Fleet, the Tyburn and the Westbourne all spilled beyond their courses, and enjoyed wild excursions through the streets of the ditch-quarters and the wharfs. More refuse was then moved by force of flood than is in a month by the municipal collectors, though, to be fair, the Noble Guild of Refuse and Shite Handlers had been on a go-slow since 1734, following a dispute over the scale of Yuletide gratuities.

The city's watergates were all choked to drowning point, each gagging like an over-eager sot on an upturned bottle of musket. Conduits thundered with the passing pressure, their stonework trembling, and voided themselves with huge tumult into the Thames, casting up mists of rainbow spray from their cataracts. Men from the Guild of Cisterns and Ducts visited each city conduit daily in turn and stood, dour and drenched by the spray, shaking their heads and tutting.

The Cockpit on Birdcage Walk became so full that the stewards had to open all the public doors to vent the water before gladiation could begin that night. Small boys had been found sailing rival armadas of paper man-o-wars from the pit rails. Even after the stewards' action, some said the only birds worth betting on that night were ducks. When it did eventually occur, the cockfight proved to be a notable and famous bout, featuring a title fight for the Bantam Weight Champion of All London. The contenders were Cocky Joe, a six-pound, experienced fighter trained by John Lyon of Poplar, and Bigge Ben, a twelve-pound newcomer presented by one Thomas Arnes of Peckham. The eventual victor, Bigge Ben, was later disqualified when it was discovered he was a cunningly disguised buzzard, and Cocky Joe reinstated, though by this time he was full of onion and three-quarters roasted.

The rain fell on all. It made no distinctions for rank, and offered no exceptions for situation. It hammered on the un-protected heads of the impoverished and loose of bowel in the jakes of Shite-berne. It drizzled off the leaded glass of the Palace Mews. It fell with a continuance and persistence that was nothing short of impertinent.

From Cornhill to Ludgate, not one thing in the whole Vale of the Thames prospered, except perhaps the osiers and wa-tercress in the marshes.

When one of the wags in the Rouncey Mare off Allhallows Walk remarked upon the fact that there was no superstition associated with so many days of rain before St Dunstan's Eve, it was volubly decided that there bloody well ought to be, and bloody well would be before the tavern closed, so long as liquor sufficiently inspired the collective imagination. In-deed, sometime after ten that night, a handsome and appropriate saying was devised by a drover of advanced years named Boy Simon, but sadly it had been forgotten by the time daylight crept in and announced the dawn of St Dun-stan's Day.

The towers and steeples of a hundred and nine churches shivered at the dismal morning and driving rain, and bells slapped out the hour of daybreak as if the water had softened their clappers. Most of the City's population grimaced in their states of sleep and rolled over. Those up and active through the necessity of their various offices shuddered grimly and went about their business in hats and hoods and long, soggy capes. A carter, late delivering for a fishmonger in Billingsgate, overturned on the corner of Windmill Street, and his entire cargo swam off through the neighbouring byways. Shortly afterwards, a magistrate in Rudlin Circus was painfully thrown when his horse was bitten by a passing turbot. The fishmonger was sanguine, however, as sales of fish had fallen dramatically in the course of the week.

One of the hundred and nine churches tolling out that lubricated morning was St Dunstan's Undershaft, near the New Gate, where the aforementioned saint's day was about to be celebrated. Dunstan, a ninth century Norfolk lacemaker, died piously during the notorious Woolcarder's Revolt of 814, and was canonised in 1853 during the Diet of Cannes. He is the Patron Saint of boundaries and hedges, lacemakers, undergarments and impalement, though not necessarily in that order.

In the damp shade of St Dunstan's porch, valiant observers of the martyr's festival (the eleventh day of May) made garlands of flowers and ribbons, and glumly offered small lace keepsakes showing the saint "being martyred on the sharpened fence" for sale to empty streets. The deluge had kept almost everyone away. Large sections of the regular congregation had found drier things to do, and a promised coach party of pilgrims from the provinces, composed in the main of folk from the popular Christian sects the Orford Doxies and the Exeter Terrestrials, had not materialised.

Even the priestesses in the Temple of the Justified Madonna across the road from St Dunstan's had decided for once to wear clothes. They stood, red-nosed and corset-clad, in the windows of the seminary, and occasionally waved encouragement to the St Dunstan's band across the street. Needless to say, the folk of St Dunstan's didn't wave back.

Two streets behind St Dunstan's, an alley too insignificant to have a name of its own led through the rents to Chitty Yard. It was raining there, too.

The yard was a paved square, forty feet across, flanked on one side by the dingy rears of the rents. To the other three it was enclosed by the back of the once-imposing Chitty House. A small fountain, in the shape of a dismayed griffon, stood at the centre and had been dry for seventy-three years. It was full now, of leaves and rainwater.

The Chittys had come into money late in the previous century, thanks to a small miniver business that had flourished at a time when cuffs and collars were worn hirsute. They had built Chitty House as a headquarters and town residence, and occupied it continuously until the last Chitty had died of fur on the lung twenty years previously. Since then, the building had been a tannery, a hostel for drovers, a bordello (twice), a store for timber, an eating house, and a singularly unsuccessful farrier's (one Joseph Pattersedge, who suffered from chronic hippophobia). Now it was empty, with its rafters open to the weather, and its environs were of interest only to vermin, weary beggars or those in need of privacy.

At dawn on St Dunstan's day, four of the latter were assembled in the hidden yard. One was a diminutive, portly Spaniard from Valladolid, who huddled from the rain under the stoop of the storehouse wing, his ruff and waxed moustache as limp as his expression. He clutched a velvet cape and a plumed hat that did not belong to him. Opposite him, across the yard, stood a rake-thin man of Suffolk descent, an imposing figure over six feet tall, dressed in a simple suit as grim as his countenance. He too held clothes that were not his. Every few seconds, he winced slightly.

The other two individuals in the yard were trying to kill each other.

Lord Callum Gull, Laird of Ben Phie, Captain of the Royal Guard, Scottish to the marrow ("and loyal to the courgette" as the old saying goes), edged around the yard with four feet of basket-hilted steel swinging from his hand. His red hair was plastered to his skull, his linen shirt was sticking to his rangy form, and his breath was rasping through defiantly clenched teeth. He knew well his Livy, his Caesar, his De Studio Militari and his Vegetius. He knew extremely well the finer points of The Art of War, particularly the one on the end of his rapier.

Sir Rupert Triumff, seafarer, Constable of the Gravesend Basin and celebrated discoverer of Australia, was commanding over a yard of sharpened metal of his own. His black locks hung in ringlets around his brow, his shirt had acquired two extra slits since he had put it on that morning, and he was humming a song about the Guinea Coast for no real reason at all. Triumff had once read the title page of Vegetius, owned a risible translation of Livy, and often quoted Caesar, even though he had never been within ten feet of a copy. He was not, at that stage, entirely sure what day it was.

Triumff danced and stumbled around Gull in a way that looked almost, but not quite, deliberate. He tossed his rapier from hand to hand. The gesture suggested he was a nimble, gifted swordsman, but in truth had more to do with the fact that he couldn't remember which hand he was supposed to be using. Each exchange of grip caused the slender witness in black to wince again.

With a snarl, Gull lunged for the umpteenth time, and added another vent to Triumff's left sleeve. Backing up rapidly, Triumff looked down at the gash, tucked his blade under his arm like a cane, and fingered the damaged cloth.

"Fuck," he remarked.

"En garde!" barked Gull, and crossed.

Triumff spun hastily, ducked, and came up again holding his sword by the blade, with the basket grip bobbling threateningly at his adversary. There was a pause. Slowly, Triumff adjusted his depth of field from his opponent to the nearer hilt, noticed the blood dribbling from his fingers, and dropped the rapier smartly.

"Poxy thing!" he said, sucking at his sliced fingertips. Blood collected in his beard, and spattered his doublet, making it look as if he had been punched in the mouth. He continued to complain through his stinging fingers.

Gull tapped Triumff on the breast-bone with the point of his sword. The Scot's black eyes always looked angry, even when he was not. It was said in the Royal Guard House that if Gull's lids were ever peeled back during slumber, he'd still glare with the liquid black eyes of an enraged bullock. Now, his demeanour perfectly matched his natural expression.

"Pick up," he said softly, his words gnawing into the air like acid, "your bloody sword, you cussed knave. Though I'll delight in filleting you, I'd rather do it while there's a blade in your hand."

Triumff looked down at the urging sword tip, and then up at Gull, and nodded.

"Right… right… of course…" he replied, turning to look for his fallen blade. To the side of the yard, the man in black covered his eyes, and started in on the Lord's Prayer, sotto voce. The man in black's expression increasingly resembled that on the face of the fountain's stone griffon, which in turn suggested that the mythical creature had been intimately violated against its will, and without much in the way of warning.

The rapier had rolled to rest in the lea of the fountain bowl. Triumff steadied himself on the griffon's beak as he stooped to recover it. He grasped the weapon in his uninjured hand and straightened up.

Even during his more sober periods, the weapon had been a bother to him. It had been a gift, a reward for his exploits, bestowed upon him by the president of the Royal Cartographical Society. It was a Cantripwork Couteau Suisse, or Schweizer Offiziersmesser, an elegant instrument manufactured to the exacting specifications of the Victorinox Cutlers of Ibach. According to the owner's handbill, which had been packed into the presentation box underneath the velvet padding, the device was capable of auto-selecting any number of tools or blades, which it deployed from its ornate brass basket hilt at the flick of a trigger built into the knurled alox handle. One deft touch made it a sword, or a bottle opener, or a device for removing stones from horses' hooves.

Triumff looked down at his weapon. He noted the Helvetic cross-and-shield emblazoned on the tool's grip, denoting the weapon's fine engineering provenance. He also noted, belatedly, that at some point during the whole dropping-it-and-picking-it-back-up-again process, the trigger had been depressed. The Couteau Suisse was currently less well suited for duelling with an incensed Hibernian swordsman, and more for removing cross-head screws. Triumff swore again. He pressed the trigger. The intricate, jinx-powered mechanism inside the decorative basket hilt whirred, withdrew the screwdriver, and meticulously replaced it with a nail buffer.

Triumff began pressing the trigger repeatedly, and, in quick succession, readied himself to open a can, pluck an eyebrow, and do a little fretwork.

He shook his head and held up his other hand.

"Hang on, hang on," he said. "Arsing thing."

Gull stood his ground, glaring.

"Ever had a go with one of these doo-dabs, Gull?" Triumff asked, depressing the trigger with an increased degree of impatience, and consequently selecting long-nose pliers, a fishing rod, a metric rule, and then an auger. "All very clever and fancy, I'm sure, but it's more trouble than it's worth."

"I'm not one for gadgets," growled Gull.

"Me neither! Me bloody neither!" Triumff agreed vehemently. He clicked the trigger one last time and let out a bright, "Aha!" as the rapier blade snapped back into place.

"Right! There you go!" he declared, flourishing the blade. "That's what I was looking for! As you were!"

The energetic flourish had made his vision spin a little. He shook his head in an effort to clear it, blinked dizzily, and took a step forward. A loose flagstone dipped under his foot, and several pints of brown rainwater gouted up his leg, soaking his breeches. He stumbled, and steadied himself, looked down at the stone, and dabbed dispiritedly at his ruined trousers.

"Watch that, Gull," he said, indicating the flagstone. "Loose flag. You could take a nasty tumble on that."

Tried beyond a threshold of patience he had been sporting to observe even that far, Gull screeched something Caledonian and pejorative, and flew at Triumff. Only fickle fortune positioned Triumff's sword correctly to block the thrust. Gull riposted, and the blades clattered again. He hammered three times more until his sword rebounded from the knurled quillon of Triumff's fluttering weapon.

"Steady on," said Triumff, as if surprised.

Gull threw himself bodily at Triumff, their swords locking like the antlers of rutting stags. He drove Triumff back four or five yards, until the discoverer of Australia slammed hard into the kitchen wall of Chitty House. There, Triumff lurched forward, sweeping his sword around at Gull. It would have been a quite magnificent touché, had it not been for the fact that the Couteau Suisse had become, by then, a letter opener.

With a strangled and vituperative curse, Triumff selected the rapier blade, again, and swung it wildly, but the distraction had been enough. The Captain of the Royal Guard parried easily, and then cut low, slicing a new pocket hole in Triumff's breeches and a flap of skin out of the thigh beneath. Triumff sucked in his breath as blood, diluted by rain, soaked his leggings. Looking down, he found that one breeches leg was stained red and the other brown with mud.

"Motley!" he exclaimed breezily, and then looked in danger of fainting. He slumped back against the kitchen wall and dropped his guard wearily. Gull's sword was immediately at his throat.

"You're beaten, you bastard," hissed Gull, "and what's more, you're pissed. You might at least have done me the honour of duelling me sober."

"Is this all because of those things I said about your sister?" asked Triumff, absently. "And if it is, can you remind me what I actually said?"

"You challenged me, you drunken fool!" Gull growled.

"Oh... really? Then let's just forget it."

Gull stared into Triumff's eyes.

"Not this time," he said. "This time you bleed. This time, I'll give you something to remember me by." Slowly, surgically, Gull drew his rapier-point across Triumff's left cheek. Dark red blood welled up and ran.

"Learn from this, you wastrel. Don't cross me, and if you do, keep up your guard," said Gull. "Though I hear it's not the only thing you can't keep up," he added.

Triumff frowned as the jibe percolated slowly through his drink-crippled comprehension. Then his eyes snapped open, frighteningly sober for the first time.

"You can stuff that opprobrious tattle up your scabby hawsehole!" he exploded. His blade lashed out in a vicious

blur that wrong-footed Gull entirely. The blow was instinctive, angry, and undirected by any conscious thought, and if
it had been struck with the rapier blade rather than a veg-
etable peeler, Gull would have been on his way to his family
mausoleum on the shores of Loch Larn. As it was, severed
air fell away on either side of the small but razor-sharp implement. There was a brief impact, a sound like cabbage
splitting, a yowl, and a spray of blood.

Gull left the yard in a bounding, frantic stride, his portly
Spanish second fluttering in his wake and squeaking, "Señor!
Señor capitan!"

Triumff slid to the flagstones, his back against the wall. He
looked down at something that was cupped in his outstretched hand.

"Gull? Gull, don't go," he called out, weakly. "You've left
an ear behind."

The man in black stalked across to the sprawled drunk.

"Agnew," said Triumff, looking up blearily, "Gull forgot an
ear."

"Really, sir."

Triumff nodded, and then put a hand to his bloody cheek.

"You'd better call me a surgeon, Agnew," he said.

"I'd rather," muttered the older man on reflection, "call
you a silly arse, sir."

At the very same moment that the Laird of Ben Phie was divorced from his left ear in Chitty Yard by means of a novelty
potato peeler, the six days of solid rain came to an end. Spent
clouds, wrung dry, slouched off grumpily towards Shoebury-
ness and the sea. A tearful sun, pale as a smoky candle,
appeared over the Square Mile. The City's mood swung.

At Leadenhalle, the cheap was reconvened amid over-en-
thusiastic announcements of apres-deluge bargains. By the

Gibbon Watergate, on the Embankment, the men of the Cisterns and Ducts Guild slouched back the hoods of their oilskins and exchanged knowing, professional nods that hid their relief. In the stable adjoining the Rouncey Mare, Boy Simon woke up and remembered his own name after only a few minutes' concentration.

The City shook itself dry. Casements creaked open in swollen wood frames. Damp boots were upturned on hearths. The residents of the ditch-quarters began to bail out their homes with a blithe London cheeriness that had been called "blitz spirit" ever since the airship raids of the Prussian Succession. The marshy reek of drowned vegetation that had permeated the City for a week began to be replaced by the reassuringly familiar odour of refuse. In Cambridge Circus, pedestrians skirted a beached sea-bass gasping out its last moments on the cobbles.

Within an hour of the sea-change in the climate, one of the Billingsgate mongers sold a pint of shrimp, and there was considerable rejoicing. Within ninety minutes, a troop of the City Militia in Babcock Gardens began the onerous, though unusual, task of returning the barge Mariette Hartley to the river three hundred yards away. Several of the City's bolder cats were seen for the first time in six days.

Two minutes before St Dunstan's clock tower struck eleven, one of the faithful finally sold a lace memento to a passer-by. The parson of St Dunstan's began a short service of thanks, and his congregation struck up with the Old Seventy-Sixth ("Though the Fence is Sharp, My Lord hath Riches Waiting"). Across the street, the Sisters of the Justified Madonna, who had ceremonially disrobed, pressed most of themselves against the windows, and shouted out messages of congratulation and other heart-warming communiqués.

St Dunstan's flock hurried indoors on the advice of the parson, all except a lingering choirboy, who was later assured by most of the congregation that he was irrevocably destined to have his eyes put out in the Fierce Smithy of Hades.

By noon, the sun had coaxed a mist of evaporation out of the Capital. Every inch of wood: every bridge-post, every newel, every beam, every door in the City groaned and sighed. From the villages and hamlets around the outskirts, it was possible to hear the complaints of the drying metropolis, faintly and distantly, like an elderly relative stumbling out of bed next door. A goat-herd in the Brent Woods, sheltering from the downpour under a broad oak, heard the faraway groaning, and cheered up, anticipating imminent relief from his misery.

At Richmond, the terraces, beds, rows, lawns, mazes, arbours and quincunxes of the Royal Palace blinked away the dew and woke up. Ornamental ponds finally stopped being choppy, and their lily pads drifted to rest, becalmed. The gardeners oiled and unleashed the mower from its lair near the boathouses. The Beefeaters started to whistle as they took off their weatherproofs and cycled off on their patrols. Maids on the south terrace began to beat carpets with wicker paddles, and maids by the wash-house began to hang out a week's worth of damp laundry. Boar and turkey, penned in an enclosure north of the Chase, noted the approach of the Assistant Under-Chef with heavy hearts, and jostled the weakest present to the front.

On a gravel walk along the paddock, Cardinal Woolly of the United Church crunched maze-wards, with two pike-men and a small, obedient civilian in attendance. The cardinal's robes were rich to the point of Papery. The civilian's hose was all but out at the knees. Tugging at his ill-fitting ruff as he followed the cardinal, the civilian moistened the end of his lead-stick on his tongue and pulled open his notebook. He was a nondescript, bearded man with tawny hair, long at the back and absent at the front. His ear was punctuated with a gold ring. His name was Beaver, and being me, your servant the writer, he will have no further words wasted upon him.

"Know then, Master Beaver," said his worship, "that the following declaration may be printed with my approval in your periodical."

"Right ho, Cardinal," quoth I (Wllm Beaver).

The cardinal continued.

"Hereby, it is made known that her most Royal Majesty Queen Elizabeth XXX, Mistress of All Britain, Empress of the Anglo-Español Unity, Defender of the Cantrips, Protector of the Jinx... and so on. You know the form and style, Beaver."

"Ex Ex Ex, uh huh, right ho," I said, nodding.

"Hereby, it is made known that Her Majesty has no comment yet to make on the seriousness of the threat made to the Channel Bridge by the Liberté Gauloise subversives, nor on the unsound rumours reaching our ears from Wiltshire. However, on the matter of the Great Masque this weekend, it is announced that it will now go ahead, thanks to the change in weather. Further, on the subject of the Spanish insistence of an expedition, forthwith, to the new-found Continent, Her Majesty is still awaiting consultation with said Continent's discoverer, Captain Sir Rupert Triumff."

"Tee-Arr-Eye-umff... uh uh. Right ho. Go on, your holiness."

"Sir Rupert maintains that the Terra Australis is a diverting realm, but largely lacking in precious metals or other exploitable resources. Further, its people are said to be ignorant of the ways of ensorcelment. Given the grave hardship of a journey to the New South Lands, he considers further missions there unworthy of the cost and effort. In this, the Privy

Council and the Church are yet to agree. There is much still to be reckoned out. And all, of course, depends upon Sir Rupert presenting his Letters of Pa... Excuse me."

We paused, at the turn of the paddock walk, as a Great Dane the size of a pony shambled across our path, trailing its lead and carrying a rose trellis in its mouth, complete with climbing rose. The cardinal sent one of the pike-men after it. We could hear his calls of "Easy boy, easy boy!" disappearing down towards the lake.

"Any official comment, your worship, on the rumour that Captain Gull of the Royal Huscarls is currently minus an ear?"

"None whatsoever," snapped the cardinal. "Ask him yourself."

"I did," said Beaver.

"What did he say?"

"He didn't appear to hear the question, sir," I admitted.

There was a splash from the direction of the lake. The hound retraced its steps across our path, dragging a chewed halberd instead of the trellis. The cardinal turned to the other pike-man. I closed my book with a shrug. The press conference was over.

The emerald privet of the Inigo Maze stood before us. A blue kite sporting the Royal Crest scudded along above it, its line secured to some moving point amid the leafy walls. We heard the unmistakable sound of female sniggering. Woolly straightened his robes, cleared his throat, and headed for the entrance arch of the maze.

"Your Majesty?" he called gently.

I felt suddenly chilly, despite the sun. I rubbed my beard in a nervous gesture particular to myself, and beat a retreat towards the gatehouse on the City Road.

* * *

Some fourteen miles west of the Palace, the timbered Royal Lodge in Windsor Great Park shook with the sound of tramping boots and yapping bow-hounds, those robust, lugubrious, liver-spotted retrievers from Abyssinia, noted for their reliability as hunting dogs, their extensive dewlaps, and their copious spittle. "Drooling like a fine bow" is a common expression across the Unity. Almost every physical aspect of a bow-hound seems to loll.

A watercolour sky of the most dilute blue washed around the swollen sun. Fine mist, like cold smoke, rose from the soggy nettles and elderbushes, around about, and wafted through the forest of beech, mature oak and hawthorn. Distantly, fallow and roe, preternaturally sensing that something was up, scattered from deer-licks into the early afternoon.

The Windsor Lodge had been built for the twenty-fourth Elizabeth as a gift from the Duke of Cartagena, one Gonzalo de Ruiz, a keen huntsman and keener suitor to the Royal Personage. Many at Court said it was the Lodge that had put the final nail in Gonzalo's coffin. This was untrue. The final nail had been put in by one Ralph Logge, a joiner from Church End, but it was a safe bet that Logge had only got the job as a direct result of Gonzalo's gift. Elizabeth XXIV was less than enthusiastic about the pastime of inserting iron-barbed darts into fleeing deer at very high velocity through holes not previously there. Poor Gonzalo, blinded by the double visors of love and ambition, failed to realise this, and would attend the Gloriana at Windsor regularly, wearing the latest chequered hunting-breeches, the most fashionable stalking-doublets, tweedy sporting hats with ear flaps, and bandoliers packed full of lures, calls, whistles, castanets and a comprehensive trousse de chasse that contained so many specialised blades it could have armed an entire company of Landsknechts and still have some bits spare to hang over the fireplace.

Gonzalo would attempt to distract Her Majesty with discourses on the correct stringing of the composite bow, the training of the dog pack, the pros and cons of the frog-crotch barb, crossbows for pleasure and profit, detecting grot-worm in the stools of bow-hounds, and sundry other secrets of the huntsman's art. Frequently, he would invite the Queen to join him for an afternoon in the Park. She always declined, having pressing business of national import to attend to in the Star Chamber. Elizabeth XXIV's private diaries reveal that the "pressing business of national import" was almost always a game of tiddlywinks with members of the Privy Council. They also relate that she referred to Gonzalo as "that smelly maniac with the arrows".

Eventually, Gonzalo became desperate for some sign of progress in his suit, and forced things by making a gift of the hunting lodge to the Queen. He had it designed by the celebrated architect Morillo of Barcelona, who devised it to be "churrigueresque". Technically speaking, this was a style characterised by twisted columns, broken and arched pediments, and pilasters with more than one capital. In practice, it was an overly enthusiastic wealth of decoration beneath which the actual structure of the building was largely hidden. Morillo assured Gonzalo that this was "the latest thing".

Elizabeth was certainly impressed by the gift. Within a week, she'd had Gonzalo beheaded on a charge of Conspiring To Mock The Royal Person. Elizabeth XXIV is reckoned to have been a mild and gentle queen, so the affair vividly demonstrates that there's only so far you should push a monarch.

On that misty St Dunstan's Day afternoon, the men who emerged from the Lodge had thoughts of the hapless Gonzalo and his ill-advised churrigueresque very far from their minds. (Apart, obviously, from passing thoughts such as "If this is a broken and arched pedimental ornamentation, where's the bloody door?" And "How the bastard do you get out of this benighted shed?")

Leading out the beaters, the pack and the hound-master was Sir John Hockrake, Duke of Salisbury, resplendent in his green stalking gaiters and leaf-pattern tabard. Salisbury, a rotund, gouty ox, was one of the richest men on the mainland, and one of the country's largest landowners to boot. His Court influence, however, was scant, as he and the Queen had precious little time for one another. It had something to do with the Queen's manners, and Salisbury's complete lack of them.

The Duke of Salisbury hawked in a rasping noseful of air, coughed, and spat what appeared to be an entire bed of shucked oysters into the nearby scrub.

"Let's be off!" he bellowed to all present, and flourished his cry with a fanfare of expelled wind that trained men with bugles would have been sore pressed to mimic. The bow-hounds set to yapping excitedly.

Roustam Allasandro de la Vega, Regent of Castile, Governor of Toledo and victor of Lille, scowled at the obese Duke as he followed him out of the Lodge. An athletic, handsome six-footer, reputed world-master with the rapier, de la Vega busied himself with checking the brace of pearl-inlaid matchlocks that his bearer carried for him. The noblest of Spanish blood ran in de la Vega's veins, but the pressure of that blood was not as low and tranquil as one might expect in a high-born aristocrat. Steadily, through the preceding century, the power of the Unity had swung further and further towards Britain and the demi-goddess Glorianas. Resentful frustration underlay most of the Spanish politicking, and behind the pleasant smiles and the charming manners of their regal scions lay rancour and unrest. In

Madrid, Zaragoza, Sevilla and Salamanca, the pamphleteers cranked out bitter diatribes about "the Virgin thief" and the "scales of partnership overbalanced". A constitutional crisis loomed across the Unity, and even the most Anglophile of commentators foresaw a time, not far away, when the Queen would have to begin to make reparations that restored the potency of the Spanish political machine.

But Roustam de la Vega wasn't going to wait for some un-specific time. He had always been a man of action, and his action always got him what he wanted.

He took one of the primed matchlocks, and trial-aimed it at a distant tree-bole. Salisbury looked at the firearm in dis-gust.

"Good hunting today, you think, señors?" de la Vega asked, by way of making things more convivial.

"Poor as I reckon for you, if you persist with that black powder nonsense," growled Salisbury. "A stout bow of Eng-lish yew is good enough for me."

"My dear Regent," said Lord Slee diplomatically as he joined them from the Lodge, pulling on his leather bow-string protectors, "I for one am keen to see your new devices in operation. I trust they will not alarm the pack?"

Salisbury stooped with a wheeze to knuckle-rub the scalp of a panting bow-hound that worried at his heels.

"These dogs don't scare for nothing," he observed, rising again and shaking the ropes of dog-drool from his hand. "Don't you fret, Slee. My men trained 'em well."

"Good, good!" smiled Slee, thinly. He and de la Vega exchanged knowing grins that Salisbury was too busy to see. They were grins of tolerance. Slee clicked his fingers and called for his bow and quiver. He tested the tension, and exchanged a little technical wisdom with the bow-master.

Robert Slee was a short, mobile man of forty-three, his patrician's profile set off by a receding head of silver hair. He owned ancestral lands in Hertfordshire and Essex, but his power stemmed entirely from a hard-won career in law, through the Inns of Court and Whitehall. He had won himself a seat in the Privy Council, and was tipped to take the post of Lord Privy Seal from Thomas Arbuthnot before the year was out. Slee's scholarship and learning was admired across the Unity. His many books and treatises were required reading for all young men with political aspirations. It was said he spoke and wrote nine languages. He had travelled extensively, and participated in some of the most formidably important legislation of the last six Parliaments. His only fault, it seemed, was his lack of charm, which was often remarked upon. Dignitaries from across Europe queued up eagerly to meet the author of such articulate writings, and they were all disappointed. In the flesh, Slee was a cold, dry, plaster-of-Paris man. No one actively disliked him, but he'd have had trouble forming a cricket side if he only called on his friends.

The Divine Aleister Jaspers, fourth and final member of the illustrious party, joined his three waiting companions from the Lodge, and took a pair of polished Swiss crossbows from a waiting bearer. An austere young man with fleshy lips and cropped hair, Jaspers wore the knee-length robes of the Magickians' Union. When the Arte of Magick had been rediscovered, the Church had been forced to accept and accommodate it, or be ousted from the structures of power. The Protestants had simply enlarged their doctrines. The Catholic Church had "fortuitously" discovered six more books of the New Testament in a cave in Sinai, all of which thoroughly expanded the motif of "moving in mysterious ways" to include Magick.

This additional doctrine was included in the very first edi-
tion of the Steve Gutenberg Bible, and its textual authority
was embraced rapidly by the Church of England, which
was, at that time, an uneasy blend of Catholic pomp and
Protestant simplicity, and formed one of the fundamental
tenets of belief. The Church of England became, in time,
the United Church, and absorbed almost all the other Christian religions of the Unity (except for various underground
movements and secret societies, and, of course, the Bollards
of Ghent, the Stevenage Prurients, and the Vatican, who
were allowed to continue as usual if they didn't bother anyone). The Church closely regulated all official usage of
Magick through the Magickians' Union, which was part
trade guild and part holy order. All members of the union
were skilled and potent users of the Arte, answering only
to the Queen, the Privy Council and the Church cardinals.
Through them, the Cantrips and the Jinx were operated for
domestic use.

Jaspers also displayed the collar pin of Infernal Affairs, the
union's disciplinary department, charged with investigating
and punishing any individuals conducting unauthorised dab-
bling in the Arte. Jaspers was reckoned to be Infernal Affairs'
finest. His twinned powers of Magick and Prosecution gave
him a status at Court far, far above his actual social rank.

"Are we ready?" he asked, smoothly, examining with
hooded eyes the oiled, machined perfection of his weapons.
To the other three, his soft voice sounded like Turkish Delight: sweet, rich, intense, and the sort of thing you can
quickly have enough of.

"I 'ope you won't be using any Goety to improve yorn
aim," commented Salisbury to the Divine.

There was a pause. Even the agitation of the hunting dogs
skirled to a halt. A shadow passed over the sun. Salisbury,

unaccountably cold for a moment, looked into Jaspers's piercing eyes. What he saw there, he patently didn't like.

Slee stepped forward quickly, and executed what was, on balance, probably the most graceful diplomatic manoeuvre of his career. He said, "Ha ha! As if!"

"As if!" joined Roustam de la Vega, catching on quickly, and adding his deep laugh to Slee's thin, piping chuckle. Only Salisbury, who seemed incapable of getting anything out of his voicebox, didn't laugh. In ten seconds, his tomato-red face had become cabbage-white. He managed a pale, valiant smile.

Jaspers smiled too, though it was not a reassuring smile.

"As if," he echoed. Then he turned, and sauntered away towards the dog-pack and the hunt-team.

Salisbury sagged, and then, as his colour flushed back, he busied himself volubly with unnecessary checks of the hounds and their handlers.

"Close," whispered Slee to de la Vega, as they stood, side by side, buttoning up their coat collars. "Your assistance was appreciated. Salisbury is profoundly clumsy in almost every respect, politics included. No wonder the Queen can't abide him."

De la Vega smiled dryly, and said, "I'm not about to marry him myself, my good Lord Slee. If it weren't for his consid-erable financial reserves I'd be more than happy to be part of a tragic hunting accident this very afternoon."

Slee allowed himself a thin smile at the delicious thought. To their left, the runners were blowing shrill whistles and calling guttural encouragements to the pack, which surged away through the sunlit mist of the forest space. As the vol-ume of the hounds dipped away, they could hear birdsong, dripping water and the crackle of undergrowth all around them. Slee and de la Vega set off after the others.

"Shall we," asked Slee, "discuss your disengaño, my dear cousin? The woods are close and deaf."

"Good," replied the Spaniard crisply, "for my words would seem calumny to most English ears, but not yours, or those of our other two... friends. We all share a certain hunger. My family, my faction... they ache for the taste of power, but we are famished of the influence that is our due. Magick, my lord, that is what we need. Without access to the Cantrips, we have no leverage. With them..."

Slee caught at his sleeve and pointed at their companions ahead through the trees.

"Do you see, Lord Regent, the way that no hound will go voluntarily within a lance-length of the Divine?" he asked.

"They are wiser than us, perhaps," said de la Vega. "I often doubt it is entirely safe to have Jaspers around, even if he is of our cause."

Slee nodded, and breathed deeply. The two men hefted up their weapons and moved on through the ferny chiaroscuro of the forest.

"So," said Slee, "you were saying?"

THE SECOND CHAPTER.

And so to Soho. Ah, Soho. What are we ever to do about it?

Number seventeen, Amen Street, Soho, was a three-storey residence built in the Neo-Rococo fashion that was typical of its neighbourhood (to wit, generously proportioned and not quite buttoned up). It stood in a quiet, well-guttered lane just off the more commercial streets, which was surprisingly decent and presentable considering that it lay only a short stagger from some of the most disreputable taverns and stews in the City, as well as the Windmill Theatre, where the famous burlesque show "All The World's A Fan-tail Stage" was now in its record-breaking seventeenth year ("Come and come again!" declared Jack Tinker in the *Daily Maile*), not to mention the Stratford Revue Bar, with its nightly presentation of such entertainments as "As You Lick It" and the ever-popular "Two Gentlemen of Vagina".

Number seventeen had been built in the time of the ninth Gloriana, and had withstood five unseasonal gales, a Great Fire, two plagues, six riots and, in its more recent history, a number of apocalyptic parties. Rupert Triumff had purchased it with some of the five thousand marks the Navy had awarded him for his part in the Battle of Finisterre.[1]

His neighbour on one side was a nondescript member of the diplomatic service by the name of Bruno de Scholet. De Scholet was abroad for much of the year, and Triumff had only met him twice. He had come round to complain about the noise one evening in 2003, and then again about an hour later. To the other side lived the distinguished composer Sir Edoard Fuchs. Fuchs had made his name and fortune in the early nineteen-eighties with some top-ten galliards and ron-deaus, but he hadn't had a notable success since the release of his "Greatest Hits" sheet-music quarto. He lived off his roy-alties and the occasional guest appearance, and was almost permanently soused on musket. Fuchs never complained about the loud parties at number seventeen. He was usually at them.

The effects of three bottles of Old Skinner's Notable Mus-ket was by that stage of the day beginning to wear off the owner of number seventeen. It was three o'clock.

Rupert Triumff lay supine and rather Chatterton-esque upon a chaise-longue in the Solar, washed in the hazy light that filtered down through the high, leaded windows. He had

---

1 With a rag-tag, badly victualled squadron (seven pinnace, three sprightly Hawkins, two luggers, half-a-dozen ketch and a galleasse) led by his own flag-ship, a hundred-gun galleon called the *Blameless*, Triumff had engaged and annihilated a flota of Portuguese Privateers off Finisterre in the summer of 2002. The pirate fleet, forty-strong, had been harrying Spanish treasure ships from the New World. The Admiralty later referred to Triumff's tactics as "The instinctive genius of a man in whose veins runs salt-water, not blood." The *Times* described it as "Typical and extremely jammy." Triumff's famous line at the hour of victory ("Oh, Spain! Sleep easy in thy bed, for England hath set thy foe to flight!") is now reckoned to be a product of dramatic licence on the part of the battle correspondent. It is likely that what Triumff really said was "Suck on it, you gob-shites!"

bathed, shaved, put on a splash of his favourite aftershave (A Scent of Man), and changed into grey netherstock hose, patterned canions, and a dark damask shirt, all topped off by an embroidered peascod doublet of beige murray. Only the small grille of black sutures across his swollen cheek hinted that the previous parts of the day had been anything less than respectable. Triumff was idly rotating the large, brass armillary sphere that stood on the floor beside the chaise with his draped hand. It thrummed like a roulette wheel. On a side table nearby sat a half-eaten nantwich. The Couteau Suisse lay in a waste-paper bin beside the door.

A few yards away from Triumff, at an oak desk lined with copies of Wisden, sat a large man with braided black locks. The man was entirely naked, his gleaming skin as dark as turned ebony, and he had the sort of gargantuan muscula-ture that would have made Rubens whistle like a navvie, and Michelangelo place want-ads for a big ceiling. Naked though he was, the man had a pair of small wire-framed spectacles perched on the end of his broad nose. He was perusing a huge book of charts.

The door to the Solar creaked open, and Agnew entered, bearing a tray of beakers. He offered them to Triumff.

"Your elixir vitae, sir," he said in precisely the same disap-proving tone of voice with which he would have announced "The Prince of Wales", or "Who, precisely, has popped off?"

Triumff took one of the gently steaming beakers, and sipped at it gratefully. At the very beginning of their profes-sional relationship, Triumff had discovered that Agnew could concoct a mulled herbal drink that almost Magickally abol-ished the effects of alcohol. Agnew, with affected ambivalence, called it "elixir vitae", and sometimes hinted that it was prepared from an old Suffolk remedy of his mother's. It was almost miraculously effective. Triumff had often been heard to joke that the Church Guild really ought to check up on Agnew for practising the Arte without a licence. He was not far wrong. The potion was Magick. Just because the Arte had been generally rediscovered during the Renaissance, it didn't necessarily follow that Magick was unknown before that time. All the Renaissance did was to popularly rekindle the practices that had become esoteric since antique times. In many places, particularly among tribal groups, or in old rural communities, many forms of Magick had survived and thrived, thank you very much, in the form of folk customs, traditions and hedgerow remedies, which is why so many country witches looked on the Renaissance as simply the rest of the world catching up with progressive current thinking. The elixir vitae recipe had been in the Agnew family for so long, indeed, they had forgotten that it was Magickal. All they remembered, every New Year's Day, was that it worked.

Triumff sipped at his beaker thoughtfully, and held out an object for Agnew's inspection.

"D'you think Gull will want this back?" he asked.

"I doubt it, sir," answered his manservant, placing the tray on the edge of the dresser. "But he will, I'm certain, be interested in acquiring some other portions of anatomy... your anatomy, sir."

Triumff waved the notion aside, and sat up with a yawn.

"What're you doing, Uptil?" he asked.

The naked man at the desk turned, and removed his spectacles with a refined gesture.

"Just looking, Rupert," he said.

"At?"

"Well, it never ceases to amaze me," Uptil replied. "I mean, your Unity is meant to be the superior power on this Earth, and you know so flipping little."

He pointed to the charts laid open on the desk. "Africa," he said, with a sigh. "One of the greatest, strangest, most complex continents on the planet, and you represent it as a fuzzy triangle full of drawings of pigs and loaves."

Triumff stood up and looked over Uptil's shoulder. "They're hippopotamuses. And huts. Look, there's definitely a door in that one."

"Well, pardon me," Uptil said, grinning. "You know, when I agreed to come back from Beach[2] with you, I thought I'd be learning great wonders and notions from your oh-so-famous Empire, which I could take back and share with my people. I've been here now, what? Quite a while. It's like living with flipping savages. You're superstitious, uncouth, blinkered, arrogant, and you generally don't smell all that great. You think Africa is full of loaves and pigs. You haven't even mastered the simple combustion engine."

"Hey," said Triumff, "we've got Magick…"

The massive autochthon looked at Triumff sadly.

"How many times have I got to explain this?" he asked. "It's your downfall, my friend. Magick is the cross you've crucified your cultural progress on, to borrow an analogy from your myths. Take my word for it. Yours would be a better world without the Arte."

Triumff shrugged dismissively.

"You saw Beach, Rupert. You saw the way we live. We

---

2 "Australia", the terra incognito, is only the working name the Unity has given to the vast southern continent Rupert discovered. Many other names vie for popularity: "Lucach", "Maletur", "New Virginia" and "The Vast Southern Continent" are all contenders. "Beach" is a literal translation of the name Uptil's people have for their land and, as such, is the best choice. As with all these things however, it doesn't stand a cat in hell's chance of being accepted formally.

kicked out the ways of sorcery three hundred years ago, and we haven't looked back."

Triumff took a deep breath, and thought for a moment of the shining glass edifices of Beach, the smooth streets, the gleaming metal horse-less chariots, the smiling, healthy, clean people. He remembered their mpIII players, their Visagebook, and their ThyPlace, their reliable sanitation, their dry martinis, their surf boards. He remembered that all of it had only been possible because there were, in essence, no Wizards of Aus.

"Oh bollocks," he sighed.

"Just remember," he added, after a moment, "just remember the real reason you're here."

"The Ploy?"

"Right, the Ploy. I'm sticking my neck right out for your folks back home, so just take it easy with the old criticism."

The sound of knocking drifted up through the house.

"Is that de Scholet again?" snapped Triumff. "We're not even having a party. If it's about the other night, tell him to sod off. If it's Fuchs after a bottle of laughing juice, tell him we've joined the Temperance Society. I can't afford to subsidise his problem."

Agnew paused on his way out. "And if it is guests, sir? Are you entertaining today?"

"I'm a bloody scream," said Triumff, flopping into his seat. Agnew disappeared.

"Better be on the safe side," Triumff said to Uptil. The big man nodded, and then slumped into the corner, an expression of sullen vacancy suddenly investing his face. He began to pick at his ear.

Agnew reappeared.

"Sire Clarence, sir," he reported.

Sire Roger Clarence, powdered, perfumed, teased, waxed, plucked, lipo-ed, laced, veneered, buffed, polished and heeled in the very latest fashion, flounced into the Solar. Clarence swam in the intermediate depth of the Court pool, and was one of Woolly's more effective facilitators. Behind him came two pike-men of the Royal Household, sweltering in full Beefeater uniform. They were meant to be in attendance, but one of them had caught the head of his polearm in the staircase ceiling, and they were both engaged in freeing it. Clarence paused in the doorway for dramatic effect, realised his dramatic effect was still outside on the landing fighting with three yards of halberd, and decided to make the best of things as they were. He waved Agnew aside with a lace nosegay so stuffed with scent it made the grim man gag, and turned to Triumff.

"Felicitations, stud," he said, "I hope I'm not intruding, but it's Court business."

Triumff looked up from the book on fly fishing he had been pretending to read.

"Well, I never," he said, smiling dangerously, "Roger Clarence, the man of whom they say in hushed whispers 'his name is not an instruction'. Come in. Can I get you a diet malmsey, or would you like something stiffer with a cherry in it?"

Clarence turned up his nose and closed his eyes in protest. "You are an awful man, Triumff. So common. So unreconstructed."

Triumff got to his feet and closed the book.

"Things must be slow at Hampton today to get you down to the sleazy end of town. Or are you slumming?" he asked.

Clarence looked at him contemptuously, and then shook open the newspaper he had been carrying under his arm. "Have you seen the rag this morning?"

Triumff took the paper and studied it. "Times Bingo… Coffers to be won?"

"The headline, you monstrous man! 'New Continent Expedition Still In Doubt.' The Council's sent me down here to gee you up. De la Vega's expedition is champing at the bit. When the hell are you going to make your report?"

"When I'm ready," said Triumff. "When I've assembled all the facts. I'm still studying the trinkets I brought back."

Clarence eyed the hulking figure of Uptil, who was staring into space with empty eyes.

"Hnh," Clarence murmured. Then he remembered himself and turned to glare at Triumff. "Well, Rupert, let me tell you, they're reaching the end of their tether at Court. They're saying your lack of enthusiasm proves there's something down there worth exploring, something you're keeping to yourself. De la Vega won't be gainsayed for long. The time will come when the Queen will grant him his Letters of Passage anyway."

"The Queen?"

"Yes, the Queen. She's getting impatient."

"The Queen?"

Clarence looked around the Solar with artificially wide eyes.

"Is there an echo?" he asked. "Yes, old Three Ex herself. Don't fool yourself, Rupert, it's been a decade since you were her blue-eyed boy. You've been away for three years, and you've hardly been a constant presence at Windsor since you've been back. De la Vega's her favourite now, and Slee has her ear. The day's long gone when you could string her along by force of your charm alone."

Triumff glowered and sat down heavily.

"Cheer up, stud. All it takes is you attending on Her Majesty for an afternoon with your report. The Council will look it over too. Then you'll be in her good books, and the whole Australia business can get under way."

"Another month–"

"One week. That's her final word. If I were you, I'd get it done and dusted before the Masque this Saturday. And please understand she's being generous. You've had a year already. God knows, if you hadn't once been her favourite, she'd have carted you off to the Tower months ago, and gone ahead regardless."

Triumff's shoulders sagged, and he looked at the floor-boards, a dismal expression on his face.

"I'll see you at Court then," said Clarence, heading for the door. "Don't disappoint her. It's your head. And remember, this was a friendly warning. She could have sent a detachment of huscarls."

Clarence paused in the doorway. He took a small fold of paper out of his tunic pocket. It was sealed with a ribbon. He tossed it to Triumff.

"By the way," he said, "that was on your doorstep."

Triumff caught the slip neatly.

"What is it?" he asked.

"Far be it from me to read another man's personal correspondence," smiled Clarence, "but it appears to be an invitation from a man asking you to meet him at the Dolphin Baths at four-thirty. There's a whole side to you I don't know about, isn't there? Vivat Regina!"

Triumff leapt to his feet, but Clarence had gone, taking his pike-men with him, and leaving nothing but a stench of cologne and a ragged hole in the plaster of the staircase ceiling.

"Clarence! What man? What man? Come back here!"

Triumff looked back from the stairhead. Agnew and Uptil were staring at him.

"Things," Triumff said to them dolefully, "are turning so pear-shaped, they wouldn't look out of place up a tree with a partridge."

THE THIRD CHAPTER.

Which doth contain a Most Engaging discourse upon modern issues of Discovery, & also a visit to the bath-house.

Almost every day, a ship of the Royal Unified Navy leaves one of Britain's harbours bearing Letters of Passage that grant it the majestic right to discover, explore and, frankly, pillage less fortunate or well-known parts of the globe. On that St Dunstan's Day alone, Sir Walter de File sailed out of Portsmouth on the *Peacespite* to see if there was anything of merit between Florida and Argentina, Lord Archimboldo cast off from Southampton aboard the *Golden Shot* in search of the South Indies, and Thomas Pickering, mariner, sailed his cog the *Batty Crease* into Toamasina and discovered Madagascar.[3]

Letters of Passage, granted by the Queen, were potent tools that gave the seafarer virtual copyright over anything he discovered in the name of the Unity. They were sweeping powers, but necessary. Without such an incentive, it was doubtful anyone would voluntarily spend two or three years in a badly caulked, leaking, unhygienic, overgrown barrel, adrift on the stormiest oceans of the world, braving corsairs,

---

3 And stayed there too, which is why Madagascar didn't appear on charts until 2046. But that really is another story.

sea-serpents, kraken, bull whales, foreign powers, Scurvy, Rickets, Dutch Wart, hostile native peoples, famine, thirst, drowning, marooning, becalming, casting-away, mutinying, keelhauling, slipping off a topgallant in icy conditions and braining yourself on the taffrail, acting as a human lightning conductor whilst on watch in the crow's-nest during a freak electrical storm, choking on a ship's biscuit, scalding to death in the ship's kettle, being operated on by the surgeon's mate after grog-rations, smoking in the Orlop next to the Powder Room, going back to check on a lit 32-pounder, happening to mention out loud that you fancied some albatross soup, or, of course, falling off the edge of the world.[4]

Voyages of Discovery were a dirty, dangerous and compli- cated business and no mistake.[5]

The procedures surrounding a victorious return however, were simple. The explorer, bearing his Letters of Passage, was given a respectable length of time to rest, recuperate and get his land-legs back, before he was required to present a report of his discoveries to the Queen. The explorer would be

---

4 No one still believed that the Earth was flat, but there were still many ad- herents to the notion that it might be unfinished in remoter areas (presumably areas where the hills and valleys still had some scaffolding up, the rivers had yet to be plumbed-in, and cherubic workmen lounged about smoking rollies out of sight of the Foreman). There were also quite a few reluctant ex-flat- Earthers around, who couldn't quite go the whole hog and conceive of an Earth that was spherical, and therefore favoured the recherché "conical" the- ory.

5 Lord Marmaduke Latimer, Privy Seal to Elizabeth XVIII, was famous for drawing up his "Compendium Of The Relative Dangerf Of Sum Profeffionef". "Nautical Exploration" came third, between "Being An Heretic" and "Being Out Of Favoure", and "Generale Seafaring" came seventh over all, behind "Fightinge In An Foreigne War On The Lofing Side" and "Contractinge Ye Buboef". Top of the list, of course, was "Being An Potentate Of The Southern Americaf".

celebrated, paid a considerable sum known as "a Regarde" to acknowledge his achievement, and would probably have the discovered place officially named after him. In return, he would formally hand the Letters of Passage over to the Queen, and, in so doing, bequeath the territory to the Unity.

Only then could further expeditions be arranged. This second wave of voyages would hurtle off along the trail blazed by the original explorer, and, using his notes, maps and gathered intelligence, thoroughly plunder, despoil and exploit the new-found corner of the world. It was the way things were done.

However, until the explorer had made his report and handed back the all-important Letters of Passage, none of that could take place. There was huge money in new discoveries, not to mention honour, prestige, fame, governships and nubile local women, and the Unity's huge Exploitation Industry therefore waited with eager anticipation for the green light on a new Continent, as did the Church, which was hungrier for fresh sources of Cantriptic power than they cared to admit.

All of this explained the mounting frustration felt at Court over Rupert Triumff. He'd been away. He'd come back, flushed with success, explaining that he had discovered new lands in the Southern Oceans. He'd brought with him many astonishing finds and trinkets, including four hundred and six new species of plant, a lot of non-placental fauna, and a noble, dark-skinned autochthon as an ambassador of the Meridional Climes. Then, months had passed, months in which he showed no signs of making his report, months in which the Letters of Passage idled in his desk under lock and key, long, slow months, which the Unity's reavers, exploiters and churchmen suffered with increasing impatience, hives, palpitations and stress-induced migraines.

No one had ever taken so long to deliver his report, not even Captain Jacob Tavistock, of the *Blue Beagle*, who came back from discovering Bermuda with amnesia, and had to have his memory gently nursed back by a team of specially trained Spanish inquisitors.

No one knew what to do about it. There just wasn't provision in the statutes to deal with a holder of valuable Letters of Passage who was backward in coming forward. They were usually all so anxious to get their hands on their Regarde, buy a big place in Oxenfordshire, and marry a girl who was either a minor Royal or blonde or, best of all, both.

When a full six months had elapsed with no sign of Triumff, the Privy Council began to look into the matter, scouring the many volumes of regulations for a loophole. They consulted the Navy, the Church and the various lords that might know. Solutions there were none. The ball, it appeared, was firmly in Triumff's court. It was up to him to take the initiative, and up to the rest of the government and other interested parties to lump it.

However, the interlude was now long enough for even a busy Queen to start noticing it, and that, as the Privy Council soon found out, was the one thing they hadn't thought of. The simple way to get around the legal thicket protecting Triumff was to erase the laws, and the one person who could do that was the Queen.

The only thing that ever weighed heavily on Her Majesty was about half-a-ton of lace, silk, gauze, kapok, sequins and pearls. Nothing else troubled her or slowed her down much, particularly not minor foibles like statutes or civil laws. It was the matter of a moment, and the work of a scratching quill, to ascribe new Letters of Passage to another explorer and expunge the life, property, rights and memory of Rupert Triumff from the land.

Triumff might have been the only person who had actually been expecting as much for a while. He knew it was just a matter of time. He'd stalled for as long as he could, hoping the Court would swallow his ploy, but now he needed something else, some more active course to follow. He needed a *new* ploy.

That was exactly what he'd been afraid of, because, unfortunately, if there was one thing he really didn't shine at, it was ploys.

Considerations of the possible size, shape, colour and cost of a potential new ploy, as well as how he might recognise it, filled Triumff's mind as he paid a shilling to the doorman and entered the warm, damp embrace of the Dolphin Bath House at twenty past four. There was the best part of another hour before they shut for the night, and late-afternoon bathers, seeking a restorative for agued limbs made rheumy by a week of heavy rain, jostled about the place. Their pallid, portly shapes could be glimpsed in the steamy atmosphere, lurking under the green-shadowed colonnades, slapping across the tiled walks, or sliding walrus-like into the pools.

The warm, wet air smelled of soaked stonework, body odour, antiseptic and wrinkled skin.

A meaty attendant with arms like hams and a tight blue bathing cap came over and handed Triumff a clean towel.

"Changing over there," he said, pointing to the doorways in the shadows of the western colonnade, marked variously Miladies and Migents, as well as three marked *Sauna*, *Jacuzzi & Cold Plunge* and *Wassail*. The attendant turned his moon-face back to Triumff. "No carousing, no splashing, no bombing and no pissing in ye pool. We close at six."

"Thank you so much, I know the rules," Triumff said, glaring. The attendant shook his rubber-capped head at Triumff and wandered away. The cap was so tight, he looked like a bald man with a frost-bitten scalp.

The Migents changing area was vacant, except for hooks full of unlaced doublets, capes, canions and wrinkled hose. Triumff stripped off swiftly, and then, with his towel knotted around his waist, crossed to the frosted window in the west wall. It was high up. He had to climb up on a bench to reach it, and in doing so knocked somebody's slashed appliqué Pansid Slops and heavily bombasted codpiece into the puddles on the floor.

Steam had swelled the window's frame into wedged plumpness, but three smart blows with the ball of his hand finally knocked it out. Cold, evening air rushed in and stung his flushed face.

"Uptil!" he hissed into the dark of the alley beyond. "Uptil!"

"Give us a hand up, mate," muttered Uptil from outside. Triumff obliged by heaving the large man up and in through the window. It wasn't easy, and it took a good few moments. Triumff prickled with agitation as he strained to counterbalance Uptil's weight, expecting an interruption at any second.

Finally, he was in. Uptil was shrouded in a hooded serge cloak. He produced Triumff's scabbarded rapier from beneath its folds, asking, "Want this?"

"Right, where am I going to conceal that?"

Uptil winked, and said, "Exactly. That's why I fished this out of the garbage."

He held out the Couteau Suisse.

"Okay, that's actually quite a good idea," Triumff admitted. "Now, stay out of sight, keep your eyes peeled, and if you hear me whistle, move like the clappers."

Uptil nodded.

"And," he added, "if anyone does see you, remember the Ploy."

Uptil nodded again.

"The Ploy. Right," he said, making his "lamps on, nobody home" face.

Triumff wandered out into the Bath Hall. No one seemed to spare him a second glance. Already, many of the bathers, sensing the approaching end of the day, were climbing from the pools and heading for the shower stalls. Triumff dropped his towel, wrapped the Couteau Suisse in it, and left it on the edge of the pool. Then he waded down the steps into the warm waters of the main bath. There was a stone seat against the side, beneath the water level, which one could sit on to bask in the relaxing heat. Triumff sat, wiped his face with a palm-scoop of water, and leant back, surveying the place with apparent disinterest.

Minutes passed. Triumff's hawkish vigil relaxed somewhat as the gently lapping, tepid environment lulled and soothed away his aches and cares. He breathed deeply and shook his head, fighting away the drowsy weight that seemed to have suffused his brain.

When he next opened his eyes, he was alone.

Triumff stiffened with a start. The steady drip of water re-sounded from somewhere, but nothing else: no voices, no sign of life. He wondered how long he had been asleep. Surely the attendants would have woken him if it had passed closing time? That implied that it was still before six o'clock. Yet where were the attendants?

Triumff tried to whistle, but his lips refused. He was up to his chest in many thousands of gallons of water, and his mouth was dry.

Then he saw the line of bubbles. They were crossing the centre of the pool and heading his way. He caught his breath.

Plip plip plip plip plip, they went.

They were ten yards away, coming straight for him. The steps out of the pool were ten yards to his right. He fancied the idea of clambering out of the pool where he was, using the seat as a leg up, but his limbs felt dull and heavy, and didn't seem strong enough to support him.

Plip plip plip plip plip, came the line of bubbles.

He became aware of how fast he was breathing.

"This is silly," he whispered out loud. "I can't just sit here, waiting to be harried by a line of bubbles."

Five yards away from him, with a last, ominous plip, the bubbles vanished.

Triumff opened his mouth and then closed it again. He considered submerging to take a look-see. By the time he had decided not to, it was academic anyway.

The swordsman exploded out of the water in front of him like a breaching whale. He was heavily muscled, and dressed in a greased breastplate and leather shorts. His face was hidden by a fierce, full-visored helmet that had been reworked to incorporate a trombone-pipe snorkel and leaded glass eyeholes. A rapier glinted in his hand, and the space between Triumff's naked body and the razor edge of the sword was diminishing alarmingly.

"Gniumpff!" raspberried the assassin tinnily through his snorkel, "Gie! Gie, goo girty gastard!"

Triumff threw his body to the left, thrashing against the slowness of the water. The stinging blade described a glittering arc, and rebounded loudly off the lip of the pool, against which Triumff had just been leaning.

"Gile get goo!" gurgled the assassin, turning after Triumff.

"Pardon?" yelped Triumff, heading out into mid-pool in a mix of headlong flight and doggy paddle.

"Gile get goo, goo girty gastard! Gore gonna gie gorrigly!"

The assassin's snorkel tube sucked and farted out the words. Water jetted out of the top of the air-pipe.

"What?" asked Triumff desperately.

The assassin ground to a halt some yards from the fleeing Triumff and waved his arms in frustration.

"Gook! Gook!" he snorted. "Gie…" he tapped himself on the breastplate.

Triumff looked uncertain. "You?"

The assassin nodded eagerly. "Gess! Gie gam gonna gurder…" he pointed to his rapier and then to Triumff "…goo."

"M-me?"

"Gess!" bubbled the assassin, clapping his hands. "Gorrigly," he added.

A FOURTH CHAPTER.

"Oh bollocks," said Triumff, and resumed his thrashing attempt at escape. Water churned from his milling limbs. The swordsman ploughed after him.

Almost at once, Triumff realised things weren't getting any better. A second line of bubbles was arcing around in front to cut off his flight. A moment later, another submarine assassin rose from the depths.

"Give gim gis gay! Gile gop gis gloogy ged goff!" the second attacker instructed his partner.

"Garden?" asked the first.

Triumff stopped and looked back.

"He said…" he began, but then he paused. "Why the bastard am I bothering to explain it to you?"

He set off again, breasting the flood, churning up sheets of spray, breaking off perpendicular to the pincer manoeuvre of the snorkel-blowing killers.

Five yards from the pool-side, he pursed his lips and whistled the first two bars of the song about the Guinea Coast.

Something flat, hard and fundamentally aerodynamic choppered out of the colonnade shadows like a startled grouse. It struck the second assassin square in the visor with a painful, metallic clang. The assassin crashed backwards into the water as if he'd ridden a steeplechaser full-pelt into an overhanging branch.

The flat, hard, aerodynamic thing whirled around, back the way it had come, still making the sound of someone thrumming their lips with their finger whilst they exhaled hard. It landed neatly in Uptil's outstretched hand. It was Uptil's "come-back", a traditional hunting weapon of the Beach folk. It was essentially a flat stick with an elbow, but in the hands of a trained caster it could not only do serious hurt, but also reload itself into its owner's hand for another go.

Triumff reached the edge of the pool, grabbed his towel and shook the Couteau Suisse out of its folds. He pressed the trigger and got to the rapier by way of only a pencil sharpener and an egg spoon. He flourished the long blade twice to enjoy the bee-buzz it made as it cut the air, and then raised the hilt to eye-level in a salute.

"Vivat Regina," he hissed, and threw himself at the remaining assassin.

The assassin had never, in all his long days as a paid cut-throat and hit-man, been attacked by a naked man with a rapier before. Come to that, he had never been asked to take on a contract wearing swimming trunks and part of a brass band on his head. The hooded man who'd hired him and his mate in a Cheapside tavern had paid well, in advance, and so he hadn't really questioned the details at the time.

Now his mate was floating face-down in the municipal baths with blood clouding the water around his crumpled visor-work after a collision with what appeared to be a flying shelf bracket, and he had his hands full with what was known in the trade as a "contrary client".

There was only one thing he could do, and thankfully (for his sake) it was something he was very, very good at.

He would have to fight him and kill him.

The rapiers flashed against each other in a series of blinding strokes, the cutlery percussion of the blows ringing around the gloomy hall. Almost from the first riposte, Triumff knew he was up against a professional swordsman. He just hoped that the odd venue (four feet of warm water) would be on his side.

It was an ungainly fight. Their upper bodies flew and twisted above the waterline, their hips and legs paddled like spoons in syrup to keep up. It was remarkably easy to outrun your lower body, and therefore fall over, and therefore die. Triumff did his very best not to do any of those three things.

It might be noted at this point that when either sober or desperate, Sir Rupert Triumff was a considerable swordsman in his own right. Currently, he was both. It was even money, whichever way you looked at it.

Uptil looked on, aghast, from the vantage of the bath-side. He yelled encouragement, advice, and a few of the ruder words in his considerable vocabulary, unable to do anything else of use, since the fighters were too close for him to risk another cast of his come-back.

Something caught Uptil's eye. Something was moving in the shadows further down the colonnade. Fearing a third as-sassin, he tore himself away from the blistering duel and moved in to investigate. He raised his come-back, catching a glimpse of a robed figure scurrying away towards the bath-house exit, too far away to get a clean cast. Uptil ran after it.

Uptil didn't like leaving Rupert at such a crucial juncture, but something forced him to give chase, something like a lin-gering impression that the robed figure had possessed the head of a cat.

Uptil didn't know much about cats, since they didn't have them in Beach. He was pretty sure, though, that cats weren't generally six feet high, and wearing a silk doublet and a cape.

There was no sign of a robed figure in the entrance hall, feline or otherwise. The front doors were bolted shut, and the three bath attendants were bound, gagged and unconscious on the floor of the ticket office. Uptil checked along both sides of the hall, his come-back poised for launch. There was no sign of an intruder.

Someone started hammering at the bolted doors. Uptil walked forward, and drew back the bolts. As the doors swung open, he nearly exclaimed loudly. At the last moment he remembered the Ploy, and settled for a hasty yelp of inarticulate fear.

In the pool, Triumff parried low against the assassin's backhand, and then struck in, slicing the end off his assailant's snorkel. The man made a noise like an un-bled radiator, and rained several more blows at Triumff, who backed and parried again deftly.

"You in the water! Stop fighting! At once!"

The words rang out in booming echoes across the bathhouse. Out of the corner of his otherwise intently occupied eye, Triumff saw Lord Gull, standing at the head of a detachment of the City Militia at the pool edge. The soldiers were all big, armoured dreadnoughts from a SHAT unit (Special Halberds and Tactics), one of the Militia's Anti-Affray Departments. Gull looked more furious than usual. If they wanted the fight stopped, Triumff knew that they would be able to do it with just two or three strokes of a skilled pike-arm.

"You want me to stop the fight?" bellowed Triumff, side-slicing with his darting sword, "You want me to stop it? No sooner said…"

He punched up, driving his basket-guard into the assassin's visored face, and then raked downwards, the length of the man's torso, with a slick blow that was almost surgical. The assassin collapsed messily into the water, which changed colour rapidly.

"   than done," Triumff finished, slooshing away from his dead foe, waist-deep in the water. "That'll teach him to call me a gastard. Afternoon, Callum. How's the ear?"

A long row of pike-heads pointed down off the pool-side at him, each one ready to thrust. Gull stepped forward between the hafts, and glanced disdainfully down at the carnage in the water. Triumff, smiling up at his captors, could see Uptil, crouching nervously at the back of the colonnade under the watchful eye of a SHAT team member.

"I'm not going to allow our personal differences to get in the way, Triumff, you piece of worthless offal," said Gull. "As Captain of the Guard, I've a job to do, and that involves arresting you for Causing An Affray In A Public Place and Participating In A Breach Of The Peace. Not to mention what looks like a double charge of Manslaughter."

"They were knifemen. Look at them. Paid to do me in. You know that damn well, Gull."

"Perhaps," said Gull, with what was almost a smile. "We'll ascertain that after the Coroner's been in and Forensic Physic have poked about. Until then, Rupert Triumff, you're coming with me to The Yard for questioning. You men, haul him out."

Huge, mailed hands reached down. With a resigned curse, Triumff allowed himself to leave the water.

CHAPTER THE FIFTH.
Concerning Forensic Physic
& gathering storms.

In the cool of the corridor outside the sweaty, red-faced hub-bub of the Affray Room, Forensic Physician Neville de Quincey took a moment to compose himself. He rootled out the bowl of his pipe with the tip of a poniard he had found on a tray of labelled exhibits, and stoked it up with fresh Virginian weed. It was a busy, rowdy evening. Cage-doors slammed, keys jangled, oaths resonated, and boots tramped all through the great stone blockhouse of New Hibernian Yard.

Things had kicked off at about five o'clock that afternoon, before de Quincey had even had time to grab a quick nantwich from the cafeteria for his tea. The witchboard operator had been taking calls all afternoon, and alerted Affray to an anonymous ouija tip reporting a significant tavern brawl in progress at the Rouncey Mare off Allhallows Walk. The Flying Squad had returned with over two dozen cursing, spitting, bleeding, reeling detainees. Statements were taken, questions were asked, blame was variously apportioned across the Affray Room, and the shouting began. Then two officers from Southwark came in with a mouldering corpse they had found in a coal house after a complaint from the neighbours, and it was time to pull on the gloves and open the instrument box.

Whilst he had been conducting the autopsy, de Quincey had heard the Rouncey Mare boys resume their fight in the Affray Room. Whistles were blown above the tumult, feet thundered down corridors, and the repetitive thwack of stout, Militia-issue cudgels became clearly audible.

Then Gull turned up with two cadavers in hopsack shrouds, two prisoners, and a tale of swordplay in the Dolphin Baths, and it wasn't even seven-thirty.

De Quincey lit his pipe and began to puff gently, leaning back against the cool hallway's red-painted stone buttress. The door to the Affray Room opened, and a storm of noise and a tall, sour-faced man issued forth. The man closed the door after him and shut back the storm.

"De Quincey?" asked Gull.

"Just collecting my thoughts, Lord Gull," de Quincey said, nursing the hot bowl of his pipe with careful fingers.

"Your opinion on the dead?"

"The Southwark stiff? Stabbed. Broad, French-style dagger, under the ribs. We're looking for a right-handed man under five three with–"

"And the other two?" Gull interrupted.

De Quincey nodded. "The killers, you mean?"

Gull stepped forward, toying with the various instruments on the exhibit tray. "Not necessarily. They could be–"

"Your pardon, my lord, you know they are. I'm aware you'd love to keep Triumff in the cells, and haul him before the Chamber in the morning, but you know it won't wash. Those two down on the slabs, I recognised them anyway, but I've double-checked, just to be sure."

"And?" asked Gull.

"I've looked through the Hilliards[6]," said de Quincey. "They're both there. William Pennyman and Peter 'The Knife' Petre. All their priors involve sharp objects and the insertion of same into unwilling members of the public, et cetera et cetera. They were contract boys, knifemen, paid to kill Sir Rupert. You ought to thank him for taking them off the streets."

Gull snorted.

"Besides, there'll be testimony from the three bath attendants. Triumff will sail out of court. That's what he's good at, isn't it?"

Gull cracked his knuckles. "I know, I know... We'll have to let him and his savage go. I just... I just would love to know who hates Triumff so much they'd put a contract out on him."

"No idea at all then?" asked de Quincey.

"Only one," said Gull dourly, "and he's the arresting officer."

De Quincey smiled.

"Leave it with me," he said. "Things are a little lunatic at the moment, but later tonight, when it's quietened down, I'll get on the ouija, make a few calls, and see what I can turn up."

"I appreciate it," said Gull.

"No problem," de Quincey replied.

Little did de Quincey know, it would be a problem. Later would not turn out to be quiet at all.

At one minute past eight, the rain began again.

Night reclined languorously over the City, its darkness swaddling ten thousand winking lights. Somewhere in the

---

6 Named after their inventor, these are the files of miniature portraits kept of all known felons.

sky's black interior, thunder rumbled like moving furniture. A cold wind took up from the south, and then, as the last, delayed chime of the hour rang away from the tower of St Mary-le-Tardy, whose mechanism is famously thirty seconds slow, the rain returned.

The reflections of street-lamps shivered and broke as the raindrops pelted down into puddles left over from the morning. An air of gloom gathered over the rainy streets. Windows closed and curtains were drawn. Fires were built up, and pots and pans returned to their places under leaking roofs.

In the Rouncey Mare, Boy Simon attempted to get a discussion going on the possibility of England becoming too waterlogged to float on the Seas, but most of the Allhallows Walk regulars were banged up in a holding tank a mile away across the City, and the notion soon fizzled out.

In the tiered stalls of the Globe, theatre-goers groaned audibly and opened programmes out into roofs for their heads. The Chamberlain's Players, ten minutes into the first act of the provocative new drama Bard Lieutenant, sighed, and struggled on manfully as their costumes and scenery wilted.

Across the river, under the gathering storm and the tremble of thunder, the rain caused harmless arcs of blue, Magickal energy to short and discharge between the high stacks of the Battersea Powerdrome. Somewhere in Woolwich, a spear of lightning lanced down into a weathervane, and destroyed the tiled roof of St Carpel le Tunnel. The church caught, and the flames quickly spread to the scalding houses nearby. A terrible stench of burning offal pudding filled the night, and drove back many would-be firefighters. The resulting inferno soon filled half a street, and could be seen from the river. Old Father Thames, oily, sluggish and rain-dimpled, became a broken mirror for the firelight.

Upriver, at Windsor, the castle staff heard the distant, disgruntled thunder, smelt the rain in the air, and set about closing shutters and fastening windows. Baskets of logs were ferried in from the stores, and the drapes and wall-hangings pulled into place. The Queen was safely at Richmond for the night, but the comfort of other noble guests meant that the Castle had to maintain peak operating efficiency.

In the Oriel Banqueting Hall, Lord Slee turned from the window, swirling a crystal balloon of cognac in his hand. Sheet lightning flashed across the sky behind him as he looked at the three men still seated at the long table, the remains of the feast spread between them. Roustam de la Vega was quartering an orange with a silver dirk, and slowly consuming the juicy segments. He returned Slee's watchful gaze with a flick of his eyebrows. Jaspers was sitting well back in his chair, like a child slid low on a throne. A glass of port hung in his hand, and he looked drunk and vacant, but Slee knew better than to write off the Divine's sharp brain. The Duke of Salisbury was busy devouring the remains of the dressed swan, left on its platter, with noisy, champing relish. He tugged at the greasy flesh and gristle, spitting out inedible chunks, his mountainous stomach gurgling like a fermentation vat. Slee looked away, in distaste.

"Well, my friends," he said at length.

"Well indeed," replied the almost disembodied voice of the Divine. "We have eaten well, talked to excess, and plotted to the point of treason."

Salisbury coughed out a lump of swan-fat.

"I don't like that word," he announced, wiping his chin.

"Then what euphemism for our scheming would you like to use?" asked the Divine snidely. "It is treason, the deepest, darkest kind of treason. There is no gain to be made by disguising that."

Salisbury shrugged.

De la Vega put down his knife and washed his hands in the finger bowl.

"I am uneasy about the complexity of what we propose, señors," he said. It is all quite... desmañado... clumsy. There is no direct action to take. We rely upon the whims of others, waiting hungrily for their mistakes and errors. Is there not a more direct way?"

"No," replied Slee, softening the negative with a smile as de la Vega looked up. "Act directly, and we incriminate ourselves directly. There is a true art to intrigue, one bedded in bluffs, deceits and guile. I won't be another Crompton Finney."[7]

Slee resumed his place at the head of the table.

"This place... this Australia... is the key to our desires," he said. "I am sure there is new Arte there, new Arte that might be ours to tap. To have it, we must be subtle. It must be given to us, and we must receive it with gratitude and feigned surprise. The skill lies in making Triumff lose his grip on the prize by his own misdeeds and foolishness. With his feuding, his drunkenness, his reluctance to conform, he is already playing for us. His disgrace, or death, will suit our purpose. Either is simplicity itself to arrange."

Salisbury chuckled through a mouthful of pecan stuffing.

"Hockrake?" said Slee, sharply. "Something amusing?"

"That last thing might already be done," the Duke of Salisbury murmured, tugging at a flopping leg of the ex-swan.

"What do you mean?" asked Slee, getting to his feet. "What have you done?"

---

7 Spencer Crompton Finney, the fifth Earl of Tewkesbury during the reign of Elizabeth XXVII, who rose in revolt against his monarch after the lamentable Leek Famine of 1911. Historians described his plot to dethrone the Queen by marching his retainers to Richmond Palace and hammering on the door as, "lacking in the finer points of everything except sheer balls."

Salisbury looked up.

"Two rowdies, from the Cockspur in Cheapside, took laughably little of my gold to do the deed this afternoon…" he said, his voice trailing off as he became aware of the fierce gaze Slee had fixed him with. Worse still, Jaspers had sat forward, alert and beady-eyed.

"I… I mean… there's no way it can be traced. The knifemen had no idea who hired them. I–"

"If your moronic action has any ill repercussions, Hockrake, rest assured they will roost only in your house. We will deny everything. You'll go to the block alone." There was a malevolence in Slee's words that seemed to echo the encroaching storm outside the castle. Slee was especially good at that.

"I'm sorry," mumbled Salisbury, averting his eyes.

"No matter, for now," Slee said, refilling his glass from the decanter. "We shall soon see if your work is useful to us. If Triumff is already dead, so much the better. If not, then perhaps it will merely add to the collapse of his reputation."

"But hear me well, Hockrake," Slee added. "I will not brook your unilateral tinkerings again. If you are with us, then you are with us in all details. Is that clear?"

"It is," replied the Duke of Salisbury, pushing the dish of exploded swan away. Thunder rolled.

"So our next action?" asked de la Vega, bursting his last segment of citrus fruit with the point of his dagger.

"If Triumff lives, we continue to harry him, and engineer for the worst each aspect of his life until he breaks. The meanwhile, we will stir trouble in the City, from a safe distance. Anything and everything that can be upset, we will throw over by stealthy manipulation. The public must be made unhappy, ill at ease… frightened. The more we trouble the Queen and the Council with petty annoyances, the more we will distract them from the true threat we pose. Is your camp, dear Regent, all set for this?"

De la Vega nodded, and sipped his wine.

"The Spanish factions are rife with dispute," he said. "I have laid the foundations of diplomatic problems that will keep them at the throats of the English Court. Tomorrow, Pedro de Gramplo will petition again for his pork subsidy, and the Escorial will announce the observation of a day to commemorate the Armada, despite Lord Sutcliffe's lobby."

"That'll really get up the Navy's nose," mused Jaspers, "and old Three Ex's too."

"Indeed," smiled de la Vega. "Further, I have pressed my contacts in the Basque region to needle the Liberté Gauloise faction into resuming their nonsense. We have supplied them, clandestinely, with black powder and Toledo steel. I'll wager a New World coffer that the Queen sends at least another division of Light Horse to France before the end of the month. Troubled times for England, times that could split the Unity under a weak Queen, or so the public will perceive. A good time for us to commit treason and still be seen as heroes."

Slee plucked a grape from the dish in front of him and chewed it thoughtfully.

"All that remains is the Church," he said. "The Arte is the one thing trusted by all. Confound that belief, and the Unity will be squalling in our hands for help."

Jaspers got to his feet and crossed to the long walnut cabinets by the wall. He bent down and produced two seven-stemmed candelabra, which he set on the table and carefully lit with a match.

"I have that part of our treason in hand," he said with a grin. "It begins tonight. Fear, devilment, superstition, Goety... the banished trappings of Magick will return and be our handmaids. By dawn, the Church will be in uproar, and the Union too, and the Court and public will be outraged by that same uproar."

He looked up, his eyes starkly blue in the flame-light. "I caution you, gentlemen, that we have, this evening, passed beyond that place of no return. Such things will come to pass tonight that we can never undo. It is too late for regret or changed minds. There is no going back. Tonight, the Unity will shake and reel. Tomorrow, we will awaken to a different world."

Slee nodded, feeling a chill in his bones. De la Vega toyed with his blade as if his mind were far, far away. Salisbury trembled so much he was unable to contain his tumultuous wind any longer. As the outburst died away, de la Vega gestured up at the ceiling lamps with his dirk.

"Why the candles, mi amigo?" he asked.

"Wait, mi amigo," replied Jaspers with a voice that seemed to have been waiting in some dank, heathen barrow for thousands of years. "Wait and see."

THE CHAPTER THAT IS SIXTH.
In which there is a great darkness.

Doll Taresheet was wetter than a mallard's bum, as the saying goes, and crosser than a cardinal on a diet of Worms (as that other fine expression has it). She pulled her shawl up over her head and scurried across Paternoster Lane, hopscotching the puddles and the near-tidal gutters. The rehearsals had gone on for an hour too long and, of course, everyone was quite het up about the looming Masque, and they had finished ten minutes after the renewed downpour had begun. The trek across town from the Wooden Oh had all but ruined her second best gown. The ruff was sagging, the bodice and support waterlogged, and the petticoats and bum roll were stained with mud, and quite ruined. Furthermore, her Chinese fan, bought with a week's pay at the East India Company auction, was well and truly knackered.

Doll vaulted the far gutter's sluice, cursed the night openly, and darted into the doorway of number five, Paternoster Lane, slamming the door behind her.

The interior smelt of carrots and mutton, and a fire crackled in the grate. She shook off her cape, and tousled her ruined hairdo so that the fine chestnut locks slumped down loosely around her slender shoulders. Mistress Mary was embroidering by the fire with a bodkin so big she could have disembowelled a caribou with it. The dowdy old woman looked up with a short-sighted frown.

"Doll?" she queried, narrowly avoiding her thumb with the stabbing spike.

"Evening, Mary," said Doll. "I'd say 'good' but it isn't. Thank heavens for your fire." Doll chafed her hands and sat for a moment on the stool opposite the old lady.

"Have you heard the news today?" asked the elderly dam, impaling her work with ruthless stabs of the bodkin. "Some fellow went mad with a sword at the Dolphin Baths. Two dead. Eviscerated, they say."

"How nice," grimaced Doll.

The old lady chuckled to herself as if "eviscerated" meant "bopped on the head with an inflated sheep's bladder" (which it does in the Welsh Marches, though the usage is offset by their understanding of the expression "bladdered").

"Are you walking out with that nice Master Rupert tonight?" added Mistress Mary, rethreading her barb.

"Ohhh," mused Doll, "I don't think so. He's… busy, very probably."

"Such a nice young jackanapes," babbled Mistress Mary, regardless.

"Well, that's one word for him," said Doll, smiling sourly. She got to her feet. "I'm off now, Mary. I'm as tired as a baited bear at a ragged staff. I've got to get some sleep. It's the Masque this Saturday."

"And I'm so excited," replied Mistress Mary. "I do love a good firework."

"Indeed you do," smiled Doll, remembering the last Great Masque Day, when they had been required to ouija for a twenty-four hour glazier because Mistress Mary's Great Apollo Rocket had blown out all the back windows.

Mary nodded, and continued to murder her embroidery, as Doll turned and stomped up the narrow stairs into the upper levels of the boarding house. On the first landing, the air stank of turpentine. She peered in through the open doorway of the rooms rented by Luigi, a struggling, bohemian artist from Italia.

"How's it going, bambino?" she called. The long-haired painter looked up from his canvas and smiled his beautiful Latin smile, all teeth and flecks of oil paint.

"You tell me!" he invited, gesturing to his canvas, which was a fine but horsey portrait of a woman in a lettice cap and frangipani gloves. Portrait work like this helped him to earn his crust.

"It's not quite La Giaconda," Doll remarked, ducking out of the doorway.

"Ahh! What do you expect?" exclaimed Luigi in her wake, waving a mahl stick and a hog-bristle brush after her. "I can only work with what I have! The plain wives of coarse gentlemen who want a portrait for their fireplace! Ugly children who won't stand still! Wedding couples where my skill must hide the bride's bump better than her gown did! Horses! Horses and dogs!"

"Yeah, it's a hard life," she replied, heading on towards her room.

"But it could be so much better!" he protested. "Come back! I want to talk to you again, my lady, about you being my model! Dolce! The wonder of it! The sublime invocation of worldly beauty!"

"Nice try," Doll called back, as she clambered up the final flight to her rooms, "but you'll have to wax a lot more lyrical if you expect me to get my kit off and pose for you with swans and all that other nonsense."

"I try my very best!" he shouted up after her. "Take me to your Leda!"

Doll went into her lodgings, and closed the door behind her, shutting off Luigi's heartfelt pleas. Every night they were the same, and every night they were just as earnest, but Doll was reasonably sure they had less to do with the painting of pictures and more to do with the removal of clothing.

Her room was dark and cool, resounding with the pelt of rain outside. She breathed a deep sigh, threw aside her fan, and began to struggle with the savagely tight laces of her bodice, aching to be free of the drenched, festooning folds of the gown.

Doll was a striking woman in her late twenties, blessed with the sort of slender yet double-D cupped figure that made men swallow hard and behave attentively. Her face had been variously described as "well proportioned", "pleasing" and "finely featured". What it came down to, in simple terms, was that she was heart-stoppingly lovely. And she was an actress, but don't hold that against her just yet.

Doll crashed down on her bedspread and wriggled off her sopping slippers, pantofles and netherstocks, which she hurled at the drapes.

"Ow," said the drapes as a slipper bounced off them.

Cat-like, Doll got up on her bare feet and tip-toed towards the window, hefting up her right fist into a stiff cudgel, which she swung at the bulging curtains at nose-height.

There was a loud crack of displaced cartilage, and a faint whiff of the great smell of A Scent of Man.

"What was that for?" asked Rupert Triumff.

Triumff attempted to staunch the blood issuing from his nose with the corner of a lace kerchief.

"Nice punch... really nice punch," he moaned.

"Oh, shut up," said Doll, pouring two glasses of musket. "I've said I was sorry. It's your own bloody fault for hiding in the first place."

Triumff shook his head. "No, no. The first place would have been the closet. I was hiding in the second place."

"Shut up," she repeated, proffering him a glass of the famous Old Skinner's.

"I've had a bad day," muttered Triumff, nasally.

"Really?"

"Gull wants to kill me, the Queen wants to see me, and two knife-boys tried to stitch me up a treat in the baths. Plus, if I don't come up with something, sharpish, Uptil's homeland is going to get chewed into little bits by the reaver-fleet. And there's something going on at Court."

"Like what?"

Triumff got to his feet, felt faint, and sat down again. "Rumours," he said. "Everybody's so tense. They say there's something not right with the Cantrips."

"Define 'not right'?" she asked.

He shrugged, and said, "Last night, before I got a little over enthusiastic and challenged Gull to a duel–"

"You did what?"

"Forget that part," Triumff said with a testy wave of his hand. "Anyway, before that, I was in The World Turn'd Upside Your Head with Johnny Hacklyutt and the boys, and he said he'd heard that something was not right with the Cantrips."

"Wow, talk about your authentic and unimpeachable source."

"I'm just repeating what he said," Triumff shrugged.

"Actually, I've heard things too," said Doll. She sipped her drink. "All these rumours are going around. Everyone backstage was gossiping."

"Rumours?"

"Rumours of bad omens. Portents. People on the ouija hearing sinister voices on crossed lines. There's talk of stuff. There's talk of Goety, and worse."

"This is exactly my point," said Triumff. "I've half a mind to–"

"You've half a mind, let's leave it there," said Doll. "And for God's sake, leave the jinxy conjuration stuff and nonsense to the cardinals and the Union."

"Oh, like they're the experts," said Triumff. "Come on, Doll. Everyone knows the Arte only lets the Church play with it. I just wish the country could forget about Magick and try and do things for itself. Machines, now–"

"You've been thinking about Beach again, haven't you?" asked Doll, cutting him off.

"What if I have? Uptil's people have got it all worked out. I have this horrible feeling I'm going to let them down badly," said Triumff.

Doll leaned across and kissed his mouth. It was one of the better things that had happened to him that day.

Doll smiled, and then blotted out her smile with a frown.

"What was that?" she asked.

An animal squalled somewhere under the window.

"Cats," said Triumff. "Cats fighting. That's all."

It wasn't. In the coal-blackness of the alley next to number five, Paternoster Lane, stood a bruiser of a ginger tom called Rusty, who owned Mistress Mary (this is perfectly correct usage. Humans, in their arrogance and lack of insight, believe they own cats, like they do dogs. The reverse is so utterly true that they entirely fail to see it). Rusty, who was ordinarily pretty confident that he was chief kahuna thereabouts in the spranting, siring, hackle-raising and territorialising departments, howled again and fled like a furry cannonball.

Under normal circumstances of alarm and agitation, Rusty would inflate himself to three times his normal size, and pull the sort of face usually only found on outraged racoons that have been mistaken for novelty pencil sharpeners. Right now, he was so scared, he clean forgot, and exited, thin and lank and jittery, into the lane.

The cause of his concern stood in the alley, pulled its cloak around its shoulders, and stamped its booted feet to keep warm. A gutter-drip spattered across its ear. It took off its glove, licked the back of its paw, and washed the droplets from its furry, whiskered cheek.

Meanwhile, in a garret in the attic spaces of a house on Fleet Street, a garret which was all he could afford unless his fortunes changed, as it is nigh on impossible to rent a decent place on the sort of page-rate the tabloids offer, not that there was much of that around, even, and lord knows he looked, sniffing out a story here and there, always coming home to this stinking garret that perpetually smelled of fried garlic and rancid poultry thanks to the tandoori three doors down, and there was no bath to speak of, and a cooked meal would be a luxury, and even the cockroaches had taken to looking in the property section of the Standard each Thursday...

In a garret on Fleet Street, your humble servant, the author, Master Wllm Beaver, sat, scribbling away by the light of the single overhead lamp. It was a piece on "Ten Things You Didn't Know About Hose", as I recall. It was destined never to be finished. My HB pencil had just broken, and a rummaging search was underway in the drawers of the desk for a clasp knife with which to re-point it before item four ("You can wear it upon thine head if you seek to obtain money with menaces from a Banking House, Real Estate Society or Postal Depot") slipped from my mind.

Whereupon, everything went black.

I, Wllm Beaver, discounted a sudden, crippling stroke, mainly because I believe it pays to be optimistic. I straightened up slowly in my chair, my eyes becoming accustomed to the gloom. The only light was the faintest outside sheen of the far-away lightning. The City, from the window, was black as pitch. There was a crashing, and the sound of voices from below as fellow residents realised it wasn't just a prolonged blink, and set about walking into things in a search for matches.

The City was utterly, utterly dark.

It wasn't local. If you'd been there, you would have seen the sprawl of the whole city in darkness, or rather you wouldn't. There was only the merest hint of something big and black against something bigger and blacker. Just the Thames, like a ribbon of mirror, glittered in the storm-light. Usually, the city at night lies like a black velvet cape encrusted with winking sequins, spread across the muddy earth by some titanic Raleigh for some celestial Elizabeth.

That night, even the poetry had been turned off. Everything in London, under the beating rain, was dark, and blind, and cold and frightened.

In the Rouncey Mare, Boy Simon believed for some moments that he had gone blind, and coped with the sudden affliction stoically, considering first how his ailment might earn him the sympathetic shillings of passers-by if he took to wearing a placard around his neck reading "God hath blinded me and made me thirsty". He also figured that being blind, he wouldn't get as much work as a drover, which, on balance, meant he would get more time to spend in the Rouncey Mare. Then he realised that it was the lights that had failed and not his optic nerves, and at once joined in the general activity of bumbling around. It is strange, but true that every time the power fails, and people are plunged into darkness, they immediately start blundering around three or four times as much as they do when the lights are on. God knows what they think they're going to achieve, apart from bruises and broken ornaments.

At Richmond, Cardinal Woolly rose from his darkened lectern in the library, and crossed himself. The void beyond the rain-spattered window confirmed his fears. He fumbled for the hanging bell-pull, and rang on it repeatedly for the domestic staff.

All the while, his lips silently moved in prayer.

At the Yard, the sudden gloom set the prisoners in the cells to chanting, and rattling on the bars with their tin cups. The only light in the Affray Room was the coal of de Quincey's pipe.

"Dear me," muttered de Quincey in the sudden silence that immediately followed the abrupt lack of light, "here's something you don't see every day of the week."

"What's that, doc?" asked an invisible serjeant named Tomkins to his left.

"Absolutely bastard nothing at all," said de Quincey.

At Windsor in the Oriel Banqueting Hall, the light had dwindled, but not died. Fourteen candle flames cast out long shadows from the table, glinting across glasses and cutlery, and hollowing the features of the four conspirators. Slee began a slow, approving handclap. Jaspers chuckled in response.

"I hope," murmured de la Vega, uneasily, "that no one is afraid of the dark."

"Only," answered Jaspers, "the whole of London."

Rupert and Doll broke their latest kiss, each assuming the other had turned off the lamp. Then there was a loud complaint from Mistress Mary below in the house, and a clatter and a curse from Luigi's apartment.

Triumff slid off the bed, to his feet, and pulled one of the blankets with him as a loincloth.

"What's going on?" asked Doll. The bedsprings broinged under her as she wriggled up on the pillows.

"Shhhh," said Triumff from the window, "the lights are off."

"I can see that," she said. "Or rather—"

"No, the lights," said Triumff in a tone of voice that Doll didn't much like. "All across the City. All the lights."

She padded, naked, across to him at the window, and huddled under his blanket. They stared out at the nothingness beyond. The storm boomed away to the east.

"The power Cantrips have failed. They must've done."

"That's not meant to happen," said Doll.

"I know," said Triumff, "but if you recall, I said that something was not right about the Cantrips. My guess is they just became really not right."

He began rummaging around on the floor.

"What are you doing?" Doll asked.

"Looking for my shoes."

"Why?"

"Because if something's not right, I can't sit around here procrasturbating," said Triumff.

"What?" asked Doll.

"It's a word!"

Doll hauled him up to face her in the dark, her thumb and index finger pinching his battered nose.

"Ow! Ow!" he protested.

"You weren't thinking of going to the Powerdrome? Not at this time of night? Not when you're in all this trouble as it is? Were you?" asked Doll.

"Doe," he answered. She released his nose.

"Good," she said, and slid her arms round his neck. "The

Union will get it all sorted out. That's their job. And we don't
need any light, do we?"

"No," he answered again.

"Besides, at least if you stay here, you can't get into any
more trouble, can you?"

THE SEVENTH CHAPTER.
Night thickens.

Dragon-shapes and bat-silhouettes swung around through the storm in the sky above the Battersea Powerdrome. On the flagstone apron in front of the drome's great entrance, hooded figures scurried out of the doorway's shelter into the wind, and formed a wide ring with their flaming torches.

The dragons came down.

Gull landed first, and then the six huscarls, slowing the wing-beats of their great wooden-framed Vincis with expertise. The torch-bearers hurried forward, taking the weight of each Vinci as the riders unbuckled their harnesses. The huge canvas wings flapped in the estuary wind.

"Stow them somewhere, out of the wind. We want them serviceable for the flight back," instructed Gull. The seven flying machines were carried away into the hallway of the drome. Gull and his huscarls marched along behind, pulling off gloves, goggles and scarves, and wiping water from their brows. The robed figures held up the torches to guide their way.

"Where's Natterjack?" asked Gull.

"Here, milord," answered the eldest of the robed figures. Natterjack was a weary, anxious-looking man with salt-and-pepper hair. "Vivat Regina. The Union bids our guests welcome and ho–"

"Save the formal guff, old man. We came as soon as the lights failed. What's the story?"

"We… don't know," admitted the Union rep. "The doors to the Cantrip Chamber are barred from within, and there's no reply to our knocking."

"When did you discover this?" asked Gull.

"When the lights failed, milord. The shift had changed but an hour before. There are five Union members on station in there. It shouldn't be possible for this to happen. There are back-ups… fail-safes…"

They stopped outside a pair of massive oak doors, dotted with iron studs, and engraved with ancient scripts that it was a good idea not to read.

"Break them down," said Gull to his huscarls.

"Milord!" interceded Natterjack. "We have sent for the cardinals. Surely we should wait until they–"

"Every footpad, cut-throat and opportunist in the City is going to think it's Christmas. We can't maintain security anywhere… including at the Palace. Break it down," Gull insisted.

Natterjack nodded, and then stood aside with his comrades.

Two of the largest huscarls approached the doors, sized them up, mentally shook hands with them and popped in gum-shields, and then laid into the solid oak with shoulders that had room on them for mantle clocks and souvenirs from Skegness. After twenty seconds of tooth-rattling impact, there was a splintering noise. Another few shoulder-barges, and the doors reached the end of their three-hundred-year-long working life.

A smell like that which permeated Wllm Beaver's garret, only a thousand times worse, welled out of the Cantrip Chamber like a fog. Huscarl and Union-man alike coughed and gagged. The two beefy huscarls, whose shoulders had beaten the doors by two falls and a submission, bore the brunt of it. Their stomachs tried to exit via their throats, but they staunchly fought back the nausea. They were tough, they were veterans, they had brawled and bashed their ways through the world's trouble spots and come out laughing. It took an awful lot to better them.

There was an awful lot in the Chamber beyond.

The two huscarls entered, looked around, looked up, saw what was making the smell, and threw up involuntarily in the doorway.

Gull drew his rapier and covered his nose and mouth with his kerchief.

"Stay back here," he instructed his men and the Union team. Absolutely none of them had even thought of doing anything else.

Gull stepped between his heaving, retching bruisers, and entered the room.

Somehow, he kept his dinner internalised.

The thirteen crystal balls, each the size of a man's head, that usually stood on the gilt frame in a careful pyramid, and focusing the pure energies of the Cantrips, had been smashed, as if by some furious hammering. Crystal shards were scattered in a constellation across the intricate mosaic floor. Shorting, unfocused Magickal energy sparked and spattered across the room, like loose, torn ribbons fluttering in the wind. There was a stench of sulphur, and ozone, and something else... something fried and burnt and blistered.

Gull looked up.

The five Union men who had been on duty looked down at him from the rafters, staring out of scorched sockets, their white teeth smiling out of blackened gums.

They had each been crisped and seared by some unimaginable heat. Then, something had put them forty feet up in the rafters to cool, like burnt gingerbread men from an oven.

Gull swallowed hard.

He forced himself to look away, and swept his gaze around the room. Someone… something had done this, yet it was no longer here. There was nowhere to hide, and no exit save the barred and bolted door. Gull tried not to think of invisible spirits. He tightened his grip on his rapier.

Then he saw the daubed writing on the back wall: tall, ugly, childish letters marked out in…

Gull's grip on his sword tightened. Something had removed gallons of blood from the five dead men before frazzling them into dried shells.

He read the slogans, shaking with both fear and anger. Somehow, the childish writing, the misspelling and the malformed letters made them all the worse.

They said:

CANTRIPS DOWN
TO HELLE WITH THE UNITTY
ELISABETH IS AN HORE
THIS FOR YOU AND YOR FAMILY TO
THIS BE MY FIRST TRIUMF

Natterjack caught at Gull's sleeve as the guard captain strode from the room.

"What does it–" he began.

"Get your men in there. The place must be cleaned," Gull told him. "Try to rig up a temporary repair if you can. The cardinals will know. I'll get on the ouija and summon guards to reinforce and support you. Be doubly vigilant…" He tailed off, realising how much he was shaking.

"What does it mean?" asked the elderly Union man in a small, frightened voice.

Gull looked at him, and said, "It means treason. It means diabolic perversion. It means Triumff is dead."

"Why?" asked Natterjack.

Gull weighed his rapier carefully in his gloved fist. "Because I'm going to kill the bastard myself," he said.

THE NEXT CHAPTER.

Bedevilment has a unique odour, something like burnt molasses, but less inviting, and by dawn the next day hints of it had spread out far across the glittering expanse of the Unity. People woke up and smelt it on the air, like they smelled stale wood-smoke the morning after the Midsummer Revels. They smelt it, and then they got up, afraid without knowing why.

From the beating heart of the City outwards, down the Valley, through the Boroughs, across the Shires and the Wealds and the Wolds and the Ridings, over fenland, farmland, woodland and heath, up scarps, over rivers, past coasts and ports and shorelines and beyond, the citizens of the Unity went about their lives and trades with little additions that morning: here a knotted brow, here a patter of rosary beads, there an anxious sigh, there a nervous prayer.

In the Suffolk village of Ormsvile Nesbit, where the geese outnumber the human residents, the smell seemed to have got in the air and the stones, and the milk.

Mother Grundy looked down at the curdy contents of the pail, and wrinkled a forehead that already needed a hem and a good iron. She extended a finger that was as true and unknobbly as a cudgel wasn't, and inserted it into the milk like a dipstick. Withdrawing it, she sucked it thoughtfully, and more wrinkles over-wrinkled themselves on top of wrinkles.

"Hmph," she murmured.

She patted Nettie the heifer on the rump to reassure her, took the offending bucket out of the dairy, and tipped the contents unceremoniously down the drain-midden.

It hissed alchemically as it gurgled away.

"Hmph," murmured Mother Grundy again, and headed for the house.

Mother Grundy was a well-worn woman of incalculable years. It was said she could remember half a dozen coronations. She didn't look old, as such, just hard and angular and lean. Her clothes hung from her rangy frame like curtaining nailed to a gibbet. Her hair was raked back over her skull in layers that looked like they had been beaten out of old pewter, and was held in place by iron pins that seemed stapled to her scalp. The structure of her face was not so much bone as a lifetime of concerns: worries over family weddings, wayward sons, idle daughters, awkward neighbours, fractious grandchildren and sick livestock. She had raised and scrimped, toiled and spun, cared and midwifed, tutored and advised. She was autumnal. She was stoic. The community clacked around her skirts like milling geese, waiting for help and counsel and titbits. She braved long winters, suffered summer heat, and abhorred both the passage of time and any wastage thereof.

Without her, most reckoned, the village of Ormsvile Nesbit would have vanished, bewildered, into the soil, a generation since.

There were a few occasions on which she was known to smile, but that morning after St Dunstan's Day was not one of them.

In the numb chill of the farmhouse scullery, she hung her
shawl on the door-peg (where it draped more fulsomely than
it had around her shoulders) and began to fill a hopsack with
various sprigs of dried herbs, a jar or two of preserved
produce, a batch of Bath Olivers wrapped in grease-proof
paper, an elderly book, a ram's-horn-shanked knife and a
flask of tea.

There was something ill abroad, as the saying went. The
signs positively yelled of it. And they weren't the usual calf
with two heads or non-laying hens or red sky type signs (as
in the country proverb: "Red sky at night, swineherd's delight; red sky in the bedroom, thatch is on fire"). They were
neither as crude nor as sensational as that. They were real
signs, bad signs, signs in the weave of the grass, the dew on
webs, the call of birds from the woods and the tang of burnt
molasses in the milk.

Mother Grundy was uneasy, and that was a bad sign in itself.

Just after eight in the morning, a crust-maker's apprentice
named Gavin met Mother Grundy on the lane out of the village. Gavin, like many pie-men, was simple. He suffered a
mild mental infirmity that meant he was blessed with several
personalities, but he was good people.

Gavin shifted his pie-tray to his left shoulder, and tipped
his cap to the woman as she strode past.

"Fine morning, Mother Grundy," he suggested as she
strode past.

"Not in the least," she answered.

"Where are you off to, then?" he added.

She paused for a moment, and fixed him with a lancing
stare.

"The City," she told him, and then continued to march away
down the misty lane between the spinneys of ash and lime.

Gavin hurried on into Ormsvile Nesbit to spread the news. Mother Grundy was going to the City. Not only was that unheard of, even a simple pie-man knew it was possibly the worst sign there ever could be.

The signs spread across the turning globe, as fast as the line of daylight crept around. An hour before Mother Grundy had even plonked down her pail under Nettie's rotund udder, the signs were already reaching more distant regions of the Unity.

In the cypress-groved hills above La Spezia, where everything looked like it had been done in egg-tempera on stuccoed wooden panels, the first light of dawn grazed against the pumice-pink walls of a lone tower that stood at the crest of a wooded slope like a finger of Battenberg cake topped off with an icing of chunky red tiles.

One strand of light entered the tower through the single slit window near the top, and found itself slalomed and bent unexpectedly by a configuration of polished lenses and mirrors, finely set in a skeletal frame of stripped yew. The light twisted, refracted, reflected, sidestepped, dropped, levelled out, cornered sharply, gasped in alarm, and finally shot vertically down onto a horizontal plate of oil-buffed glass.

Giuseppe Giuseppo leaned forward in the chair he had set by the plate an hour before dawn, and watched the column of light, slowed by its tortuous path through the apparatus, drip like neon honey onto the smooth surface. It twinkled into intangible ingots of photonic gold, and then settled gently into a fanned-out specimen of the captured spectrum.

Giuseppe Giuseppo blinked his sleepy eyes for a moment or two, and then looked more closely.

At least two members of the spectrum were missing, and three others were in the wrong order.

He rose from the high-backed chair, and reached out to adjust the setting of the device, but withdrew his fingers from the brass handles at the last moment, and sat down again for a closer look. Giuseppe knew he had adjusted and re-adjusted the settings to the point of obsession the sunset before. Nothing had disturbed his apparatus in the night, the lenses were all clean and the wood unwarped.

It was the light that was wrong.

Giuseppe swallowed hard, and hurried across to his study desk. He lit a lamp, and leafed through his book of tables and notes, throwing aside blueprints for wide-bodied gliders, bathyscaphs, retractable quills, airbags and roll-bars for racing landaus, methods of refrigerated food preservation and golf-ball embossers. After a few minutes' scrambling, during which the genius outpourings of over a decade spilled onto the floor in a thick drift of parchment, he found what he was looking for, stuffed between an essay on "The Potentialities of Telephony" and a treatise he had composed on the "Elektrifikation and Harmonisation of Gauges" for a system of railed omnibus that hadn't even been built.

It was a book, quarto in size, bound in dark and patchy kid-skin, and held shut by a loop of black ribbon. With reverential fingers, Giuseppe slipped off the ribbon, turned open the cover, and began to skim through the vellum pages of tight, precise ink-script, cursing as he always did in such moments; that clever-clever mirror writing was so difficult to speed read.

There were, perhaps, two dozen copies of Leonardo's *Principia De Tenebrae* extant in the known Unity, and no reason to suppose any existed outside its territories. All, except this one, were in the possession of cardinals and senior divines of the Church, and all, except this one, were incomplete, printed editions. This manuscript draft, in the Master's own hand, had been in Giuseppe's family since the Re-Awakening. The story went that the old Master had given it to Giuseppe's forebear Niccolo for safekeeping when Niccolo had been apprenticed to him as a paint-mixer. The Church, Giuseppe was sure, would rack him, spit him, draw him, eighth him, burn him as a heretic, demolish his tower, torch his vineyards, and contract out plagues of locusts on all his friends and relations if they knew he had a copy. Much had been surmised over the years about what the Father of the Arte had "edited out" of his manuscript before committing it to print. Many were the rumours of an unexpurgated manuscript somewhere on a dusty shelf in a gloomy corner of a forgotten library in the back end of the Unity. After all this time, few believed those rumours could be true.

After a few moments struggling and squinting, Giuseppe called the Most Important Book in the World a very rude name, and stormed downstairs to fetch his shaving mirror.

When his housekeeper, Maria, arrived an hour later, she found Giuseppe in the tower room, under the distracting swing of the pendulums, packing such items as a scroll-butt snaphaunce revolver into an open valise.

He barely looked up as she entered, but gestured to a drawstring purse of coins on the desk beside him.

"Go to the port quickly, please," he told her. "Find me a berth on the next merchantman bound for England."

She began to object, but cut it short as he turned to look at her. She didn't like the look of the look.

"How long will you be gone?" she asked instead.

"If I don't come back," he replied, "I doubt you'll notice."

So the ripples spread.

Five hours after Mother Grundy had set the pail beneath Nettie, the dawn finally arrived, out of breath, through the evergreens of the Senenoyak forests and twinkled off the shore-waters of Lake Tenantochook.

The sky was as clear blue as only a sky can be, and by anybody's standards, seemed the biggest, handsomest, fittest sky in the whole world. Rakish, adolescent mountains, capped in serious ice, and bearded with emerald goatees of fir and spruce, struck muscular poses against the fierce blue, happy and proud that they were not yet tainted with a paleface name.

Beneath their taut shoulders, the lake, which would have been a sea in any other part of the world, was transparent green, like bottle-glass. Salmon cut through its clarity like chromium torpedos. Grizzlies the size of fur-upholstered garden sheds prowled the shoreline, being mythic. Wolves, grey as slate, large as ponies, padded through the forests, and sang to the setting moon. Snow-hooded eagles with beaks like halberds and wings like top-gallants waited patiently for the chance to symbolise monumental capitalist democracy, and caught salmon the size of sofas to pass the time.

Tatunghut watched the light approaching, and reached into his pouch-bundle for something reassuring, but found only tobacco leaves, a sucking pipe, part of a dried sidewinder and a beaver's tail.

He pulled a thick blanket around his shoulders, dragged back the drop-hide door, and crept out of the lodge, heading for the lake-edge.

The calls of the loons sounded ill at ease to him. From his people's encampment, dogs woke and growled and yapped

---

8 In the Senenoyak language, Tatunghut means literally "Runs With Scissors". Chinchesaw, on the other hand, means "One Hand Clapping". He had had his name changed by deed poll from "Wahanoka" ("Swarthy Caribou") at the age of twelve because he fancied something a little more interesting, and was tired of the older boys "accidentally" calling him "Wohonako" ("Does It With His Horse").

distractedly. Tatunghut looked down at the water that lapped around the toes of his moccasins, glad he had chosen to wear the ones with the fur side inside and the caulked side outside.

Something unwelcome was edging across the Land of his Ancestors, something insidious and cunning that carried the unmistakable scent of manitou.

Chinchesaw strolled down across the beach to join him, hands on his hips, breathing in the morning breeze through a cheerful smile.

"You're up early, Tatunghut[8]," he said.

"Bad wind," replied the long-limbed shaman, gravely.

Chinchesaw nodded sympathetically. "Too much buffalo, I expect."

"No, no," said Tatunghut, holding up a hand that had been known to divert storms and flummox cougar. "Something bad is stirring. Far away, across the Great Water, in the Distant Place. Something bad."

Chinchesaw considered this for a few moments. As far as he and most of the Senenoyak People cared, the strange, hairy, rough-voiced men who came across the Great Water in wooden islands from the Distant Place deserved as much badness as could be sent their way. They were full of vulgar customs, crude habits and dubious ethics, and could kill you from four bow-shots away with a piece of lead the size of an alfalfa sprout. What's more, they could not be deterred from the belief that the Senenoyak and their neighbours in the Plains and the Uplands wanted to exchange things for strings of glass beads. However, Chinchesaw knew Tatunghut. He knew how seriously the shaman took the unseen workings of the manitou.

"You're not thinking of... going there, are you?" he asked, nervously.

"Going there?" asked the shaman.

"To do something about it. It'd be just like you, Tatunghut, going off on a wild vision quest to fight the demons that plague another people. The Distant Placers can face their own problems. Don't you get tangled up in their affairs. Besides, they're an ugly, smelly lot."

Tatunghut managed a smile.

"Rest assured, brother, I won't go," he said. "It is too far, and even if I did go, I would get there too late. It is a task for their shamans. I just hope by the Great Spirit that they have noticed this Badness in time."

"I'm sure they have," said Chinchesaw in encouragement.

"Maybe," Tatunghut said, sighing deeply. "They seem so dull-witted and insensitive. Maybe they are unaware of the stirrings in the Spirit Plains."

The wind coursed across the lake, tugging at their plaited hair. Chinchesaw brushed a few loose strands of hair out of his kohl-edged eyes.

"They do have shamans," he said. "I've heard talk of them. They call them…" The young brave was silent for a moment as he searched for the word.

"Kardenowls," he said at last. "These Kardenowls will know what to do. You mark my words. Don't you worry about it."

"I suppose so. It's just…" Tatunghut paused. "I have such a great reservation."

Chinchesaw brightened.

"Well, quite," he said. "So why on Earth would you want to leave it?"

THE NINTH-EST CHAPTER.

As the varied thoughts of Ormsvile Nesbit, La Spezia and Senenoyak turned towards it, London woke, coughed, scratched its arse, and got up.

Carters, drovers and pedlars rattled and hacked despondently across the wooden bridges into the City, and were greeted by an offputting and rancid smell (something like past-it eggs or retired fish or a very, very blocked privy) that had welled up through the streets in the night, and refused to dispel.

The markets were unusually quiet that morning. Everybody was breathing through their mouths, and no one felt much like calling their wares. Pulling himself from his sacking bed at the back of the Rouncey Mare, Boy Simon felt like going to church for some unaccountable reason. His head still rang with the echoes of a night full of terrible dreams. Unfortunately, he found the doors of St Dunstan's locked, since the parson of St Dunstan's was still abed after too much porter at the Saint's Day feast the night before. Once again, though indirectly, drink thwarted the old drover's attempts to clean up his act, and so he meekly turned on his shabby heels and arrived back at the tavern for first orders.

Talk in the tavern was low and morose. Most of the regulars had only just got back after a night in the cells and a morning at the Assizes, and most of their reserves of beer-money had gone on fines or bail or bribes. Those in the know reckoned that Sublime Lore lay at the root of all the problems. "Magick stink" they called the ripe fog in the street outside. There had been word of "wicked business" over in Battersea during the night. Someone mentioned "The Beast" and "The Last Days", and someone else grimly misquoted the Revelation of John the Divine. Another round of frothy porter and fruity musket was ordered and consumed. Someone hypothesised about the result of the coming Saturday's match.

Then the talk *really* got serious.

Circling flocks of gulls, driven up the estuary by coastal storms in the night, mobbed and shrieked around the dome of St Paul's and all the roofs and spires eastwards as far as Ian Paisley Park. The scribes and paternosters in Creed Street hurried to work through an unseasonably heavy and viscous campaign of saturation defecating.

Climbing out of his modest private carriage by the steps of the Cathedral, Cardinal Woolly found himself face to face with beady-eyed, inquisitive herring gulls and terns instead of the usual petitioning knot of crippled pigeons. He shooed them aside as he thumped up the steps, and they broke around him in a deafening chorus of seafaring oaths, and shat on his coach.

The Cathedral had been closed for the day, and two young divines stood guard at the west door to let the cardinal through. He nodded to them distractedly.

Once inside the vast darkness of St Paul's, Woolly allowed himself a moment's pause and reflection, letting the soft calm of the place filter through him and slow down his agitation.

The Cathedral's shadows were soft and velvet, the light stained into muted colours by the arched windows. Far off, the choir breathed out a liturgical moan that seemed to have been planed smooth by the action of the heavy air. In moth-soft voices, they were intoning the chant "Pax Vobiscum to the Left Hand Side".

A distinguished group of elders awaited him in the sacristy. Cardinal Gaddi stood in quiet conference with two representatives from the Curial Office, toying nervously with the tassels on his biretta. There were a number of diocesan commissioners, significant deacons and divines, the priests of nineteen parishes and two senior intendents from the Church-Guild School at Westminster, including Praetor Enoch.

A catechism of greeting nods and responses ruffled through the group at the cardinal's entry.

"Thank you all for attending," began the cardinal. "As you know, this past night has seen most unwelcome events spoil the spiritual calm of our city."

"And further afield," put in a voice from the crowd.

Woolly looked up and recognised the Bishop of Reading.

"Indeed, my friend. We must, this morning, begin work to execute a policy that will at once smoke out this heresy, quash it, and maintain the security of the Church and State the while."

"No kidding," said the Bishop of Reading.

"I propose the initial work to be divided thus. Praetor Enoch – turn all the efforts of the Guild to ascertaining the precise nature of the Arte abused so last night, and attempt to trace from whence it could have come."

The praetor nodded.

"I ask the curial officers and the commissioners to liaise with all aspects of the Church to keep us all informed of developments. It is more than likely that clues and evidence of this conspiracy may lie in some of the more remote parishes, where such things might be plotted away from the busy eye of the City."

Woolly noted the assent of the blue-robed officers.

"For the rest of us," he continued, "I urge you all to return to your dioceses and prepare for wonderment. Calm your congregations, soothe away their fears. Announce the special celebration of any minor saints to take their minds off it... Praetor?"

The praetor shrugged, and said, "St Oscar and St Raquel are coming up. Traditionally we don't do much for either. Nothing big until Occimanificaniment, which is the second Sunday coming, and then St Rufus, really, but..."

"Give it a go. Oscar and Raquel. Observational knees-up, Bring and Buy, feasting and altar wine. Each of you, make your flock too preoccupied with putting up bunting and having a good time to think about what's been going on."

There was some nodding and a few exchanges of ideas. Then, Cardinal Gaddi's voice rose over the murmuring.

"It seems, brother cardinal, that the source of this problem lies within our brotherhood," he said.

Silence fell upon the group.

"Only one of the Church could have the ability to perpetrate such a crime. I am sorry to seem so bleak, but there is no other explanation."

Woolly nodded.

"I'm afraid I concur with you, brother," he said. "This has come from within. None of us are above suspicion. We must all be especially vigilant."

Gaddi smoothed his collar distractedly.

"What I mean to say is, how are we going to combat a cancer within the Church?" he asked.

"We could try a guided missal," suggested the Bishop of Reading.

"We combat it with the very body created for such a purpose," replied Woolly. He turned to the young man standing to Praetor Enoch's left, who had been silent since the meeting had begun. "Brother Divine?"

"Infernal Affairs has already begun its investigation," replied Jaspers with a smile that made Woolly think of predatory fish, and sympathise with convicted heretics. "We will be merciless."

The curial meeting broke up shortly afterwards. Everybody seemed anxious to be off. As it clattered down Hercules Street on its way back to Richmond, Cardinal Woolly's carriage passed Neville de Quincey, who was trudging home after a long night-shift at the Yard. The cardinal, struggling to compose an encyclical bull on the nature of the emergency, which was turning out to have very little that was encyclic about it, and a great deal that was bull, didn't notice the drab, weary, pipe-puffing man as he went past.

De Quincey was tired and irritable. The bad night had got worse and worse, and he'd been forced, eventually, to turn one of the Yard's cellars into a makeshift morgue to cope with the overspill of bodies the Militia had brought in.

Most if it had been quite literally an overspill, too: six knifings, two batterings to death, one garrotting, one throwing bodily from the upstairs window of a high-class stew called the Ruff House, one shooting by a wide-bore pepperbox in a spontaneous duel, and one pinning to an oak door with a crossbow bolt through the bread basket, not to mention the awful victims of the incident at the Powerdrome.

The mood of the City had been ugly the previous night, cranky and spoiling for a brawl, and the dead represented only those outbursts that had ended in actual killings. The

Yard's cells were packed to overflowing with offenders, and the magistrates were going to have a busy morning. And it would only get worse. Masque Saturday was coming up.

Most of the boys at the Yard had put it down to the blackout and the whiplash of reactionary lawbreaking that it had caused, but de Quincey knew there was more. There had been the look on Gull's face for a start. And Masque Saturday...

The City seemed to shiver in the stinking cold, and de Quincey shivered with it, aching for his bed.

Triumff, heading home for Amen Street just after eight, bought two apple fritters and a paper cone of custard from a street vendor, and gingerly began to consume the piping-hot wares as he crossed Irongate Wharf and headed down the Embankment. It was a very roundabout route back to the lanes of Soho, but Triumff liked to be close to the river, which in turn was close to the sea, whenever his mind needed clearing. It was like being connected to the source. This was the case most mornings, particularly after a heavy night. It was even more the case this morning. He was as sober as a judge, bright-eyed and wide awake, but he was suffering with an idea-hangover from the night before. The things he had thought and conjectured about during the blackout hadn't agreed with him. He'd certainly had one too many unpleasantly strong ideas. That was always his trouble. Once he started on the strong thinks, he didn't know when to stop.

A dull coal of possibility throbbed in his brow, aching likelihoods pincered behind his ears and the base of his skull, and a tense nervous conclusion lacerated his temples.

He stopped by the railing over the Petty Watergate, and looked out across the grey flood. It was choppy and frothy, and thick with leaves and branches downed upstream by the night's storm. Seagulls turned and banked around the river piles and bridge supports. A Thames barge, its one-hundred-and-twenty-ton cargo sliding effortlessly down-river under the vast tanned canvas expanses of the spritsail, strolled past on the ebb, foam scrolling around its chined bilges. Triumff watched its graceful passage, and longed to be aboard, heading for the open sea. Even a shallow-draught would suit him now: a sturdy boat and a sheet of canvas to catch the winds and carry him away from this pestilent rat-hole of intrigue.

He ate another fritter.

A high-sided covered wagon clattered to a halt some yards down the waterfront. Triumff shot it a cursory glance and then gave it a second, slower appraisal. It was dirty grey and spattered with mud as if it had just come up from the Wharfhead, but the twin team were big, restless thoroughbreds, and there was a sparkle to the brasses that no amount of boot polish could disguise. The carter sat rigid on the buckboard as his companion slowly dismounted, and began to cover the distance between the wagon and Triumff with measured, purposeful strides. He was a big man, dressed in give-nothing-away dark hose and tunic with a short, black cape.

Plain-clothes, assessed Triumff. He swallowed the last chunk of fritter and began to stroll deliberately in the opposite direction.

The footsteps behind him went up a gear. Triumff accelerated a tad, and began to whistle the song about the Guinea Coast to off-set his increase in speed. The footsteps behind stopped walking and began to trot. Triumff broke into a loose jog, and risked a look back. The man was right behind him, beginning to run.

"Rupert Bartholomew Seymour Triumff?" he began.

The cone of warm custard smacked him in the face and put him off running altogether. Triumff exploded into a gallop.

"Oi!" bellowed the be-custarded man, and the cry was followed by a sharp blast on a silver whistle.

Triumff vaulted the gate at the end of Petty Walk, and sprinted away from the river, the fritters lumping up and down uncomfortably in his stomach. Passers-by on the street looked at him curiously as he thundered past. As he turned off onto Rake Lane, he glanced back again and saw the sides of the wagon drop down, the canvas awning skirt back and a lance of six armed men disgorge from its interior. Each was the twin of the man he had engulfed in custard: tall, broad, professional and dressed in simple black clothes. They hurtled up the lane after him, each one pulling a concealed short sword and buckler from the shoulder-scabbards under their tunic coats. Triumff caught a glimpse of breast-plates and other Secret Service-style body armour under their doublets. He swore, and began to run for real.

Streets and startled faces flashed by. Triumff doubled back into Cod Street, and almost went down under the wheels of a thundering wool-cart. He pulled back at the last minute, and dashed through a cobbler's shop, knocking a rack of clogs flying. The cobbler spat out a mouthful of nails, and rose from his bench, hefting his mallet, and wiping his hand on his apron front.

"What's your game, guv?" he enquired in less than friendly tones. Triumff flew past him into the back of the shop, dodging around a startled woman at the stove, and leaping over a toddler playing with old heels on the scullery floor. He slewed to a halt. In front of him was a solid wall with two small window lights at the top that you couldn't have squeezed a rabbit through, even if they hadn't been grilled up.

He turned back, desperate, to the anxious woman, who had collected up her child in smothering arms.

"You won't scream, will you?" he implored.

She shook her head, screaming. The cobbler was right be-side her.

"What's your game?" he repeated, raising the mallet.

"A back way! There must be a back way!" yelled Triumff. Outside, boots banged across the pavement.

"In the pantry," began the cobbler, pointing, "but—"

Triumff didn't wait for the rest. He bolted left into the clut-tered pantry and threw himself at the wooden door in the rear wall.

It thumped open, and out he went.

Into nothing. A sixth sense, one that had kept him shy of musket balls, grapeshot and wooden splinters off Finisterre, made him duck when the beakers flew in tavern brawls, and took him home safe down streets adjacent to footpad prowls, made him hang onto the door handle. His feet pedalled in empty air, and he felt himself go. The door swung back and he regained his footing on the pantry sill.

The back of the shop, and all the shops in the row, dropped down six yards into a garbage-choked watercourse of mossy brick, where stagnant water gurgled down towards the Thames. The gully was four yards across. On the far side, at the level of the pantry, a broken iron railing led into a dingy alley that ran down the back of the next street along the wa-terlane. Triumff turned back, his heart thumping.

The first of his burly pursuers slammed into the pantry, and skittered on the tiles. He regained his footing quickly and advanced on Triumff, brandishing his short sword meaning-fully.

"You!" he growled. "You're coming with me."

His stance spoke of trained excellence in the venerable dis-cipline of sword-and-buckler work. He kept the small shield low and steady like a chafing dish, and criss-crossed the blade. Triumff knew his style of fighting was old-fashioned, traditional and deadly.

Triumff drew his Couteau Suisse and hastily selected "rapier". The blade, when it finally deigned to put in an appearance, was a foot longer than the man's sword. The rapier was a modern, stylish sidearm that was beginning to become fashionable. Triumff was a student of the Spanish school of fencing, and was extremely well versed in the "immortal pasada". He hoped a bit of the immortality would rub off on him now. Triumff raised the rapier in front of his face so that the point scraped the pantry ceiling, and saluted.

"Vivat Regina!" he snarled.

The gallant lunged with a stabbing thrust. Triumff leapt back, and then essayed a stroke that took a line of jars off an upper shelf. He cursed, side-stepped the man's next brutish lunge, and decapitated a candle stick.

"Shit!" he declared.

There was no room in the confines of the pantry for the geometric time-and-distance keeping of the fencing system. With his short steel and burly frame, his opponent had the distinct advantage.

Triumff was forced backwards, dangerously close to the sheer drop as his opponent assaulted with vigorous strokes. He tried to parry and riposte, but there was no room to accommodate his blade.

Triumff knew it was time for something more drastic. "Rapier" wasn't the only blade variant in the Couteau Suisse's range of extensions.

He clicked the trigger, and the long blade retracted as another took its place. He was already swinging his next blow.

The blow bounced off the raised buckler with the sound of a dull gong. Triumff found he was wielding a basket-hilted soup ladle. Cussing even more colourfully than before, he managed to thunk the ladle across his opponent's ear, before being obliged to use the long-handle scoop to deflect and parry three swift cuts.

Their weapons locked. Teeth gritted, they pressed against one another's guards. Triumff threw the man backwards and pressed the trigger again.

"Oh, you beauty," he said in delight.

The Couteau Suisse had become a cutlass: short, thick and slightly curved, a weapon Triumff was very familiar with, a weapon designed for God's single purpose of clouting Portuguese pirates on the bonce.

"Yaaa-hah!" cried Triumff, and lunged. The man tried to block with his blade, but Triumff got past it and slid a long, useless blow off the man's cuirass. The short sword whipped around laterally at waist level, and Triumff almost doubled up to avoid it. He sliced again, and their blades met. The serjeant threw Triumff off with a flick of the wrist, but the effort wrong-footed him, and he flew awkwardly into the dresser shelving to his left. Triumff bounded forward with a jubilant cry, and punched the wrought hilt of his Couteau Suisse into the man's armoured chest. The wind barked out of him, and he flailed backwards out of the pantry.

There was a very solid crack. Triumff edged forward. His assailant lay comatose on the tiles, and the cobbler stood over him with his mallet in his hand.

"Thanks," said Triumff in surprise.

"Wrong bleedin' fellah," replied the distracted cobbler.

Outside, his wife screamed again. The other hounds had entered the shop. Triumff took one last look around at his options. Then he took a deep breath and a short, fierce run, and jumped out of the back door.

He sailed over the gully with a whoop, and came to a bone-jarring rest on the far wall, clutching the ancient railing, his feet dangling over the drop. His sword bounced from his hand, and clattered down onto the alley floor on the other side of the wall.

His breath had been all but knocked out of him, and his ribs and arms burned with bruised pain, but there was no time to recover. Under his weight, the railing was slowly tearing out of the mouldering brick with a wretched squeal. His feet floundered for purchase on the wet moss of the wall. He was sliding inexorably backwards.

As the railing ripped out of the bricks, he got his left arm free and clamped it over the wall. The iron bars dropped into the muddy residue at the bottom of the trench. A fingertip at a time, Triumff crawled up over the wall, and flopped down the other side.

About the same moment, two of his pursuers reached the pantry door and bellowed oaths after him. Triumff got to his feet and picked up his Couteau Suisse, laughing the insults off. Then one of the men fired a quarrel at him from a hunting crossbow that had been slung over his shoulder. Triumff ducked. The bolt buried itself three inches deep in the brick wall behind him.

"Bloody hell!" Triumff exclaimed, and ran off down the alley before his adversary could reload.

There was a scream, a thud and a dreadful commotion behind him. One of the men had attempted to duplicate his leap. Triumff left it all behind.

At its far end, the alley opened into Wine Office Court. Triumff knew it reasonably well. He could cross to the gateway onto Pickadel Lane, and turn west towards the crowds of Fleet Street and relative obscurity.

Two of the buckler-boys entered the gateway, panting, and split to each side to flank the exit. They looked at him grimly, and raised their swords. With a disheartened sigh, Triumff flourished obligingly, and reached out a hand to the barrow-load of casks to his left: six stacked casks, full of sherry. He'd once seen Captain Pennance Perkins cause a landslide of gunpowder barrels that had decked a squad of Portuguese ratings, like skittles in a skirmish, on Lisbon harbour. Inspired by the memory, Triumff sliced through the barrow strap with an auguring gouge of his cutlass, and the casks tumbled free like loose boulders on an Alpine pass.

The first one bounced off his foot. Hopping, Triumff remembered, and then yelpcd, a swear word he hadn't uttered since someone had thrown a hedgehog at him during an unfortunate misunderstanding at a morris dancing festival (for the record, it had missed, but he had later sat on it).

Vaulting the scudding casks, the first swordsman was on him. Triumff was so furious with the pain in his toes that he decked him soundly with a left hook to the chin. His partner ploughed in before the other had hit the ground. Triumff salchowed and met his lunge with a reflex riposte that would have brought a round of spontaneous applause from the College of Expert Fencing, Toledo, where they are usually so busy witlı barbed wire and timber posts that they seldom get to see a good swordfight.

Triumff got in over his assailant's buckler and under his guard, and raked down his right side with the cutlass blade. It sliced through his assailant's tunic, and cut the straps of his cuirass. Cursing, the man backed off. It was difficult to fight with twelve pounds of loose steel flapping around your stomach.

The only things proximal to Triumff's stomach were a silk doublet on one side and two semi-masticated fritters on the other. Neither slowed him down at all. He used the left hook again, and it worked as well as it had the first time.

He was badly out of breath, now. His bruised arms and body throbbed, and his toes felt as if they'd been branded.

He leaned on his sword for a moment, and then began to hobble out of the Court.

A tall, solid man with custard stains down the front of his tunic stood in the shadow of the gateway.

"Just my bastard luck," moaned Triumff with feeling.

The serjeant stepped forward. He was significantly over six feet tall, with a grizzled, craggy countenance, a jaw like a galleon's keel, cropped hair that hinted at military service or head-lice, and cold, cornflower-blue eyes buried in slits like papercuts.

He raised a large pistol that was as heavy and complicated as an ornamental foot-scraper, and pointed it at Triumff. With his other hand, he held out a leather wallet in which a silver crucifix was pinned on a purple rosette.

"Serjeant Clinton Eastwoodho, Curial Inquisitory Agency," he growled, without any apparent motion of his lips or jaw-line. "It wasn't nice what you did with that custard."

Triumff lowered his Couteau Suisse and breathed hard. "Look, what does the Secret Service want with me?"

Eastwoodho exposed his clean, even teeth. To a crocodile, it might have been a friendly grin.

"If you'd stayed put when I challenged you, mister, you might've found out the easy way. Now, though…" he said, his voice trailing away in the time-honoured tradition of silent threat, as used and abused by heavily armed bruisers who have cornered their palpitating prey.

"Sorry about the custard," said Triumff lamely. A thumb that could have successfully arm-wrestled an Irish mercenary without calling on the rest of the body for help pulled back the hammerlock of the gun. There was a significant click.

Eastwoodho's words crackled softly like burning leaves.

"This is a Fulke and Seddon all-steel ten-shot pinfire harmonica pistol," he said, "the most powerful handgun in the

Unity. From here, it could take your balls clean off."

"Is there any way I could get out of this without bleeding profusely?"

"Shhhh!" rasped Eastwoodho in annoyance. "I haven't finished. Now, do you feel opportune, punk?"

There was the sound of a wet impact. Eastwoodho staggered backwards, wiping his face. Overhead, a seagull cawed and clacked with glee.

"Yes, I do," replied Triumff, in answer to Eastwoodho's question, and sprinted off in the opposite direction.

Just then, one of the Wine Court officers opened a side door to find out what the noise outside was all about. Triumff, moving at close to thirty knots, missed the bemused officer, and hit the door face first.

He was going to swear, but unconsciousness got there first.

OF CHAPTERS, THE TENTH.
Divers journeyings & wakings up in Predicaments.

At noon, on the high road to London, just past Leveller's Crossing, Mother Grundy frightened away a trio of bandits with some clever prestidigitation involving a hawthorn twig and a pinch of ground bladderwort. Two of them reached the decency of an elderberry thicket before naked fear defeated bowel motion in a best-of-one willpower contest. The third fell on his back in the cart ruts and whimpered up at the gaunt woman.

"Spare me, mistress," he implored.

"Well, of course I will," Mother Grundy snapped. "I haven't got time for this. I have very urgent business in London."

She looked skyward, triangulated the relative positions of two starlings and a swift, and tutted loudly. The barley in a nearby field was swishing in all the wrong ways.

"It's getting worse," she said to herself and marched onwards.

The robber got to his feet shakily and watched her disappear into the wooded distance. He felt sort of sorry for London.

An hour earlier, but also at noon, Giuseppe Giuseppo was carefully covering the advance of two rough-house sea-dogs with his raised snaphaunce.

"Please, my friends, let's not do anything foolish," he warned softly.

They chuckled, and took another step towards him across the sun-bright poop deck.

"Now, now," said Giuseppe with a smile, and then he fired twice. A poniard and a marlin spike flew out of surprised hands. The sea-dogs looked at each other, crossed themselves, jumped over the rail into the sparkling Ligurian Sea and began to breast-stroke towards the Golfo di Genova.

Giuseppe turned, shaking the soot from his firing caps.

"Best speed for England, Captain," he called cheerfully at the master of the Battista Urbino, who was cowering in the wheelhouse.

The ship's master, an anxious Corsican with a personal freshness problem that had just got several degrees worse, bumbled agitatedly out of the wheelhouse with raised hands and a raised voice.

"Signore Giuseppo," he frothed, "you have just reduced the crew complement of this sturdy caravel by forty per cent!"

"A fact," Giuseppe said with a winning smile, "that is surely your fault for hiring worthless, criminal scum."

The master shrugged, and said, "Maybe, but without them, I doubt we can even return to La Spezia in one piece. If the headwinds are kind, we might make Antibes in two days." He ground to a silent halt, glumly. "England is, I fear, out of the question."

Giuseppe looked around.

"There are still three of you," he began.

The master sat on a tar barrel and stoked his pipe. The mate and the blotchy cabin boy clambered out of the hold, and sat down nearby: a full meeting of the remaining crew.

"Do you," asked the master, between sucks on his clay pipe, "know anything about the square and lateen rigging of a caravela redonda?"

"No," replied Giuseppe, his encouraging grin never leaving his face.

"I thought not," reflected the master. A cloud passed across the Mediterranean sun, and the wind got up a little. Canvas banged and flapped above. The sea spray divested itself of its salt, and plugged their nostrils with it. "Master Verrochio, set course for La Spezia. On the double."

The mate trudged off to the wheelhouse.

Giuseppe leaned close to the ship's master.

"Do you," he asked, "know anything about familial homunculi, the binding of elemental servitors or astral provenance?"

"No," replied the master frankly.

"Of course you don't. They are known only from the pages of Leonardo's original *Principia*. Knowledge of them is beyond even the Church. Be so good as to have my green sea-chest brought up on deck, the large one with the brass clasps. We'll get to England, Master Luccio, and I'll pay you double into the bargain."

There was something about Giuseppe's eyes that robbed Master Luccio of any argument.

"Who'd be a sailor?" he mumbled to himself.

Giuseppe overheard.

"I would," he replied.

Triumff woke up slowly, rolled over, and fell out of bed. His head ached terribly, and his nose had all but lost feeling.

Twice in twelve hours it had received a blow heavy enough
to stun an ox, and he hadn't even begun to list the other
parts of his frame that smarted, throbbed, pulsated or just
plain hurt.

He made use of his time on the floor to assay his surroundings. Oak-panelled walls, plastered ceiling, a cot bed draped
in what looked like horse blankets – used horse blankets – a
heavy-looking closed door and a pair of barred windows.

He clambered to his feet, but only because the stone floor
was cold and unyielding. Eighty-five per cent of his body
voted against being vertical, but his goose-pimples vetoed the
motion and sent an order to his legs.

He swayed towards the windows and looked out. It was
early afternoon by his estimation, but of what day, he didn't
care to hazard. Two floors below him was a shady courtyard,
dark stone pathways snaking between shrubberies and well-
tended borders. Globes of stone punctuated the ends of low
walls. A statue of Eros doing something erotic by himself
stood in the centre. Around the sides of the courtyard,
anonymous windows looked out from indeterminate wings
of the building. A figure stood on the pathway below his window. It was Eastwoodho. He looked up, somehow aware of
the gaze on the back of his head. He smiled up at Triumff,
winked one papercut eye, made a finger-flintlock and shot it
– pow! – up at the prisoner with a laugh that the window-
panes silenced.

Triumff turned away. Where was he? He felt he should
know. At one time or another, he'd woken up in most of the
royal and semi-royal Palaces in the Home Counties, and had
managed to work out where he was. He fumbled his way
towards the identity of his surroundings. Hampton?
Penshurst? Brayfield Wilmscott? Buddleyby Castle?
Tavingham? His fastest ever recognition had been Luckhouse

Place (four minutes seventeen seconds) after a telltale glimpse of the snorting basilisk weather-vane on the morning after the Treaty of Sidmouth celebratory revels in 1999.

Triumff sat on the cot and rubbed his forehead.

A key clacked in the lock and the door opened. A mousey little man in the blue robes of a curial divine stepped inside, and looked Triumff up and down. Triumff returned the up-and-down look as coldly as he could.

"Good afternoon, Sir Rupert," said the divine. "Cardinal Woolly will see you now."

Triumff got to his uncertain feet. Richmond, he realised.

Cardinal Woolly was a dark bulk against the ogee windows of the Great Library. The perspective of the book-shelves on either side swept down to pin-point him. The windows framed him and cast a long, portly shadow backwards across the room. For sheer compositional drama, Woolly couldn't have chosen a better place to stand. The divine closed the door, and Triumff was alone with the Church elder.

There was a painfully long pause.

"Sir Rupert?" asked the dark shape.

"Yes, indeed," Triumff replied nasally, wishing there was somewhere he could sit down before his legs gave way.

There was another eon-long pause.

A reading chair on castors trundled across to him, by itself.

"Sit down, please, before your legs give way," said the cardinal.

"Okay," Triumff reasoned, sitting. The chair trundled him closer to Cardinal Woolly's shadow. He slid helplessly across to the edge of the desk. Triumff didn't like that much. He didn't like any fancy showing off with the Arte.

"Neither do I," commented the cardinal.

"I'm sorry?" asked Triumff with a frown.

"I don't like any fancy showing off with the Arte either," explained the cardinal.

Triumff was on his feet again.

"You're reading my bastard mind!" he exclaimed. "I won't have that... I won't have your prying–"

"Please be seated, Sir Rupert. I meant no disrespect," Woolly interrupted. Triumff found that the chair was nudging against the backs of his knees like an eager, friendly bow-hound. He sat again.

"Thank you," said the cardinal. "Certain simple jinx enable us to skim the surface thoughts of our fellow man, Sir Rupert. We cannot detect the mind's deeper secrets. Rest assured, I am not picking your brain."

"Good," said Triumff firmly, gripping the arms of the chair hard, and glancing around the Library nervously.

"Much as I'd like to," added the cardinal. He stepped nearer, still eclipsing the luminosity of the windows. He held something out in front of Triumff's nose. It was a ragged foolscap sheet of parchment.

"What's this?" asked Triumff.

"You tell me."

The sheet filled Triumff's field of vision. Reluctantly, he looked at it. He saw spidery script, executed, it seemed, by a hand twice damned by palsy and a rotten dip-pen. He tried to make sense of the language, but recognised only a few of the characters. Then a drum-like pulse began beating in his temple, and he was swept up by a giddying rush of nausea. He looked away, his head swimming.

When he looked back, the cardinal was folding the parchment away and tucking it out of sight in a folder on the desk.

"Ugh..." began Triumff, but didn't really know what else to add. The cardinal handed him a goblet of water, and he sipped it gratefully. The nausea retreated.

"I'm sorry about that. Are you feeling better now?" asked the cardinal.

Triumff nodded. He felt that if he opened his mouth, he'd reunite his morning's fritters with the open air.

"The feeling concerning the fritters will soon pass," said the cardinal. You experienced a condition known as Thaumaturgic Reaction. It is a little like an allergy. In simple terms, it is the instinctive physical revulsion of the non-initiated to pure Lore."

"What was that?" asked Triumff, daring at last to speak.

"A page from the *Unaussprechlichen Kulten*," said Woolly. "You don't want to know what it concerned. Consider it a test, Sir Rupert. If you had displayed anything except genuine revulsion, I would have known in an instant that you have dabbled in Goety." The cardinal sat at the desk, and Triumff saw his face for the first time, illuminated by the light of the desk lamp.

"I haven't felt that crook since a night last year in the Mermaid. The eight bottles of musket were a personal best, but, on reflection, the rogan josh might have been a tad foolish, followed, as it was, by a nasty bout of a condition known, in the vernacular, as Bombay Doors. Are you familiar?"

The cardinal smiled, but Triumff could see how pale and drawn he looked. Dark circles of insomnia ringed his eyes. His flesh looked pallid and damp.

"So," said Triumff, getting back to the point, "you get the CIA to pick me up, and then you test me for Goety. May I ask why?"

The cardinal clasped his podgy hands together and steepled his fingers.

"Last night, the City went dark," he began.

"I noticed," interrupted Triumff.

"Someone employed the vilest Goety to desecrate the Cantrip Chamber at the Powerdrome. Some Guild men were slain in the incident."

There was something about the cardinal's lack of specifics that made Triumff shudder.

"But why?" he began.

"Your name was implicated in the affair, erroneously, I was quite sure. You understand, I had to be certain."

"Thank goodness," breathed Triumff. "The last thing I want is to go ten rounds with some cheery Infernal Affairs inquisitors."

Woolly raised one large hand to his head, and gently stroked his silky coif.

"You are innocent," he said, "but it's not as simple as that. The event is the most significant symptom of the greatest crisis that has stricken the Unity since it began. Intrigues are afoot to undermine the sanctity of the Throne and the Church. The Cantrips are threatened."

"You're talking conspiracy," said Triumff.

"Indeed I am. These are lean and dangerous times, Sir Rupert. One may not trust even his closest brethren and friends. You are, I'm afraid, caught up in this dangerous web most entirely. Your position at Court is fragile to say the least. Someone has seen fit to single you out as a scapegoat, and few would be prepared to listen for long enough to hear your side of the story."

"Except you?"

"Had I not instructed the agents of the CIA to collect you without delay this morning, you would now be in the hands of an unsympathetic government department... or dead... or *both*."

"I was nearly dead anyway, Your Grace," said Triumff. "Eastwoodho and his boys don't know the meaning of 'care' and 'gentle restraint'. I'd bet they're not too hot on 'fragile' or 'this way up' either."

Woolly nodded.

"Thankfully, they are agents of the Curial Bureau, and not employees of Her Majesty's Postal Office," he said. "However, I apologise for any trauma they might have caused. Believe me, it is preferable to the alternatives. On the City streets this afternoon, agents of the Diocesan Office are falling over investigators from the Church-Guild, Infernal Affairs inquisitors are bumping into Militia officers, and civil servants from Whitehall are colliding with aldermen from the Mayoral Chambers. Every authority in London is sniffing around for clues, and one whose scent is as strong as yours might find it hard going on the streets."

Triumff raised his eyebrows, and said, "I can handle such–"

The cardinal cut him off. "Lord Gull, commanding the Militia inquiries, has already set a price of one thousand marks on your head, whether it is attached to your body or not. You are just as popular with the other agencies."

"Oh Jesu…" breathed Triumff. Then he looked again at the pasty cardinal. "But you're acting alone, aren't you? You and your CIA? Even the other Church agencies don't know you've got me?"

"That is correct," said Woolly.

"You don't even trust the other segments of the United Church!"

"Until I am satisfied with the nature of things, I don't trust anything, except myself, a select core of the CIA, and Gloriana."

"And me?" added Triumff, hopefully.

"And you, Sir Rupert. Now I trust you too. Welcome to the most exclusive club in the Unity."

Triumff stood and wandered across to the nearest book stack, running his fingers absently along the row of vellum spines.

"So where does that leave me? Vis-à-vis paddles and creeks located near to sewer outfalls, I mean?" he asked.

"I am too… well known to conduct an investigation, in person. The officers of the CIA are also well known to the other Church bodies. Besides, most of them are too stupid to be useful. I need a friend on the streets, one who knows London and how it works. Someone who might slip in and out unnoticed where even the best disguised officer of the Church would stand out and be noticed."

"You want me to do your dirty work for you?" Triumff asked, uttering the words with slow incredulity. "Bollocks," he announced, and added for good measure, "and anyway, isn't the most wanted man in London a bad choice for an espial?"

"If he was Sir Rupert Triumff, yes. But if he wasn't…" The cardinal rose from his seat and crossed to the corner of the room. He tugged on the bell-pull. When he turned back, Triumff saw with no little shock that there was genuine pleading in his face, pleading mixed with fear.

"Please help me, Rupert," he said, "I… the Unity needs you."

"Well…" began Triumff.

"In return, Sir Rupert, I could see that all your ambitions at Court and beyond were realised. I could protect any interest of yours at home and abroad," the cardinal interrupted.

"Any interests?"

"Any," the cardinal nodded.

"Are you sure you can only read my surface thoughts?" asked Triumff.

Woolly smiled.

"Quite sure," he said.

The door to the Library opened, and Eastwoodho stepped in. He came to attention with a smart clack of heels.

"Sir!" he snapped.

"Conduct Sir Rupert to the Mews, serjeant. Operation Original Sin commences as of this moment."

"Sir!" exclaimed Eastwoodho again, like a flintlock going off. Triumff walked towards the door that Eastwoodho held open for him

"Don't foul it up, Triumff," added the cardinal darkly, "I'm counting on you. And rest assured that some Cantrip-gate scandal will bring the Unity crashing down as sure as an uprising."

"One thing," said Triumff, from the doorway. "How do I know I can trust you?"

"You don't," replied Woolly. "But consider this: if I was part of the conspiracy, you'd be dead already."

Triumff followed Eastwoodho out of the Library. He didn't feel all that reassured.

THE ELEVENTH CHAPTER.
On cipher-names & sundry;
also, a musical interlude.

The Mews lay a short stroll from the Palace quad, across the greenery of the kitchen garden. It was a long, half-timbered bunker of converted stables. A light drizzle fell on the pair of them as they walked down the gravel path.

"I guess this sort of thing is new to you, right?" asked Eastwoodho.

"Delightfully so," replied Triumff grumpily.

The Secret Service agent stopped in front of the hammered oak doors of the Mews, and rang the four wire bell-pulls in a special order.

"Don't be rattled by this place. And don't wander off," he said.

The doors opened.

The well-lit interior smelled of cloves and gunpowder, and the floor, walls and ceiling had been whitewashed antiseptically. They entered, and Triumff followed the big man down the central aisle. On one side, two agents were testing matchlock carbines cunningly disguised as lutes in a sandbagged range that had once been a horse stall. Plaster dummies wearing ruffs exploded with serious completeness.

To the left, brawny men in hose and little else threw each other around on straw mats and yelled monosyllabic oriental howls. Triumff winced.

"Special Forces boys," muttered Eastwoodho proudly, "Green Garter. Toughest hombres in the Unity."

A little further on, a party of plaster courtiers sat around a banqueting table on which lay a wax suckling pig with an apple in its mouth. The fuse on the apple was nearly burnt out.

"Cover your ears," advised Eastwoodho. Triumff obeyed.

There was a flash, and the banquet came to a sudden, outwardly expanding end. A singed ruff floated down in front of Triumff's nose.

"Charbroiled," said Eastwoodho with a sick grin. They crunched on over plaster fragments. In the next silo, a foppish gent executed another plaster dummy with a crossbow that had, until moments before, been his codpiece.

"Just a little prick with a poisoned quarrel. That's all it takes."

"So I noticed," said Triumff, uncomfortably.

Next door to the codpiece surprise, four men in plate armour and houndskull helmets were rappelling down from the roof.

"In case we ever have to mount a raid into the cone of a volcano," Eastwoodho explained helpfully.

"Does that happen much?" asked Triumff.

"Not yet," smiled the CIA agent.

"Gosh," said Triumff. "It's exciting being you."

Eastwoodho looked at him dubiously with his papercut eyes.

They moved on. Triumff looked in awe at the machines of destruction being employed all around him. The seat of a sedan chair suddenly rocketed skywards on the end of a belling steel spring, and after a short round of congratulatory applause, the agents set about recovering the plaster passenger that was jammed head-first into the ceiling. A debonair gent unfixed his ruff and sent it skimming through the air, whereupon it decapitated yet another dummy at the end of the next stall. The whirring disc of razored lace returned to his hand neatly.

"This is the dirty tricks department," remarked Eastwoodho with some glee.

"You don't say."

They turned the end of the stall rows into what had once been the tack room. Eastwoodho held up a restraining hand, bringing Triumff to a halt. Before them, between two deep trestle tables lined with gadgets and machine parts, an elderly man with a stooped frame was priming the pan of an ivory-handled baltic-lock fowling piece that had been set on a tripod stand. He stood back and squeezed the trigger via a length of silk cord. There was a loud retort, and the gorget of a plate-armour suit thirty feet away was thoroughly perforated.

"Armour-piercing balls," said Eastwoodho.

"Really?" asked Triumff. "What's his name?"

Eastwoodho turned to him with an unfriendly grin.

"No names, no pack drill. Careless talk," he said, looking at Triumff significantly. "He's Kew. That's his cipher-name. We all have cipher-names. This week, they're based on English horticultural gardens. Mine's Winkworth."

"What does that make me?" asked Triumff.

"Agent Borde Hill," said Eastwoodho. "That's all you need to know on a need-to-know basis."

"What about, let's say, introducing a want-to-know basis here?" suggested Triumff.

"No need," smiled Eastwoodho, "you know?"

"Not entirely."

By then, the stooped man had wandered across to them. He was carefully wiping his hands on a silk kerchief.

"This the dupe?" he asked Eastwoodho, as if Triumff was made of plaster.

"Tri–" Triumff began.

"Agent Borde Hill," cut in Eastwoodho firmly. "Agent Borde Hill, Kew. Kew, Agent Borde Hill."

Triumff shook hands with the stooped man, who promptly wiped his palm again.

"Cold-smelted carbonide spheroid. Ten by twenty-six hundred muzzle velocity, but the trick is in the rifling." he said, gesturing towards the fowling piece. "Impressive, what? It'll shear through a gorget, a spaulder or a breath at up to sixty yards. Knock through two inches of plate at twenty. And you might as well wrap your privates in tissue-paper for all the stopping a mail fauld will afford."

"Ouch," muttered Triumff, with compassion.

"Would you like to see the stealth plate-mail?" asked Kew keenly.

Eastwoodho leaned forward. "Operation Original Sin is a go as of fifteen-thirty, Kew. We'd better get on with the show. Tri–Agent Borde Hill hasn't got time to waste."

"Pity," mused Kew, moving across to the trestle tables. "Now pay attention, Borde. This is a rum do, and no mistake. Item one."

He held up a stubby-looking clay pipe. "A stubby-looking clay pipe? Yes, and no. Depress the underside of the bowl, and you reveal a lodestone and miniature windvane."

He demonstrated. Triumff frowned. He was still frowning at the stubby looking pipe when Kew moved on to the next item.

"Item two: a conventional buckler of the ecu target variety. Pull out the bevel here and the rim circumrotates. Look here."

He held it up for inspection. Triumff wasn't quite sure what he was supposed to be looking at.

"Adjustable codex," Kew explained, "suitable for all Agency ciphers. State of the Arte. Eastwoodho will provide you with the logs. Read them. Then eat them."

"What is this?" asked Triumff.

"Poniard/flintlock combination piece," replied Kew, assuming Triumff had meant item three and not the situation in general. "Single shot, and the blade is edged with diamonds. It'll cut through most anything. Item four."

He held up a mandillion doublet, "Lined with sprung wire, it'll stop a sword edge or a musket ball. Item five: your false papers and letters patent. Louis Manticore Cedarn, actor/wassailer/troubadour. You speak French? Of course you do. Try and live the part if you can. We've written up an accompanying biography. Your cover will be an appointment as a lutenist with the Curtain Company at the Swan. Research says you can play a lute. You can pick up a standard-issue lute from the quartermaster. Don't forget to sign for it. If you lose anything, there'll be a slew of re-requisition orders to fill out."

"Louis... come again?"

Kew didn't.

"Your contact's name is Wisley," he said. "He'll be your only link to the Service. You can pass intelligence reports back through him. Item six: a signet ring full of arsenic tincture for tight spots."

"Suicide?" breathed Triumff reluctantly. He was still staring at the Hilliard of the clean-shaven, blond young man that featured prominently in his "papers". "This doesn't look a bit like–"

"And item seven: a razor and a jar of peroxide bleach."

Triumff suddenly felt very attached to his beard.

"Oh no you don't…" he began.

They did.

At four minutes past six, the man who would, reluctantly, be Louis Cedarn, actor/wassailer/troubadour, descended unceremoniously from a passing unmarked phaidon outside the porch of the Swan Theatre in Southwark.

Cedarn picked himself up, and gathered his scattered belongings up out of the gutter.

"Thanks, guys," he yelled at the disappearing phaidon.

Cedarn ran his hand through his newly blond locks. His scalp stung, and the cold Thames wind bit into his raw chin. His clothes felt unsuitable and didn't fit very well. He hobbled up the steps to the Swan in shoes that sported frilled rosettes on the toes and were a size too small, and knocked.

"Here we go," he whispered to reassure himself.

There was a rattle of chains and dead-bolts, and the door opened a crack. A long nose poked around the jamb like a surfacing periscope.

"Theatre's closed," it told him.

"I'm expected," Cedarn began as the nose showed signs of withdrawing. "I'm… Louis Cedarn. Lutenist. Er… Bon soir."

The nose looked him up and down.

"You're the Frenchie lutenist, then?" it asked.

"It would seem so. Monsieur," Cedarn said, smiling what he hoped was a winning smile. It didn't necessarily win, but it got him a place in the quarter-finals.

"You'd better come in while I find someone who knows about you," the nose said, withdrawing and opening the door a little wider. Squinting, Cedarn ducked inside, following the nose. He banged the bowl of his lute against the door frame, and cursed. The instrument had turned him into a wooden hunchback, and he'd clouted it into just about everything between Richmond and Southwark. He'd given up checking it for damage, as most of the bumps and scrapes he'd caused were invisible amid the scar tissue of a long Service career. It was an eight-course Tavistock Lute-O-caster in sunburst peach, with a Service serial number stencilled on the fretboard. It had seen active duty on nine prior missions, including a stake-out at the College of Minstralcy during the notorious Quadrillegate affair, where it had been instrumental in depriving the spy, Guido Resticulati, of consciousness. It was nominally kept in an open "D" tuning, but this was subject to humidity and dry rot, and it looked more like a long-necked tortoise that had been through the Peninsular War than a vessel of St Cecilia's Art.

In the gloom of the stage-door entrance, Cedarn found that the nose belonged to a gangly man of ill-kempt appearance. They eyed each other cautiously.

"And you are?" asked Cedarn.

"Bonville de Tongfort. Stage manager. Stay here, I'll get the boss." De Tongfort strode off into the shadows like a long-legged wader on the Thames flats at high tide. Cedarn looked around. The hallway was choked with miscellaneous scenery flats, racks of costumes and lantern boxes with big reflectors. He leaned his lute and bag against a section of forest, and sat down on a stool beside a length of plyboard battlements.

"Down there," he heard de Tongfort say presently, and footsteps approached. He got up. A barrel-chested man wearing a hearty grin and a fully sequined, taffeta gown emerged through the archway of a makeshift church.

"Basil Gaumont," announced the petticoated man brightly, "your humble servant! Captain of the Swan's valiant Company, an impresario of sorts, as I style myself! Actor, manager, dramaturge, darling of the theatre-going world, what can I say. I am famous for my Paris, my Caesar, my Zeus and my

Oberon. And my Dido's pretty flaming good, too. You're the lutenist fellow, Cedarn?"

"At your service," smiled Cedarn nervously, with a bow. "Monsieur," he added.

"Good fellow!" rejoined Gaumont, clapping him hugely in the small of his back. "Let me show you the boards. We have a big do coming up."

Cedarn followed the swishing train of the dress down through the backstage stores, past whole landscapes of scenery, and under the mass of winding gear and pulleys that operated the drop-curtain and all the stage effects. The complex ropes and wires reminded him pleasantly of a galleon's rigging.

They stepped out onto the stage, and Cedarn got a good look at the tiered gallery stalls, the pit and the high walls of the wooden polygon. It all looked rather open and worrying from the little apron stage. He'd been to the Swan dozens of times before he had suddenly become Louis Cedarn. From the galleries, as one of the roaring eighteen-hundred-strong crowd, everything looked exciting and glamorous. From down here, it was grubby and threadbare, and not a little ripe with the smell of tallow, greasepaint and sweat. It was as reassuring as looking into the mouth of a primed bombast.

"Ahhh, it quite knots your belly with pride, doesn't it?" beamed Gaumont.

Cedarn nodded. Something had knotted, but it wasn't his belly, and it wasn't with pride.

"This way," said Gaumont, plucking him by the sleeve of his mandillion. Cedarn allowed himself to be led back through the facade into the smoky confines of the tiring room. A dozen pairs of eyes turned to look at him. Five women and seven men, all thoroughly made up in grotesque face-paint that enlarged their lips and eyes, were sitting around in their underwear or less, smoking, laughing and drinking. All of this ceased as Cedarn entered.

"This is Louis. He'll be joining our merry company of players as lutenist," announced Gaumont to the ensemble.

"Hello. Er... bonjour."

A few of the gathered players nodded in return.

"I 'opes you play well, Frenchie," said a man in a false moustache and little else, sitting in the corner. "We 'ave need of a fine dose of playing to please our public. Especially on this coming Saturday."

"Oh, well, you know," Cedarn began.

"That's Edward Burbage, our star player. And, of course, the rest of the bold company. They'll make you welcome, I'm sure."

Someone belched, and there was some sniggering.

"Is there no performance tonight?" asked Cedarn nervously.

"Jesu, no," said Burbage, rising and wiping droplets of wine from his moustache. "We were meant to start a run of *The Gentleman Fop of Innsbruck* on Friday, but there's some business concerning the company of the Oh, and so we're resting."

"The Oh?" asked Cedarn, his curiosity suddenly piqued. Doll was a member of the Wooden Oh company.

"It's flooded, and can't be used for a week. By arrangement, their company will use our premises to begin their rehearsals of *Dutiful Husbands at Their Duty* tomorrow, along with their preps for the Masque," Gaumont explained, "so we all have to bunk in together to make sure we're ready for Saturday's show."

"It'll give us time to rehearse up a supporting piece on our programme while we brace for the big event," said Burbage.

"A little musical farce I've been working on," said Gaumont. "That's where you come in, with a few tunes, sir."

"What's the piece called?" asked Cedarn.

"*Lark Rise to Camel Toe*," replied Gaumont.

"Oh," said Cedarn. He wasn't really paying much attention to the talk of plays. A large number of awkward possibilities were beginning to run through his mind.

"Would the Frenchie like a drink?" asked a bosomy actress to Burbage's left. Her grubby lace underskirts and whale-bone-reinforced stomacher strained anxiously around her well-upholstered frame.

"Why, ask him yoursen, Mistress Mercer!" mumbled Burbage through a swig of musket.

With a shy grin, she stepped forward, holding a beaker of wine. The boards creaked under her advance.

Mistress Mercer... *Mary Mercer*, thought Cedarn. She who was called the Beauty of the Stage, for whom lords and potentates swooned and threw coin. Close-up, she was a rather frightening matron, with a sad, eager look in her eyes. Cedarn supposed that to look exotically nubile and desirable from forty yards away across a theatre pit, she would have to possess exaggerated attributes that scuppered any close-quarters charisma. Like the Theatre itself, Mistress Mary Mercer was a tremendously disappointing let-down in person. Time could not wither her, nor custom stale her infinite variety, but they'd both had a bloody good try.

"Voudrais-vous... uh... desirai un cup de drinkie?" she asked with an embarrassingly demure turn of the head. An ogress with the coquettish mannerisms of a five year-old child.

"Thank you," Cedarn said anyway, reaching out for the cup.

"Wait there," called a voice from the back. De Tongfort stepped across the tiring room with a purposeful grin. "Let the fellow earn his first share of the company vittals." He held out a sheaf of tatty sheet-music. "Let him play for his cup. Come on, now, Frenchie."

There was a chorus of approval and some slow hand-clapping. Cedarn took the sheaf of music and swallowed hard.

"Well, now, really," he began.

"Come on, Frenchie! No excuses!" bellowed Burbage.

Cedarn set the music on the top of a tea-chest, looked at it in alarm and took up his lute. He tested the courses, and tried an open chord. The silence was overpowering.

"Come on!" Burbage insisted.

Louis Cedarn had never had a lesson in his life, but as that life had only begun three hours earlier, it was hardly surprising he hadn't fitted any in. Rupert Triumff, on the other hand, had been schooled on the lute since childhood, and had spent many a drunken afternoon with his neighbour Edoard Fuchs manufacturing delicious melody.

He played "St Layla's Galliard" and "Coverdale's Jig" and followed them with "Come To Me, Oh Lover, And Groove Upon My Love". The flabbergasted company stomped and shouted, and rained applause that showed no signs of abating.

Louis Cedarn smiled appreciatively, and sipped the first of many cups of wine. Unseen by him, on the far side of the wings, Gaumont watched him with narrowed, dangerous eyes.

THE TWELVTH CHAPTER.

"Of course I'm worried," said Uptil. He sat back in Rupert Triumff's chair in the Solar of seventeen, Amen Street, put his hands behind his head and managed to look anything but.

Doll sat glumly on the bench seat nearby, and toyed distractedly with the lace trim of her gloves.

"You don't seem very worried," she said. "He could be dead."

"He could be," remarked Uptil smoothly. "He could be dead drunk. You know what he's like." Uptil stretched and looked out at the damp evening that pressed itself against the Solar windows. The third quarter of eight had just chimed from St Ozzards, and it was turning into a soggy, unattractive night.

"I must say," said Agnew, sipping peppermint tea in a dim alcove on the other side of the room, "that on this occasion, I share Mistress Taresheet's concern. It has been my…" Agnew paused and rummaged mentally for just the right word. He gave up.

"…honour to serve Sir Rupert for more years than might be considered sensible. For all his failings, his one admirable quality is his ability to survive. He does it on wild oceans, leagues from land; he does it in battle; he does it in taverns when the drinks go down and the knives come out. I've seen him. Often. Too often, perhaps. But what with Lord Gull, and the business at the Baths yesterday, I truly feel he has sailed too far over the dangerous side of common sense. Today, this house has had more than the usual number of visits from the Militia and the Guild Officers, even by Soho standards. There is a price on his head. One would assume that is the result of misdeeds that we have yet to learn about. Whether by his own hand or another's design, Sir Rupert is in grave circumstance."

"I keep thinking I should go back to Paternoster Lane, in case he turns up there," murmured Doll.

"Didn't you say the Militia had it staked out?" asked Uptil.

Doll nodded.

"They left a man watching the house after they searched my rooms this morning," she said. "I think he was meant to be inconspicuous, but you can't help standing out with a halberd."

"There's no point going back, then. If Rupe's rolled up at your place, in whatever state, the Guard will have him," Uptil said, boinging a letter-opener experimentally on the side of the desk. Doll shivered despite herself. That was something Rupert used to do. The spring-bounce noise made him laugh every time. Right now, it was the saddest sound she could have heard.

"After all, what can we do?" Uptil went on. "Go out looking for him?"

"We could."

"Oh, right. And if every investigator and blood-hound in the City can't find him, what hope do we have?" Uptil said.

Doll was about to answer, but she was interrupted by a loud knocking at the downstairs door.

Agnew rose.

"I'd better get that," he said, brushing out his sleeves in a businesslike way and heading for the stairs.

"The Ploy," Doll squeaked at Uptil, who had almost forgotten.

"Yeah, yeah, yeah," he grumbled, dropping off the chair and scurrying into the corner of the room.

Agnew led Lord Gull into the Solar a moment later. Raindrops twinkled like diamonds on his coal-black cloak.

"All his known associates in one place. How convenient," mused Gull. "Good evening, Mistress."

"Lord Gull. Twice in one day. A lady could get the wrong idea."

"Let's hope not," said Gull, looking around. "So, he still hasn't returned?"

Doll took a step closer to the lean soldier.

"Lord Gull, I want to know, why are you so desperate to find him?" she said.

"Treason," answered Gull succinctly.

There was a pause.

"Remind me again when you last saw him," Gull said.

"During the early Flirtacious Period," Doll replied.

"When?"

"First thing this morning before he left."

There was a second loud rapping from the downstairs door.

"No rest for the domestic," muttered Agnew, and disappeared again.

A distinct chill greeted his return.

"The Divine Jaspers," he announced.

Jaspers stalked into the Solar, glancing around at those present with hooded eyes. He put down his ebony cane, and removed his kid gloves with elaborate slowness.

"Gull."

"Divine, our investigations cross again."

"What a busy day we're all having. There's nothing like an abominable crime to make everyone pull together," Jaspers said, wandering over to the desk and helping himself to a glass of claret. "I take it you've ascertained that the traitor has not returned to these lodgings?"

"If he had, Divine, he would be under Militia arrest. There is no reason to detain you."

Jaspers looked at him with one raised eyebrow.

"We're turning London on its head looking for this vile man," he said. "I do hope that when he's found all the representative bodies will be allowed to question him."

"After due process," Gull replied. Doll could see that the guard captain was stiff and tense. He clearly liked the Magickian as little as she did.

"He will be found, and this treason laid to rest," Jaspers said, turning to smile at Doll. "You must find yourself a new amore, my lady. Triumff's life as a free man is over. In fact, his life is over, full stop."

Doll turned away.

Gull straightened his collar and turned to go.

"I'll take my leave," he said. "I care little for the company here."

That was brave, thought Doll. Lord Gull certainly had courage.

"Do you anticipate a swift closure of this affair, my lord?" asked Jaspers, toying with his wine glass.

Gull turned at the door and faced down the adept with a confident stare.

"The Militia received, this night, a warrant of permission from the Privy Council to conduct a Cantriptic postopsy on two knifemen killed whilst trying to slay Triumff, yesterday," he said. "Their bodies are in our custody. The affair is just now underway at the College of Westminster. I am certain of some advancement before the night is older."

Jaspers put the glass down roughly, spilling some wine. "The College is going to question the dead on your behalf?" he asked.

"Praetor Enoch himself," answered Gull. "It is all agreed. Those two dead ruffians are potential sources of information as to Triumff's private doings. If we can establish who meant to kill him, we might close on his present whereabouts. It has taken us all day to get the Council's permission."

"I..." began Jaspers. "I have things to attend to." He strode out, brushing past Lord Gull. The temperature in the room rose several degrees. Doll felt her goosepimples dissipate.

"That man puts the 'un' in funny," she said.

Gull turned to her.

"Lord Gull," she said, "I know you hold Rupert in very low regard, but I care about him. I would like to be informed of any developments in this matter."

Gull looked at her for a moment.

"I will see that you are, Mistress," he said, in a tone that was almost kind. Then he was gone.

"Rupe's in it up to his neck," said a voice from behind the drapes.

Doll looked across at the emerging Uptil, anxiously.

"He most certainly is," she admitted.

Jaspers emerged from Triumff's house onto the darkened Amen Street, and threw himself into the saddle of his waiting horse. It reared up, and he forced it down and around, and set off towards Westminster at a full gallop.

From a nearby alley, feline eyes watched him go. Feline eyes that were six feet off the ground.

An hour earlier, as the sun began to set on the choppy waters of the western Mediterranean, a voice from the crow's-nest of the *Bright Ducat*, a sturdy brigantine flying a bloody ensign, sang out, "Sail!"

Torquil Lapotaire looked up from the binnacle, and wandered over to the rail. Lapotaire was a small man, smaller by far than his grand piratical reputation. His beard was banded out in black ribbons, like the tail of a kite.

"Ahhrrr," he said softly, then added for good measure, "where?"

The sail was pointed out, a dull square adjacent to the dimming horizon: a caravela redonda, making good speed. Lapotaire rubbed his hands together, and thought of coffers of moidores. He ordered them to come about and cut off the vessel. The tang of gunpowder filtered into the night breeze as the guns made ready. Lapotaire freed his sabre in its scabbard, and took out his spyglass. *The Battista Urbino*, read the plate on the approaching caravel.

Lapotaire was about to say something buccaneerish when he noticed the glow around the caravel's wheel house. He trained the spyglass in. There was something wrong with the ship.

Then Lapotaire realised that the caravel was racing towards them under full sail… against the wind. Corposant crackled around the ratlines, and St Elmo's Flame bloomed from the masthead. Lapotaire watched with grim fascination, and saw something vile and unearthly clinging to the rigging of the phantom ship. It looked back at him with a grin.

"Break off! Break off!" he yelled, and the *Bright Ducat* heaved to as the caravel shot across its bows like a rocket, its sails glowing luminously.

"Bugger that," said Torquil Lapotaire. There were far easier ways of earning a dishonest living.

Night cloaked the London Road. The whole world was abed, and a mighty comfortable one at that.

Mother Grundy had no time for sleep. She didn't stop as, step after determined step, she marched on for London.

THE NEXT MOST CHAPTER.
Athwart a Cedarn cover.

Big Ben struck nine. One hundred yards north of the clock tower, the College of the Church Guild shone with candlelight from its leaded panes.

Waiting nervously outside the praetor's chambers in the Seminary, Neville de Quincey heard the last stroke of nine peal away into the evening air. He didn't like this sort of business.

The screen door to his left clicked open, and Praetor Enoch emerged, dressed in the full regalia of a Guild ceremony.

"It is all prepared," he told the physician. "Thank you for waiting."

"Not at all, praetor," said de Quincy. "There's just a docket to sign, and you can get on with it. Receipt of bodies, that sort of thing. Just to keep the morgue files straight."

Enoch nodded and signed the document on de Quincey's clipboard.

"You will probably feel more comfortable if you withdraw and return in, say, two hours, after I have completed my work. I can furnish you with my findings then. Otherwise, you might find the atmosphere accompanying the postopsy... unnerving."

De Quincey nodded gratefully.

"I'll pop back at eleven, then?" he said.

Enoch showed him out. "One last thing, doctor. Their names?"

"Oh," said de Quincey, "William Pennyman and Peter Petre. Do you need to know any other details?"

The praetor shook his head.

"Return at eleven," he said.

De Quincey hurried away into the night, heading for the nearest brandy-serving tavern. Enoch strolled back through the apartments to the lead-lined chamber behind the collegiate hall. He muttered a short prayer, and blessed the vestments as he placed them around his neck.

The bodies lay on catafalques carved from Egyptian basalt. They had been stitched up and cleaned, but the welts of their wounds spoke of miserable deaths. One had drowned, his face broken by the heavy impact of visor driven into bone. The other had been battered facially and then ripped open. The stink of medicinal alcohol hung in the close air.

Enoch began.

The State Magick was not black. It was a dour, industrial grey, a plain, functional, even terse process. There was no room for fancy poetic flourishes, and experience had taught the Guild elders that the excesses of Goetic black practice only ended in tears.

Enoch's incantation was as rudimentary and unexciting as a reading from the instruction manual for an ironing board. Cantriptic energy oozed through the chamber. The Praetor cracked his knuckles.

"I am Enoch, praetor of the Guild College of Westminster, Divine of the Lore. I have recited the Massachrondic Litany in order that I might speak with you, you being William

Pennyman and Peter Petre. Do you understand what I have told you?"

The electrical polarity of the chamber switched. The air tasted of wet iron. Ectoplasmic dew sheened the metal surfaces of the walls.

"Do you understand?" he asked again.

A smashed jawbone moved, grinding.

"Yeth," said a breathless voice.

"Good. To whom do I speak? State your name."

"Wiwiam Peggyman, thir," replied the corpse.

"Tell me what you sense."

"My faith... it'th all cwacked up. It'th a meth. I'm dead, ain't I?"

"You are," said the praetor. "I will not hold you here long, William." Enoch circled the bodies and looked down into Pennyman's ruined face. The open eyes were glazed like buckets of milk, and showed no spark of consciousness. With a ghastly crackle of ricted muscles, the mashed mouth moved.

"Whad'you wan tho know?" asked the dead man.

"I make my enquiry on behalf of Her Majesty's Government," said Enoch. "I have a signed authorisation, to wake you, from the Privy Council. Arbuthnot himself has inscribed the wax with his ring. Do you want to see?"

"Naaahh," replied the corpse, brokenly. "I caanth wead anywayth."

"Yesterday at six, you and your accomplice attempted to slay one Rupert Triumff at the Dolphin Bath House. On whose instruction?"

Psychometric mist rose and shimmered in the chamber.

"Thome fat geether came to uth in the Cockthpur Tawern down Sheapthide. Didn't git hith name," said the corpse.

"Can you describe him?" asked the praetor.

"Rich, thmart clotheth… an awithtocwat like you, thir," William answered. "Let'th thee, he 'ad a pinky wing marked with a thmall 'n' thape."

"The letter 'n'?" Enoch asked, frowning. Then a thought burst through his jumbled mind like a tackling prop forward. "Perhaps, William, it wasn't an 'n'. Perhaps it was a trilithion. A pair of sarcen stones with a capstone across the top."

"Come again, thir?" asked William.

"Have you seen pictures of the old Druid stones on Salisbury Plain?"

There was a slow, lingering silence.

"My mother uthed to thow me engwavingth of 'em when I wath a lad," said William, his airless voice subsiding into silence. Enoch looked down and saw a single tear rolling down the dead man's cheek.

"Thir? I don' like being dead," added William Pennyman.

Enoch took a deep breath. The corpse had already entered the second stage of awareness. It would take all the praetor's skills to keep him together long enough to finish the questions.

"The stones, William. The stones in your dear mother's pictures. Could they not have been the mark on the gentleman's ring?"

"Why, yeth, they could have bin," he answered.

Enoch nodded.

"Would you tell Thir Wupert, I meant him no 'arm? Pleath, thir? Would you? I don' mean to be a burden… It were jutht a job… good pay…"

"I'll tell him, son," said the praetor heavily.

Pennyman's body began to shudder and shake. Enoch stepped back. He hated this bit.

"What'th happening, thir? It'th gone all cold… I don' want to go, thir… thir? Pleath?"

"It is the final stage, William. I am losing touch with you. They're calling you back." Enoch closed his eyes.

"I don' want to go…" said the voice, before grinding into silence. Enoch realised he was breathing hard. He stepped forward and closed the dead man's re-dead eyes.

"Rest in peace, my son," he said, gently.

The Privy Council and Gull's cussed Militia will be bloody grateful for this, thought Enoch as he stood back sadly. When they ask me to dabble so, they have no idea what it takes.

"Learn much, Praetor Enoch?" asked a voice. Enoch jumped, despite himself. Jaspers stood in the chamber doorway, flushed as if from exertion.

"Divine? This is unexpected, and unconventional. You know the college is closed during this type of audience," said the praetor.

Jaspers stepped into the room, swivelling his ebony cane, and asked again, "But did you learn much, *praetor*? This is the first time in thirty years the Privy Council has allowed a revivication in the name of the law. I'm fascinated. I'm also deeply disturbed that you carried on without informing me or inviting me to be present. You know how serious this affair is."

Praetor Enoch was a strong, courageous man. He looked Jaspers in the eye and said flatly, "The work was initiated and ordered by the Militia. These cadavers are their property. I was obeying the letter of the law. There was no need to inform you."

"But what did you learn, old man?" asked Jaspers.

Enoch looked around. He was in a lead-lined chamber of solid granite. The nearest human being was over a hundred yards away. That had been his instruction when the order arrived. He hadn't wanted to spook the young initiates.

"Don't threaten me, divine," he said, bunching his knuckles.

"I'm sorry, Praetor. I don't know what came over me. You must understand, I am just so anxious to fathom out this treason so that the Queen may sleep safely in her bed."

Enoch looked at him cautiously.

"I… I understand, Divine," he said. "It is a heavy burden. I will inform the Militia representative in an hour when he returns. In the meantime, you may as well know, it was Lord Salisbury who fashioned the attempt on Triumff's life last evening."

"Hockrake? Are you sure?" asked Jaspers.

"The man Pennyman recognised his signet ring. The dolmen sigil of the Duchy of Wiltshire. Our plot, as they say, thickens…"

Enoch's voice trailed off. There was a taste like bile in his mouth. More than anything, he was surprised.

"How did you… Why did I tell you that?" he asked.

"A jinx of truth. I conjured it as I came in, old man. I could have made you tell me anything," said Jaspers. "Which initiates you'd interfered with, for instance."

Enoch started forward, breathing hard. He was weak and drained from the exertions of the revivication Cantrip.

"Damn you, Jaspers, you'll never get away with this infringement of–"

"Infringement?" Jaspers interrupted. "That's the least of my concerns. You know of that fool Hockrake's involvement. I can't let you live."

Enoch tried to duck past him, but Jaspers rose to block him and threw him back. Then the smiling Divine struck one of the corpses soundly with the end of his cane.

There was a kaleidoscopic flare of bubbling light, and a smell of ground pumice. Peter Petre lolled up on his slab, and stumbled to his feet. Blood, diluted pink by medicinal alcohol, spooled from his smashed lips. One of his eyeballs rotated in its socket like a compass hunting for true north.

"That Arte… it is black," said Enoch in horror.

"Indeed. Not white, nor grey," Jaspers smiled. "I have made a very close study of all the mantic arts, praetor… the pyromanti, geomanti and idromanti we all study in the guild, and also the negromanti we do not. It is a shame, for that is the most delicious sort."

Peter Petre staggered towards the shrinking praetor.

"How do you like my Goety, praetor?" asked Jaspers.

"It is you!" howled Enoch, as Peter Petre killed him. It was a long, slow, drawn-out killing, and involved nothing more than frenzied tearing by a hideous strength not sired on Earth. Jetting arterial sprays spattered the ceiling and far corners of the room. Enoch could not scream. He was enveloped in a cone of silence that Jaspers had manufactured with a twitch of his cane.

When he was sure Enoch was dead, Jaspers strolled from the room. At the door, he gestured with his cane again. Everything organic in the lead-lined chamber combusted in a ravenous blaze of lambent flame.

Jaspers shut the door on the inferno.

"I will keep my secrets," he mused.

Some minutes later, initiates from the college dorms ran across to the chamber-hall, roused by the sight of blue flames licking the tiled roof.

They found Jaspers, sobbing, at the steps of the hall. Horrified, several ran off to raise the Brigade.

"It was terrible," Jaspers told the others tearfully. "I warned the praetor, but he would not listen. I told him that the devil Triumff would have inlaid black Cantrips of destruction into the bodies of those he had slain, but he insisted on his ability. When he cast his jinx upon them… The fire… I tried to save him… It was too much."

Someone put a blanket around the divine's wracking shoulders. The Brigade bells jangled through the darkness. All agreed it was the second great disaster in as many nights.

The flames leapt up to the heavens. For a while, the safety of the City around was in doubt, but the Brigade trained two Worm's Drive Fire Squirts at the combustion, and by eleven, only the white-hot core of the seminary chamber still broiled in its lead-lined casket.

As he was led away by sympathetic hands in search of brandy and a soft seat, Jaspers took one last look at the hundred yard flames, and smiled, an expression that his dutiful companions were all too shaken to notice.

De Quincey saw it.

He was quaffing a second welcome cognac in the Shades when he heard the rattling bells. Racing outside, he was greeted by an angry, amber glow against the sooty night, rising from behind the Parliament House. He swore, and broke into a run towards the college.

It was chaos, and the frantic initiates at the gatehouse would not let him pass. But from the shadows of the gate, he saw Jaspers. He saw the smile and shivered. He saw it all too clearly.

Triumff woke up with his face pressed to cold glass. Beyond the distorting pane, London lay asleep, except for the churning gout of flame over to the east.

He scrambled up, his head spinning. The cupola on the top of the Swan Theatre, which was used to store the pennants and banners, had ended up serving him as a place of rest. It wasn't ideal, as he had to sleep semi-vertically in the confined area, but it was better than sleeping below in the cramped tiring room. Mary Mercer was two sheets to the wind and after his body, and, after his success with the lute playing, he was convinced that most of the Company wanted to have congratulatory sex with him. The rope, canvas and moths of the cupola would do.

He looked out at the torching blaze. Westminster, he guessed. Glory, what *now*?

There was a tap at the door.

He breathed in, remembered his name was Louis, and opened the clasp.

Gaumont looked in at him, tired but alert. He was dressed in longjohns and a nightshirt, and he held a glowing lamp.

"You've seen it, then?"

"Y-yes," said Cedarn.

"Don't worry, Borde," said Gaumont, climbing up into the cupola alongside him and shutting the hatch, "I'm Wisley." He reached into the pocket of his nightshirt and pulled out a silver cruciform on a purple rosette. Across the rood was the inscribed eldritch logo of the Curial Inquisitorial Agency. "Agent Wisley, CIA deep cover."

"Agent Borde," said Cedarn, wishing he had a glitzy badge to flash around.

"Good to be working with you on this one. It's a bad show all round. I have to say, Operation Original Sin is the toughest number the Spymasters have set me on yet. The place is going to hell in a hand-basket, and we don't even know where to begin to look."

Cedarn nodded.

"I'm lost," he admitted. "I have no idea what's expected of me. I'm hard up in a cinch and no knife to cut the seizing."

"Sorry?" queried Wisley.

"It's a nautical expression. I, er, heard it on the boat coming over. From La France." Cedarn covered himself hastily.

"Right," nodded Wisley. He peered out of the cupola windows. "It's the Church-Guild School, all right. That's a fine mess. If the Arte's gone bad, what hope is there for the likes of you and me?"

Triumff didn't much like contemplating such subjects in quite such a cramped space, quite so far off the ground, quite so late at night with a complete stranger.

"Bastard all," he reasoned. "What a night."

Salisbury awoke, alone and cold, in some small hour of the morning. The Palace of Windsor was silent all around.

Salisbury turned over with a grumble. He was cold and a-sweat with bad dreams. He snuggled down belligerently into the pillow, but something made him open his eyes and look up.

The knife was an inch from his eyeball. It glinted in the grey darkness.

Salisbury froze, terror icing its way across his bulky extent. Jaspers was standing over him. Then, with yet greater shock, Salisbury saw that the blade was actually grown from Jaspers's outstretched fingers.

"You're a stupid, lardy moron," Jaspers told him.

"W-what?"

"Tonight, your foolish nonsense nearly cost us all. This is the very last time I'll warn you, Hockrake. Next time I'll send something in my stead, something from the furthest necromantic reaches of the cosmos, something that will eat you, soul first."

"I-I understand," said the Duke of Salisbury, gagging on his fear.

Jaspers's strangely sharpened fingers cut a slit through his pillow, and downy feathers puffed out. Then he disappeared, just like that, as if he had never been.

Salisbury lay very still for a very long time, staring up at the indistinct paintings on the ceiling of the chamber. Slowly, he began to see more and more of them, as their details became plain. Then he realised it was because the sun was coming up outside.

THE FOURTEENTH CHAPTER.
What happened on Friday.

There are few things more likely to get you out of bed of a Friday morning than the sound of someone nailing a dead cat to your front door, except, perhaps, the sound of someone nailing a live cat to your front door.

The intermittent thumping that accompanied the former endeavour echoed up through the boards of number seventeen, Amen Street, Soho, and jabbed rudely between Uptil's consciousness and a rather good dream about a motor launch, the Barrier Reef and a girl called Ruuti.

His sleep-dilated mind constricted tightly as he snapped awake, and he groaned. The boat, the reef and Ruuti waved goodbye from the receding edge of Dreamtime, and left him, alone and annoyed, in a grimy, uncivilised foreign land that he was really beginning to loathe, though his entire capacity for loathing was temporarily directed towards the steady *thump-thump* from below.

Shoulders slumped reluctantly, Uptil slapped flat-footedly down the staircase, rubbing the sleep from his eyes. Yawning, he threw open the vibrating front door.

The man outside with the hammer pulled up mid-swing,

and caught the head of his tool in a protective, cupping hand inches from Uptil's face.

"Od's bollocks!" he exclaimed, and then jerked backwards involuntarily as he realised how muscular, alien, naked and angry-looking Uptil was. Then he swore loudly, and shook his hand as the momentum from the hammer belatedly travelled up his arm and arrived in his brain.

There were three men on the doorstep, common mongers or journeymen by their clothes, and a stiffened English Domestic Shorthair crucified under the knocker. Two of the men looked at Uptil apprehensively, while the man with the hammer did a little jig with his hand in his armpit, and muttered a few words that were low on letters and high on dudgeon. Uptil slid his just-awake stare around until he was nose to nose with the feline door-hanging. He blinked. The cat didn't. It seemed likely that it had fallen foul of a stage-coach some considerable time before its crucifixion, and its grimace was just the sort of expression Uptil assumed cats made when their alley-singing was interrupted by three tons of horse-drawn criticism.

It looked as if it was even less happy about the whole affair than Uptil.

"What the bloody hell do you think you're doing?" Uptil wanted to say, but realised he couldn't. Habit had conditioned the Ploy into him to an almost Pavlovian degree. He settled for giving the men, and the cat, his most unforgiving glare.

"Let that be a warnin' to yer!" said the man with the hammer as he regained his composure.

Uptil considered this and looked at the crucified cat again. He'd never even considered keeping a cat as a pet. He had no idea that such an activity was so frowned on by Londoners. He'd certainly take their advice and never do it now.

Uptil nodded, smiled and went to shut the door. The trio peered at him warily through the closing gap.

"D'ye unnerstand, savage man?" snarled the man with the hammer, with mounting confidence, before the door could entirely shut.

"Course he don't," put in one of his colleagues. "He's a savage man and therefore born without much mind for reasonin'."

The other two agreed keenly.

Uptil re-opened the door and the exchange. If he'd had sleeves, they would have been rolled up by now. Banging their heads repeatedly against each other, or the footscraper, surely wouldn't constitute an infringement of the Ploy, he decided. Rupert could always write it off against ignorant native confusion, and besides, it would improve the way Friday had started.

"Would you gentlemen be so good as to appraise me of your business here?" asked Agnew, appearing suddenly. He was wrapping tight the cord of his dressing gown. He looked even less amused than Uptil or the cat.

"Tis a warnin'!" repeated the man with the hammer, waving said item threateningly in the direction of the gaunt manservant.

"I don't think so," replied Agnew, studying the new decoration on the door. "I'm rather inclined to suppose it is an abuse of a poor, dumb animal and an act of vandalism to private property. Do you know how long it will take to repair iron-tack holes in finished oak of this quality?"

There was a pause. One of the men, who happened to be employed as a joiner when he wasn't involved in cat-hammering expeditions, looked up helpfully and began to say, "About a seven-night, with good grout an' a willing hand," until the others shushed him.

"We knows who's owse this is, mister, and we knows wot he's done," said the man with the hammer, through clenched teeth. His teeth were as white and regular as a fire-damaged portcullis, so the words experienced no difficulty getting out.

Agnew folded his arms patiently.

"Then enlighten me, please," he said, "before I am forced to fetch a big stick, lend it to my naked friend here and turn a blind eye."

Keeping the hammer handy, the leader of the trio took a step forward and said, "I be Bruvver Bob. This be Bruvver Thomas and Bruvver Colm." Brother Bob nominated each man with a wave of the hammerhead.

"Mornin'," said Brother Thomas (the sometime joiner).

"Mmmm," nodded Brother Colm, less cheerfully.

"Are you monks?" asked Agnew.

"You what?"

"Or friars? Monastics of some kind? Or are you… brothers?"

Short, red-haired Bob looked at gangly, balding Thomas and pudgy, grey-haired Colm. They exchanged frantic, cataplectic looks.

"I said we was," Bob began.

"You share the same parents?" asked Agnew.

"No, mister. No, we don't. My dad's old Handy George," Thomas said, "and Bob is the son of–"

Brother Bob told him to shut up.

"Then on what basis do you call yourself 'brothers'?" asked Agnew.

"We are," Brother Bob explained curtly, "bruvvers in the sensa fraternity, sworn, devoted acolytes of a secret trust, conjoined in the 'armonious relation of a brevrin o' true men."

Agnew nodded. "You're members of a secret society."

The trio looked at him nervously.

"You won't tell?" asked Brother Thomas.

"Which society?" asked Agnew with a sigh.

"We can't be tellin' the uninitiated that sorta thing! Pox on you, for yourn impertinence! Why, I'd bleedin' die afore I blabbed o' the private and most secret knowings of our bruvvcrood."

"It's the Housing Committee, isn't it?" asked Agnew flatly. They shuffled awkwardly.

"*Isn't it?*"

"Yes," peeped Brother Bob.

"Honestly, you will drive me to an early grave with your agendas and minutes, and association meetings. If it's not the state of the cobbles, it's the provision of street lighting, and if it's not that, it's a torch-bearing mob with a petition about unsound guttering. What is it this time? Not enough wall-mounted cats on display to meet by-law requirements?"

Brother Bob straightened up and adjusted his cartwheel ruff.

"I," he began in stentorian tones, suddenly reinforcing his ramshackle accent with a bold over-elocution that disembowelled itself on his terminal aphesis. Agnew winced. "I am Chairman-Elect of the Owsin' Committee's Moral Turpitude Action Group."

"We meet of a Thursday in the room over the Chuffing Pheasant," put in Thomas, by way of a gloss.

"Don't tell 'im that, you twonk! It's a secret!" Brother Bob said, turning back to Agnew as Brother Thomas rocked backwards with a reddening hammer-mark in the middle of his forehead. "It's come to our Action Group's attention, as it as to the City at large, that tewible anus doin's are bein' perpetrated in this town. The college went up in smoke last evenin'. You musta sin it. There's evil wizardry abroad, bein' done by evil wizards specially trained in fiendishness."

"And?" asked Agnew.

"It frettens to corrupt this 'ere nayberood, and we won't be standin' for it," said Bob.

"*And?*" Agnew asked again.

"Well… Sir Rupert is to blame, inne?"

"No," said Agnew firmly. "Good day," he added, and slammed the door.

He reopened it a moment later as Brother Bob was taking a show-of-hands vote about continuing with the hammering.

"So what's this poor cat got to do with it?" Agnew asked.

Brother Bob set his head on one side in the sneering manner of a master craftsman judging the work of his most unpromising apprentice. "Don'cha know anyfing? Tis a warnin'. To demarcate for de attention o' de public the property known to be ripe with de curse o' bedevilment and tewible anus doin's."

"Why a cat?"

Brother Thomas edged forward with an air of certainty.

"Has to be," he said. "Says so in Committee Ordnances. Point of Order One Seven Six and after: 'An cat or similar shall be used to denote an offending property, due to the traditions of superstition associated therewith'."

"Thank you, Bruvver Thomas," said Brother Bob. Brother Colm nodded in serious approval.

"The only superstition associated with cats I can think of is that a black one crossing your path brings good luck," remarked Agnew.

"Aha, but nailed to yer door! A black cat nailed to yer door brings bad luck."

"Particularly, I would think, if you were a blind door-to-door salesman with a hard knock," Agnew replied, and then chose his next words carefully.

"Bugger off – and take your cat with you."

He slammed the door again. In the hall, with the murmurings of the Housing Committee still audible through the door, Uptil looked at Agnew and sighed.

"We have to find Rupert," he said. "This is getting beyond a joke."

Agnew nodded.

"Let me get my coat, and have a cup of tea," he said. "That always helps my thinking process. Then we'll begin to search."

Uptil followed him down the passageway into the kitchen, saying, "I wouldn't mind a cup of that stuff too, if it's as good as you say. I can't even begin to think where we'll start."

Agnew spooned out two heaps of what looked like gunpowder from the caddy.

"We start at the front door," he said, "and move out from there."

A dishevelled Friday plodded wearily across the City. In the scalding houses of Eastcheap, the butchers grumpily swept out the grisly by-products of their hog-trade into the gutter to make sure that Pudding Lane lived up to its name, but their hearts weren't in it. Many of them wished they were cast away with the offal on a drifting Thames dung-boat rather than living in the City. The thinning pall of smoke over Westminster only served to remind them of the bleak outlook.

In the blackened wreck of the college seminary, the Militia inspectors made themselves as busy as they could with tweezers and magnifying scopes, but there was a nasty quality to the air that wasn't just the fumes of the dead fire, and they all longed to be elsewhere. De Quincey had brought his outlining chalk, though he was sure there would be nothing worth drawing a line around.

He retreated to a bench in the west corner of the college quad from where he could oversee the work, and smoke a comforting pipe. Even here, half a furlong from the husk of the chamber-hall, he had to brush the seat clear of glass fragments before he could sit. The building's demise had been volcanic.

Gull was due to arrive shortly, and de Quincey didn't relish the prospect of making his SOC report. Its brevity was going to be matched only by its lack of an enlightening narrative. There had been nothing left in the leaded chamber, apart from some traces of adipocere and glomerated fat: no sign, no clue, no cause, no answers, except, of course, for the plaintive, emotional statement of the divine, Jaspers, corroborated by over a dozen traumatised initiates. Jaspers made the deceased praetor out to be a meddling, incompetent fool, who carried on with the perilous business in the face of reasoned advice. The few short minutes in Enoch's company the night before made de Quincey doubt that character sketch very much.

De Quincey knocked out his pipe on the leg of the bench and got up. Gull and two huscarl wing-men were stooping like hawks down into the quadrangle, the vast wings of their Vincis beating against the pulls of wind and gravity. De Quincey began to walk across to them. Steely yet unsubstantiated worries filled his mind, but he didn't know who to tell, or even how to begin to tell them.

All the same, he couldn't get the image of the divine's laughing, firelit face out of his mind.

To the north, Mother Grundy sat on a fallen gatepost at the edge of the Moorfields Bog and ate the last of her Bath Olivers. The City was only a few hours away. Thunderclouds, heading in from the Shires, rolled overhead on their way to

London. They would be there before her. Something was drawing them on.

Far, far to the south-west, Giuseppe Giuseppo licked the salt-spray from his lips, and looked out into a Channel thick with fog. The bells of low-water buoys tinkled through the dead air. The rigging of the *Battista Urbino* creaked softly. It was taking longer than he had hoped.

On the apron stage of the Swan, Louis Cedarn was re-stringing his lute.

Who was it who said that "Theatre is the blessed balm to all life's cruel workings"?[9] Or that "The play doth rightly smooth back the cares of this work-a-day life"?[10] Or even "On this stage of wooden fancy, the muse doth wrap us in a cloak of imaginings that our finest dreams might be made flesh for one jewel hour"?[11]

As Wllm Beaver Esq. strode purposefully across the threshold of the Swan, such thespian mottos filled his eager mind, and a thick sheaf of scribbled paper filled his breeches pocket. He hummed a cheerful tune. The City was in emotional tatters, the cornerstone of Magickal power was a smoking ruin, as rumour had it that some Goetic bogey-man had been unleashed to stalk the London streets. As far as Wllm Beaver was concerned, however, this was a good, fine, promising, happy day. To him, the Swan, and all it represented, was a million miles divorced from the horrors of the world and that damned traitor-culprit, Rupert Triumff, who everyone said was the root of all the evils.

---

9 Lady Scritti of Trabant, after the first night of *Titus Androgynous*.

10 Cyril Scrope Esq., after three bottles of sack.

11 I honestly do not know, but he sounds like the most tremendous twat.

Wllm Beaver Esq. is, of course, your loyal servant the author, i.e.: me, in case you had forgot, the sheer wonder of this gripping narrative being enough to dazzle and distract you.

"Excuse me," said I, Wllm Beaver, to the blond man with the lute, "I'm looking for Messrs Gaumont or de Tongfort. Are they about?"

"Probably," the lutenist told me. "Try over there." He pointed the neck of the aged lute at the door to the tiring room. It was a little before eleven-thirty, and few of the company were up.

I, myself (Wllm Beaver), nodded in a friendly way that tried to suggest comfortable familiarity with the Way of the Boards.

"Rehearsing, I imagine," I said with a grin.

"Sleeping, farting or receiving extreme unction if yesternight was anything to go by," said the lutenist. "All three at once in some cases, I suspect."

"Uhm," said I, not quite certain what one might retort to that.

The lutenist stood up. His second B snapped around like a coach whip and whined softly.

"Louis Cedarn," he said, holding out his hand.

"Oh, right. William Beaver. Pleased to meet you. Lovey."

Cedarn looked at me strangely.

"Actors do call each other 'lovey', don't they?" I checked anxiously.

"Not the ones I've met. But don't ask me. I'm new here, monsieur."

"Are you French?"

"For a limited period only," said Cedarn in a low growl, before adding quickly, "Beaver... Beaver... You write for the broadsheets, don't you?"

Your author felt quite proud at this recognition from a foreign talent, and confirmed it.

"The stuff you come out with sometimes..." said Cedarn.

"You are familiar with my work?"

"I have bowel movements like the next man. Passes the time. That article you wrote about Rupert Triumff's homecoming and discoveries."

"Sharp journalistic scrutiny? Fluid articulate prose? Consummate handling of factual material enmeshed in a lyrical weave of wit?" I suggested.

"'Bollocks' was the word I was searching for," said Cedarn, "and that was just the tone. Your facts were pretty threadbare. He had two ships, not six. He was away for three years, not two..."

"Must've got my notes muddled there," stammered I.

"Yeah, right. As for the stuff about what he found. I don't know where you got that from... except, maybe, the bottom of a cask of musket."

I cringed painfully, and stammered, "You've no idea what it's like. Deadlines approaching... editors balling you out and screaming for exclusives... copy-choppers wanting glitz and glam and sex."

"That would explain the stuff about 'dusky aboriginal maids' then, would it?" asked Cedarn.

"Yes. Sorry. I..."

I broke off and thought for a moment. I looked more closely at the scruffy lutenist.

"Why are you so concerned about it?"

Cedarn shrugged.

"I... um... know him," he said. "Quite well. He was awfully upset by the stuff the papers came out with."

I leaned forward with a keen, bright look in my eyes, as my journalistic instinct went into overdrive.

"You know him? You don't know where he is, do you?" I asked. "The whole blessed City is after him… I mean… What's he really like? Did he tell you anything? Does he, you know, *dabble*?"

"No. And no and so on. I haven't seen him for ages." Cedarn sat back down and secured the loose B. He strummed the courses and began to twist the pegs into tuneful obedience. He seemed to me anxious, as if he had nearly undone himself with a slip of the tongue.

"What are you here for?" he asked sharply as the strings wailed into harmony, urgently changing the subject.

"I'm known for my…" I replied, and stopped. If nothing else, I had recognised that I was in the presence of a man to whom bullshit was transparent. I didn't want to push my luck, or get off on the wrong foot. "They're looking for stand-up acts to please the rabble at the interval. Just a little divertissement, really. I want to broaden my horizons. The papers aren't my first love. I have ambitions… to be a comic."

"Well, you're a funny guy," said Cedarn, mordantly.

"Yeah?"

No, said Cedarn's threatening look. I felt small and grubby. I sighed. This wasn't going the way I had imagined things would go. I glanced around, trying to identify the nearest exit I could slope out of. The wings and flies were a forest of flaking, painted coulisses and jumbled chunks of mise en scène.

"Hang on," said Cedarn, softening. "How do I know? I haven't heard your stuff."

"Would you like to?" asked your loyal servant, me, Wllm Beaver, re-igniting his smile.

"Not on an empty stomach. What's the deal here?"

I moved back across the apron to the lutenist, and said, "I spoke to Mister Gaumont last week, in the Boar's Head. He seemed to like my one-liners."

"Had he been drinking?"

"Like a fish. But I look at it this way… Is the audience ever sober?"

Cedarn chuckled.

"No. Never," he said. "That's a promise. So what did Gaumont tell you?"

"That he'd give me a spot in the interval as a warm-up for the third act. Ten minutes, he said. Politics, social comment, penis jokes. As long as I didn't pillory the Queen or mention the Triumff scandal, he said it would be fine."

"It will be. I'll find him for you." Cedarn said, getting to his feet and holding out the Service-issue lute to me. "Look after this, will you?"

I took the lute like a trainee animal-handler with a turtle phobia.

"Thanks," he said.

"I understand there's also to be a visiting company," I said. "The Wooden Oh troop have been flooded out, and–"

"That's right. They'll be here before noon to set up. A stay of execution for the Swan Players. I don't think they've even learned their lines." Cedarn said, pausing on his way to the tiring room, and turning to regard me and my lute-husbanding skills.

"Look," he said, "could you do me a real favour?" The roar of the greasepaint and the smell of the crowd, the eldorados of my life, were so close, I could almost taste them. They didn't taste very nice in point of fact, but I was sure I would get used to them. Like scotch. I was damned if I would let anything jeopardise their acquisition at this eleventh hour. I was determined to know the right people, make the right moves, grease the right palms, and do just about anything and everything I could to endear myself to anyone and everyone who could bunk me up the ladder of stardom, one rung at a time (though I drew the line at getting anything pierced, and other peoples' beards brought me out in a rash).

I smiled Cedarn a smile so broad each point ended in an ear-lobe.

"Anything," I said, selflessly.

In an unmarked sedan chair, parked unobtrusively down a rent-passage behind the Swan, Serjeant Clinton East-woodho lowered his telescope and noted down the time in blue pencil in his blue-pencil log.

Eleven forty-six, he wrote. U*nknown subject entered Swan seventeen minutes ago. Believed to have spoken with Agent Borde.*

Eastwoodho underlined the word *spoken*. He sat back in the darkness of the shuttered box, and sucked grape juice through a straw from his Service-issue flask. The bourbon he'd laced the juice with at a frozen five-thirty that morning crept sluggishly into his body like warm quicksilver.

He stretched, as best the box would allow, and reached over to his waiting telescope. Then, with a snap of his hand, he lunged around and drew his pistol from the holster on the seat nail. The all-steel weight of the ten-shot pinfire harmonica felt good in his hand, and a frighteningly brief blur was all that linked its position in the holster to its place in his hand.

The scent of gun-oil wreathed the close air.

"Boom boom boom boom," he breathed, through his teeth, pointing the massive handgun through his spy-slit.

"I gotcha, punk," he murmured. "Do you feel opportune?"

Eastwoodho lowered the gun. The view through the spy-hole had suddenly got interesting. A blond gent in Frenchie clothes, carrying a lute, had just emerged from the Swan, and hailed a sedan. Already, he was moving off down Pawket Street towards the Colchester Road.

"Oi!" bellowed Eastwoodho from the sedan chair.

The two army bruisers, who were leaning on the wall nearby, smoking roll-ups, leapt up and accelerated away with the chair.

"That chair! Follow it!" yelled Eastwoodho through the sideflap. *Officer Eastwoodho. In Pursuit. First and Pawket* he wrote on his message slate and tossed it out of the window to his runner.

The chair-boys he was chasing were good. They jogged into the slow lane on Skinner's, and then cut a daring sharp right across the traffic onto Mermaid. A keg-wagon had to break sharply as they cut it up, and almost jack-knifed. Traces and wiffleboards tore loose, and upset barrels exploded on the road. His own chair-men were highly trained and fitted with the latest in anti-slip boot soles. They leapt the debris, dodged the prancing horses and the bellowing drover, and banked hard into Mermaid.

Ahead, the quarry rounded into Cordwainer Street, the chair leaning out dangerously with the torque. Eastwoodho lit his blue-lensed lamp, hung it out on the roof of the chaise, and began ringing his handbell. People stopped and looked. They got out of his way quickly, and he liked it like that.

From Cordwainer, they really picked up speed, and began to close on the suspect vehicle. The runaway's men were panting and red in the face. His CIA men were known for their high performance and road-holding. Eastwoodho had his gun ready.

Without warning, the quarry cut left into Swithen's. Eastwoodho's vehicle overshot, did a heel-brake turn, ran backwards, and pelted off after it. A dangerous corner down into Craven Hill almost had them spinning out. The right shoe of his front runner pattered out across the cobbles, but he managed to right himself and keep up the pace. Eastwoodho rang his bell so hard, the clapper flew off out of the window.

They drew alongside the quarry: chairs and runners bobbing and thundering down Broderers Lane, neck and neck. Eastwoodho leaned out of the window.

"Pull over!" he yelled. The blond man in the other chair looked across at him and shrugged in confusion.

"Me?" he mouthed.

Eastwoodho reached for his gun, but heard his front chairman gasp in alarm. The end of the lane was the site for an occasional market, and Friday was one of those occasions. The stalls narrowed the lane width to single file. The thoroughfare wasn't wide enough for both speeding sedans.

"Brakes!" screamed Eastwoodho. They skidded, and knocked sideways into a stand of vegetables.

Eastwoodho screeched, leapt out of the pranged chair and spat out a lump of rogue aubergine.

The quarry had fared no better. Trying to pull clear, it had caught on the awning of a lace-maker's stall, and the chairmen were currently trying to reverse out of a pile of ruffs. Eastwoodho ran across to them with his gun braced in a straight-armed, two-handed grip.

"Hands up! Now!" he snarled. The chair-men obliged, and the sedan thumped heavily onto the cobbles.

"You in the chair! Step out! Keep your hands where I can see them. Step out and place your hands on the hood. Now!"

The blond man in French clothes clambered out of the sedan as instructed.

"Trying to give me the slip, eh, punk?" Eastwoodho began. He narrowed his papercut eyes.

The blond wig slipped off.

"I think that was sort of the idea," smiled I, Wllm Beaver. "Now what happens?"

THE FIFTEENTH CHAPTER.
More of what happened on Friday
(which includeth a great, great SECRET*).*

At roughly the same moment, as the disjointed strokes of
noon began to peal out across the City from an unnecessary
number of clock-towers, another sedan came to rest in
Oxstalls Lane, Deptford, and the fare climbed out and
awarded his chair-men a handsome tip.

"Suck a peppermint comfit after eating garlicked sirloin,
and you might pick a few more fares," he said.

The fare was dressed all in black, with a high, goffered collar, and a felt cap scrunched low on his head. It was turning
into quite a warm day, and the clothes were heavy and hot,
but Louis Cedarn preferred their stuffy weight to the possibilities of discovery, followed by death and several other
unpleasantnesses that he could amply imagine.

Returning to Deptford, thriving little boom-town Deptford,
was like coming home for the man Cedarn used to be.

He stood for a long moment on the cobbles of Oxstalls
Lane, and watched the bustle all around. Since the first days
of the United Fleet, it had been a place of chandlers, caulkers,
hemp-dressers, joiners, and all the associated industries of
sail. Just now, as clocks and hollow bellies announced

lunchtime, a legion of such artisans scurried to and fro, mixing with, and through, knots of sailors on furlough. Loud and raucous, the seamen caroused rather more aimlessly down the busy street, with the eager intention of replacing the grim shipboard regimen of burgoo, botargo and banyan days with boiled brisket, floured hobs and frothy porter. Cedarn could hear a hurdy-gurdy wailing out the song about the Guinea Coast from a tavern by the Creek-Bridge.

Kentish matrons in straw hats and broad, white aprons, like galleons asail, tacked down through the market stalls with baskets of fish, cherries and marrows on their arms. Less dowdy ladies, the powdered bawds, rested their décolleté bosoms on the sills of tap-room windows and stew balconies, and winked or called cheerfully to the passing mariners. Ragged wharf-brats ran tops and hoops through the alleys between the riverside rents. A tame monkey gibbered and chirruped from the awning of a knife-sharpener's shop. Rising up behind the Deptford streets, to the west of the Creek, stood the merchants' Private Dock, the Royal Dock shipyards, the warehouses and excise barns, and a vast, gently rocking forest of masts and stays.

Cedarn's nose breathed in the smells of sea-breeze and estuary mud, timber shavings and pitch, and his ears soaked up the multi-lingual chatter of the cosmopolitan thoroughfare. It all made him feel rather homesick for distant places, even though he hadn't actually ever been to some of them.

Reluctantly, he broke his reverie and strode down the street onto Butt Lane, which ran through to the main London Road. On either side were wide market gardens, ripe with manure, trim orchards, herbal plots of madder and woad, and the wide tenter-yards where cloth was stretchered. A twin-gabled victualling house stood at a bend in the land with a walled garden to the rear. By its sign, it

promised "Fine foods and suppage in the Roman Mannere".
Cedarn stooped in under the low door and took a seat at an
empty table. The restaurant was filling up with a noisy
throng of merchants and gentlemen traders, dining on spiced
faggots, spaghetti, olive bread and gnocchi. A young girl in a
long smock brought him a menu slate and a bowl of pitted
olives.

"Is the padrone in?" Cedarn asked her. She studied him
suspiciously for a moment, and then replied that she would
fetch him.

Cedarn sat back and studied the menu. It was inscribed
with the house name – The Go-Betweene – at the head,
under which was the scrolled legend: *"The Pasta is a Foreign
Countrye; they chew things differently there."*

A plump, balding Italian in a gooseturd-green doublet
wandered over to the table, wiping his chunky hands on a
dish cloth.

"Signore? You ask-a for me?"

Cedarn looked up and returned the man's curious stare
with a soft smile.

"Drew Bluett. Since when did you become Italian?"

"You make-a the mistake, signore. I am-a Guido Severino,
host of this-a–"

"Drew, pull up a chair and lose that ridiculous accent,"
hissed Cedarn.

The man obliged, quickly, sitting across the table from
Cedarn, and keeping his head and his voice low as he scru-
tinised him with angry bemusement.

"What's your bloody game, mate? Do I know you from
somewhere?"

Cedarn nodded, still smiling, and said, "From Aleppo, and
Gravelines, and an evening in Monte Cabiarca when the
Prussian flag caught fire a little."

The man's eyes widened in slow realisation. He gawped, blinked and then began to chuckle in wonderment.

"Rupert–"

Cedarn hushed him.

"Call me Louis," he said. "Like you, I have found it expedient to be re-christened. Is there somewhere we can talk?"

To the back of the Go-Betweene, the walled garden held trellised vines and plum trees en espalier. Kitchen smells mingled with the garden scents, and almost-warm sunshine bathed the grass. Drew Bluett latched the back-door behind them, and then whooped and howled and hugged his guest.

"What is it? Five years?" he asked, laughing.

"Yes, but it feels like less somehow," said Triumff. Bluett punched him playfully on the arm.

"What about this Frenchie crap? This cutesie blond bob?"

"And this Roman nonsense? 'I ask-a you, signore'... Honestly!" said Cedarn.

"A man has to survive. Italian food is the very fashion now, not that I expect you to know that. You always were miserably behind the times. This is a trattoria, in the Roman style... all prosciutto, saltimbocca and chintz table-cloths. The punters expect the accent. It's all part of the ambience."

"Do tell."

"So... why are you here? Catching up on old times at last?" asked Bluett.

Triumff shook his head.

"I need help, Drew," he said. "I'm trying to stay alive, and you were always good at that."

Drew Bluett had served the Unity with distinction for twelve celebrated years. That is to say, Drew Bluett hadn't done so much as Tom Dabyns, Truffock Roundeslay, Joachim Brukk, Geriant Malpowys, Steffan Droigt, Baldesar Boccho... Triumff forgot the rest. Bluett's talent was espial, that so-called second oldest of professions (the first, of course, being cave realtor), and in the guise of three dozen or more fictions, had plied his art of intelligence across the courts of the European Unity. They had met in Venice in ninety-six, and their paths had crossed many times since. Twice, Rupert Triumff had run Bluett's coded letters of espial down the Channel in a fast sloop, and delivered them to anonymous spymasters and case-officers at nervous midnight trysts. Once, with only a rapier, a burning artillery linstock and a leaking dorey, he had pulled Bluett from the clutches of a torturer of the Prussian navy, and rowed his comatose form to safety across the Monte Cabiarca Sound, while two Prussian galleasses burnt and foundered at their moorings. This had been during the six-month Prussian Uprising, when the *Blameless* had been blockaded in Gramercy Harbour, and Triumff had had nothing better to do.

Since such glory days, times had changed. The Privy Council – with Lord Slee its chief mover – had become alarmed at the autonomous power of the intelligence community, and had cooked up ways of curtailing its powers, or turning them in ways the Council could control. Then came the infamous "Sedangate" affair, when Lord Effingham, Her Majesty's Comptroller of Espial, had been disgraced and banished.

This was a shameful matter, blown up into lurid myth by the pamphleteers and tabloiders. Effingham had been caught kerb-crawling in his sedan chair off Holborn, propositioning gigolos in cipher. In the wake of the scandal, Effingham had died in exile, a broken man (when a harpsichord mysteriously fell on him), and his espial "Circus" had been dismantled. In a house-cleaning purge authorised by Effingham's Council-sponsored replacement, Lord Blindingham, the Circus's many brave agents were deemed untrustworthy, and either hounded from the country, or suffered long, fabricated treason-trials and came to sticky ends, thanks to Lord Slee's newly imposed capital punishment of hanging, drawing and syruping.

A few, a very few, turned to their hard-learned skills, and melted into the fabric of British life as different men. In the power vacuum that followed, the previously impotent CIA rose to dominance as the new Secret Service. Many at Court believed it wouldn't be long before they too found themselves on the business end of a "treason-purge" from the Privy Council. In his present circumstances, Rupert Triumff found that last concept fundamentally reassuring.

Drew Bluett had been one of those who had survived it all. Quiet hearsay, from one confidante to another, had allowed Triumff to learn of Bluett's new station in life, running a victualling house cheekily named after his old profession. Triumff had remained, dutifully, out of contact. He had reasoned that Bluett would ill-favour a visit from his past life, and the potential damage that it might do.

But now, Triumff had a reason.

"You're in a pretty fix, by all accounts," mused Bluett, sitting on a bench under the plum arbour and uncorking a bottle of cassis. "All London is a-chatter with your... 'treason', Rupert. They say you've made a pact with Beelzebub and plan to threaten the Queen's person. They say you're specially trained in fiendishness. They say you've brought back new Magicks from your new continent."

"Do they?" asked Triumff, all but growling. It wasn't a question. He took the glass of liquor that Bluett offered, and downed most of it in one gulp.

"Let me tell you, Drew, of some secret things," he began.

So it was, in that walled garden in Deptford, that Rupert Triumff unfolded his deepest confidences to Drew Bluett, confidences that, until then, had been known only to

Triumff, Agnew and Doll, and Uptil, of course. Only one other great secret in the Unity was known by so few personages, and that was the secret conspiracy of Slee, Jaspers, Salisbury and de la Vega.

In this momentous hour, a close-kept secret grew a little larger. A cloud passed in front of the sun and the garden grew chill. Triumff shuddered, and felt as if all London was hushed and listening. He waited for a moment as the hubbub of Deptford around about filled his ears and reassured him, and then he drank another glass and began.

"The voyage to the South was arduous," said Rupert Triumff. "I would that others knew of its perils, but it was necessary to burn my logs and claim they were washed over-rail in a squall. Months we sailed, not knowing to where, out of sight of land or friends or even other ships. There was a time when I would have welcomed the sight of a pirate sail. Forty men sailed with me on the *Blameless*, forty good men. Piers Packenhamme, Morris Roughly, Tom Tibbert and Swainey Gould. Old Roger Frizer... remember him? South of the Tropics, we were becalmed for weeks. Illness wracked the ship, and twelve men died, Piers among them. Two others went so sun-mad they mutinied, and were taken by sharks as they tried to swim for home. All the while, I buckled under my responsibilities, knowing what the Crown expected of me, new lands, yes, but more than that: new Magick, new wonders for the Church to employ. Before I left, I had an audience, in camera, with a senior prelate of the Guild. He implied that the Arte was burning out, and only a new lease of Magicks would save it. He urged me to bring back miracles. I needed that sort of burden as much as I needed a brimming privy."

Triumff sat back on the bench and sighed.

"So it was, we found the new land," he continued, "this Australia. It was paradise. A bright, big country of multiple delights, a New World with its own proud people."

Drew nodded. "These autochthons. I have read the reports of your endeavour in all the journals. You have made a fine discovery."

"It is a rod for my own back," Triumff replied, sadly. "Beach, for that is the name of the land in its people's tongue, is a worthier world than ours by far. It's noble and clean, and civilised beyond compare. And the things they can do…"

"Their Magick?" asked Drew.

Triumff shook his head, and said, "No Magick, Drew, no Arte. The folk of Beach renounced the Magick way centuries ago, seeing it for the curse it was. No, they have based their beautiful world on industry… on machines. They have advanced the rude skills we left to languish when Leonardo and his kind re-midwifed the Arte. While the Unity buried itself in centuries of misbegotten sorcery, Beach grew up healthy and strong, and able, by the power of their own minds and hard-working hands. Their entire continent is pure and uncorrupted by the stink of Magick."

Triumff realised that his glass was empty. He took the bottle from the bench-seat and refilled it with slightly shaking hands.

"So now, on my return," he continued, "I was faced with a dilemma. I had no Arte to bring back, no new Cantrips, no new jinx. But what I had… Ahh, what a thing! News of a noble world, secrets of technologie that would baffle and illuminate the Unity. And I realised my duty."

"Duty?" asked Bluett.

"To keep it from the Church and Court," answered Triumff. "Once they knew of it, an armada of reavers and wreckers would put out from Plymouth and Southampton, and all points east, off to despoil and break and invade and steal. They would want it for themselves. At worst, my friends, those folk of Beach who had treated me with kindness and generosity, would be enslaved and murdered, and driven from their cities, like the noble kind in the Indies and wherever else the Unity stains the map. At halfway best, they would fight back, and war would wreck the globe. We would have no shield against their machines, and they no shield against our Arte. I held a million lives in my own two hands."

Triumff was silent for a moment.

"So it was, I devised my Ploy," he said.

"Ploy?" asked Bluett.

"To return, victorious, yet not so," said Triumff. "To bring back trinkets and stories to please the Court, yet not so much they would itch to learn more. I thought of simply staying there, but that, I knew, would only draw down the inquisitive to finish my work. I had to make my passage back and discourage further missions. I took with me certain marvels of Beach that might amuse, and also Uptil, a prince of his people, who wished to learn of our wretched world. He was sworn to act the ignorant savage, so that our story might be given weight. We were to say that Australia was but a little place, devoid of civil life or enviable riches, a place not worth the further efforts of discovery."

"But your crew? Could you trust them to–" Bluett began.

"My crew?" interrupted Triumff. "Nine fellows stayed in Beach, reported dead on my return. Those few that made the trip back fell prey to the rigours of our hideous passage home before I could even begin to wonder at their trust. Only myself, Uptil and two others were alive by the halfway mark of our journey. Roger Frizer was one, and a boy called Lot Passioner. We were half-mad, half-dead, tempest-tossed and out of vittals. The cussed ship made north only through the seamanship of wind and flood. We were all but corpses in the shivering cabin. I sometimes wish that we had perished there and been spared this intrigue of homecoming. But off the Azores, leagues wide of our way, we were sighted by a Spanish brig, the *Clemente*, and taken under line. Their captain was a bold, honest man, who knew our name and our business. They cared for us and offered a skeleton crew to steer the Blameless back homeward, in companionship. The boy Lot lasted another week, but his scurvy could not be repaired, and we cast him into the deep with all honour. Old Roger saw the Scillies pass and even saw the rock of Plymouth Ho, but the voyage had tried him to the bloody limit, and he died in sight of land, choking on the medicinal alcohol that had become his only comfort. So, the *Blameless* was brought to the quayside with only two crew. I believe God was spitefully assisting in my damnable Ploy."

"But your return was triumphant!" said Bluett. "I read it so! You were feted, paraded…" Drew's brow furrowed.

"It was seemly so to do. We rested in Trinity House for a month, secretly put up and nursed. Then Admiral Poley presented me with a new crew, and we sailed out and back into harbour, spruced up and fighting fit, to the cheers of a crowd harried out for the occasion. It was Poley's notion, assented to by the Court. It was an exercise in propaganda, to increase the splendour of my success and celebrate the balls of the British Mariner.

"Then began the gossip, and the questions, and meetings with this press agent and that fop from the Admiralty," continued Triumff. "So, Uptil and I wove the Ploy to perfection, and our story was caulked against the storm of interest, despite the public fantasies in the press. I was a hero, I'd done my bit. A new land was added to the Unity map, and new titles strung upon the Queen's style. Never once was mention made of further voyages. All agreed Australia was a delicious trinket, but not worth the sailing to. I honestly thought we'd got away with it."

"But?" asked Drew.

"But I reckoned without the inveigled ambitions of the Court. Slee, I think, is foremost in this, but that so-called seaman de la Vega rat-arse is burning with it too, I'm sure. Each passing day since my return, the Court has pressed me to make my report and sign over the Letters of Passage. I feel it is only because de la Vega wishes to make a victorious voyage of his own, and bathe in such glory, but I've almost run out of tactics to delay them. The Ploy is about to fail, and then Beach will become another sad victim of the Unity's lust."

The garden had grown suitably cold and shadowed.

"And this is why you've sought me out?" asked Drew Bluett.

"No," said Triumff, "well, not entirely, anyway. This madness that afflicts the City, the business at the Powerdrome, at first, I thought it was a skilful attempt to discredit me through treason, so that the Letters might be taken off me by legal sleight of hand while I languished in the Marshalsea. Other things are afoot, however. Woolly himself detained me and disguised me in this wise. From him, I know there is more to it than Australia. Some black conspiracy is abroad in London, and I'm just a scapegoat. I'm on the run, friendless, and I know my life will only be safe if the hidden enemy is put to rout. That's why I've come."

There was a long silence, broken only by the clatter of pots from the Go-Betweene's wash-house.

"Let me see what I can do," said Drew Bluett finally. "Some of the old Circus Performers are still at large, like me. They keep their ears to the ground, if only to watch out for themselves. If there is some conspiracy, they may have heard. Where can I find you?"

"As Louis Cedarn, lutenist, at the Swan," said Triumff.

"Then I'll come to you soon, with what intelligence I can rake up," said Bluett.

Triumff took Drew's hand and shook it.

"It's a lot to ask, I know," he said.

"Think of it as payment for an artillery linstock, well used, and a pile of Prussian embers," replied Bluett. There was a look of boundless, epic friendship in his eye that seemed to need a sweeping orchestral score to accompany it.

However, accompanied only by the sounds of a hooting goose, in the madder plots over the wall, Cedarn turned and walked away.

The street lamps were lit by the time Cedarn tried to slip into the back way of the Swan. There was a bustle of activity from the direction of the stage boards, and voices were raised, rehearsing lines. Behind the cyclorama, the read-through of a stichomythia was going particularly badly, and brutal threats were being made.

Spying down from a turn in the gallery, Cedarn saw me, your servant Wllm Beaver, in the back row of the lower circle, watching the players go through their paces on the brightly lit stage. From that distance, he couldn't be sure if it was the rehearsal for the multiple-killing sequence of a re-venge tragedy or an escalating creative difference. He made his way down to the circle.

"Can I have my lute back?" he asked quietly, slipping into the seat beside me. I turned to him with a look that would have been withering were not both of my eyes blackened and swollen.

"You tricked me, Louis," I snarled painfully.

"Get in a fight, did you?"

"That's not funny," I said. "The man who chased me was most upset. And he was built like a flying buttress. Worse still, Gaumont says I can't go on until my bruises are gone. He says the audience will laugh."

"I thought that was the idea," said Cedarn.

"With me, not at me," I said, handing the lute back.

"I won't forget this, you know," said Cedarn, trying to sound sincere.

"Neither will I," said I, Wllm Beaver, gruffly.

"Where have you been?" asked Gaumont, as Cedarn ran into him as he tried to slip through the backstage darkness.

"Business, Wisley," said Cedarn, with all the serious "I-know-what-l'm-doing" brusqueness he could muster.

"Brief me later, then. The powers that be want a report," answered Wisley.

Cedarn nodded and edged past the hem of Gaumont's gown. He met de Tongfort, on the back stairs, coming down.

"Where the hell have you been?" snapped the stage manager. He had the advantage of height on the stairs, and Cedarn thought for a moment that the stringy man was going to swing for him.

"Dentist. I had a tooth-ague."

De Tongfort watched him closely as he slid past, and continued to watch him as he disappeared up the stairs.

In the flag-store of the cupola, Cedarn threw himself down onto the sacking and sighed. A few hours' sleep in this pleasant darkness and he could–

Something very cold and hard pressed against his cheek.

"You played me for a fool, punk," said an asphalt voice.

"Sorry," said Cedarn, his words muffled by the sacking he was face-down in.

"Got a reason?"

"Tell Woolly I'm on to something, but I need more time. And I don't need a Fulke and Seddon dowhatsit man-lamer poked in my ear, thank you very much," said Triumff, still chewing on the sacking.

There was a grunt, and the chilly threat withdrew. When Cedarn looked up, he was alone in the cupola.

"I wish he wouldn't do that," he murmured.

An hour passed, and hunger got the better of him. Luteless, he crept down the rickety stairs. There was a noise of carousing coming from the tiring room. Rehearsals were over for the night, it seemed. As he made his way towards the rear door, he saw the property and costume crates that had arrived during the day, stacked up in the underway. "WOODEN OH COMP" read the stencil on the sides.

"Shit," he breathed, and his pulse quickened.

Someone embraced him from behind, and he went over into a pile of folded drop-curtains, under what seemed like a ton of giggling blubber. It felt like he had been flying-tackled by a sperm whale.

"Oh! Oh! Mais oui, oui! You naughty little Gallic charmer, you! You shan't escape this time, oh no! Oh non non!"

Crushed, Cedarn smelled beery breath, sweat and powder. Mistress Mercer bore down on him, pinning him to the curtaining, writhing and pinching, and groping and goosing.

"Get off!" he gagged, "Please… Mary… madame… Get off-ay moi, s'il vous plait!"

"Oh, speakez la Frenchie to moi, do, you exotic elf, it fires my blood. Oh! My loins are quite a-quiver with your Romance tongue!" announced Mary.

"That's just your imagination, mistress. Please…" Cedarn said, managing to prise himself around, but Mary Mercer flopped over at the same time so that they were nose to nose, with Cedarn beneath.

He looked up into blood-shot eyes, well-gone with musket, and choked on the brewery fumes that billowed from her rouged mouth.

"Be gentle with me… now!" she squeaked, and kissed his mouth. She kissed. He didn't. Sometimes these things can be a one-way matter.

Just as he was hoping to come up for air and wondering if her tongue was going to puncture one of his lungs, a lamp shone across them both.

"What is– Oh! Sorry!" said a voice from behind the lamp. Cedarn and Mercer looked up, and blinked into the light. Now he wore as much lipstick as her, though not all of it was on his lips. Some of it was on his oesophagus.

"I didn't mean to interrupt," began the voice.

The light shone down into Cedarn's face.

"It's you!" said the voice.

"Oh no…" Cedarn breathed.

"What the hell do you think you're doing?" asked Doll Taresheet.

"I can explain," said the man in the dripping cloak.

Robert Slee looked up from his writing stand, and took off his reading glasses. Rain tap-danced on the window behind him.

"I don't want you to, sir," he replied coldly. In the lamplight, he looked even more anaemic and reptilian than usual. "I disapprove of our meeting in person. You know that. There are channels for communicative purposes. Confidential ones. Go through Blindingham, if you must. Windsor has ears and eyes everywhere. This is dangerous."

"And important," said the rain-soaked man, brushing droplets of water from his hair and wishing there was a fire in the study grate. "If I sent a cipher down the usual route, you wouldn't get it until Monday. Things are moving too quickly for that."

Slee blotted his ledger carefully and stood up.

"Talk, then," he said. "Quickly. And then begone."

"Woolly has placed an espial at the Swan."

"Yes… that fool Gaumont. Old news."

"No, another. A lutenist from France, though if he's truly French than I'm a harlot."

Slee raised an eyebrow and said, "Someone in your line of work should be more careful about the way he describes himself."

"Very funny, my lord. This new man may be a danger. Gaumont is soft and stupid, and no threat, but this one… Cedarn he is called. He seems sharp and quick. Whatever else, he is an unknown quantity. Woolly would not have sent him in if he wasn't good. I fear they are on to the Play. He may be there to break it."

"Unless you've been talking rashly, no one but you and I know of the Play," said Slee, his voice rising in anger.

"No one but you, me and your circle of allies, you mean," replied the visitor, veiled sarcasm in his words. "Can you trust them all?"

Slee thought of a fat, farting, uncouth Wiltshireman, and let the notion simmer in his brain.

"Perhaps not," he said. "If the Play is compromised, we will all die on the scaffold. See to it that this espial is taken off, quickly, before he can bleat to Woolly, and do us harm. See to it."

"O'Bow, p'rhaps?" asked the visitor.

"I don't care how," said Slee. "In truth, I don't want to know. Just be away and do it."

"As you command," said Bonville de Tongfort, pulling his cloak up around his neck.

CHAPTER SIXTEENTH.
Which is set upon Friday night
& Saturdaye morning.

Cat's eyes watched the moonlit Swan. Cat's paws did up the fastenings of its doublet, and it walked slowly around to the rear door of the theatre.

Tide bells clanged in the darkness, and moorlines hummed away from the fo'c'sle spinners. The air smelled of rain, though it was temporarily between showers. A pewter moon made occasional appearances in the puffy blackness above, edging the scudding cumulonimbus with silver traces.

Giuseppe Giuseppo watched his cargo-trunks being winched away onto the quayside by hulking porters, who would, no doubt, take a fair chunk of his gold away with them for being roused this late.

"It's been an education," said Master Luccio frankly, his shoulders relaxed for the first time in three days.

"For me, too." said Giuseppe, smiling at Luccio, and shaking his moist hand. "Will you wait in port until I return?"

"I'd rather not," said the master. "No offence, signore. You've given me a sack of coin and tested my nerves to the limit. I'd best be off to do something safer. Shark fishing with my wedding tackle as bait, maybe. Perhaps making rude signs at the British Admiralty revenue cutters."

Giuseppe nodded with a smile.

"I understand," he said. "You've been brave enough for one lifetime."

"You, I sense, are going to have to be brave for several more," said Luccio. "God speed, sir."

"God, Master Luccio, has little to do with it," said Giuseppe.

On the quayside, he turned to wave once again to Master Luccio, but the man had gone below decks. The Battista Urbino rocked gently in the harbour swell, and rain began to fall again.

"England," Giuseppe said, smiling up into the drizzle spattering off his face.

It was just before one of the clock. Plymouth had collapsed in a drunken stupor an hour since.

An Admiralty man in mouse-beige velvet and an oilskin stumbled over to him with a clipboard held in still-dreaming hands.

"It's bloody late for this kind of show, signore. Couldn't you have dropped anchor in the bay and waited til dawn to come ashore?" he asked.

Giuseppe shook his head. He was wider awake than he'd ever been.

"Urgent business. What must I sign, how much do I owe, and where can I get a fast coach and a steady team?" he asked.

"At this time of night?" asked the official with a "you-must-be-sodding-joking" absence of usefulness that made the English despised the world over. "You must be sodding joking."

* * *

De Quincey had found that a stack of leather-bound statutes made a surprisingly comfy pillow for one in the furthest stages of fatigue, and was just beginning to drool on paragraph one hundred and thirty-five (The abatement of public fornication) when a thump at the door started him back to the painful reality of two-fifteen AM in New Hibernian Yard.

"Woff?" he slurred, his lips numb with sleep. He wiped the spittle off his slashed sleeve.

"Sorry to wake you, sir," began Serjeant Burnside, poking his head around the ward-room door.

"No, you're not, Burnside."

"Yes I am, sir," contradicted the thick-set huscarl. "It's just that we have a matter in interview room three that requires your attention."

"I'm coming," sighed de Quincey, rising and pulling his popinjay mandillion off the back of the bench. It was close to freezing in the stone hallways of the Yard, and de Quincey followed Burnside down the passageway, shivering. Low moans from seriously unhappy prisoners floated up through the brick.

"Quiet night?" de Quincey asked through a yawn.

"Until now," said Burnside. "Bob Lucky's team picked this one up in Drury Lane just forty minutes since. She was frying a pair of cutpurses."

"She?"

"Old girl from up east," said Burnside.

"Frying?" asked de Quincey.

"Magick, sir. All blue and crackly, Bob said."

"Great," heaved de Quincey, rubbing his eyes and finger-combing his bird's nest hairdo. "Have you informed Infernal Affairs or the Guild?"

"Not yet, sir," said Burnside. "After last night's little three-and-nine, I thought you'd want to talk to her first."

They had come to rest outside the riveted door of interview room three.

"Right," said de Quincey, taking a deep breath. "Give me her charge sheet."

"There, sir." said Burnside, handing the parchment over.

"Grundy, Mother… No known priors. Nothing at all, in fact. She quiet?"

"She is now, sir," said Burnside.

"Go and get me a coffee, Burnside."

"Yes, sir," said Burnside. "I've laid on some nantwiches, sir."

"Don't expect me to eat them, then. And Burnside…"

"Yes, sir?"

"It's two-and-eight, not three-and-nine," said de Quincey.

"Yes, sir," said Burnside.

With what must have been his hundredth weary sigh of the week, de Quincey opened the heavy door and stepped into the room.

It was as cold as… some place de Quincey had no intention of going in the next life. Present in the starkly blank chamber was a duty guardsman in full breast and gorget with a horrendously bladed lugged partisan, the stenographer at his portable lectern, and Serjeant Lucky, sitting across the table from a pinched, elderly lady who had all the physical presence of a gardening implement.

Lucky looked up.

"Let the record state, Chief Investigator de Quincey entered the room at…" He glanced at the hourglass on the desk. "Two nineteen." There was some scribbling from the lectern.

"Carry on, Lucky," de Quincey nodded, closing the door, and standing back for a while to get the measure of the suspect.

"So, tell me again, missus, what were you doing to those chuffing foisters in the lane?"

"I'm not your missus," replied the old woman.

"No, indeed! My missus has got a bit more meat on her, if you takes my meaning. Not that I don't admire the more willowy figure, you understand, but, well, my missus is built for comfort, not acceleration…"

Lucky tailed off. It had been a long night for him, de Quincey could tell. He hardly possessed the keenest investigative mind at the best of times, and these were not them. De Quincey hazarded that Lucky's mental state was currently as marshalled and organised as a Bacchanalia with St Vitus Dance.

"Where was I?" murmured Lucky, largely to himself.

"At the end of your tether?" suggested the stenog.

Mother Grundy seemed to smirk, though she rapped twig-fingers on the tabletop with impatience. Lucky looked around at de Quincey, his expression of the imploring variety.

De Quincey sat down in the chair that Lucky had vacated.

"Let the record state: de Quincey takes over interview at… two-twenty. Delete that garbage about Lucky's wife, please, stenog," said Lucky, relieved.

There was some hasty scratching.

"Changing the police records now, eh?" asked Mother Grundy in a voice that sounded like an un-oiled weathervane squeaking around in the wind.

"No. Just trying to save time and get to the real point. You're being evasive, ma'am," said de Quincey.

"Am I?" she asked.

"Yes you are. Just then in fact. Now I haven't yet been fully acquainted with the affray that led to your detention. Would you like to tell me what happened in your own words?" asked de Quincey.

Mother Grundy pattered her fingers on the tabletop again, and said, "This is wasting precious time."

"Let it waste. Either you tell me, or you wait while I read off the stenog's report," said de Quincey.

"Very well. I was going down this street—"

"Drury Lane, sir," put in Lucky, his notebook open.

"And these two imbeciles leapt out and said… I think it was 'Give us yorn purse, old hag'…"

"Why do you say they were imbeciles?" asked de Quincey.

Mother Grundy looked affronted. "Because any but a fool knows it is wrong to tangle with me."

"Where are you from, Mother Grundy?" asked de Quincey.

"Ormsvile Nesbit, Suffolkshire."

"Where you are justly famous, I'm sure."

"You can be sure of it, sir," said Mother Grundy.

"But perhaps your fame has not yet spread to the City, ma'am?"

"Perhaps not. Perhaps that would explain why there were so many fools on the road to London," she agreed.

De Quincey nodded, and said, "Undoubtedly, ma'am. So what did you do to these… imbeciles then?"

"I wrapped them in a sheath of phlogestonic flame," said Mother Grundy proudly.

"All blue and crackly it were," put in Lucky over de Quincey's shoulder.

"Thank you, serjeant."

"And their flesh was burned like old steak and their eyes did melt—"

"Yes, yes. Shut up now, Lucky," said de Quincey.

"Shutting up, sir."

"So you admit to using bedevilment to spurn your attackers?"

"Indeed. I am a warlitch," the old hag admitted.

"I beg pardon?" asked de Quincey.

Mother Grundy looked across at him witheringly. "I know full well that warlocks and witches are forbidden. I am a warlitch. It's a loophole," she said.

"Of course."

"Why are you smiling behind your hand, Mister de Quincey?"

De Quincey hadn't been aware that he was, but he was.

"No reason," de Quincey said. "Tell me now, what were you doing in Drury Lane?"

"Apart from frying imbeciles?" she asked.

"Apart from that."

"I have a great urgency. There is a grave matter in this noisome City that I must attend to."

"And that is?" asked de Quincey.

There was a long pause.

"Someone is using the Arte necromantically to destroy the Bonds That Should Be Unbroken," said Mother Grundy.

De Quincey felt a chill in the small of his back.

"What makes you say that?" he asked.

"I have felt it. I know it. Bad things are going on. I have seen the signs. I must be allowed to stop them before they get out of hand," she said.

De Quincey looked around at the others present. The guardsman was impassive, the stenographer busy. Lucky had his eyes closed and clearly wanted to be elsewhere.

"Another question, ma'am," said de Quincey. "If things really need your attention as you say, why didn't you fry the officers that tried to detain you? Why didn't you just blast past them and carry on to stop these grave matters?"

"Because I'm no murderess. Stupid they may be, but these boys are not villains. They are officials of the State. I am bound by the rule of law," said Mother Grundy. "Do you think I would still be sitting here if it was simply a matter of toasting my captors and leaving? I may be a warlitch, but I'm not a monster. As soon as you have finished all this nonsense, I will be about my business. And you will thank me for it."

"Well," said de Quincey, and then stopped, a thought having occurred to him. "What signs have you seen, Mother Grundy?"

"Corn weave, ash-tree bark, skylark song, mole burrows, flocks of sheep, furling clouds... things you wouldn't read or understand," she said.

"So how do you know what you're looking for?"

"Because of dreams."

"Dreams?" asked de Quincey.

"Burning dreams that come even when I'm awake," she replied, "dreams from the sinistral side of the mind. A sunfire, a raining cloud, a blameless son, a false face, a swan, a king with a dagger, a clown with a bow. And a name... One name. A stone. A jasper."

De Quincey sucked in his breath. He was suddenly profoundly aware of his heart, beating in his chest, thumping like a marching-drum.

"Get out. Get out of here now," he hissed at Lucky, the stenog and the guard. Nonplussed, they obeyed, clunking the door shut behind them.

"Tell me more about the jasper, ma'am," said de Quincey.

Tantamount O'Bow took to criticism like a duck to lava. In the opinion of Boy Simon, and the other regular topers in the Rouncey Mare, there was a particular word that described the comments on O'Bow's singing, made by two yeomen visiting the hostelry that night. The word was "inadvisable". At the time when its use was most apposite, Boy Simon and his cronies were too busy hiding behind furniture to bring it to mind, but they remembered it several days later, and had a drink to celebrate its recovery.

O'Bow had been busily doh-reh-me-ing his way through a spirited, if tortured, solfeggio when one of the yeomen had been heard to remark, "Truly, the fellow is blessed over-much with the favours of the Terpsichorean Muse." His companion had sniggered.

Silence had fallen on the Rouncey Mare, the kind of silence that usually came between the stubbing-out of a last cigarette and the chorus of hammer-clicks from a line of waiting matchlocks. Charged bumpers halted inches from open mouths. The innkeeper slowly sank down to a crouch behind the oak bar.

"Turpsy Korean?" asked O'Bow. His head twitched to the side, though his eyes never left the yeoman pair. O'Bow never looked angry. It was rumoured (generally at a distance from O'Bow measured in leagues) that he was too stupid to appreciate the concept of anger. His face always had a perky yet vacant glaze that hinted at homicidal idiocy and invited spontaneous, unrepentant apology from the world at large. It was the kind of expression that Vesuvius might have worn just prior to engulfing Pompeii, if it had had a face.

O'Bow invited the yeomen to explain the meaning of the words. They did so, haltingly, with reference to the employment of irony and sarcasm.

"Czar chasm?" asked O'Bow.

At that point, the braver of the two yeomen decided that laughter was the best medicine, and explained that, in their opinion, O'Bow's singing was – ha ha ha! – a pustular chancre on the cloaca of London's cognoscenti. He said this with an expansive laugh to all around, which begged for good-humoured support so that they could all joke it off and get on with remaining alive.

"Conk-nosed scenty?" asked O'Bow in the deathly quiet. "Who are you calling a conk-nosed scenty?"

This was, O'Bow explained, fighting talk where he came from. No one disagreed. No one was actually sure where O'Bow had come from, though they were all fairly certain that, wherever it was, it must have been happy to see him go. As most of the mother tongue, even the politer bits, seemed to be fighting talk to Tantamount O'Bow, the occupants of the Rouncey Mare had no doubt that "conk-nosed scenty" was actually heavily-armed-and-insultingly-provocative talk in O'Bow's book. "Conk-nosed scenty" was suicide by mouth. "Conk-nosed scenty" was indisputably inadvisable. To a man, the regulars dropped to the saw-dust-covered floor, leaving the yeomen marooned in a sea of quivering tables.

With one meaty paw, Tantamount O'Bow lifted the twenty-pound bain-marie off the carvery hearth, emptied its scalding contents over one of the yeomen, and then swung it like a tennis racket at the other, who took its cast-bottom full in the face and chest, and cleared three tables and a spitted calf. Then, for good measure, O'Bow thumped the pan down twice on the head of the whimpering, blistered man at his feet. The bain-marie was not quite the same shape when he returned it to the hearth.

There was a spontaneous round of applause, and the regulars emerged from under the tables. They'd seen the same sort of show a hundred times before, but it was always a good idea to clap. There was such a thing as escalation.

There was a whip-round, and congratulatory drinks were bought for O'Bow. They covered a table top. O'Bow was just getting into his stride and dealing with them when a tall, slender man entered the tavern and approached him directly.

"Dung Tongue-Fork," nodded O'Bow, pledging the new-comer with a raised cannikin.

"De Tongfort," corrected the incomer, eyeing suspiciously the two astonishingly broken men being stretchered out of the Rouncey Marc. "How goes it with you, my friend?"

"Fair to mandolin, and please you," replied the humanoid leviathan with a twitch. "Why comes you to the Rouncey this eve, my lesbian friend?"

"Thespian," said de Tongfort, sitting down opposite O'Bow. "I have employment for you, but I'd rather not discuss it in such populated environs."

"There bain't be nothing wrong with these envy irons," replied O'Bow, mid-quaff. "They won't be a-listening to the likes of us. We're bein' dusk Crete." As if to prove his point, O'Bow looked up and twitched a glance at the tavern around them. The tavern quickly found other things to look at.

De Tongfort leaned closer, as close as the stench of O'Bow's breath would allow.

"There is a fellow at the Swan," he said, "a Frenchie called Louis Cedarn. He came to us a lutenist."

"And you'd be wanting this nist back then?"

"Which nist?"

"The one the Frenchie came a-looting?"

"Well…" said de Tongfort, struggling but inspired, "… we've given up the nist as lost, but we could do with having him punished. In the finite sense."

"Fie night, eh? My pleasure. But it'll cost," said O'Bow.

"There's a dozen sovereigns in it for you," said de Tong-fort.

"In what?"

"In… this purse," said de Tongfort, producing it. O'Bow took it, weighed it in his hand and nodded.

"How will I knows him?" he asked.

"Blond, cocky, foppish clothes. He has taken to living in the Swan's cupola. You know what a cupola is, do you?"

O'Bow looked at him wearily.

"I'm not stupid," he said. "I know full well what both of them is."

THE SEVENTEENTH OF CHAPTERS.

Dawn came up over London town, a mackerel sky smoked to kipperhood by the rising sun. Yawning, Agnew nudged Uptil awake.

"What? What bloody what?" gurgled Uptil, his eyes still closed. He'd only sat down on the slatted bench a moment before, but his head was so heavy he would have fallen asleep on a bed of nails. Under a bed of nails even.

"Shhh!" warned Agnew. The Thames ferry, Gogmagog, was approaching the south shore, and they shared it with a gaggle of up-with-the-dawn drovers and late-back-for-barracks sailors. No one was paying them much heed. Pinkish light filtered down across the estuary, and rudely loud gulls mobbed in the wind above the ferry. There was a chalybeate taste of spindrift in the air, borne down from the coast.

"Sorry," whispered Uptil, pulling his cloak tighter around his bare muscles. "I forgot where I was."

"Try not to," warned Agnew. "The last thing we want is the Ploy to get as lost as Sir Rupert."

The ferry edged up close to the landing strip. Reluctant longshoremen waited for the out-flung ropes. There was a rocking to and fro that only their kinaesthetic sense registered, and then, with a bump, they moored. The drovers and sailors and stop-outs flocked down the duckboard ramps.

"Come on," tugged Agnew, and Uptil trailed along in his wake.

"When you said we'd trawl London until we found him, I didn't think you meant it literally," Uptil murmured as they plodded down the gangplank.

"You wanted to find him," replied Agnew.

"I assumed there would be intervals for sleeping and eating. You may be able to survive on a flask of tea, but I need refuelling and a stationary pillow," said Uptil.

Agnew turned and gave Uptil his most long-suffering stare. Uptil just soaked it up, oblivious. The quayside was cold and unforgiving, and he ached so much he wanted to die. That was before he even considered the entreaties of his rumbling belly.

"I admit," said Agnew, sagging a little, "that we have achieved the square root of bugger all in our search so far. I fear I am running out of ideas of where to look for our misbegotten master."

"Good. I'm running out of consciousness. Let's go home," said Uptil.

"I really thought we'd got somewhere at the Star. And Mr de Vries at Grey's Inn seemed a hopeful lead. But now I'm really down to the last of my knowledge of Sir Rupert's life and doings," Agnew said, rubbing his reddened nose on his hanky.

"So let's go home and sleep on it. I'll wager Rupe is tucked up in his Amen Street four-poster right now," said Uptil.

"There is one last place – that's why we're here," Agnew replied.

Uptil wilted further, looking around for a bollard to sit on. Agnew led him over to a pile of lobster baskets, and they slumped together into its damp, wicker clutches. The elderly manservant reached into the folds of his cloak and produced a stoppered costrel. He took a long swig, flinched, and offered it to Uptil.

"What is it?" asked the Beachovite.

"Just take a sip..."

Uptil did. He swallowed, and then shuddered for some time. When he had finished shuddering, he was aware that his toes were still clenched.

"That's not tea," he commented accurately.

"Elixir vitae, concentrated," said Agnew as his breath returned properly. "It hits the spot when all else fails. When tea fails, anyway. So now... one last hunt?"

Uptil stretched and stood up.

"Okay," he said, "one last hunt and then home to beddy-boos. Where are we?"

"Deptford," said Agnew.

"Uh, why?"

"Last possible lead, my titanic friend. Our last chance. If this fails, we say 'oh well', and forget Sir Rupert entirely."

Agnew led the cloak-swathed autochthon down the quay and into the empty streets of Deptford. Oxstalls Lane was devoid of everything except a water-butt and a slumbering sailor who'd missed his bunk by about three hundred yards.

"Come on," whispered Agnew. "Down this way."

Down this way, Oxstalls snaked around into a rutted track, marked *Butt Lane*. Uptil plodded along in the mud after Agnew, grimacing at the dawn-chorus. If life with Rupert Triumff had taught him anything, it was that dawn and its accompanying ornithological cheeping was the sign of a good night overdone. For many, the daybreak song of birds was a symbol of rebirth and reawakening. For Uptil, birdsong and the encroachment of light were symbols of a jug too far.

"Where and why are we going?" Uptil asked, squelching through the Butt Lane mud.

"There," pointed Agnew. The building ahead was a nondescript walled affair with a placard out front. The shutters were closed, the gates shut, and the building seemed to be breathing the deep breath of slumber.

"Who lives here?" asked Uptil.

"With luck," said Agnew, "if my information is correct, an old and secret friend of Sir Rupert's. I propose we reconnoitre the place first."

They left the wet mud of the road for the wet mud and wetter grass of the paddock adjacent to the walled property. The air was ripe with the smell of damp herbs.

"Give us a leg-up, and I'll take a look," Uptil suggested. Reluctantly, Agnew made a stirrup of his hands, and hoisted the bulky man up the wall. Uptil scrabbled at the wet brick and slippery creepers for purchase.

"Okay," he grunted, with his armpits and chin over the top of the wall.

"What can you see?" whispered Agnew, beginning to shake with the effort of holding up Uptil's weight.

"A garden. Some fruit trees. Back door to a kitchen. Gnngg."

"Gnngg?" asked Agnew.

"I was losing my grip. I don't think there's anyone up."

"Well it is five o'clock in the morning."

"What did you say?" asked Uptil, trying to glance back down at Agnew.

"I didn't," Agnew replied.

The support gave way, and Uptil slithered back to earth with a yelp and several handfuls of Virginia Creeper. Agnew stood with his back to the wall, facing a thick-set, balding man, who had come out of nowhere with a pair of leather breeches, and a cleaver of significant size.

"We didn't mean to wake you, sir," Agnew began.

The man took a step forward.

"You CIA? Militia operatives? Or are you…" he asked, before pausing, and squinting down at Uptil, and then back up at Agnew.

"You're Agnew. Triumff's man. And this must be the fellow from Beach," he said, lowering the cleaver and expelling a relieved breath. "I thought you were government agents or worse. Sorry about the cleaver. I sleep with one eye open these days."

"I presume you are Mr Bluett?" asked Agnew. "Your appearance is somewhat different to that which I remember."

"I'm known as Severino now, but you're right," answered Bluett, "and I can guess what you're looking for."

"Any word of Master Rupert would be most appreciated," said Agnew. "Have you seen him?"

"Of course he has," snapped Uptil, getting to his feet and brushing himself down. "He called me that fellow from Beach, not Australia or the Terra Incognita. How long ago did Rupert leave here, Mr Bluett?"

"You'd better come inside," said Drew Bluett.

Doll pinched at his shorn, bleached locks.

"It's not really you, is it?" she ventured.

"No. Neither is playing at sodding espial, working for Woolly or any of this cloak-and-dagger stuff," said Rupert. "I'm really scared, Doll. I don't think I'm in control of anything any more."

Daybreak was slicing open the envelope of night, in a wide tear across the City, and a clambering sun began to illuminate Doll and Rupert, who were sitting together by a puffing brazier in the litter-strewn arena of the Swan.

There had been a certain amount of shouting and yelling and running backwards and forwards the night before, the sort of business that would have made the basis for a good Aldwych farce if anybody had been taking notes. After ten minutes of dodging the bitter salvos Doll fired at him, the stage rigging she swung at him, and the scenery flats she toppled at him, Triumff had managed to calm her down to a just-less-than-piercing shriek and impress upon her the seriousness of his disguise.

Doll's relief at seeing him alive overcame her fury at seeing him hiding out under a peroxide crew-cut and a promiscuous actress, and they kissed and made up, not altogether unsuccessfully. Then her rage, and the stinging realisation that she seemed to have been worrying about him whilst he had been having a whale of a time, in turn, overcame her fluttering relief, and there was a little more stomping and snarling. Luckily those in the Swan who overheard her angry attack had dismissed it at once as a creative difference and hadn't paid it any mind, and hadn't noticed that she was saying things like "Where have you been, Rupert?" and "Triumff, you bastard, do you know how worried I've been?" Gaumont, brushing wigs in the property wardrobe, had chuckled at the sound of the argument, unperturbed. He had a certain fondness for the sound of creative differences, as a parent does for the sound of his children squabbling at play. Wllm Beaver, who had slid into sleep in the gallery seat, roused briefly at the uproar, but was soon snoring again. Of de Tongfort, there had been no sign.

The shouting had gone on for another fifteen minutes. After that, there was a truce as they carried Mary Mercer to the tiring room and dropped her on her cot. The drink and confusion had rather got the better of her, and she'd opted for the unconscious approach.

When he had finally got her sitting down and listening quietly, it had taken rather longer for Rupert to recount his recent doings to the bewildered Doll. She listened to his tale, and took it rather well.

"I thought it was better if you didn't know where I was," Rupert explained. "It kept you out of danger. Whoever's behind this plot has made damn sure I'm the fall guy. There are people, people like Gull, who would run me through as soon as know me."

"Infernal Affairs, too," said Doll. "Some lizard called Jaspers came round a couple of times yesterday. He was so creepy."

Triumff yawned and rubbed his eyes.

"The worst of it is, I've got nothing," said Triumff. "Not a clue. Woolly got me in here because he thought the theatres were somehow caught up in the conspiracy. But I don't even know what I'm looking for. Maybe it was all a ruse by Woolly to get me out of the picture. Or maybe he's playing me off somehow. Maybe I'm another pawn in his game. I wouldn't be hugely shocked if it turned out that the CIA were behind it all anyway."

He threw a stick in the spitting fire.

"I've been in some fixes before," he continued, "some as deadly as this. But there's always been an obvious plan of attack, a sensible course. There have always been facts I can marshal and details I can assess... the speed of the wind, the run of the tide, the number of guns, the strength of the enemy. I take the facts on board and work out a solution, but this is a whole different thing. I don't know who the enemy is, what he wants, what I have do to beat him, or how I will know I have, if I do. I know who's trying to kill me, but they may not necessarily be the enemy. I know who's keeping me alive, but they may not necessarily be a friend. I'm stuffed."

"You look stupid too," said Doll. Triumff looked up with a hurt expression, but found her smile. It was a brave smile, one that fought through tiredness to make it onto her face. He savoured it.

"I live in hope of Drew coming up with something," he said, dredging his weary mind for reassurances. "Trouble is, though I trust him, I have no idea how much else of the Intelligence Service I can trust."

"The cardinal, the CIA..." she ventured.

"I think if they really cared about me they wouldn't have buried me in this pantomime. It would have been far safer for me if they'd kept me under house arrest somewhere rural and quiet. No, this..." – and by "this" he seemed to mean his bleached hairdo – "this marks me out as nothing more than a fall guy. It's hardly the greatest ever disguise. By keeping me in circulation, Woolly wants to draw the conspiracy out. If I get a knife through the ribs in the process then that's just hard knocks, as long as I've pointed out the traitor, or at least writ his name in my blood on the cobbles of whatever back-alley I die in."

"Is pessimism part of your cover too?" Doll asked.

Triumff growled a no.

"Then what happened to the hero of the high seas, the valiant sail-dog who was the talk of London, and the Queen's favourite, the man who'd laugh in the Devil's face, slap his cheek and leave him to pay the bill?"

"He retired hurt," said Triumff, sourly.

"And what happened to the man who used to hum that daft song about the Guinea Coast in the dark?" she asked more softly.

Triumff smiled, despite himself, and leaned slowly towards her.

"Oh, you know… he's not far away," he murmured hoarsely. Their lips closed to a distance of about an inch. Pheromonal boarding parties prepared to cast across mooring lines.

"Did you find him?" asked a bleary voice from nearby.

Triumff and Doll pulled away from each other, and looked around.

Your loyal servant, I, Wllm Beaver, stood on the other side of the brazier, yawning and trying to flatten my ruff. I looked, all told, like a circus troop had used me as a mattress for a week or two.

"Excusez-moi?" asked Louis Cedarn.

I tried to stifle my yawns.

"The man. Did you find him? He was knocking on the stage door just now. Bloody woke me up. He was looking for you," I said, my facial bruises even more livid after a night's rest. I believe I resembled a mandrill.

"What man?" Cedarn asked, rising to his feet.

"The man. The man." I wasn't fully awake. I coughed and yawned some more.

"What man?" Cedarn asked more forcefully than before.

"The man at the door," I snapped. Really, I thought, how much more explaining did I need to do? A man. A door. The former knocking on the latter.

"Did you let him in?" asked Doll.

"Of course," I said.

"Where is he now?"

I stopped yawning and looked at Cedarn as flatly as my traumatised cheeks would allow.

"I don't know," I said. "I assumed he would find you. He was looking for you."

Cedarn scanned the empty, silent structure of the theatre around us. The only things moving were the pigeons in the rafters and the racing clouds in the mauve sky.

"What did he look like? Shortish... heavy-set... Italian?"

"No," I replied confidently, gazing down into the brazier and warming my hands. "Great big bastard. Built like a brick... uh... privy."

"The guy that smacked you yesterday?" asked Cedarn.

I looked up, and said, "Oh no. Bigger than him. Really big. He had a scar on his face."

"A scar on his face," Cedarn echoed.

"Well, it was more like his face was a scar. Right mess, in fact. Urgghh!" I said, shuddering at the thought. Then some slow realisation crossed my fuddled brain. "I say... He was pretty unwholesome altogether, in point of fact. And rude. I... I suppose I ought not to have let him in at all."

"Stay here," Cedarn instructed.

"What is it? Do you know who he's talking about?" asked Doll. There was worry in her voice.

"I hope not. Stay here." He turned to me, Wllm Beaver. "Stay with her."

"Right ho," I said, nodding, and immediately occupying Triumff's seat by the brazier and beginning to warm my hands for real.

"Be careful, Rupert," said Doll, gazing after Cedarn as he stalked towards the stage.

"My middle name," Cedarn called back bravely, though his heart wasn't in it. He climbed up onto the apron and disappeared into the left wing.

"So, you're an actress?" I asked brightly, turning to Doll.

"Not now," she hissed.

The wings were gloomy and unfriendly, and there was a pungent, pervading stench of tallow. Triumff edged forward, feeling his way along flats and over rope-coils as his eyes became accustomed to the dimness. His heart felt as if it was beating up into his throat. He drew the poniard weapon that old man Kew had given him.

In London, scars were two-a-penny. Indeed, you might be hard-pressed in certain streets to find someone without one. Triumff knew for a fact that the Militia didn't class a scar as a "distinguishing feature".

The way Beaver had described the man, however, rang unpleasant bells in Triumff's mind. He could think of six or more ruffians whose faces were a mess of scar-tissue, and over a dozen who were bigger than the undoubtedly impressive Eastwoodho. Only one man fulfilled both criteria: O'Bow.

Triumff had met O'Bow once, face to scar-face, and had seen him at work four times across crowded taverns. The face-to-face meeting had been eight years previously, when he had been called as a character witness at the inquest of Midshipman Pyker, slain in a tavern brawl in Deptford. Pyker had served on the *Blameless*, and the prosecution had been trying to prove that the midshipman was of sound mind and wouldn't therefore "throw himself into a fireplace and flagellate himself unnecessarily with a poker" as the defence contested. Unnerved by the feral blue eyes that gazed at him out of a puckered, fleshy face, from the dock, Triumff had done his best to commemorate Pyker as a bright, stable young man.

All the while, those blue eyes... that knotted, misshapen skin...

The case had finally been thrown out through lack of... what was it again? Lack of witnesses.

Tantamount O'Bow.

Since those strained hours in the Chancery rooms, Triumff had seen the monster on several other occasions. On each of these – at the Mermaid twice, once at the Rouncey Mare, and once again at the Spread Eagle – O'Bow had vividly demonstrated how a twenty-one-year-old, handsome midshipman might have been turned into a blackened mass of tenderised pulp.

Triumff had always, always stayed well clear of such demonstrations. He couldn't shake the memory of those blue eyes, that cratered, puffy face, or of Pyker's cadaver on the mortuary slab.

He had often wondered how O'Bow had come by that mass of scarring. It looked like someone had branded him full in the face with a white-hot skillet. Triumff had sometimes wanted to shake the brander by the hand, even though he felt sure that would mean shaking hands with a corpse.

His eyes were used to the darkness of the early morning theatre, and he was no longer bumping into things. The poniard was comforting in his hand. He eyed his surroundings, confidently recognising this scenery flat, that rack of lanterns, this dangling pulley...

That enormous silhouette.

The blow took him by surprise, and off his feet. With a gagging yelp, he smashed backwards through a plyboard section of the Castle Dunsinane, his chest hot with pain.

He lay still for a moment, assuming he was dead.

He wasn't. He crawled through the splintered wood and settling dust, groping for his poniard. His chest hurt like nobody's business.

Except Tantamount O'Bow's.

"Frenchie looter," hissed a voice that could only have issued from damaged, twisted lips.

"What is this... why?" Triumff managed, each breath, each word, an agony.

Something massive lumbered through the wreckage closer to him.

"It's a job," said the voice, dismissively.

A hand as big as a warship's anchor took him by the collar, and hoisted him aloft. Swinging gently, Triumff found himself face to face with those blue, burning eyes. No face, no scars. It was still too dark. But the eyes burnt like sapphires in the gloom.

"Is you…" There was a long pause as O'Bow's memory rattled and composed itself. "Is you… Louis Cedarn?"

"No," said Rupert Triumff. Telling the real truth was much easier than lying.

"Oh!" the formless monster said, pausing for some time. He stank of ale. "In that case, I apologise for committing my axe to a strike at yourn person. I'm most particulate about who I kill."

"Oh, good," said Triumff. He was sure he could taste blood in his mouth.

"I'm looking for a Louis Cedarn, who I mean to kill," continued O'Bow, showing no signs of putting Triumff down. "You fit his prescription, so I exhumed you were he."

"I'm not," said Triumff. He hit the floor hard, bouncing off unprepared knees and elbows.

"So sorry," said his attacker, moving away.

Triumff sprawled on his hands and knees for a long moment as he struggled to recover his breath and fight off the pain. He clutched at his chest, feeling the sharp coils of the sprung wire exposed by the axe-blow. Kew's reinforced doublet had saved him from the worst of the biting blade.

"So where might he be?" rasped O'Bow, suddenly at his ear.

"No idea," said Triumff, freezing.

"I might always finish you for being incooperative," said the voice in his ear.

"Why do you want to kill him? He seemed like a nice enough bloke to me," said Triumff.

"Probably is, probably is. However, I am prequired to kill him anyway."

"Oh dear," sympathised Triumff. With a shaking thumb, he slowly drew back the hammer of the flintlock that was built into his poniard.

"That is indeed the shame of it," O'Bow went on. "Have you any eye dears where I might locale him?"

"He's right here, you ugly bastard!" screeched Triumff, stabbing the poniard around at O'Bow and pulling the trigger. There was a dry puff.

"Oh shit," exclaimed Sir Rupert Triumff, wrenching back the hammer for a second try. An avalanche seemed to be falling on him.

An explosion, deafening in the confines of the space between their two, thrashing bodies, rang out like a salute.

Triumff launched himself backwards out of the monster's grasp, and began to run through the backstage confusion. He smacked his forehead on a swinging pulley, and barked his shin on a bull's-eye lantern. Neither stopped him.

He fled around behind the cyclorama, and hit the stairs into the gallery at a run. Something hit him rather faster.

He went down, thrashing and struggling, aware that his efforts were futile. O'Bow weighed more than three hundred pounds. A fist caught his jaw and snapped his head back hard into the edge of a step. The massive axe-head buried itself an inch from his left ear. He stabbed out again with the poniard, remembering its diamond edge that could "cut through anything". It cut through nothing but air. A paw like a bear's snatched at his wrist, caught it, and slammed his hand into the stairs beside his head. Pain cut loose his hold on the poniard, and it skittered away.

He looked up into the ruined face of the man about to kill him, and, with a last reserve of willpower, punched his hand up into the branded features. Most of his fingers accidentally went into O'Bow's snarling mouth, and O'Bow's mouth began quite deliberately to bite.

There was a sudden explosion of splintering wood and distressed musical whimpers, as if a tea-chest full of chords had just detonated.

Triumff found himself pinioned beneath three hundred pounds of dead weight.

He pulled himself out from under O'Bow's body, which lay like a downed titan across the stairs. Above him stood Doll, ashen-faced and frantic, and your humble servant Wllm Beaver, holding the remains of the Tavistock Lute-O-caster.

"Needs must, I suppose," I mumbled, shrugging while still holding the remains of the lute. Lost for words, Doll dragged Triumff to his feet and into her arms.

"I hope you weren't too fond of it," I added, laying the smashed instrument to rest on the face-down bulk of Tantamount O'Bow.

"Not as fond as I am of staying alive," Triumff managed, cuddling Doll. He looked down at his hands, wrapped as they were around Doll Taresheet, counting the fingers. All ten were there. The capstone of his signet ring rattled loosely on its hinge.

"Good grief," Triumff mumbled. "He swallowed my arsenic."

I frowned down at the ring. "So I didn't actually... with the lute, I mean... you would've... that is..."

"Thank you," said Triumff, "I have no doubt your intervention helped enormously."

I looked at the hugging couple for a moment, a satisfied look on my face. Then it changed to one that was part realisation and part confusion.

"She called you Rupert," I said.

"When?" asked Triumff over Doll's shoulder.

"Back then, before…"

"I mean…" I added.

"But that…" I interrupted myself.

"Surely…" I stammered.

"Don't tell me you're…"

I fell silent, and stared at Rupert and Doll until they broke from their embrace and looked back at me.

"You're Sir Rupert Triumff, aren't you?" I asked, a journalistic hunting instinct brightening my previously bleary eyes.

"Yes," said Sir Rupert Triumff, honestly.

CHAPTER EIGHTEEN.

Saturday unfurled itself.

Absent that special morning were the usual breakfast-time comments such as "This tea tastes like dish-water", "Where's my bacon?" and "Just a few more minutes". Instead, curious remarks crossed London's breakfast tables, remarks like, "Is this the fly edge or the hoist edge?", "Have you seen my best ruff?" and "Get that taper away from the bloody Catherine wheels!"

It was Masque Saturday, and the City was preparing to have an Extremely Good Time, which was fine provided your concept of an Extremely Good Time involved flags, patriotic songs and a potentially lethal combination of fireworks and alcohol.

The morning poured itself across the City, robust and full-bodied. Apart from a few determined individuals, who were resolutely intent on properly finishing off Friday (most of these were to be found in the Rouncey Mare), London was up, and busily getting on with Saturday, which was going to be fun with a capital eff.

Sometime around dawn, the City streets had begun to extrude bunting: bright, flapping, tricolour bunting that apparently had been pulled from the shadows of each street corner the way stage conjurers produce coloured hankies from the mouths, ears or armpits of surprised volunteers from the audience. Suddenly clad in miles of bunting it had not known it contained, the City could do little more than applaud the trick with a mystified expression on its face.

After the bunting came the flags, thousands of them, hung, tied, wrapped or otherwise suspended from every available surface above the streets. Pennants and streamers swam like eels in the breeze, banners and gonfalons swung like veils from gutter-lines and eaves, burgees and swallowtails snapped like whips from chimneys and wash-ropes, Guild and Union emblems hung resplendent in the morning light.

Every household seemed to have found a flag, pulled it out of an attic box, darned it, and hoisted it to the roof. Anything fitted the bill: jubilee jacks, crosses, ensigns, pennoncels declaring "Happy Birthday" or "Merry Christmas", oriflames, quarantine burgees, and clubhouse guidons. The winds crossing London found themselves unexpectedly detained by new acres of bagging, furling cloth. The noted wit and bon viveur, Sir Thomas Decretz, declared that the City-folk had suddenly become damnably vexillopathic, but rather underscored this quip by making it while he was rummaging through an ottoman for his Uncle Albert's regimental banderole.

Apart from the very real danger that the entire City might take off if there was an unnecessarily strong gust of wind, there were threats from other quarters. Caches of unexploded fireworks mined the City more thoroughly than any bombardier could have planned. It would be a miracle, particularly given the anticipated alcohol consumption, if they all went off as intended.

Members of the City fire brigades sat around in their stations, grimly sipping coffee, and preparing to intercede when
the merrymaking in the streets turned from "Ooohh!"-ing
and "Aaahhh!"-ing to "Er, wasn't that your house?"-ing.

Detachments of Militia routinely stopped platoons of
troops hauling artillery into the streets.

"Isn't that an excessive number of guns for a salute?" the
Militia men would ask, resignedly, but there was no gainsay-
ing the enthusiastic troops.

"Of course we haven't been authorised," they'd say, "but
it's the Masque Holiday, innit?"

"Aim for the sky," they were told.

"Of course we will," was the response, as the soldiers
handed round rum for the umpteenth time, continued down
the street, came back for the cannons which they had left behind and smiled, completely unreassuringly, at the Militia.

A profusion of floral sprays decorated every surface not occupied by a ratty flag or a box of festive explosives.
Somewhere, vast meadows, glades and dells must have been
denuded of flowering undergrowth. The demand for bou-
quets was so great that by the time the florists got to
Denmark Hill, they were putting up nettle nosegays, which
frankly lacked in everything except effort.

Triumff led Doll and me, your reliable servant, Wllm
Beaver, from the Swan to a tea shop called the Conifer in
Skitter Lane. Since before six, it had been doing a roaring
trade in sweet tea and filled cobs with all those up early on
flag-hoisting, spray-nailing or firework-priming expeditions,
which was nearly everybody.

Behind its leaded, sooty windows lay a modest chamber
where even the air seemed to have been stained brown with
tannin. A rich mix of camomile and lavender filled the room,
oozing out of the steamy clouds that billowed from the

hearth kettles. Two dozen or more patrons sat in the dim booths, smoking, draining china cups of hot brown fluid, and discussing such things as the subtleties of halyard tugging, the bannerol versus the pencel as a patriotic statement, and whether a privy would offer sufficient protection in the unlikely event of, hypothetically let's say, all twelve Grand Combustive Number Four Sky Rockets being ignited simultaneously.

"A pot of Assam and a plate of fruit cake," Triumff told one of the serving girls, once he had got her attention away from a conversation about waft, waif and flaunt.

"Excitin', innit?" she asked him with glee as she took his order.

"You've no idea," he said with a thin, artificial smile.

Triumff took Doll and me to the back of the shop, and installed us in a booth that hid us from the street windows and casual glances.

"I'm not sure I should be associating with you," I mumbled wearily as the tea arrived. I gingerly kneaded my bruised, swollen face.

"Your choice," said Triumff, passing me a steaming cup, "but drink this before you go. You've had a rough time, and your nerves need calming."

Your humble servant took the cup, silently, and sipped, deep in thought. Triumff and Doll began to devour the cake in a way that suggested eating had just become a timed sport.

"You're a member of the fourth estate, Beaver," said Triumff through cake crumbs. "I assume, therefore, that you can string a word or two together. I have a story for you. It'll make your reputation, and I'd be obliged if you took it down for my sake."

I looked at him, any amount of curiosity, and any number of questions in his expression.

"By tomorrow, I might be dead. I'd be happier about that if I knew someone was going to relate the truth after my death," said Triumff.

They ordered a second pot and another cake. I produced a pencil and my notebook.

"Tell me all about it, then," I said.

At Richmond, grumpy workmen did the rounds and shook fried moths from the lantern boxes. There were over four thousand lantern boxes, so that meant a lot of moths, not to mention the number of stubby wicks that had to be tweaked to ignition readiness.

Behind them came the groundsmen, raking up fallen leaves and a not inconsiderable number of dead moths from the dewy lawns. The park braziers sparked and burnt with a strange, lepidopterous odour.

The cavalcade began to roll through the Palace gates: carts and wagons laden to axle-warping with foodstuffs, wine, and enough theatrical equipage to put on the complete plays of Jonson simultaneously. Gaggles of musicians flocked in with the carts, some playing jaunty tunes on their instruments as they strolled along. The carters gave the players sour looks; they had been on the move since four in the morning, and the last thing they felt like was a jolly almain. Palace stewards bustled through the mob, organising, advising and directing, each of them beginning to realise, with a sick feeling, that what had looked terrific on paper was going to be a logistical nightmare in practice.

Rain-clouds admonished the sultry skies, but their threats were empty, and the sun seemed to have got all dressed up for the occasion, roughly pushing aside all hints of inclement weather.

It was going to be a fine Saturday, no matter what. Twenty miles south of the Capital, amid the slumbering corn fields of the North Downs, Giuseppe Giuseppo clambered down from the wagon he had been riding in, and looked out into the middle distance. London seemed as far away as the sleepy sun. Out here, on the Downs, there was nothing but the breeze, the nodding corn, an occasional droning bumblebee and the promise of the perspective-eating trackway.

"Well?" he asked the carter, one Chub Blackett.

Chub proffered a clump of torn-up cowgrass to his horse and said, "Sure and be as right as rain in a day or twa."

Giuseppe swallowed hard, and wondered if his command of English was failing him.

"I have to be in London at once," he reminded Chub, smiling.

"As if," said Chub, scowling as his panting horse refused the cowgrass.

"Sir, I don't think you understand. Forgive me if my English isn't making my purpose clear. I must be in London with all haste. It is vitally important."

"As if," replied Chub, stroking the sweat-drenched flanks of his weary workhorse.

"But–" said Giuseppe.

"Listen now, mister. This horse has run as far and as fast as it will and no more. If I put the lash to him now, he'll drop rightly dead at once."

"But–" added Giuseppe.

"Innt no point complaining. I can gets you to London for Sunday, like enough. If yorn wants to get theres sooner, you's must have to pace it out yournsel."

Giuseppe mopped his brow with his cuff and studied the horse. Its chestnut coat was sheened with perspiration. Chub had been driving it at a gallop since they had left the coast.

It looked back at the Italian traveller with fathomless dark eyes, and Giuseppe knew that further argument was useless.

"Free the horse from the harness," Giuseppe instructed the carter simply.

Chub looked at his passenger for a moment with hand-shaded eyes, and then obeyed without comment. He led the horse away from the wagon to the roadside, where it began to graze in a half-hearted way.

Giuseppe climbed onto the driving board and reached over into his luggage. After a moment, he produced the little, potent book and a small felt bag of coins. He tossed the latter to Chub, who caught it smartly.

"What's this?" he asked.

"For the cart. Now I recommend you look the other way. Over there, for instance," Giuseppe said, indicating the misty distance beyond the corn, which Chub dutifully began to regard.

"And don't look back until I'm gone," Giuseppe added, turning the fragile, wriggling pages of the notebook.

Chub had had a funny feeling about the Italian since he first met him, so he obeyed the instruction unswervingly.

He looked out over the Downs, across the corn to the point where it met the sky. Bees hummed past. Behind him, he heard, although he did not want to hear, a muttering of Latin phrases, followed by a creak of wagon-wood. The air around him, around the Downs, seemed fulminous and heavy, suddenly, charged with an electrical murkiness, and there was a smell of syrup, or was it molasses?

Then there was the sudden rattling of a wagon in motion, a rattling and a squeaking, but no hoof-beats. His horse started, nostrils flaring, but he shushed it down with an experienced hand, his eyes never leaving that distant spot. The hairs on the back of his neck stood up.

The noise of the wagon receded and was gone.

Chub slowly turned around. He was alone with his horse in the middle of the golden ocean and the early morning.

"As if," he murmured to no one at all.

Lying on the nape of the Downs, on the London Road, Smardescliffe is, if you didn't know, pronounced "Smarly", and has been since before they started taking preparatory notes for the *Domesday Book*. On Masque Saturday, however, the only thing pronounced about it was the anti-Goetic fervour that throbbed in all Smardescliffian veins.

By the church gate, opposite the cross of St Cunegund (the patron saint of being patronising), on the village sward, the Mayor stood in conference with the Baker, the Butcher and the Landlord of the Cat and Stoop. The Mayor had leant his pitchfork against the gate for the time being, but the other three had fast holds on their own makeshift weapons, variously a rusty haulm shear, a pig stick and a cooking apple on the end of a piece of string. Frankly, the Landlord of the Cat and Stoop wasn't quite sure what he was going to do with the be-stringed apple in the event of a fight, but he wanted to show willing, and, besides, he felt that the confidence with which he hefted the thing suggested it was a devastating, exotic weapon, whose secrets he had learned from some far-travelled great-uncle, and which could bloodily rout any foe in seconds, in the hands of a trained expert, ie him.

The Butcher, a vast man, who looked like one of his bled carcasses dressed up in an apron, was rhubarbing on about deviltry, evil times and making a stand. Blood-letting was first nature to him, and he was secretly very pleased that this national emergency had come along and given him an excuse to bluster and threaten people with a piece of sharp iron.

The Baker hadn't even cut so much as a thatch spray with his shear, let alone another person, but he was quite buoyed up by the Butcher's bullish gusto. He stood, legs apart, shear over his shoulder, eyes hooded, imagining that he cut quite a heroic, dashing figure. He didn't, of course. He looked like a skinny Baker trying to look relaxed about struggling with a heavy piece of rusty metal. But no one told him. "Live and let be" is the Smardescliffe village motto.

The Mayor had thought about telling the Baker he looked like a prat, but he was staring with ill-disguised fascination at the Landlord's cooking apple. He had even blanked out the Butcher's unstinting and inflammatory monologue.

Eventually, as the Butcher paused to draw breath and wipe the drool from his lips, the Mayor spoke.

"I quite agree, Master Butcher," he said, having no idea what he was agreeing to. "In these dark times it is our duty as seniors of the parish of Smardescliffe to stand together and defend our lands, our country and the honour of our Queen against the vile perculations of Beelzebub, whose infamy has risen to plague this fair isle."

"And on such a day as this," put in the Landlord of the Cat and Stoop, swinging his apple dangerously, "when we should all be celebrating the coronation of our Gloriana. Why, it makes my blood fret and boil." He punctuated his comment by slapping the apple hard into his open palm. They all looked at him. They all wondered.

"They say London has already fallen," said the Baker, shifting the shear to his other shoulder with a wince. "Demons prowl the very streets, eating people. Bedevilment is abroad. The Queen, I hear, is besieged in her Palace, with only the Royal huscarls around her, blading off the Hades-born scum."

"Would I were there, by the side of the noble huscarls, for the honour of Her Majesty," the Butcher said, twisting his pig-stick significantly in the clenched meat of his fist. There was something unpleasantly rectal about the gesture, and the other three looked away.

"Our duty is here, defending our own parish against the foes of England," the Mayor reminded them all, examining the privet of the church hedge.

"Of course," said the Butcher.

"If we cannot look after our own, then we have no business taking our war to London," said the Mayor.

"Of course," the Butcher nodded.

"The Queen expects as much. If each town looks after its own sanctity, then Her Majesty may rest easy. She will have an intact kingdom to rule once the danger is passed."

"Of course," said the Baker, assuming the Butcher had forgotten.

"You can wager that the damn folk over in Nether Pluxley aren't doing as much. Like as not, they're all hiding under their beds," said the Landlord of the Cat and Stoop. The apple smacked into his hand again. The Butcher looked down at his pig-stick and wondered a bit more. Pluxley, incidentally, is pronounced Plexcliffe.

"That's Nether Pluxley for you," said the Baker, quite getting into this macho posturing bit. "Shirkers."

"Shirkers," they all sneered in agreement.

"Well," said the Mayor, "we have militia stationed at every entrance to the village, and everyone is braced for any attack. We all know the signs to look out for. The moment the demons appear, they will be destroyed."

"Bled dry," affirmed the Butcher gruffly.

"Sheared," added the Baker enthusiastically. The apple slapped around into the Landlord's palm again.

"Indeed," said the Mayor.

"Reminds me of the Armada watch," ventured the Butcher. "Alert night and day, signal fires waiting to be kindled. Hungry for marching Spaniards to drive off."

They all nodded. The Butcher was forty-six, and the threatened Armada was four hundred years previous, but no one wanted to point this out to the Butcher. There was a dried sheen of something on the pig-stick, which quite curtailed comment.

"I almost might wish the Spaniards had invaded," added the Butcher in the silence.

The Mayor looked at him.

"I relish a good fight," the Butcher told him.

The Mayor nodded in agreement, and wondered how easy it would be to oust the Butcher from the Parish Council. Then he wondered how hard he'd have to jab his pitchfork in order to penetrate the Butcher's blood-scabbed apron. After that, he wondered how much he'd have to pay the Baker and the Landlord of the Cat and Stoop to corroborate a story of the Butcher suddenly going berserk through demonic possession. Not much, he concluded.

Then, a sudden shout was heard in the lane, and they all looked around. The Verger was sprinting down the bank from the high road, the hem of his robe gathered up in his hands, his hairy white calves scissoring frantically.

"D!" yelled the Verger as he approached across the Sward, sweat dripping from his nose.

"D!" he added as he fell against the gate, panting.

"D… what?" asked the Mayor, reaching for his pitchfork.

Regaining his composure, the Verger turned to look at them. His face was blanched white with terror. The Mayor took a step back. The Butcher curled his lips into a snarl. The Baker almost dropped his shear. The Landlord of the Cat and Stoop slapped his apple.

"DEMON!" completed the Verger, and fainted. As he hit the ground, he extended a telling finger helpfully towards the north road into the village.

"Slap him," suggested the Butcher, "repeatedly."

But the Baker caught his arm and turned his attention to the road. The cart thundering down the track had no horse, but the gentle slope could not explain its accelerated progress.

"By Our Lady," said the Mayor, gawping.

The Butcher, the Baker, the Mayor and the Landlord of the Cat and Stoop took up their weapons and blocked its path.

"Stand ready now," hissed the Butcher through fused-together teeth.

"I'm ready for anything," said the Baker, who wasn't.

The Landlord of the Cat and Stoop spun his apple in slow, hypnotic arcs.

Giuseppe Giuseppo halted his careering wagon before the four armed men. It skidded up five feet from them. The harness, which had been mysteriously suspended in mid-air in front of the cart, flopped to the earth. The air was heavy with a syrupy aroma. The Mayor, the Landlord, the Baker and the Butcher all distinctly heard the snort of horse-breath. The Baker sensed that his bladder control was about to knock off for the weekend. He held out his shear, crossed his legs, and hoped that he retained some vestige of macho posing. He didn't, but, no one noticed.

They were all too busy looking at the foreigner on the horse-less wagon.

"Good day," said Giuseppe Giuseppo with a warm smile, rising from his seat. "I am Giuseppe Giuseppo, late of La Spezia. I must apologise for my unseemly mode of transport, but I am in haste, and must be in your fair City of London with all despatch. Is this the road?"

"What business have you in London?" asked the Mayor, coldly, the pitchfork shaking in his hands.

"Nothing less, in truth, than the life of Her Majesty, your Queen."

"Get the bastard!" squeaked the Mayor.

The Baker pitched forward, overbalanced by the weight of the shear. The Butcher pretended to trip, and accidentally drop his pig stick, and cursed profusely. The Mayor lunged at Giuseppe, who ducked. The pitchfork smacked smartly into the side of the wagon.

"Demon!" declared the Mayor, running out of breath and pitchfork handle at precisely the same moment, and therefore hitting the side of the cart with stunning force.

"Are you all right, sir?" asked Giuseppe Giuseppo in concern.

Then a cooking apple on a piece of string struck him soundly in the face.

Dazed, Giuseppe fell backwards off the cart, his head glancing off the edge of the off-side front wheel. By the time he hit the ground, he was unconscious.

The Baker helped the Mayor to his feet. The Butcher looked at the Landlord, who shot him a wide, cocksure grin that quite belied his astonishment.

"Very impressive," said the Butcher.

It bloody was, wasn't it? thought the Landlord of the Cat and Stoop, but he didn't say anything.

Bells had started ringing across the City. As it had been decreed that all the belfries of London should mark the festival at six in the evening, the cacophony was a little premature. The most likely explanation seemed to be that parish bell-ringers in north London had decided to get in a little last-minute practice, and their peals had set the whole place off in a frenzy of not-to-be-outdone ringing. Even the Sisters of the Justified Madonna had got out their tambourines. Under a table in the Rouncey Mare, Boy Simon awoke, and couldn't believe how loud his hangover was.

On Thames Street, de Quincey led Mother Grundy through the seething crowd and the campanological on-slaught. According to a clerk at New Hibernian Yard, Lord Gull was due to inspect the Militia watching the bridge.

En route, de Quincey and Mother Grundy had been forced to abandon their carriage at Wafer Lane due to the congested traffic, and they hurried along on foot, pushing their way through the press, ignoring the hundreds of attempts to sell them flowers, flags or fireworks.

"Not today!" de Quincey told the umpteenth hawker with a sprig of nettles. Up ahead, he could see the Militia post. There were six men there, each holding a halberd and a sprig of nettles. As they saw de Quincey approach, they tried to hide the sprigs in embarrassment.

"Where's Lord Gull?" snapped de Quincey as he made it through the crowd.

The men shrugged.

"Where is he?" de Quincey repeated with more urgency.

"He's gone," said one of the pikemen. "He was here, but he went, not five minutes ago."

"He took a wherry down Richmond," said another, kicking his sprig out of sight discreetly behind a box of firecrackers on the kerb, "for the Masque."

De Quincey spun around, lost for words.

"Then what now?" asked Mother Grundy with astonishing calm.

"Richmond," replied de Quincey.

There wasn't a waterman in sight on Three Cranes Pier. A queue of hopeful passengers stood on the boards, having their names taken by a young girl, who occasionally turned and wailed "Oars!" futilely at the empty river.

"Oy!" they said as de Quincey pushed past.

"Police business," de Quincey growled back. He reached the girl. "How long?"

"Name?" asked the girl, her pencil poised above her fares book.

"How bloody long?" screamed de Quincey.

"Twenty minutes, at the very least," she said, "It's a busy day. It's Masque Saturday."

De Quincey took off his cap, then jumped up and down on it.

"No need to be like that, I'm sure," said the girl, moving on.

"De Quincey!" His name rang out across the pier. De Quincey stopped jumping and looked. Mother Grundy stood beside a battered old dorey, which was up-turned on the pier like an exhausted turtle, an exhausted turtle with holes in its shell. "Give me a hand with this," she ordered. Her words were as sharp as a rapier thrust, and just as chilly.

De Quincey left his trampled cap, and hurried over. "What good's this?" he whimpered. "It's got holes in it, and there are no oars."

Mother Grundy fixed him with a look that had driven three generations of Ormsvile Nesbit children to school, no matter how brilliant their acting.

"Do you always go to pieces in a crisis, Mr de Quincey?" she asked.

"I don't know. I haven't been in many."

"Help me with the boat."

"But–"

"It's got holes in it, and there are no oars. I know. Complain in the rain and you just wet your head."

"I'm sorry?" asked de Quincey.

"It's a saying," Mother Grundy explained, "and not a popular one in this City, I'll be bound. Perhaps this one will be easier to understand: find a way, not a fault."

De Quincey looked down at the dorey, and almost grizzled for the first time since his sixth birthday, when a horse had eaten his new kite.

"My mother used to say that," he admitted. "I never knew what it meant."

"Then learn, Mr de Quincey," said Mother Grundy.

Together, they overturned the dorey and slid it down into the water. It began to sink, quickly.

"Get in and bail," Mother Grundy instructed.

"Okay," said de Quincey, meekly.

"Hey!" cried the girl on the pier.

"Is for horses," Mother Grundy told her. The girl frowned and looked around at the queue, who all shrugged.

"My feet are getting wet," said de Quincey, bailing for all he was worth.

"Then bail harder," Mother Grundy hissed, climbing in beside him. The dorey went down another three inches.

"Oh God," said de Quincey, soaked by the spray he was making. "If I'm bailing, I can't row, and I can't row anyway because there aren't any oars!"

Mother Grundy just stood in the stern. She said something quiet and complicated. The boat sank a little more.

"Hmph," said Mother Grundy, "it works all right on the millpond back home. Perhaps the spirits of the Thames are a little hard of hearing."

She said whatever it was again, louder.

De Quincey fell over as the dorey suddenly began to move. It shot away from the slip like a skimming pebble, bouncing off and through every wave of the river. A foamy wake sprayed out behind them.

"Uh... uh..." said de Quincey, struggling up in the violently shaking boat, but he was too wet to do any better.

"That's more like it," smiled Mother Grundy.

"By Our Lady," breathed the girl on the pier. The queue all nodded in agreement.

Upstream, in mid-Thames, Gull consulted his notebook itinerary. Facing him, the two watermen heaved on the wherry's oars.

"Fast as you like," said Gull. "I have many things to attend to."

Both watermen felt like exchanging rude remarks, but their fare was a big man, and he wore his sword like he knew how to use it. They nodded instead, but there was deep and multiple meaning in the nods.

"Begging your pardon, sir," said one of them, suddenly catching sight of something astern.

Gull raised himself from the bench seat and followed the waterman's gaze. Three hundred yards behind them, de Quincey was approaching the wherry in an oar-less dorey with only a thin, grinning old lady for company. De Quincey wore an expression that was part child's glee and part complete bemusement. There was no obvious motive power for the dorey, but it was coming at them as if it had been shot from a cannon, skipping the water like a porpoise.

"Easy oar," said Gull in astonishment, getting to his feet. Both watermen had already forgotten they were meant to be rowing anyway.

The dorey hove alongside and stopped abruptly, causing de Quincey to sit down again hard. Its sudden lack of forward motion was met by a resumed downward motion.

"Permission to come aboard," said de Quincey, a glazed, inane look on his face.

Gull and the watermen helped de Quincey and the old lady to hop across onto the rocking wherry.

The dorey sank.

"Mr de Quincey. Please explain… everything," said Gull sternly.

"Mother Grundy can do that," said de Quincey, flopping into Gull's seat, and emptying his boots over the rail. "Mother Grundy can do anything. Lord Gull, Mother Grundy."

Gull turned to the old lady, but she waved him back, peering intently after the bubbles that marked the dorey's departure from active life.

"In a moment, Laird of Ben Phie," she said, before sprinkling the water with a handful of flowers from her purse. "Father Thames, I thank you for your aid. Flow softly on in peace."

"What are you doing?" asked Gull.

"Being polite," she replied.

"You won't get a straight answer out of her, chief," said de Quincey. "I haven't yet, and I've been with her for hours. Careful now, or she'll issue you with a saying."

Gull wasn't listening.

"When you've finished being polite to this body of water, try being polite to me," he said.

"There isn't time," said Mother Grundy, turning to the Captain of the Royal Guard. "We have a nation to save."

THE NINETEENTH CHAPTER.
At Richmond.

Murmuring armies choked the fields and lawns around Richmond Palace. It was nearly two in the afternoon.

Better than twenty thousand people were converging on the splendid Palace from all compass points. Fifteen hundred of them were invited guests: ambassadors, clergy, nobility, foreign potentates and senior military staff. A further three thousand were the augmented Palace staff: full-time retainers, huscarls, militia men, ladies-in-waiting, maids, gentlemen-ordinaires, stewards, chefs, servers, musicians and a large number of temporary helpers-out.

The balance were Londoners, spilling from the City in gaggles of extended families, clubs and works outings, dragging with them carts of food and drink, explosives and makeshift musical instruments. None had been invited, and none would get any closer than the meadows beyond the Palace walls, but that was close enough for them. Simply to be within a mile of the Queen as she celebrated her coronation filled them with a sense of pride and place, and of patriotic importance. Besides, Her Majesty's fireworks were bound to be the biggest, the best and the most "ooooohhh!"-worthy in all the land. They trampled down the grass, dug in, lit fires, and popped corks. All any of them could see was other people doing the same thing, except for the really lucky ones, who could see other people doing the same thing and the Palace wall. Everyone assured everyone they were with that they had definitely got a good place.

People carpeted the area. They covered the twenty acre Green and, beyond Trumpeters' House, could be seen right up Richmond Hill. The Shene was covered with them, and the towpath, and they were beginning to intrude on the Deer Park and Richmond Park itself. Some were even clinging to the branches of the one hundred and thirteen elm trees on the Green.

High above, on the flat roof of the Palace's East Wing, Cardinal Woolly lowered his spyglass, and stepped back from the parapet, handing the instrument to the waiting steward.

"More than last year," mused the steward, cheerfully.

"More than ever," reflected Woolly. He glanced along the length of the roof, noting the huscarls patrolling at regular intervals. Each carried a Swiss crossbow fixed with a telescope spotter. Woolly nodded to himself.

"When Lord Gull arrives, conduct him to my presence immediately," Woolly ordered. "I want to go over the security arrangements again."

"Of course, your Reverence," answered the steward, following the cardinal back over the roof walk to the tower stairs.

Three deacons from the Curial Office stood waiting for him at the base of the tower flight, in a corridor packed with men moving mahogany pews. There was a lot of groaning and grunting, and "down your end"-ing. The corridor looked like a log-jammed river.

Deacon Spench sashayed through the wooden tide, and made it to the cardinal's side. He carried a leather clipboard, complete with a purple silk place-marker, which he consulted regularly.

"We've all but cleared the upper auditoria and the Green Rooms," he said. "The Head Housekeeper thinks there may be some more benches in the storeroom of the Addey Camera. They may need a bit of a dust-down, but they'll have to do." He consulted his seating plan carefully. "Either that, or the parties of Viscount Hailsea, the Earl of Slough and the Sardinian Ambassador will be on canvas chairs at the back of the third file."

"Find them proper seats, Spench," the cardinal told him. "We don't want to go to war with Sardinia. Or Slough, come to think of it."

They began to jostle down the crowded passageway.

"Items ninety-six to one hundred and three are ready to be dealt with in your suite," Spench told him.

Woolly's suite was thick with knots of waiting men and pipe smoke. Woolly took a minute or two to issue lists and back-stage medallions to Messrs Holbein, Bailey and Blake, the official portraitists of the occasion, who stood near the door next to a pile of easels, smelling of turps.

"Approved sketching only, gentlemen," Woolly cautioned them, "no cartoon opportunities, please. I don't want to see candid vignettes of pie-eyed nobility appearing in the broadsheets on Monday."

The artists nodded and collected up their clattering equipment.

"The players," intoned Spench, leading Woolly across to a second group, "Gaumont of the Swan, Flitch of the Rose, Huntingdon of the Mermaid, Trobridge of the Oh, and Baskerville of the Lord Chamberlain's Men."

The player-managers got hurriedly to their feet, from the chairs they had been lounging in, and ignited professionally competitive smiles of adoration. Except Huntingdon, who cast a nervous, involuntary glance of guilt at the un-stoppered decanter of brandy on the cardinal's desk, and hoped that his breath wouldn't give him away.

Woolly noted it all. It would have made him smile if he hadn't been in such a serious, businesslike mood. He noted the way they jostled for position to be in front, to smile broadest, to look relaxed and reliable, despite the sneaky elbow-prods and shoulder-barges each was giving the others. It might have been a mistake to try to involve all of the City's theatre companies in one blockbuster presentation. They were the most competitive, jealous bunch of people in London. Still, Woolly could well-remember the outrage and back-biting that had followed his choice of Chamberlain's Men to stage last year's entertainment alone. Anything was better than that, even this.

"Thank you for attending, gentlemen, I know you all must be busy with last-minute preparations," Woolly began, cordially. He knew there was nothing better than a good bit of simpering when it came to getting on the right side of thespians. The quintet launched into a chorus of "Don't mention it"s and "Not at all"s and "Heavens! Compared with the work you have on your shoulders, your Reverence?" Woolly acted up his best smile and allowed the hubbub to die away.

Then the cardinal got down to business.

"I trust," he said, in a voice that suddenly hinted at tumbrels and gibbets and keen axes, "that everything is in order?"

"Oh yes!" said the quintet, one body with five mouths.

"Good. We will commence at ten. We will only commence later if the dinner runs over-long, and only then if I signal you in person. Understood?" asked Woolly.

"Yes, indeed." said the five-mouthed creature.

Woolly turned from them, strolled to his desk, and slowly, pointedly, re-stoppered his decanter. There was a thick silence, broken only by the susurrating din from outside the windows.

"Gentlemen, I very much appreciate the work you have put in complying with my request," said the cardinal. "I know it is against your natures to work together to please the public."

There was a pause, and then Woolly smiled to show them it was a joke. They exploded into raucous hilarity to compliment the cardinal's fine wit. All except Huntingdon, who managed only a snigger, due to the fact that he was half-dead with relief.

Woolly smiled his false smile again. They smiled back. You ought to sign me up, thought Woolly, I'm acting better than you ever have.

"However," said Woolly, "for the purpose of this evening, I must perforce appoint one of you in overall charge. This will rankle with the others, I know, but it is necessary. For the sake of efficiency, in what will doubtless be a thoroughly hectic night, I must deal with one spokesman, one that the others will obey at all costs. It can be no other way, and I will come down most firmly on any that disaffect this request of mine. Is that clear?" The creature nodded its heads.

"I intend to be as fair about this as possible. Deacon Spench? Your biretta?" The deacon stepped up, and handed his hat to Woolly. The cardinal produced five twists of paper from the pocket of his robes. He dropped them in the cap and agitated it gently. "Spench?"

With a breezy smile, Spench reached gingerly into the cap, and pulled out one of the scraps. He untwisted it with slow, clumsy hands, shooting cheery "nearly there" grins at the uncomfortable players.

Spench opened the paper twist at last, squinted at it, turned it up the right way, and read out, "Basil Gaumont."

Gaumont smiled with genuine pleasure, and found himself on the receiving end of four nasty looks.

"Mister Gaumont it is. My thanks, gentlemen. That will be all. I will go over the last details with Gaumont now, and he can inform you momentarily."

Huntingdon, Trobridge, Baskerville and Flitch took turns to shake the cardinal's paw, and then shuffled out.

Woolly led Gaumont over to the comparative privacy of the desk, and set down the biretta.

"My apologies for that palaver," he said. "I had to be seen to be fair. I didn't want you troubled by bickering in the wings."

"Understood. Many thanks, your Reverence."

Woolly's voice dropped to a murmur. "How goes it, Agent Wisley?"

"As well as can be expected, chief," said Gaumont. "The whole affair's looking most vulnerable, but if Lord Gull's boys do the stuff security-wise, we shouldn't be open to compromise."

"Anything I should know about?"

"Nothing springs to mind."

"What news of Agent Borde Hill?" asked the cardinal.

Gaumont frowned, toying idly with the paper scraps left in the biretta, and said, "I'd say he was a dead-end. He seemed to come up with nothing. I've reported back the sum of his espial thus far, and none of it amounted to much. I don't know where you got him from."

"Neither shall you, Wisley," said Woolly. "His origins are particularly sensitive, and higher than even your clearance allows, I'm afraid."

"Say no more," said Gaumont.

"Where is he?"

"That's the thing. I haven't clapped eyes on the fellow for hours," replied Agent Wisley. "Not since last night, in fact. Must be here somewhere, doing his thing. Damn fine lutenist, I'll give him that."

Woolly scratched his chin thoughtfully, and said, "If you see him, send him to me at once. Invent some story to cover it. It is important I speak with him."

Gaumont nodded. He looked down at the twists of paper. "Well heavens! These all say Basil Gaumont!"

"Of course they do," said the cardinal.

Woolly dismissed Gaumont, and moved to consult with the kitchen staff. The ice-sculptor was looking morose, and his shoes were sopping wet. A bad sign, Woolly noted.

Eastwoodho entered the suite, and stood waiting by the window drapes like an off-duty Rhodesian Colossus.

"A moment, gentlemen," Woolly told the kitchen staff, and crossed to the massive CIA agent. "Report?"

Eastwoodho shook his anvil of a head.

"Borde Hill gave me the slip again just before dawn," he said, "after I'd located him following that litter business. He's a tricksy gent. There was some altercation in the theatre. I went in to investigate, and he must've slipped out the back door. Sorry, sir."

"Did you find no clues at all, officer?"

"Nothing, sir," said Eastwoodho, "except a broken lute."

Down by the massive pavilion on the Palace lawn, three huscarls were chasing a popping, sparking Catherine wheel, which was fizzling explosively across the grass. The various stewards and musicians around about applauded and cheered them on.

"Catch it! Stamp on the bloody thing! Keep it away from the main cache!" the officer of the watch was bellowing.

One of the huscarls managed to reach it with a flying tackle, and clamped his barbute over it just as the main charge went off. The helmet lofted twelve feet into the air, excreting blue sparks in a trail behind it. Then it dropped and bounced off the sprawled huscarl's head with a dull *thump*.

"Ooooohhhh!" said the onlookers, and applauded again.

The officer of the watch thundered over to the huscarls, and embarked on a fierce diatribe about smoking on duty. De Tongfort turned from the brief spectacle, and glowered at Cedarn.

"You're late," he snarled.

"Sorry," said Cedarn, adjusting the ruff of his musician's uniform.

"Where's your lute?"

"I was coming to that." said Cedarn. "It's warped. The wet weather. Can't play it."

De Tongfort looked him up and down, an expression of contempt flickering across his face.

"There are two spare in the trunk behind the front stage," he said. "Get one. Tune it. Get to your place. Or I'll have your head on a stick."

Cedarn nodded and moved off. De Tongfort watched him go. No one saw the ugly puzzlement in his eyes.

Once armed with a lute, Cedarn climbed around behind the stage area, and entered the makeshift tiring room, formed by the rear folds of the long pavilion. A chaos of jabbering, half-naked bodies met him. The air was dense with drifting face-powder. He found Doll, sewing up a torn gauze attifet.

"Anything, love?" he asked.

She grimaced and shrugged.

"Nothing," she replied. "I don't even know what I'm meant to be looking for."

"We'll know it when we see it," said Cedarn. "You know the signal. I'll be watching you. Keep watching me."

He kissed her.

"And break a leg," he added, with the most encouraging grin he could manage in the circumstances.

He turned away, and then turned back and kissed her again. He hoped it wouldn't be for the last time. On the Green outside the walls, the Bracket family – John Senior, John Junior and little John, wife Martha, sister Delia, Grandma Sweeney and tiny Nell – were in the middle of their damp nantwiches, their third flask of tepid musket and another round of "What a good spot we picked, right by the wall, thanks to me getting us off so early" self-congratulations, when John Junior, a six-foot-four blacksmith and head of the family, suddenly said, "Oy!" and got to his feet.

He marched away from his bemused family, and approached the man who was in the middle of climbing the outside of the Palace wall, hand-over-hand, on the trailing ivy.

"You can't do that!" John Junior protested. "We was here first! You ain't allowed to go in. Now be off! Get yourself another spot, and stop jumping the queue."

The man halfway up the wall turned his head and glowered down at John Junior.

"Shove off or I'll kill you without conjunction," he said simply.

It may have been the cold blue eyes, or the vivid scar tissue. Whatever, John Junior suddenly felt smaller and punier than a six-foot-four blacksmith should, and went back to his nantwiches meekly, though he didn't eat many. O'Bow disappeared over the high wall.

Your servant, me, Wllm Beaver, settled into my pew seat with relish, and consulted my gold-embossed programme. I found myself sitting next to the Countess of Hardwick's party. They were all looking across at me as if I was something they had almost stepped in.

"Afternoon!" I called, convivially. I looked back at my programme. Sire Clarence was due to be seated to my left. I sighed.

The traffic on the road into the Shene was interminable, and stuck solid. Militia stewards were flagging carts off the road, and indicating overspill fields along the edge of the Richmond Wood, a good three miles short of the Palace.

"We've got business at the Palace!" yelled Drew Bluett from the duckboard of his cart. The steward on the track beneath smiled, oblivious, and continued to wave them off the jammed road. Behind them, the traffic was urging them to get a bloody move on.

"We'll have to park here and go ahead on foot," said Drew, steering them off into the field. Agnew nodded, and turned to rouse the slumbering Uptil in the back of the cart.

"Are we there?" asked Uptil, rubbing his eyes.

"Not even close," muttered Agnew.

The Private Guild Chapel of the Palace was as quiet as graves ought to be (but probably weren't in these dire times). The incense and the smell of candle-smoke almost, but not quite, hid the syrupy smell rising from behind the vocational screen at the side of the pulpit.

Jaspers sat back from his kneeling position in front of the small brazier, his hands almost translucent with Goetic shine. Slowly, with reverence, he took up the three small, grotesque icons that he had just blessed, and placed each one in a drawstring pouch. He hung the pouches around his neck, beneath his doublet.

"What in the name of mercy—"

Jaspers turned sharply, teeth bared in anger. He was still weak from the effort of his just-finished observances, and the intruder had taken him unawares.

Cardinal Gaddi stood in the screen's doorway, eyes wide, lips dry and quivering.

"What are you doing in here, divine?" Gaddi asked, stepping forward. "I came down for preparatory prayer and smelled... I couldn't say what!"

"Don't you know, it's rude to interrupt a man's private devotions, cardinal?" Jaspers asked, getting to his feet.

"Don't give me that!" said Gaddi. He was a slight, nervous man normally, but some sense of utter wrong made him fluff with courage. "I know that smell... that damned smell. You little bastard... What have you done? What are you doing here?"

Jaspers stood ready, but knew that his legs were weak and trembling. He'd hated having to conduct the final rite in the Palace, but there had been no other choice.

"Get out of here. Leave me. Forget what you have seen." Jaspers said, trying to use the Summarian Voice Of Command that had served him so well, so often. He was too hoarse, however, too drained, and he couldn't fix the pitch or the timbre.

"You dare to try novice Goetic tricks on a cardinal? You pathetic little traitor!" said Gaddi, in disgust. "I could do the Voice when I was nine, and I soon learned why I shouldn't do it at all!" The cardinal stepped forward again, bunching his little hands into mean, resolute fists. "I'll have the guards on you!" he exclaimed. "I'll have you hanged and drawn! They'll watch your twitching corpse roast in the banquet fires tonight! They'll rejoice when they know that the source of the treasonous blight has been revealed!"

"Leave me," said Jaspers again. The cardinal's outburst had given him just enough time to focus his waning energies.

Gaddi trembled and took a hurried step back. He felt his guts tighten. He had never heard the Voice used with such power and authority before, not even when his old collegiate masters had used it to demonstrate the curse of Goety to frightened novices in Elementary Arte Science classes. He suddenly realised that he wasn't dealing with a misguided dabbler at all.

"Guards! Guards!" he began, and then choked, because no sound was coming from his throat, except for a hollow gurgling. De la Vega slid his rapier out of the back of Gaddi's neck, and the little man pitched forward onto the chapel flagstones. Blood splattered up from the impact.

"Thank you," said Jaspers, relaxing.

De la Vega stepped into the gloomy side chapel, and closed the screen door.

"Such business is regrettable so close to the appointed time," he remarked, wiping his sword and sheathing it. "I take it he caught you unawares?"

"I had just finished the rite. I was weakened, unprepared," replied Jaspers.

"It is a good thing Slee asked me to check on you," said de la Vega. "He and Salisbury are in position. Slee requires your presence."

Jaspers stepped over to Gaddi's corpse.

"I must dispose of this," he said. "A dead cardinal is hardly the thing to be found in the middle of tonight's affairs."

De la Vega nodded, and looked away, as Jaspers uncorked a phial of alchemical liquid he had concealed in his pocket. There was a sharp hissing and a foul, saprogenic odour filled the room.

It hung there, staining the air, long after the two men had slipped silently away.

* * *

There were big rats in the Palace attic spaces, big juicy rats the size of cats. But not this cat. Eight feet from nose to tail-end, it padded along the darkened rafters like a ghost. Big as they were, the rats scurried out of its way. They may have been rats, but they weren't stupid.

St Cunegund's struck five o'clock. The strokes rang across the Sward, but went unnoticed by the townsfolk of Smarde-scliffe, who were in the middle of the biggest and best coronation revelry they had ever staged. The Verger was holding audience by the village pump, retelling, for the up-teenth time, how he alone had alerted the militia to the demon on the cart.

The Butcher was explaining, to anyone prepared to listen, the finer points of running a demon through with anything from a meat-hook to a sharpened thistle. In his opinion, those who lived by the Sward, died by the Sward. People were taking notes and fetching him drinks.

The Baker, a confirmed bachelor for all of his thirty-nine years, was busily copping off with the youngest daughter of the village weaver, in the hayrick behind the bakery. She had never, it turned out, done it with a "real hero" before.

The Mayor was showing off his bruises to the members of the Women's Institute. For all the "oooohhhing" and "aaaaahhhing" going on, he might as well have been letting off fireworks.

"How's the prisoner faring?" asked the Mayor of the Butcher as the latter stumbled past, looking for somewhere to throw up.

"Sent the Landlord of the Cat and Stoop to check on him a while back," answered the Butcher, swallowing hard, and drifting off into the hedges to the left.

"Ladies! I will return!" announced the Mayor, stepping down from the seating podium, negotiating the bunting, and marching off towards the village tithe barn.

"Oooooohhhhh!" they all said, to a woman.

"They say the Landlord was the real hero of the hour," one said as the Mayor disappeared.

"With an apple on a string!" said another.

"Exotic technique taught to him by his long-lost great-uncle," explained the Landlord's wife.

They all looked at her in wonder.

The Mayor pushed open the great doors of the tithe barn, and stepped inside. Hens clucked around his ankles, and the dark, sun-shafted interior was heady with the smell of drying corn.

"Landlord?" called the Mayor, softly.

He called again.

This time, there was an answer, a muffled "Mmmmggfff" from behind the bale stacks. The Mayor sought it out.

The Landlord of the Cat and Stoop was lying face down in the straw, trussed to a pitchfork handle. He looked like one of the butcher's roast swine with the apple in his mouth.

The Mayor of Smardescliffe pulled the apple out of the struggling man's jaws like a cork.

"Sneaky devil gave me the slip," coughed the Landlord of the Cat and Stoop.

"Oh bollocks," the Mayor informed him.

One mile downstream, Giuseppe Giuseppo pulled himself out of the River Smarde, and spat out a hollow reed and a lungful of brackish water.

He crawled up the bank, hacking and sneezing. The late afternoon sun beat down on him, weakly.

Giuseppe rolled onto his back, and pulled the Most Important Book In The World out of his doublet pocket. It was sodden, the pages were stuck together, the ink had begun to run, and London was still twenty miles away, across the long, slow fields of the Downs.

SOME MORE OF THE PREVIOUS CHAPTER.
Further matters at Richmond.

De Quincey had never seen so many people in one place. It made his head spin, as if it wasn't spinning enough already. He'd always thought of himself as a solid, two-by-four sort of fellow. It came as a rude shock to discover that he was actually as riddled through and through by the woodworm of perturbation as the next mortal.

"Keep up, de Quincey!" Gull barked, snapping the forensic scientist's attention back to the moment. He scampered a little to catch up with Gull and Mother Grundy, who were striding up the Richmond Royal Stairs, a narrow defile of sixty-seven steps that linked the Palace with the Queen's private landing stage on the Thames. At river level, they were flanked in by stone walls, the jetty and the enclosed scent of the river. Now, they took the stairs up, and gained a view over the northern reaches of the Palace grounds, thick with surging crowds.

So many people...

De Quincey had affected to spend the previous Coronation Day, the Great Masque, with his mother in the comparative quiet of Wanstead. They'd clinked a few glasses of tawny port in honour of the day, and spent the rest of the afternoon ministering to the needs of the rose-bed behind her cottage. The suburban quiet suited him well. He'd been told all about the crowds and the hubbub, and the confusions of the occasion, but it had been a distant thing that had passed him by.

He had hoped to be in Wanstead among the roses this year. Now, he was in the thick of far more dangerous thorns.

"There are so many people," he murmured as they topped the stairs and crossed the riverside walk. Neither of his companions saw fit to answer him.

The huscarl posted at the annexe doorway recognised Gull as he approached, and snapped to attention, his pike quivering upright in the air. Gull swirled past him in a storm of cape, and Mother Grundy followed him as if caught in his slipstream.

De Quincey felt as if he ought to say something encouraging to the alert soldier.

"A lot of people," he managed with a friendly frown and a nod to the crowded lawns.

"Sir," replied the huscarl, mouth tight and serious beneath the visor-lip of his Coventry sallet. There was a limp sprig of lucky nettle pinned to his tabard.

"De Quincey!"

De Quincey broke into a nervous little run, and entered the Palace.

The North Processional was a panelled corridor a quarter of a mile long. Travelling down it meant passing beneath the following eyes of thirty Glorianas, each framed in gilded foliage, each rendered in the manner of her age. There was Elizabeth III, one lace glove spread on a map, the other languid on the Orb of State; there was Elizabeth IX, a Mannerist Madonna, her elongated, dreamy face averted heavenwards; there was Elizabeth XIV, Barbizon-style, a dot in the middle of the rolling landscape; there was the Moralist Elizabeth XX, with her rosy cheeks and her comical courtiers; there was Pre-Raphaelite Elizabeth XXV, dressed as a winsome Maid of Orleans with a dainty, lethal estoc and a consumptive frailty; there was Elizabeth XXVI, a Futuristic blur of speeding gown and streamlined tiara; there, apparently, was the De Stijl Elizabeth XXX.

De Quincey felt their regal gaze on his hurrying back. He felt, in the same moment, an acute kinship with the courtiers and royal servants, who had, in past ages, felt the burn of those gazes in actuality. How many intrigues, conspiracies and potential insurrections had those courtiers put down in the name of their monarch? How many times had the Crown teetered on the brink of downfall, only to be wrested back by the diligent loyalty of men and women like him?

The notion churned his troubled mind still further. History, with whom he was at least on nodding terms, was full of brave legends and worthy tales: Lord Bartleby and the Redditch Uprising, Gilead Warner and the Baron's Revolt of '73, Jakob Smallwood and the Prussian Betrayal. Noble men, noble deeds...

What of him? What of Neville de Quincey? Thus far, he had played his part as well as any ill-prepared understudy, who suddenly has the script of a lead role thrust into his hand. He was certain that the association he had made between his own troubling observations and Mother Grundy's dreams was of vital import, but now things dragged on. The excitement of the urgent river chase had emptied to make space for Lord Gull, the thronging Palace and all the other trappings of reality that had poured in on him. He was aware of how small and insignificant he was, and how laughable his speculations.

For all its heroes, how many also-rans had fickle History forgotten? How many dramas had been played out in the secrecy of the Royal Palaces, their protagonists long-dead and un-remembered? He wanted to be a Bartleby, a Warner, a Smallwood, immortal ever-after in song and statuary, but all he could see was a little plot in the Wanstead Parish cemetery, remembered only by a spray of fresh-cut roses.

Then, as he reached the far end of the North Processional, he realised that he wasn't really interested in fame at all. He wanted to live, but even more than that, he wanted to be right. He wanted to be right, at the right time, which, with any luck, was right now. And if he was a catalyst in the making of a new English legend, then so much the better.

Gull and Mother Grundy had come to a halt in the processional ante-room, where Gull conversed briefly with a waiting steward, and then sent him off into the depths of the Palace.

"Why do we wait?" asked de Quincey, voicing what Mother Grundy must have been thinking.

"The steward has gone to fetch Cardinal Woolly," Gull told them. "We wait for his arrival."

"How long?"

"Soon," snapped Gull, looking at de Quincey sharply.

"Hmmph. Take the street of by-and-by, and you arrive in the house of never," Mother Grundy intoned.

"Very true," de Quincey agreed, pushing past Gull towards the door.

"Where are you going, man?" asked Gull dangerously. "Don't tell me you're acting on every daft adage this old dam utters forth?"

"Yes, I am," said de Quincey directly. He caught Gull's deadly look, and his eager resolve wilted slightly, but not entirely. "Begging your pardon, sir, but the Palace is packed out. It might take ages for word to reach the cardinal, and ages on top of that for him to attend you here. Wait for him, by all means. We needn't all wait. It can't hurt if I take a little look around. I'll report back in a quarter of an hour."

"And I'll go with him," said Mother Grundy.

Gull draped his cloak over the back of a chair.

"No. No, no, no," he said. "The greatest turmoil of the century hangs about us, not to mention the biggest party of the year, and you two would have me believe that an unimpeachable member of the Church is behind this evil. If Woolly's going to swallow this story, I'll need you with me to make it ring true."

"That's why we'll be back before his worship arrives," said Mother Grundy. She rummaged in her hopsack, and produced a little whistle carved from a chicken's shin-bone. "And if we're not, sound this twice. We'll hear it. We'll come."

Gull took the whistle, and somehow managed to contain his anger. There was something in Mother Grundy's tone that helped in this.

"Be quick," was all he could say.

De Quincey led the old lady out into the corridor to the east. Rush matting deadened the sound of their hurrying feet.

"Your master is a surly oaf," said Mother Grundy.

"That's how he got where he is, mistress," replied de Quincey. He paused by an open casement that overlooked the front lawns. Darkness, wispy and unemphatic, was beginning to settle across the vast, busy area. Thousands of tapers and lamps were being lit, making a carpet of fireflies across the crowd and the tents. Through the din of voices, he could hear a tune from the players' pavilion.

"'Tarleton's Resurrection'," he mused, "one of my favourites. I play the viheula for recreation. I'm not very good, but this is a tune that I like to pass the t–"

"Don't ramble, de Quincey," said the old woman. "Rambling's fine for country walks, and no good for conversation."

"Do you make these up?" he asked.

Her gaze said everything. It spoke volumes: twenty-six or more hand-tooled, leather-bound, marbled and lavishly illustrated volumes.

"Sorry," he said, "I'm rather nervous."

Three huscarls were passing around a between-shifts pipe at the end of the corridor. De Quincey flashed his medallion of office at them.

"We're looking for Divine Jaspers of the Church Guild. Any sign of him, chaps?" he asked.

They shook their heads.

"If you see him, report it to Lord Gull. He's in the Processional ante-chamber."

The huscarls nodded their heads.

De Quincey took the smoking pipe from the man nearest him.

"Sorry," he said, "I'll have to confiscate that. Fire hazard."

Closing the next pair of doors after them, de Quincey paused, and dragged hard on the stem-pipe.

"Ooooh, I needed that," he said. "Left my pouch at the Yard." He paused, noticing Mother Grundy's surly look.

"Am I going to get another stern adage about tobacco and the ills of the flesh? 'Need the weed and heed not what they plead' or some such?" he asked her, tetchily.

"Only if you don't give me a toke of that," replied Mother Grundy. She smiled, for the very first time in their acquaintanceship.

"I'm rather nervous too, Neville," she told him.

Louis Cedarn set down his lute. "Tarleton's Resurrection" was one of his favourites, but his heart hadn't really been in it. The musicians' tent was an amber den of starched ruffs and rosewood sound-boards, thanks to the tapers around them. Score sheets fluttered in the evening breeze, and three dozen music stands cast spidery shadows up across the tent wall.

From where he sat, he had a good view of the stage, and, beyond that, the well-lit, open-fronted pavilion tents in which the Unity's finest were rowdily assembling. The most splendid area of the pavilion was still empty. The Royal party was minutes away from arriving. Charcoal embers fluttered up into the night air. There was a rich smell of cooking from somewhere to the south-west. Fire-eaters and tumblers cavorted like devils on the open lawn in front of the stage, earning a smatter of applause, and a hearty laugh or two.

Jean-Baptiste Couperin, the music master, took a note from a page runner, read it dutifully, and turned back to the poised musicians. Cedarn took up his lute again. His heart pounded against his ribs.

"Mesdames, Messieurs," he announced, "we 'ave time for one furzer galliard, zen we will commence the Royal Salute. Ze time is almost upon us. Attendez!" He rapped the top of his lectern with his baton. The tapers fixed to the corners of the lectern fluttered.

"Ze King of Denmark's Galliard... if you please," he said.

The baton swung almost hypnotically. Music blasted into the night like fireworks.

Doll sipped a beaker of hot-water-and-honey to ease her throat. The tiring tent was a tangled knot of nerves and creative differences. She eyed her splendid reflection in the tall mirror, adjusted her gauze and her golden half-mask, and took a deep, counted breath. Her lines swam in her head like a shoal of minnows, darting away every time she reached for them.

She was proud of the fact that she had been given all the really stonking lines of the "Goddess of the Day" sequence. She prayed they would not leave her when the moment came, the moment in front of a thousand or more nobles and the Queen herself.

Across the tent's hubbub, she could see Mary Mercer and Alice Munton, her partners in the scene, and London's most noted actresses, hugging and reassuring, and cooing at each other. Never spare a minute for me, eh? Doll mused bitterly. Me, the non-star, the no-name. Damn your bitchy eyes!

De Tongfort was by her side suddenly.

"Ready?" he asked, gloomily. "Three minutes, no more, then the Queen's in place. You won't shame the Oh, will you?"

Doll felt her nerves strain like lute strings.

"Of course I won't," she said, her voice hoarse again.

De Tongfort walked away, towards Master Horace Cato of the Swan, who was to take the part of Orion, the hunter. Cato's clown act was famous across the City, but he had wangled himself a serious part in the Masque. His gold-painted laurels and cute toga barely contained his plump girth. She watched as de Tongfort whispered to him, and handed him a long, ash arrow for his hunter's quiver. The arrowhead, flashing in the lamp-light, was a barb of steel.

Her pulse quickened.

She stepped forward, about to make some excuse to be elsewhere, when a hand caught her shoulder. Turning, she found herself facing the tearful Alice Munton and Mary Mercer. Alice was a slender, painted Diana, Mary a barely decent hillside-worth of Artemis. They clutched their bows and arrows to their bosoms.

"Dear sis," began Alice, "best of luck." She hugged the unprepared Doll, and kissed her cheeks hard.

"And from me, dearest daughter of the stage," said Mary, clutching Doll to her ample bosom. "I know we've all been at odds in the past, but now's the time to make amends. Bless you, my dearest! Let the muse inspire us all!"

"Thank you. And you," said Doll, with the most overblown emotion she could summon. Bloody actresses, she thought, so over the top at times like this. They'll hate me tomorrow. Still, just for now, I'm one of them, an equal.

It made her feel good. She felt her own tears rise. Doll took up her own stage bow and quiver, and followed them to the edge of the wings. She glanced back. Neither Cato nor de Tongfort was in sight.

The Palace gates were, according to Drew Bluett, shut tighter than a Vestal's knickers. Uptil was busy musing on Drew's colourful description as the weary trio pushed to the front of the crowd by the gatehouse. Under the moth-bothered lamps, a squad of huscarls made threatening "be off with you" noises to the gathering throng. The sounds of music and laughter, and hundreds of voices filtered through the heavy gates.

The exodus to Richmond and the Shene had brought London's beggars with it in droves. They shuffled through the crowd, rattling their clack-dishes hopefully. None of them tried to approach the big autochthon.

Drew and Agnew elbowed past a mule that was dragging what appeared to be an entire family on a low travois.

"But I've got an invitation!" complained the scruffy wretch leading the mule. The guards asked to see it. "It was lost in the post," the man began, hopefully.

Drew approached the guard captain, a pear-shaped man, who stared out of the grille of his ill-fitting zischagge like a cornered weasel.

"What's your story?" he asked, his hand on his sword hilt. The huge huscarl at his elbow looked more than capable of managing the two-hundred-pound pull necessary to fire his longbow. The longbow was even taller than Agnew.

"No story. Just let us in. It's more important than you can know."

"Heard it before." said the huscarl. "Be off."

"Really," said Drew, "I can't impress upon you enough–"

"You can't impress upon me at all," said the guard captain. "Ronard?"

The bowman nocked an arrow as long as a good-sized sword.

"I want to speak to Cardinal Woolly," said Drew, "by order of the Secret Service." He showed his ring to the man.

"Got that out of a cracker, did you?" asked the guard captain, laughing. The bow string next to him tightened.

Drew turned back to Uptil and Agnew. "I'm sorry," he said, "I just don't carry the clout I used to. The time it'll take to persuade this oaf, we'll still be here in the morning."

"So what now?" asked Agnew.

"We could rush them," Uptil suggested.

They dragged him off around the corner of the Palace wall.

"It was only an idea," put in Uptil disconsolately, in the shadow of the stone buttress.

"This way," Drew said. "When all else fails, there's always another else."

There were many times more blisters than feet inside Giuseppe Giuseppo's shoes. He sat down on a milestone that read "LONDON ~ 14 M" and rubbed at his calloused heels. A pastel night with pretty stars blessed the Downs. It was getting cold, and the clarity of the night air was ruined by each foggy breath he exhaled.

It was about then that the boy came up the trackway, leading his mare. The boy was no more than nine years old, a sallow, wet-nosed child tugging at the reins of a horse so massive that it had bearded hooves.

"Child," said Giuseppe warmly, rising to his aching feet. He was very aware of how bedraggled he looked.

"Hunff!" sucked the boy in alarm. His horse, knowing better, idled forward, sniffing affectionately at the Italian's limp ruff.

"How much for your horse?" Giuseppe asked.

"T'ain't for sale," said the boy.

"Where are you taking him?" asked Giuseppe.

"Back from mark– oh damn!" the boy answered.

Giuseppe smiled.

"So she is for sale?" asked Giuseppe, sliding a ring off his finger. It was his wedding ring, pure gold. He sighed thoughtfully, remembering his dear Eloise, dead these three years.

"For your horse?" he asked, holding out the ring.

The boy took the ring, bit it, rubbed it, sniffed it and licked it.

"T'ain't real gold," he said.

"Why, it is! I transmuted it myself!" Giuseppe snapped. "Now, your horse?"

The boy slowly held out the reins. The horse seemed tremendously pleased, as if she realised how important she was about to be.

Giuseppe took the reins, and gently slid up onto the horse's back.

"My mother warned me about you," said the boy.

"Indeed?"

"You're Old Nick," said the boy, "out on the road after dark, ready to bargain us mortals away for the price of a soul."

Giuseppe shook his head, laughing.

"But I paid you," he said. "And no souls were involved. A ring for a horse. You and your mother can sleep well tonight."

"Mmmmm…" said the boy.

"Thank you," said Giuseppe, pulling around on the reins.

"You're not Old Nick, then?" asked the boy.

"I'm Old Giuseppe," said the Italian, riding off into the dark.

The boy tossed the ring over in the air, smiled, and began to scamper home.

Once he was out of sight, Giuseppe reined up, and took out the Most Important Book In The World.

"I must be in London faster than even you can carry me," he told his new purchase, turning the pages.

Then he began the incantation.

The Militia guards posted at the Woolwich Crossing barely had time to grasp their pikes as the demon stormed through, fire licking at its heels.

"Like a great horse," said one.

"Like Old Nick hisself," said another.

"It's good, isn't it?" smiled your most humble servant, Wllm Beaver, who is also me, as the tumblers tumbled in the fire-light.

"Oh, wonderful," answered Sire Clarence, popping a sweet into his mouth. "I do hope that bore Woolly has arranged something a little better than this for tonight's show, or old Three Ex will have his head as a novelty doorstop come to-morrow." The boiled sweet clacked against his teeth like a stone.

"She wouldn't really execute a cardinal, would she?" I asked breathlessly, opening a paper packet of roasted and sugared macadamia nuts I had bought from a passing vendor.

Clarence cast me an arch look.

"Listen, stud," he said. "You claim to be a journalist. Don't you know anything about the current state of Court politics?"

In point of fact, I, Wllm Beaver, did. I knew a tremendous amount, and I'd learned it all by acting excessively dumb in the presence of supercilious Court officials. Therefore, I chomped down on a macadamia nut-cluster, widened my eyes to agog-ness and said, "No?"

Clarence leaned close to me, a sly grin on his face, his cheeks sucking at the sweet as if he was an asthmatic bullfrog.

"All this business," he hissed, glancing around and waving cheerily to the Countess of Hardwick's party in case they had thought about eavesdropping, "this dreadful week of murder and satanic who-knows-what. It's just the tip of the... of the... What are those cold things called that float around the oceans with only their heads poking above the flood?"

"Dead sailors?"

"Icebergs. It's just the tip of one of those. It's been going on for months... a year, maybe, ever since that rogue Triumff got back from his adventuring."

I fought to keep a telltale knowing look from my face.

"Triumff's up to his chin in this, you mark my words," said Clarence, "and he's in it with Woolly. The knives are out for both of them." Then his voice dropped even lower. I, Wllm Beaver, struggled to make sense of the nobleman's lip movements.

"They say the Church is a spent force," Clarence whispered. "They say the cardinals have formed a treasonous pact behind Woolly to regain their power foothold before the

Queen abolishes the Church entirely and hands over the running to the Lay Guild. They say that Triumff is the key."

"How so?" I asked, picking macadamia shards from between my teeth.

"He's brought back Magick, hasn't he? Magick from his New World. The Magick invented by those delicious ebony fellows like the one he brought back with him. That's what they need... new Magick."

"Surely the Church has got oodles of Magick?" I asked.

Clarence rocked the sweet back and forth on his tongue, saying, "It's all but spent. What's the greatest scandal at Court just now?"

"Lord Fotheringay and the dachshunds?" I suggested.

"Apart from Lord Fotheringay and the dachshunds. Wiltshire! Wiltshire!"

"Oh," said I, trying to play down my excitement. I knew I was on to a huge scoop.

"That ridiculous arrangement of stones up on the land owned by that fat pervert, John Hockrake, the Duke of Salisbury," said Clarence. "Druid Magick. Old Arte. The pagan stuff you need a strong stomach and a forty-generation yokel lineage to use. Hockrake tried to get it working again, as a new source of Magick power. The whole thing was a mess. There was some kind of accident... A lot of uncontained Magick got spilled. Disastrous. They say the Cantriptic slick washed as far as Bristol."

"I'd heard talk, but it was denied. The cardinal even denied it in my hearing," I said.

"Well, he would, wouldn't he? That kind of failure is embarrassing for a man in his position," Clarence said, rolling the sweet along the roof of his mouth thoughtfully. "The Church needs a new source, you see? And Triumff is it. Why else would Triumff have waited so long to deliver his Letters of Passage to the Queen? Woolly's told him to hold off until they can rattle the City so hard with Arteful mischief that the population begs the Church to act. They appear to save the day with all their lovely new Arte, and no one is any the wiser that it was them doing it in the first place."

"A fascinating theory," mused I, Wllm Beaver.

"Fact," said Clarence. "The Queen knows, you see? Old Three Ex is on to it. She's wise to Woolly's game, and she's waiting for him to play out enough rope to hang himself with."

I nodded, sitting back. I didn't want to disabuse the nobleman of his theory, but I did wonder if it would still be intact by the time the night was done.

I was about to ask another question when some new tumblers scampered onto the lawn. One of them was a very muscular fellow, who had apparently forgotten to put on anything except a codpiece and the contents of a bottle of oil. I had to slap Clarence hard on the back to dislodge the hastily swallowed sweet.

Over the lawns, the musicians' tent was striking up the Royal Salute, and the atmosphere in the crowd became electric.

There was a disconcerting background odour, behind the cooking, and the perfume and the sweat, an odour that made me feel uneasy, although I didn't know why.

It was the smell of molasses.

THE TWENTY-FIRST SPLENDID CHAPTER.
Just before the Curtain rises.

The upper corridors of the Palace were dark and chilly. De Quincey lit an oil lamp and carried it before them. The noise outside, below, was rising in intensity. De Quincey froze as Mother Grundy caught at his sleeve.

"There's something just ahead," she whispered.

A faint light filtered back down towards them along the corridor, followed by a cool breeze.

De Quincey handed the lamp to Mother Grundy, and took out his poniard. He wished he had been wearing his sword. His fingers trembled around the hilt of the dagger.

"Stay here," de Quincey began.

"Don't be brave," she warned him.

"That's not going to be an issue," de Quincey muttered as he crept forward.

The large windows at the end of the corridor were wide open, overlooking the vast spectacle beneath. A shadow lurked in the window space. There was a scratching noise.

De Quincey leapt forward.

He was about to shout, "The game's up", but, the words drained away down his throat.

Somewhat surprised by a man with a knife coming purposefully out of the dark at him, the artist had fallen off his canvas stool and collapsed in a heap with his easel and pots on top of him. He held up his hands, his teeth clenched around a long brush.

"And you are?" asked de Quincey, trying to make it look deliberate.

"Golgein!" said the man through the brush. He spat out the instrument and reached into his doublet front.

"Steady!" de Quincey warned him.

"I'm Holbein! Hans Holbein! Just an artist! I'm authorised... Look!" He showed de Quincey his official medal.

"Oh," said de Quincey, examining it by the light of the lamp Mother Grundy helpfully raised aloft.

"It all seems to be in order," nodded de Quincey, wincing at Mother Grundy.

"I was just doing a general view of the scene from up here before going down into the crowd for a few portraits. That's all right, isn't it?"

"Yes, yes," said de Quincey.

"What do you think, then?" asked Holbein, getting to his feet and holding up his canvas. "I was busy scumbling it when you surprised me."

"Were you? Very nice," said de Quincey.

"Indeed it is," added Mother Grundy. "Very nice."

"Have you, erm, seen anything this evening?" de Quincey asked, helping the artist to re-erect his easel.

"Like what?" smiled Holbein. He gestured out of the window at the firelit scene below. "Anything in particular?"

"Have you seen the Divine Jaspers of the Church Guild?" asked Mother Grundy.

Holbein frowned.

"I've seen just about everyone who is anyone here tonight," Holbein answered, puckering his forehead in thought. "Jaspers... Jaspers... Youthful bloke, fleshy lips?"

"That's the one," said Mother Grundy.

Holbein reached down into his knapsack and took out a thick sketch book.

"Let's see, then," he said, flipping the pages. "Lord Gorse there... not bad that, if I say so myself. Richard of Brook-shottes. I really got the nose, don't you think?"

De Quincey nodded impatiently as the pages of pencil roughs flicked over.

"Lady Mary Lusterman. Quite a bosom, eh?" said Holbein.

"Very nice," said de Quincey, wishing the artist would get a move on.

"What I wouldn't give to paint her nude," snickered Holbein.

"Wouldn't you get cold?" asked Mother Grundy. De Quincey nudged her.

"Here we go. Jaspers. That's him, isn't it?"

"Yes!" said de Quincey, taking the sketchbook.

"I caught him earlier, just before I came up here. He was chatting to these folks here. I got them all rather well, didn't I?"

De Quincey held the book closer to the light. "Lord Slee... Regent de la Vega... Lord Salisbury."

"Quite some company this vile divine keeps, Mister de Quincey."

De Quincey nodded and breathed out hard.

"They were chatting together out of sight behind the kitchen tent," Holbein explained. "I saw them, and thought I'd do a quick sketch. You see, a true artist captures the off-guard moments, the intimate things. Anyone can do rousing posed shots of the Court watching the fireworks. I think a true record of an event like this is in the informal moments."

Hasty though Hans Holbein's sketch must have been, there was no denying the subtlety of the rendering. The four ill-matched men were huddled in the folds of the tent, masked by the shadows. Slee was talking and the others were listening. De Quincey felt his stomach turn uneasily.

"Their apparent nervousness... Their guarded manner... That's not artistic interpretation, is it?" he asked.

Holbein looked wounded.

"Of course it isn't, of course it isn't," said de Quincey, nodding hastily.

Mother Grundy leaned over and pointed to something around the Divine's neck.

"What are these?" she asked.

"Pouches. Three of them. Little drawstring doodahs," said Holbein. "Didn't have time to sketch them in properly. Why, is it important?"

De Quincey looked across at Mother Grundy. "Is it?" he asked.

"A sorcerer... a dabbler in Goety... might keep talismans in pouches like that," she said.

"He might keep his change in there too," de Quincey ventured.

"Three pouches? No. He wouldn't want them to touch his skin, but he'd want them close to his heart. The pounding of the heart muscles keeps the Magick in them vital," Mother Grundy explained.

"Oh dear me," said de Quincey, sitting down heavily on Holbein's stool.

"I say, this all sounds very exciting," said Holbein, his eyes gleaming, "more exciting than sketching rich folk for a pittance at any rate. Is there anything I can do?"

"You don't want this much excitement," de Quincey told him. He looked over at Mother Grundy. The lamplight made her look more skeletal than ever. "We should tell Gull about this."

"We should keep looking. There's no time to go back," said Mother Grundy.

De Quincey got to his feet, saying, "Master Holbein, how would you like to perform a duty of national importance? Hurry down to the ante-room off the North Processional and show this sketch to Lord Gull. Tell him we sent you."

"Will do!" said Holbein eagerly. He hurried away down the corridor.

De Quincey looked around at Mother Grundy, and was alarmed to see her swaying, holding a hand to her brow.

"Mother Grundy?" he asked.

"I'm sorry," she said. "It just hit me. Like a heatwave. That smell, do you sense it?"

De Quincey sniffed. He could smell cold, damp darkness, and woodsmoke and food cooking, food that must have been basted in molasses.

"It's started," she said. "The devil has begun his business."

"I say," said Holbein, returning out of the gloom. "All the doors are locked."

The first icon crumbled to dust in his fingers.

Jaspers brushed his hands and sighed. Blood pounded in his temples.

Behind him, a fanfare began to trumpet out into the night. Jaspers rose from behind the shelter of the stone buttress, and retraced his steps, back through the dark to the VIP tent. He slipped in through the rear flap, holding it aside for other noblemen on their way to the latrine. The open-fronted tent was smoky, and stank of spilled wine. Jaspers resumed his seat next to Salisbury.

"Good piss?" asked Salisbury, knocking back some wine.

"Quite satisfactory, thank you," said Jaspers.

Jaspers watched how the fat man's hands trembled around his goblet. He knew that Salisbury dearly wished that either Slee or de la Vega had taken charge of the Divine, but they were both required in the Royal Pavilion.

Jaspers leaned over, and filled his glass from the jug on the table.

"I know you don't like me, Hockrake," he said, "but try not to be nervous or we're all dead."

Salisbury nodded. He looked across at Jaspers. Their eyes met properly for the first time ever.

"You frighten me, sir," said Salisbury. "I'll be plain. We're in this together and all, but you frighten me."

"So I should," said Jaspers. "I'm the most dangerous man in the Unity." He chuckled and moderated his tone to mollify Salisbury. "Relax. As you say, we're in this together. We'll have to trust each other if this is going to play out to our advantage." He raised his glass and his voice.

"A health to Her Majesty!" he said.

Salisbury clinked his trembling goblet with Jaspers's as the nobility around them answered the toast.

"So, your little toy?" he asked quietly under the din.

"Has sealed tight every door in the Palace," finished Jaspers. "Our main players are trapped on this public stage. A few minutes more, and we reach the culmination of this business."

De Quincey tried the door again.

"We could break it down," Holbein suggested.

"Indeed, if you want a broken shoulder bone," Mother Grundy told him. "These doors aren't locked, they're shut Goetically."

"Which means?" asked de Quincey, knowing full well what it meant.

"Which means, Neville, we're trapped up here," said Mother Grundy.

On the carpeted walk beside the Royal Pavilion, Lord Slee shook hands with another group of dignitaries, and then crossed to Cardinal Woolly, who stood by the steps of the great tent, admiring the roof of the huge marquee that had been painted with verisimilitude summer clouds. Gold dust coated every surface like a yellow frost.

"Your worship," said Slee.

"My lord."

Slee handed Woolly a sealed tube of parchment, saying, "The Speech of Thanks. The Chancellor asked me to pass it to you." Woolly nodded and tucked the tube into his waistband.

"A fine night. The Royal Pavilion looks glorious. That touch of gold will complement Her Majesty's hair. You've done well, if you don't mind me saying," Lord Slee said, smiling.

"Thank you," said Woolly. "I trust it will go well."

Slee smiled again.

"I have no doubt," he said, and turned away.

Ten yards took him around behind the Pavilion, and into the awning of the players' tent. De Tongfort was waiting.

"It's all set, my lord," said de Tongfort.

"Cato has the arrow?" asked Slee.

"Aye, and I see the Divine is in place. Have you passed the item to that fool cardinal?" asked de Tongfort.

"Lower your damn voice!" hissed Slee. "Yes, I have. Now wait and be ready. Is that fellow Cato prepared?"

"I gave him the blessed arrow. He suspects nothing. I told him it was from the Queen's quiver, and that she would favour its use in the pageant. He took it gleefully," said de Tongfort.

"And the venom?" asked Slee.

"Carefully painted on the barb."

Slee took the half-empty bottle of poison from de Tongfort, and slipped it under his cloak.

"Where's de la Vega? Have you seen him?" he asked.

De Tongfort nodded and said, "He met a steward who was looking for Woolly. He went into the Palace."

Slee looked across at grim, looming Richmond.

"I–" he began, but was cut off by another fanfare.

"Here comes Her Majesty," said de Tongfort.

The cavalcade flowed out of the Palace like a burning river. Pages, trumpeters, hautboys, awning-bearers, an echelon of huscarls in glittering plate, standard bearers holding aloft the lion of England, the swords of Spain, the Royal coat of arms that combined the phoenix and the pelican, the complex blazon of the Unity, and every other subsidiary emblem in the Commonwealth. In the midst of the triumphant march, luminous, and beautiful, was the Queen herself.

A hush fell on the gardens, broken only by the strident trumpets. The river flowed, burning bright, into the Pavilion, and three thousand people bowed.

Taking her seat, Gloriana spoke.

In his place in the musician's tent, Cedarn could neither see nor hear Her Majesty. He waited. Master Couperin took up his baton.

"Ze Royal Salute, s'il vous plait!" he announced.

This is it, thought Louis Cedarn.

The Palace undercroft smelled of damp and rainwater. Agnew found a lamp from somewhere and lit it.

"How did you know about this?" Uptil asked Drew Bluett, his voice a carrying echo in the stony vault.

"Older days, older duties," replied Drew, leading them down the dripping tunnel. "The intelligencers of the Court needed secret ways into the Palace for private audiences. This isn't the first time I've run these rat-holes."

"I was most impressed by the door to this passageway," said Agnew, "so seamlessly flush with the wall from the outside."

"When the spymasters build a secret tunnel, Mister Agnew, they build it properly," said Bluett.

Uptil paused, cocking his ear to the cold, mildewed roof above them.

"I hear a fanfare," he said.

"It's just the wind," grumbled Drew.

"No, it's a fanfare. It's all getting underway up there."

"Then we've no time to lose," Drew said.

He stopped.

"What is it?" asked Agnew.

Drew grunted, and said, "The door, it's stuck solid, as if it's locked. That's impossible. My key should fit this."

"Let me try," suggested Uptil.

Behind them, something heavy slapped down onto the wet stone of the floor.

"A-hem! Gentlemen?" said Agnew.

Drew and Uptil turned from the jammed door and saw the huge shadow that loomed behind them.

Tantamout O'Bow slowly slid the hand-and-a-half sword from his belt.

"Hello," he said. "So nice to make your attainment.

"Bye the bye," he added, conversationally, "you're all going to die."

* * *

The door to the Processional ante-chamber swung open and de la Vega stepped in. He closed the door, carefully, behind him.

"My Lord Regent," said Lord Gull from the fireplace. "You have a key, then?"

"I do not understand, Lord Gull," frowned the Spaniard.

"The last few times I've tried that door, it's been locked fast," Gull said with a shrug. "I supposed you to have a key, as you entered so easily."

"So I do," nodded de la Vega, stepping forward. He stood next to Gull, and warmed his hands at the fire. "A cold evening, Lord Gull, is it not?"

"Cold as death," said Gull cheerfully.

"Your quaint English expressions," de la Vega said with a smile and a wag of his finger at Gull. He crossed to the drinks table and poured two large glasses of port. "One for you, my lord?"

"My thanks, sir," said Gull, not moving.

De la Vega picked up the two brimming glasses and returned to Gull.

"I regret that you and I have never had the time to converse much, Lord Gull," he said. "We are alike, you and I."

"How so?" asked Gull.

"Warriors born," said de la Vega, handing one of the glasses to Gull. Neither sipped. "They say you are the greatest swordsman in the Unity. They say the same of me in Toledo."

"Two strong swords to serve Her Majesty are better than one," Gull mused.

"Just so," de la Vega said, looking down into the contents of his glass. "I intercepted a steward you had sent to Cardinal Woolly. He claimed that you believed the Divine Jaspers was a danger to Her Majesty."

"That is so," said Gull. "I trust you sent him straight to the cardinal."

De la Vega shook his head. He looked straight into Gull's black eyes.

"Well, Lord Regent," said Gull. "I suppose then we are about to discover who really is the best swordsman in the Unity, aren't we?"

"Indeed we are," said de la Vega, setting down his glass, "indeed we are."

CHAPTER NUMBER TWENTY-TWO.
Of divers various FIGHTS.

Amid the thirty-seven thousand, one hundred and sixty-three people gathered within a mile of Richmond Palace, there were five fights in progress. It was four minutes after ten o'clock in the evening, which meant that was pretty good going.

Fights one and two were happening outside the Palace walls. At the gate on the Green, members of the Militia were engaged in a rowdy brawl with some drunken Admiralty subalterns. The latter were insisting they had an urgent message to take to Admiral Poley, who was within, and the former were insisting that the latter should pull the other one. Fists were now being employed in this pulling, which was none too gentle, and the watching crowd had begun to go "oooh" and "aaaah", until the Militia lost patience and involved them in the fight too.

Out on the Shene marshes, sloping down beyond the edge of the Deer Park, the Hotchkine and Scubbold families had embarked on a physical altercation concerning the whereabouts of a bottle of musket. Apparently, at some point in the evening, said bottle had "rolled" out of the Scubbolds' hamper and been half-drained by Grayham Hotchkine. As Grayham had lost most of his teeth, liquid refreshment seemed his only option, but the Scubbolds, to a man, a woman and a red-spotted setter, had deemed it unwise for him to finish the musket off.

Bloody though both parlous disputes were, neither was as fundamental to the continued fortunes of the Unity as those that raged within the Palace walls.

On the stage of the Royal Pavilion, Master Lucas of the Chamberlain's men, Master Graves of the Oh and Master Cato of the Swan were in the middle of the carefully re-hearsed "Battle of the Glorious Dawn" before the excited crowd. Prop swords swung and sparked and clacked, and there was a lot of grunting and oathing and straining, punctuated regularly by one or more of the combatants stepping forward and delivering a soliloquy to the crowd. Said crowd was particularly delighted when Master Lucas delivered a swinging slice to Master Graves, causing the latter to back flip off the stage onto a hidden crash-mat. They were so delighted, in fact, they thumped their tankards on the trestle tables until Master Graves got up, took a bow, and did it again.

The Queen, it was reported, was tankard-thumping as loudly as anyone. It seemed she approved of this dramatic opening to the Masque performance.

It is interesting to conjecture, therefore, how much the Gloriana, and indeed the crowd in general, would have clapped had they been able to witness the fight that was currently in full swing in the ante-room of the Palace's North Processional.

This unseen combat was distinguished by two key factors: firstly, it was between Lord Gull and the Regent of Castile, two of the most admired swordsmen in the Unity. Any display given by these two sword-masters would have ordinarily drawn crowds bigger than the Masque had.

The second factor was that the fight was in brilliant, unrehearsed, bloody earnest.

Consider yourself lucky, then, beloved reader, that you get a chance to witness this otherwise unwitnessed clash of Titans.

It was an affair of the coldest, most steely nerves. Both warriors had more than his life to battle for, the fate of the Unity lodged in their hands. Yet both entered the fight methodically and correctly, drawing swords, nodding, appointing and saluting before it began. Vital though their fight was, neither saw fit to spoil it by rushing in with ungentlemanly haste before the other was ready.

In truth, they both wished to savour the battle. It wasn't often that either of them got to test his skill against an equal.

Gull unsheathed his rapier. It had been made for him by a Dresden sword-cutler named Isaach Spaaatz, and its S-swept hilt and curled quillons were of blued steel, inlaid with silver wire and pique dots. In his left hand, Gull held the matching dagger.

De la Vega's sword was a cup-hilted bilbo with a guard of quite exquisite pierce-and-chisel work, demascened in gold and silver. His coat of arms was inscribed on the ricasso. The blade was of Toledo steel, and a good six inches longer than Gull's. He held it with a Continental grip, his first and second fingers hooked over the quillons as if it were a hugely-needled syringe.

He looked across at Gull.

"I have no main gauche, señor," he said.

Gull frowned and looked down at his companion dagger for a moment. Then, with a flick of his wrist, he sent it away. It thumped into the wall panelling, and reverberated like a recently vacated diving board.

"We are even," said Gull.

"I salute your fair play," smiled de la Vega.

Gull nodded, a quick, perfunctory movement, and raised his sword so that he looked through the looped guard at his opponent.

"Vivat Regina," he saluted.

De la Vega chopped at the air in front of his own nose twice.

"God damn the Queen," he said. "En garde."

Gull flèched immediately, a short, stamping run and thrust that de la Vega volted and parried.

They broke and circled. De la Vega swung in with a return thrust that Gull met with a deft parade. De la Vega's blade slid off this defence, but he brought it in again with a remise that struck twice against the forte of Gull's blade. Slightly off balance, Gull sliced around, over de la Vega's ducking head, and executed a balestra that made them clash together and lock blades at the coquille.

They pushed away and broke again. De la Vega chuckled. "Now we have the measure of each other, Señor Gull. Now we can begin properly," he said.

They exploded at each other, their blades moving faster than the eye could see: clashing, singing, sparking.

It is safe to assume that only twice before in History had two such gifted swordsmen duelled. Neither of the other bouts matched this in splendour.

One had been between Jovan Knekt of Dusseldorf, who had trained on the system of L'Épee under Girard Thibault for twenty years, and Clovis Pappenheim, who had been schooled in the Naples Method for seventeen summers. They were both recognised as the very greatest swordsmen of their age, and had each defeated at least two hundred experts in the run-up to the grand final of the Antwerp Fencing

Tourney. This took place in 1843, and the final was over in three seconds, or twenty-nine strokes, whichever you care to measure it by. Both scored a perfect impale at the same moment. The fight is well documented, and ended with the cries of the Antwerp Judges, who exclaimed, "Fluke! Pure fluke!" as Knekt and Pappenheim hit the mat of the piste, simultaneously.

The other had been between the samurai Go San Do and the ronin Chee Fu, in Feudal Japan, around about 1230. The fight lasted three days, and the carefully recorded steps of the grand masters now form a fundamental part of the week-long Ceremony of the Clashing Swords in Otinawa. They both managed a perfect disembowelment and decapitation at the same moment. Documents show the reactions of the Shogun of Okinawa, who shouted, "Jo gon jo hona aky hu!", which literally translates as, "Fluke! Pure fluke!"

We can assume, gentle reader, that the duration of this fight will be somewhere between those two, lauded extremes. It has already lasted longer than the three seconds of the Knekt/Pappenheim clash, and it had better not out-do the Do/Fu battle, otherwise the civilised world may well be a profoundly different place by the time they have finished.

Just forty seconds into the blistering duel, and Gull found himself consistently and energetically volting to avoid the extra, stabbing length of de la Vega's bilbo.

De la Vega's onslaught was unstinting. There was no time to break cleanly and reprise. With his longer reach, the Spaniard had Gull on a permanent defensive.

Fair play, thought Callum Gull sourly as he parried vigorously. I ditched my main gauche at your suggestion. Would you have snapped six inches off your foible if I'd brought it to your attention?

De la Vega feinted with a stamping appel, and hooked a thrust in under Gull's guard. The bilbo's blade bit into the flesh of Gull's right underarm. He cursed and leapt back.

De la Vega broke off and circled, grinning.

"Touché," he remarked.

Gull could feel the blood dribbling down inside his doublet. If nothing else, the wound was going to hinder his sword work. It had been a calculated and cruel blow, unsporting. That made him cross, very cross indeed. Only one thing, one man, made him crosser.

For a moment, Gull thought about the man who made him crosser than anyone else.

Huge, seething anger flooded his mind, but he harnessed it and set it to work for him, cancelling the pain and spurring his muscles on.

He went for de la Vega like a tiger, a tiger that had been given a rapier and schooled to perfection by Thibault of Antwerp.

He drove the Regent back across the ante-room until he crashed into the drinks stand, overturning it, and shattering its crystal contents. The strong smell of liberated brandy filled the room. De la Vega barked an eager curse, and tried to parade and sidestep, but Gull would not loosen his grip on the offensive. He turned aside de la Vega's inquisitive, urgent blade, and thrust in hard. The entire foible of his rapier ran through de la Vega's left bicep.

Pain rattled up out of de la Vega's throat, and he pulled himself off the Scotsman's sword with a twist of his upper body and two rapid, backward steps, hacking with his weapon to prevent a remise.

Gull kept the space between them to a sword's length, prowling forward across the broken crystal on the mats. De la Vega backed away until he felt the cold marble of the fireplace press into his shoulders. He flexed his left arm, wincing.

"Touché," said Gull, returning to the en garde position casually.

"You fight with vigour and determination, señor. Me sorprende... I have heard many tales of your ability with the rapier, but I believed few of them. Tell me, is it really patriotism that fires your passions so?"

"A man can be inspired by a love of his country. Isn't that what spurs you on, Regent?"

De la Vega shook his head. "This country?" he asked. "No me interesa. My beloved Castile, however... Oh yes."

"Is that what this is all about? This treason that you're clearly part of. Is it the age-old complaint of underling Spain, out to spill blood to right itself at Court?"

De la Vega licked his lips and gestured ambivalently. "Nothing so simple, or so singular," he said. "Tonight, there is afoot such business as will make the stars in heaven shake."

"Business set in hand by you and Jaspers, I'd wager," said Gull, "though not alone. There must be others, but I have no doubt that Jaspers is crucial to your treason, or you wouldn't have risked exposure by coming here to silence my suspicions."

De la Vega returned his gaze, but said nothing.

"So, will you put up your sword while I summon the guard?" asked Gull.

De la Vega took a deep breath and straightened up. "Todavía no he terminado. The fight is in its infancy," he said.

"But, you're bleeding," said Gull.

"So are you. A mi no molesta en absoluto."

"If that's the way you want it," said Gull. "En garde!"

* * *

The fifth fight underway in the minutes after ten that evening was taking place in the dark, smelly arena of the Palace undercroft, and, in its way, it was every bit as fundamental to the future of the Unity as the dazzling swordplay in progress in the processional ante-room.

Drew Bluett just had time to draw his heavy-bladed Venetian storta and bellow, "Get behind me!" to Uptil and Agnew before O'Bow was on him. The first sweep of O'Bow's huge hand-and-a-halfer slid the entire length of the storta's blade as Drew deflected it, and only the finger-ring and knuckle-bow prevented it from shearing the digits of Drew's sword hand.

Drew was stronger than the average man, and his bulk counted well against most ordinary opponents, but there was nothing ordinary or average about Tantamount O'Bow. He was no great swordsman, but he swung the huge blade as easily as if it had been a smallsword or a light estoc. Drew was a reasonably accomplished swordsman, if a little out of practice. However, even a swordmaster like Roustam de la Vega would have thought twice about trying his luck with O'Bow. With the sword whirring around his head, he was about as easy to attack as a sharpened windmill in a force nine gale.

"Who are you? You're not Palace Guard!" yelled Drew as he fended away the rain of metal. "Why are you doing this?"

"Needs musk when the devil dives!" O'Bow answered, rather mysteriously. "I am on a mission of grating portents, and must mortally slay any who hinder me, what-so-whom-ever."

"I wasn't hindering you!" cried Drew, backing away across the dirty undercroft.

"I'll be the jug of that!" exploded O'Bow, and fetched Drew a massive crack across the side of the head with his sword.

Drew cartwheeled back through the damp air, demolished a small stack of very rotten barrels, and lay still in the debris.

O'Bow crossed over to him and knelt down, laying the point of his sword at Drew's throat.

"Become informatory, and I'll let you live," he said. "I seek a Frenchie looter, named Looey Cedarn. Name his whereabouts."

There was silence. Drew Bluett was profoundly unconscious with a deep, bloody gash across his scalp, and he wasn't about to name anything.

"O'Bow," said a voice behind him. The giant turned and stood up to find Agnew facing him. Uptil was paused undecidedly in the shadows behind the manservant.

"You know me?" asked Tantamount O'Bow.

"I know of you, sir. My master, Rupert Triumff, has told me of you on several occasions."

"I see my repudiation proceeds me."

"It does. Now it seems to me you mean to kill us, but you also seek a man named Cedarn. Might it not change your attitude to us if I told you we too were seeking the knave?"

O'Bow nodded slowly. In the dim light, his terrible scars looked like pleated pink silk.

"And why-for would you be of finding the fellow?" he asked.

Agnew stared into O'Bow's blue eyes without a flicker. "To kill him," he said.

Uptil stiffened, and tapped at Agnew's elbow. Agnew ignored him.

"You too, eh?" asked O'Bow, lowering his sword. "And what's your despot with him?"

"He's a Frenchie looter, as you say," said Agnew. He's caused us many problems. We've been hunting for him for several days."

O'Bow cracked his knuckles, and crossed to the door of the undercroft.

"It seems we have adjoining courses," he said. "Best we should belabour together til we smoke him out." He looked across at Drew's crumpled form. "My apology for dinting your companion. My attack on him, it now seems, was most prehensile."

Agnew and Uptil crossed to Drew's side.

"See what you can do with the door," said Agnew. "It's stuck fast. We'll tend to our friend."

"What are you doing?" asked Uptil in a tight whisper as they crouched together next to Bluett.

"Do you have a better idea?" asked Agnew. "He's laid poor Bluett out. Unless we can divorce him from his sword, we don't begin to stand a chance against him. I had to do something to stop him killing all of us."

Uptil sighed and looked down at Drew.

"Nasty head wound," he said. "We need to get a surgeon to him as soon as possible."

"First chance we get," Agnew concurred. "I'd love to know what this monster has got against Sir Rupert. Just how many people has he managed to offend since we last saw him?"

Drew stirred and groaned. He looked up at Agnew.

"Mr Bluett. Do you understand what I'm saying?"

Drew nodded, blinking.

"We have managed to converse with Mr O'Bow, the gentleman that struck you," said Agnew. "He has agreed to join forces with us, as he too wants to eliminate the Frenchie looter Cedarn. Is that clear?"

Drew nodded again. Dazed and in pain though he was, his years of espial training helped him to sift out the pertinent truth behind Agnew's bald statement.

"Help me up," he said. He was unsteady, but his eyes burned fiercely. Agnew tore a strip from his coat and made a makeshift bandage for his head.

"Upon your feet again, I see," said O'Bow from the doorway. "It gladdens my heart. I must extrude great hominids of apologism to you for my crudities."

"Your hominids are gratefully accepted, Mr O'Bow," said Drew, leaning on Agnew for support. "That door's locked, is it not?"

There was a deafening crash, and O'Bow removed the entire door from its frame. He held it up in front of them and tried the handle.

"It is indeed," he agreed.

The ill-assorted quartet entered the next chamber, a huge, echo-booming, dark kitchen. The space was cold and empty. Bizarre, haunting sounds murmured into the room. They were coming from outside, noises from the huge party, filtering down through the enormous chimney places above the dead grate.

"They must be using the kitchens in the west wing to provide for the Masque. How's the door?" asked Agnew.

The door out of the kitchen was an even heavier oak section than the one in from the undercroft. O'Bow stepped away from it, shaking his head.

"Locked too," he noted. He cracked his knuckles again, and flexed the muscles of his shoulders with a Hercynian shrug.

"Wait! We can't go through the Palace tearing every door we come to off its hinges," said Drew.

"Do you have an alternating presumption?" O'Bow asked him.

"I do," said Uptil. He gestured towards the huge fireplace. "We could climb."

O'Bow showed far too many teeth. Uptil thought for a moment that he was going to bite him.

"A very fine presumption indeed!" he exclaimed.

"Let's go," said Drew.

They climbed onto the hearth block, and looked up into the flues. Blackness stared back.

"Tell me, Mr O'Bow," said Agnew, matter-of-factly, "what is the nature of your dispute with Cedarn? Is it personal?"

"It is now," said O'Bow. "At the original, I was hired to do him away, but he was deviate, and gave me a slip. That made it a matter of distinctive personality."

"Hired, indeed?" put in Drew, testing the bricks of the flue wall. "By whom?"

"That mister Dung Tongueford. Bournevile Dung Tongueford. He has me for errands, some off times." O'Bow said, reaching into the flue and pulling himself up out of sight. Loose bricks, mortar and soot trickled down.

"What's the matter?" asked Uptil quietly, noticing the look on Drew's face.

"I knew a man, a Bonville de Tongfort, back in the old days of the Circus, when Milord Effingham was running Intelligence," said Drew. "He was a rat of a man. I thought he might have perished in the Purge. I might have hoped he had. He crossed me more than once."

"This is the same man?" asked Uptil.

"I've no way of telling," Drew replied, "but the de Tongfort I knew was in the dirtiest of Dirty Tricks. You could always trust him to procure the lowest jakes-scum for a sleazy mission. O'Bow's just the sort of element de Tongfort cultivated. Oh, but this affair stinks more and more as we go along. If it is the de Tongfort I know, I'll be happy to have a reckoning with him."

"Are you going to attend on my behind?" O'Bow called back down the flue to them.

"Let's follow him," said Drew. He caught Uptil's arm, and

said, "If I can get his sword away from him, do you fancy your chances, mano-a-mano?"

Uptil nodded. He knew that of the three of them, he had the best hope of laying the huge thug out. Uptil was a cultured, refined soul, who disliked physical violence, but he kept himself fit, and his musculature testified to his strength. Besides, he had more than enough reasons to bury his knuckles in O'Bow's twisted face.

"I'll give it a go," he replied.

They scrambled up the chimney, the noises of the great party washing down around them, like the voices of ghosts.

Above and outside, the revelry was reaching its peak. On the stage, the players were in the middle of a sophisticated comedic interlude, involving five clowns and some buckets of porridge.

Doll watched from the wings, minutes away from her grand entrance.

In the Royal Pavilion, overlooking the stage, Cardinal Woolly sat three places to the left of the Queen. He was oblivious to the laughter and applause around him. Tense worry gnawed at him.

A row behind him, Lord Slee sat and observed with equal concern. De la Vega had been missing for twenty minutes. It wouldn't be long before the Queen noticed, and asked for him. If there was some trouble... some hitch...

Slee took a sip of water to clear his mouth and his head. He nodded, and joined in the laughter as his immediate neighbour drew his attention to the antics on stage. His eyes weren't on the clowns, though, they were fixed, hawk-like, on the VIP tent facing the Royal Pavilion across the apron staging. He could see Salisbury and Jaspers, distant faces through the smoky taper-light. As if cued by some invisible

nudge, Jaspers looked back and made eye contact. He nodded across the lawn to Slee, and held up an open hand just
over the table. Five minutes more.

Slee's mouth was dry again. He glanced at the Court personages around him, and watched the way the firelight
glinted like stars off the Queen's tiara as her head moved in
laughter, like stars.

There is fortune in stars, and the greatest fortune of all was
spelled out in those that danced around the Gloriana's vulnerable head.

In the musicians' marquee, Louis Cedarn scratched at his
chin. His stubble was beginning to grow back. It itched. His
whole life itched. If he didn't scratch it soon, he'd go mad.

He set down his lute, and edged his way between the waiting musicians towards the exit.

"Monsieur Cedarn," called Master Couperin from the
lectern, "qu'est-ce que vous faites, maintenant?"

"A moment, master," Cedarn called back. "I must visit the
latrine."

Outside, at the back of the tent, it was dark and cold. Triumff snorted in the cool air a couple of times to clear his
lungs of the greasy smoke of the marquee's atmospheric fug.
He edged his way down towards the rear of the players' tiring
tent.

It was a long jump, far longer and more hazardous than anything de Quincey would ever have dared attempt under
normal circumstances. His feet slithered for purchase on the
roof tiles, and, for a moment, he thought he was about to
plunge back into the darkness below him. He managed,
somehow, to hold on, and slowly got to his feet. Mother
Grundy was crouching next to him on the roof.

"You made it, then?" she asked.

"You're more sprightly than you appear, madam," he said, breathing hard.

"I like to keep fit," she said. "Besides, this does seem to be the only way back down, doesn't it?"

"Are you both all right?" Hans Holbein called softly from the window above them.

"Yes!" de Quincey called back. "Stay where you are. We'll be back for you."

Without thinking, he took Mother Grundy's hand and led her up over the sloping darkness of the roof. After a moment, he realised what he'd done, and realised too that Mother Grundy hadn't pulled her hand away. For all her bluster and drive, she was clearly as nervous as he was. In a strange way, this comforted him.

The far slope of the roof took them down to a two storey gutter from where they overlooked the stage of the Masque. They had a clear view of the Royal Pavilion and the adjoining marquees. Down on the stage, clowns were brawling.

"Can you see Jaspers?" asked Mother Grundy.

"I can't really see anyone properly," he replied. "Is that him? No, no, it's the Earl of Richborough."

"Don't move," said a cold voice from behind them.

The huscarl marksman slid down the roof to them, his sight-mounted crossbow ready with an arrow that never wavered from them.

"Who are you?" he asked. "What the blood and mercy are you doing out here?"

"Listen–" de Quincey began, hoping that the truth would be the best option. His Militia credentials wouldn't explain why he was crawling around on a roof within bow-shot of the Queen's person.

But Mother Grundy squeezed his hand to silence him. She looked at the huscarl, and said, "Put it down."

Those quiet words were the most commanding de Quincey had ever heard. His spine tingled.

Without question, the huscarl set his weapon down in the gutter.

"Now sleep," Mother Grundy said, her words as commanding as before. The huscarl laid down and began to snore.

De Quincey looked at Mother Grundy with his eyebrows raised.

"The Voice of Command," she explained, "an old trick, and one I don't like to use too often. It's too close to Goety for my taste."

De Quincey took up the huscarl's crossbow, and trained the telescope spotter on the scene below. After a moment, he said, "There! There he is! Next to Lord Salisbury in the VIP tent."

"Let me see," she said.

He was about to hand her the weapon, but then stopped, saying, "He's getting up. Moving out of the tent. I've lost him!"

He looked around at Mother Grundy. He didn't like the look in her eyes.

Below them, Slee saw Jaspers move out of the tent opposite. He clenched his fists. It was time.

Jaspers reached the back of the players' tent, and sat down on a trunk, smiling to himself. He took one of the velvet pouches from around his neck, and opened it, sliding out the talisman. He held it up to the candlelight and smiled again.

"That's nice," someone said, "and clearly very Magickal. What's it for?"

Jaspers looked up. Louis Cedarn was smiling straight back at him.

CHAPTER TWENTY & THREE.
The Ploy's the Thing.

"You've made the most appalling mistake, my friend," said Jaspers, "and it's not one you'll live long enough to regret."

"I know you," said Cedarn, nerves that had seen him through nineteen sea actions showing no sign of breaking. "You're Jaspers of the Guild. I wondered which wretch from the Church was behind this. I should have guessed."

Jaspers got to his feet, confident but curious.

"Do I know you?" he began, staring at Cedarn's face. "Of course I do. Blond and beardless, but it is you, isn't it, Triumff?"

Triumff nodded.

"De la Vega was right about you. He will be pleased. He said you were a dangerous element. Of course, you're only in time to receive the proxime accessit. You're far too late."

Triumff's punch knocked him to the ground. The talisman bounced from his fingers across the grass.

"Late for what?" asked Triumff.

Jaspers reached for the talisman. Triumff stood on his hand.

"What are you trying to do here, you bastard?" he asked.

Triumff was thrown off his feet by a blow to the back of his head. He sprawled into the flaps of the tiring tent, and struggled around, his head spinning.

De Tongfort encircled Triumff from behind and put his rapier across Triumff's throat.

"So, you're Triumff," he said. "I might have known. Are you all right, your worship?"

"I'll live," said Jaspers, getting to his feet and retrieving the talisman. "Take him off somewhere and kill him. Swiftly. I have a schedule to keep."

"Come on," said Triumff, "you've got me cold. At least let me watch this. I'd hate to die not knowing what I'm dying for."

Jaspers nodded to de Tongfort, who kept the blade pressed against Triumff's Adam's apple.

"Then observe, Sir Rupert," said Jaspers. "I am about to re-lease Goety undreamt of, and the Queen is about to die."

They came up through a fire-pit in the Clavier Banqueting Hall. It was dark there too, but the light from outside flooded in through the windows.

O'Bow was waiting for them.

Agnew dusted himself down and helped Drew to a seat. Uptil stood by O'Bow, and the pair of them stared out into the party.

"Any lotion as to where the Frenchie might be?" asked O'Bow.

"No. None."

O'Bow frowned and turned away. By the fireplace was a table lined with racks of musket. O'Bow put his sword on the table and took up a bottle, uncorking it with his teeth.

Uptil licked his lips. He took a deep breath, knowing that the moment was upon him.

He grabbed O'Bow's sword, hurled it away across the room and swung his hardest ever punch at the Irishman.

O'Bow took the entire table of racks with him, and they all hit the wall in an explosion of smashing musket flasks and flailing limbs.

"That's for Drew," Uptil explained, picking up the stunned O'Bow by the collar. He hit him again, knocking him across the banqueting table and through the candle sticks.

"That's for Rupert," he added, rounding the corner of the table.

O'Bow's punch doubled Uptil over, knocking the wind out of him. He fell to his knees at O'Bow's feet, gasping like a punctured bellows.

"That's for starters," said Tantamount O'Bow.

Agnew and Drew leapt at him, but he threw them away like a stripper discarding her clothes. Drew landed on the floor by the window, too stunned to rise. Agnew landed, seated, in a chair by the door. There was a terribly disappointed look on his face.

"So," said O'Bow, lifting Uptil by the throat with one hand, "you're betraylors after all."

"I'm sorry," said Agnew, rising to his feet. "Please, spare my friend Uptil." He balled his fists and assumed a boxing position. "I'll give you a fight if you want it."

O'Bow threw Uptil's limp body aside, and marched towards Agnew.

"Do not revoke me," he said. "I'd make minx meat out of you."

Agnew threw a neat punch that smacked O'Bow in the face. O'Bow didn't move. Agnew winced and shook his injured hand. O'Bow smiled and slid his ballock knife out of his belt. He held it up, and the light glinted off it.

"It's pig-sicking time," he declared.

The Cat pounced.

It came down from somewhere in the rafters like a bolt of tawny lightning, and O'Bow disappeared beneath it. Agnew gasped despite himself, and backed away from the thrashing bodies on the floor: O'Bow, and a huge cat every bit as large as him, a cat with fingers, and a doublet and breeches.

The fingers sprouted claws from under the nails.

The screaming began.

"Then where goest honour and duty?" Doll asked of the crowd.

"By whichever means, it goest swiftly," rejoined Alice Munton. "Dear Goddess, tell us how we may receive your bargain."

Doll opened her arms and gestured to the multitude. At her feet, the hunters of love – Artemis, Diana and Orion – sat, looking up at her with adoration in their eyes.

"*Peace, ho!*" cried Doll, "*I bar confusion,*
Tis I who must make conclusion,
By honour, mercy, duty, right,
Look not to the dame of night,
But to the Goddess of the day!
Gloriana! Sweet Gloriana!
A nobler brow never held 'loft crown,
A nobler hand ne'er ruled this town!
This town, this burgh, this demi-land,
Of all towns sweet, none can compare
Proud Rome, Vienna dear, wat'ry Venice
Where the throats of gondoliers hymn to the beauty
Of the Great Lagoon, Noble Madrid,
fair Barcelone, and Paris, Jewel of the Continent!
None is as fine as this sweet London,
Hung as if a locket on the silver Thames."

Doll stopped, because the crowd had broken into such applause that it drowned out any further words. She stood, her arms still wide, waiting for it to subside. She glanced down at Alice and Mary.

"Wonderful, wonderful," murmured Mary Mercer, her eyes wet with tears.

Alice was so pale with emotion she couldn't speak. Doll looked at Horace Cato – Orion – with unease. He was staring at the Royal Pavilion, his hand clenching and unclenching at his bow.

The applause began to drop.

"But what is the beauty of the silver Thames,
To this, the perfection of worldly contents,
The Gloriana Divine, the Goddess of the Day?
If truth be true, And our hearts united in this Unity,
Then let us crown her crowned head again!"

The applause was even greater now. The cheering was picked up by the multitude outside the Palace walls, and the Richmond Shene shook the night with rejoicing. Noblemen in the Royal Pavilion were bowing to the Queen, and throwing their hats up into the night air like dud fireworks.

Doll waited again, breathing so hard, the effort lifted the gauze of her attifet.

She wondered where Rupert was.

Triumff's guts were shifting uneasily in his torso. He was standing behind Jaspers in the fly of the tiring tent, with de Tongfort's sword pressed against his neck. Jaspers was moaning something at the talisman in his sweaty hands, and it was this indistinct noise that unsettled him. He felt like he had done when Woolly had tested him with the obscene parchment. There was Goety flowing through the air, of that he had no doubt.

From where he stood, he could see Doll on stage, searing the crowd with her words, Alice Munton, Horace Cato and Mary Mercer at her feet.

Jaspers raised his hand and crushed the talisman into dust. The remnants sifted out of his fingers like sand, wafting away on the night breeze.

He stood and turned to face Triumff.

"All done," he said, through a leer, but his face was pallid and damp, as if he had run a marathon in a fur coat.

"What's all done?" Triumff asked.

"Look at Cato," Jaspers told him, "the plump fool. There's a venomed arrow in his quiver. In a few moments, he will use it."

"Cato is party to your plot, then?" asked Triumff.

Jaspers laughed at him.

"Him? Not willingly," he said, "but I have just sent an arch demon of hell into his unsuspecting soul. It will tell him what to do."

Triumff looked through the flaps at Cato. He looked hot and uncomfortable, distracted and bothered. His hand on the bow was trembling, and he was reaching towards the quiver slung over his pudgy buttocks. Triumff realised that no one in the audience would notice. They were too busy clamouring for Doll.

Cato drew an arrow from his pouch.

Triumff gently reached down with his left hand, and took hold of the pommel of the Couteau Swiss that was hanging from his belt. He pressed the trigger.

The weapon did not develop a rapier blade as he had hoped. It seemed incapable of doing that to order, or at the right moment.

It did, however, produce a ten-inch straight knife for carving roast meat. Four inches of it went into de Tongfort's thigh.

As the man howled, Triumff threw himself back against de Tongfort as hard as he could. De Tongfort's blade sliced a line over Triumff's ear, but he was too slow to stop the full force of the sea captain's assault.

The pair of them crashed to the ground. Ignoring the blood that was streaming down the side of his head, Triumff pounded his fist repeatedly into de Tongfort's face and stomach. Once de Tongfort was winded and gasping helplessly, Triumff leapt off him and snatched up the traitor's rapier. He turned. Jaspers was gone.

"Doll! Doll!" he screamed through the tent flap at the stage. The crowd drowned him out.

Artemis, Diana and Orion had all nocked their arrows, ready to fire them into the air, symbolically, as soon as Doll came out with the "Let us signify our love / And mark like cupid our desire / That Gloriana is most loved of all / Our Queen, our thirtieth Elizabeth" speech. But the crowd was roaring too much. She had to wait.

She smiled at Alice and Mary, ready with their up-pointing bows.

Horace Cato was ignoring her, nocking the barb that de Tongfort had given him. He was aiming up into the sky.

Maybe she had misread his odd behaviour…

She thought she heard someone calling her name over the din. It was her imagination, surely.

Then she heard something else, someone whistling the first few bars of the song about the Guinea Coast. Piercing, it cut through the noise of the crowd.

Doll went cold. Her pounding heart felt like it was hesitating.

It was the signal they had agreed. Doll looked around.

Horace Cato was lowering his aim.

THE TWENTY-FOURTH CHAPTER.
Never mind the bal-rogs.

Doll balled her fist, swung hard, and mashed Cato's nose. He flew backwards onto the stage.

His arrow sailed through the air in the opposite direction, and punctured the back of the scrolled throne, six inches above the Queen's head.

There was a sudden, complete silence.

It was followed by absolute pandemonium.

It seemed like everybody, every one of those thirty-seven thousand one hundred and sixty-three people in Richmond was either screaming and yelling, or running about, or both.

Doll backed away, her mouth wide.

Alice Munton was bawling like a baby.

Mary Mercer had fainted.

Horace Cato was writhing on the stage, nose a bloody pulp.

The musicians and the players had spilled out of their tents onto the stage, babbling and shouting as Militia men tried to push through them.

Rupert Triumff, sword in hand, leapt the colourfully decorated troyes and pushed his way through the mobbing crowd onto the apron. He grabbed Doll and hugged her.

"Well done, my love," he said into her hair.

"Oh God…" she began, pointing.

The players, the musicians, the Militia and the screaming women backed away.

Horace Cato wasn't himself. Whatever the Divine Jaspers had put into him to pollute his mind was trying to get out, or at least make itself more comfortable. Things bulged beneath his skin, and there was, in the horrified silence, a sound of bones grinding and moving. Cato got up. He swayed. He swelled. He stretched and contorted from unholy internal pressures.

Everyone, except Doll and Rupert, and a few members of the Militia, screamed and ran.

What had once been Horace Cato became an eight foot thing of gristle and breathing flesh. Air sucked into and out of it through a multitude of skinny flaps. Its arms were mostly bone and reached to the floor. Its legs had splayed like a tortoise's. Its head had extended, as if a horse's skull had pushed up through its neck to stretch and fill the skin of its head.

Suddenly it had jaws like a water-horse. It opened them, and Triumff and Doll watched as fangs erupted into place from the gums. They distinctly heard each one spring out like a nail hammered through a plank. It roared, and windows in the Palace shattered.

Triumff pushed Doll aside, and thrust de Tongfort's rapier at the creature.

The sword blade struck the beast. It melted.

Blobs of molten steel dripped onto the stage and burned through it. The creature shambled forward. It was bigger now, growing steadily. It was becoming a serpentine thing, with the tail of a crocodile. Horns sprouted from its brow.

Two members of the huscarl militia charged in downstage, and rammed their pikes into the monster. It swung around, opened its long jaws, and incinerated them with an exhalation of flames.

Triumff backed away. "Oh . bother," he murmured.

"Give me that," snapped Mother Grundy, snatching the arrow from de Quincey.

"Give that back! I must do something!" de Quincey wailed.

Mother Grundy took the quarrel, kissed the barb and muttered at it. Then she took the charm from around her neck, and began to tie it fast to the arrowhead.

"What is it?" de Quincey asked, gazing down at the stage below in horror.

"A draconian fiend," she replied.

"A dragon? A sodding *dragon*?"

"A fire-drake," she said. "It has been conjured here, and put in that poor devil's flesh. Such a thing hasn't walked in God's air in many an age. I only know its like from books. It is one of the pit fiends, perhaps a bale-rogue, or bal-rog as the Babylonians called it."

"It will burn our souls away!" de Quincey announced, unable to tear his gaze from the rapidly growing reptilian beast.

"It will most likely try," Mother Grundy agreed.

She passed the arrow back to de Quincey.

"I hope you're a good shot," she commented.

De Quincey had never fired a crossbow before in his life.

"Of course I am," he decided.

Triumff backed away across the stage as the blasphemous monstrosity advanced. He had thrown the hilt of his melted sword at it, and then snatched up a taper-brand from the footlights. He swung it at the creature, trying to drive it back.

He thought about the Couteau Suisse banging against his hip, but it was evident that even the finest metal blades were as useful as sugar-glass.

An atrocious, rattling hiss issued from the creature's deformed maw. Triumff felt it shake the organs in his chest. He glanced to each side, yelling to those miltia and noblemen who had been brave, or foolish, enough to stand with him.

"Get back! Get back! Get Her Majesty to safety!" he shouted.

He caught sight of Doll, a little way behind him.

"Doll! Get out of here, I beg you! Run!" he insisted.

The creature swung its bulk around on its elongated, scrawny limbs. A roaring cone of flame belched from its jaws, and Triumff threw himself flat to evade it. The taper bounced from his hand.

The monster was right over him. He scrambled and slithered, but it was futile. Foetid breath, rank with the smell of bitumen and burnt sugar, stung his eyes.

Triumff tried to think of something philosophical and uplifting, but his mind had seized up like a rusted lock, and refused to turn. Eyes wide, he scrambled backwards, looking at the vision of hell as it swept its jaws down at him.

The impact was sudden, and made a very distinct, pop.

The creature convulsed.

The head of a crossbow quarrel poked out of the centre of its throat, sticky with lime-green ichor.

Triumff stared at it in fascination, noticing the tiny charm wound tightly around its point.

The creature fell to its knees so hard that the stage shuddered and cracked. Triumff threw himself out from under it, and almost off the side of the apron. The creature sank backwards, and thrashed its tail, ripping down scenery flats and strung lanterns. It threw up its huge skull. Its mouth opened wide to the night sky, and screamed in Horace Cato's voice.

Triumff felt hands grab at him and drag him back off the sill of the stage. He couldn't take his eyes off the screaming beast.

The scream continued, and rose in pitch, powered by a lung capacity far greater than any human's. Tongues of blue flame licked around the creature's open mouth, and its wound. It raised its swaying arms, and held them aloft like the twisted ribs of a great fish.

Then it imploded.

Triumff's ears rang with the sound. It was as if nature had opened up to consume the creature. Every taper, every lamp, every candle in the arena went out, their flames sucked into the implosion. Then the awning collapsed across the stage, mercifully covering the rotten, liquescent remains left in the wake of the detonation.

It was, thereafter, abruptly very cold, and very quiet.

Triumff looked up, and saw it was Doll who had dragged him off the stage. She was pale and shocked, gazing at the destruction before them. He pulled her to him, and held her tight as she started to shake.

Cardinal Woolly began to bellow at the shocked crowd of nobles and guards that stood around in the ruins of the Pavilion. Lord Crowsley, Lord Greff and Admiral Poley sprang into action, formed up an honour-guard of gawping huscarls, and escorted the Queen to the safety of the Cairngorm Tower. The Queen said nothing, but as she hurried away, Triumff caught her gaze. She looked back through the thicket of Militia around her.

Sir Rupert Triumff nodded a head-bow to her, but she was gone a moment later.

Woolly stepped down into the centre of the torn-up auditorium.

"Lights! Get some lights here!" he said. "Find me the guard captain! I want this area secure now!"

They could all hear the rumbling confusion in the distance as panic cleared the Shene and Richmond. Most of the Masque guests had fled, taking their chances with the milling crowds beyond the walls.

The Palace grounds were a tattered wasteland of over-thrown seats, torn decorations, spilt food and discarded programmes. Those that remained stood in quiet, astonished huddles, unable to take in the events that had unfolded around them.

Triumff looked around as Woolly clasped his shoulder. The cardinal was shaken, and clearly torn between fear and anger, but there was a bright, grateful look in his eyes too.

"Not quite as good as last year, your worship," Triumff murmured. Huscarls hurried around lighting tapers.

"When I learn who is responsible for this–" Woolly began.

"The Divine Jaspers, for one," Triumff interrupted.

"The damned Church!" spat Lord Slee from nearby. "I might've known. And what is your part in this evil sham, Woolly?"

Woolly swung around slowly to face the Chancellor. Triumff thought the cardinal was going to strike Slee.

"I believe Lord Slee is about to remark upon the obscene and incriminating parchment concealed about your person," said a thin, panting voice from nearby.

They all turned.

Lord Callum Gull approached them across the stage. His rapier dragged from one hand, and he clutched his belly with the other. They could all see the blood soaking his arm and doublet front. His countenance was pale, his walk unsteady, and he was breathing hard, his face knotted in pain.

"It implicates you as the ringleader of this obscenity, cardinal," Gull said, sucking in each breath. "It is a damning document. Lord Slee knows that it will have you dragged to the headsman in the morning. He knows it, because he placed it there."

"This," said Slee, his lips curling back across his teeth, "is the most outrageous slander I have ever heard! Trust you to have a lackey come out on cue and defend your black-stained soul! The man is a liar, and you, Woolly, are the blight of this land!"

"I'm many things, Slee," said Gull, thumping down the stage steps, heavily, "but I'm no liar. This is your handiwork. You were in this with Jaspers, and with that bastard son of Castile, de la Vega. De la Vega told me all this himself."

He paused.

"Just before he died on the steel of my rapier," he finished.

"Nonsense! Lies! Conspiracy!" cried Slee, wheeling around and staring at the shocked, silent crowd gathered around them. "De la Vega is a loyal man! I am a loyal man! These devious murderers are in this together! See how they conveniently cover their backs, and silence loyal subjects who might expose their treason!"

"There were four traitors, actually," said de Quincey as he and Mother Grundy strode in through the gap beside the VIP tent. De Quincey was looking fiercer than Gull had ever seen him. He carried a crossbow in his hand.

"And you, sir, are?" asked Cardinal Woolly.

"Neville de Quincey, Police Surgeon," he said. "This is Mother Grundy, from Suffolk. She has been most efficacious in combating this evil."

"Mother Grundy," the cardinal said with a nod.

"Your Worship," responded the old woman. "Neville here is quite correct. And a damn fine shot, if I might add."

"We were following up investigations with Lord Gull," said de Quincey. "We have evidence that shows the conspiracy was led by Lord Slee, Regent de la Vega, the Divine Jaspers, and Lord Salisbury."

"I can corroborate Jaspers's involvement," said Triumff, "and you'd better hunt out a stage manager from the Swan called de Tongfort, too. He's one of Jaspers's henchmen. The son of a bitch gave me this," he added, touching the wound on his scalp.

"Clap Lord Slee in irons," said Woolly, in a voice that was so quiet it was terrifying.

"You bastards!" yelled Slee, pulling a long dagger from his cloak. His face was livid, and the veins on his temple pulsed visibly. "Any man that touches me will die in agony! This blade is laced with venom!"

The nobles and huscarls around Slee backed off, unwilling to enjoy a slow, screaming death. Slee broke from them, and ran. He hurtled through the Royal Pavilion, tore an exit through the canvas with his blade, and sprinted into the dark gardens beyond.

A shadow stood in his way.

"Aside, I say! I'll kill you!" Slee shrieked, foam flecking his lips.

Eastwoodho shook his head slowly, and thumbed back the hammer of his sidearm. His eyes narrowed to papercuts.

"Are you feeling opportune?" he asked.

Slee went for him like a rabid animal.

"I guess not," said Clinton Eastwoodho.

Everyone in the shattered arena jumped at the sound of the gunshot from beyond the tent.

Woolly turned away, and fixed his gaze on Salisbury, who still sat, alone, on the bench in the VIP marquee. Every eye followed the cardinal's gaze.

Salisbury got to his feet, raised his glass, and toasted the company. Then he emptied it down his throat.

"Take me away," he sighed. "I've got no stomach for this."

The guards surrounded him.

Mother Grundy approached Cardinal Woolly, as de Quincey helped Lord Gull to a seat at the stage edge, and saw to his wounds.

"The Divine must be found with all haste," she began.

"Because he has one more of those trinkets," Triumff finished, joining them.

"Indeed he does, young man," said Mother Grundy, turning to him.

"He could be anywhere," said the cardinal, wiping his brow. "Thousands of people are fleeing Richmond at this very moment. A creature as gifted as Jaspers could lose himself among them. Where would we begin to search?"

"The river," said a small voice from behind him.

As you will have realised by now, gentle reader, my part in this Night of Infamy is nowhere near as heroic as Sir Rupert's, Doll's, Mr de Quincey's or Lord Gull's, but this was my moment of greatness. I urge you to savour it. I certainly do.

"When the panic began," said I, Wllm Beaver, "and the mob was fleeing hither and yon, I saw the Divine. He was racing for the Richmond Royal Stairs. There were boats at the quay there, I believe–"

"You old goat, you, Beaver!" cried Triumff, interrupting me to be sure, but nonetheless clapping me on the shoulder. I had hoped for "William, you Achilles, you!" but I can't complain. Well, I can. "You old goat, you!" won't look that great on a headstone in Poets' Corner.

"If he's already on the river, we won't catch him now," the cardinal began. "I'll–"

"We will, sir," said de Quincey, approaching them. "Mother Grundy knows how. If she'd... er... do it again. Ma'am?"

Mother Grundy nodded. "Of course, Neville. Make haste now, make merry come supper."

Cardinal Woolly frowned, working that through.

"I'll go with you pair," said Triumff. "I have unfinished business with Jaspers."

"Weren't you tending to Lord Gull, Police Surgeon de Quincey?" Woolly began.

"I can do that," said Doll. "I've been with Rupert long enough to know how to tend a sword cut." She crossed to Lord Gull, who looked up at her with a faint smile.

"Can I trust my life to Triumff's girl?" he muttered.

She glared down at him.

"You're in no position to be choosy, Gull," she replied.

With a chuckle, Gull got to his feet, leaning on her for support. He threw his bloody rapier across the arena to Triumff, who caught it neatly.

"That might help," he called.

Triumff nodded.

"It might indeed," he called back. "Ready?" he asked of de Quincey and Mother Grundy.

The three of them hurried away towards the Royal Steps as Woolly watched them go. His shoulders, which seemed to have been holding up the burden of the entire Earth, sagged.

He looked around and saw me, Wllm Beaver, pulling out his notepad and pencil.

"Not now, Master Beaver," he said, "not now."

"Don't flinch! Be a man!" Doll told Lord Gull.

He looked up at her, an eyebrow arched.

"Let me see," she murmured, and managed to move his arm aside.

The wound to Gull's stomach was deep and bloody.

"He didn't let you off easily, did he?" she asked as she dressed it.

"No," sighed Gull.

"Then why do you smile, Lord Gull?" asked Doll.

"Because the Queen is alive. Because I won. Such things make it worthwhile for a soldier to smile."

"And my name's Callum, Miss Taresheet," he added.

"Is that so?" She sniped at him. "I'm Doll."

He smiled again. "Rupert Triumff is a fortunate man," he remarked obliquely.

A shadow fell across them.

"Miss Taresheet? Where might I find Master Rupert?"

"Agnew! What are you doing here?" asked Doll.

"My best, lady. And Master Rupert?" he asked again.

"Gone to the river," said Doll, "chasing that vile Jaspers. Agnew?"

She called his name, but he had already gone.

The elms were swaying and singing in the wind, and the Palace walls were dark cliffs beyond them. Agnew hurried over to the figures huddled in the lea of the wall.

"So where's Rupert?" Uptil asked anxiously.

"Gone after Jaspers, on the river." Agnew said, glancing around.

"Then we have to get after him," said Uptil. The figure behind them growled softly.

"Where's Master Bluett gone?" asked Agnew.

"He said that he had his own business to attend to," said Uptil. "We can't afford to wait for him. Let's go."

Bonville de Tongfort limped silently down the damp stone steps of the Maze Approach. The swell of noise from the

Palace grounds and the Shene outside was fading.

He felt sick. His leg hurt like a bastard from the stab-wound Triumff had given him, and his face and stomach ached.

He felt alone, but he wasn't.

"De Tongfort?" a voice called from the dark undergrowth by his side.

De Tongfort spun around, his rapier up and glinting in the starlight.

The storta swung out of nowhere, whistling in the still air.

Bonville de Tongfort felt his toes clench. This was remarkable, because his head was currently detached, and heading for the ground.

There was a thump, followed by a slower impact.

Drew Bluett leaned on his sword and sighed, his weariness and the pain of his bruises overwhelming him like a tide.

"Got you at last," he breathed.

THE TWENTY-FIFTH CHAPTER.

At Battersea.

The sky above the City was lit volcanically, and gunpowder scented the down-river wind. News of the calamity at Richmond had not yet reached the City, and the festivities were continuing unabated.

Ferocious fireworks of every conceivable colour and magnitude fractured the night sky, supplemented by cannonades from the troops and retainers along the riverside. The London sky glowed with the warmth of a thousand bonfires and a million tapers, not to mention one or two burning buildings.

From the prow of the speeding wherry, Triumff watched the vast display, smiling as dying firerockets hooted and wailed down out of the multi-coloured, smoky night. The bright waters of the Thames mirrored every flash and star, and surge and detonation above. It reminded Rupert of the heart of a naval engagement.

It also took his mind off the fact that they were moving, oarless, down the river at something close to ten knots.

Triumff moved back from the prow. Mother Grundy was sitting, arms folded, in the stern chair, watching the passing banks. De Quincey was sitting in an oarsman's place, trying in vain to stoke and light his pipe. The wherry's slipstream kept extinguishing his tinder strikes.

"No sign," reported Triumff, sitting by de Quincey. "He could have put ashore already, anywhere. We might have passed him."

"To keep this far ahead of us," said Mother Grundy, "he must be using a similar means of propulsion."

Triumff began to ask her about that, and then thought better of it. There were some things he felt he didn't need to know.

Mother Grundy held out a skinny hand. In the open palm lay a small gemstone. It twitched slightly, with a life of its own.

"This lodestone is responding to the Goety he has left in his wake. He's still ahead of us, have no doubt."

"But this far down-river," de Quincey began, giving up on his pipe altogether. "We'll be under the Great Bridge in a minute or so. Is he heading for the sea, do you think? A waiting ship to speed him away?"

Triumff shook his head.

"I doubt that," he replied. "Jaspers was so confident of success, I'd wager he made no contingency for escape. No, my guess is, he's set upon one last mission... an act of malice, of spite... in revenge for his scuppered plan."

De Quincey frowned at Triumff.

"You've got an idea, haven't you?" he asked.

"There's a place he has struck at before," said Triumff, "somewhere rich in arcane power, somewhere his particular talents can do the most harm."

"The Powerdrome," said Mother Grundy.

Triumff nodded, and said, "It has to be."

"Lord save us all," murmured de Quincey.

Above them, coloured fire continued to split the sky, as if the heavens themselves were at war.

Dominating the great curve of the Thames at Battersea, the Powerdrome had been designed by Sir Christopher Wren in 1671. It was as famous a landmark of London as the White Tower or Hardy's Column. The three great smoke-stacks, provided to vent off the exhaust of the Cantriptic reaction, made it look for all the world like a giant, upturned milking stool.

It loomed over them, impassive and silent, its stonework flickering in the sidelight of the firework bombardment.

The wherry bumped gently against the low quay, and Triumff sprang nimbly over the rail to tie up the rope that de Quincey handed out. Mother Grundy leaned over the stern, and fluttered a handful of dried petals into the dark water.

"What is she doi–" Triumff began, but shut up when he caught de Quincey's look.

Together, they helped Mother Grundy onto the landing, and made haste towards the drome's entrance yard.

A full ten yards from the edge of the quay, they passed another wherry. It was leaning on the stones, its belly raked and broken from its passage across the landingway, a passage evidenced by long gouges across the quay.

"He was in a hurry," mused Triumff with an unconvincing grin. "He didn't even stop when the water ran out."

De Quincey scratched the back of his scalp nervously, and swallowed hard. "He's… er… not going to be easy to tackle, is he?"

"Nope," said Triumff, unsheathing Gull's beautiful rapier, "but then neither am I." The naked weapon didn't make de Quincey feel very much better.

"A word of caution, Sir Rupert," said Mother Grundy quietly. "Over-confidence is the handmaid of disaster."

"Really?" asked Triumff.

"I mean it, sir," she insisted, and there was a quality to her voice that left neither man in any doubt that she did. "A man with a sword, even a brave man, is no match for that creature Jaspers. Please, attempt nothing rash. Be advised by me as we go. I may be a frail old dam from Suffolk, but I know my Arte. My knowledge may be the only weapon we have."

"And," she added, completely unnecessarily in de Quincey's opinion, "even that might be far from enough."

They passed under the arch of the river gatehouse. The drome's great yard opened before them, and beyond it, the massive entranceway yawned like a mouth.

The curtain walls shielded them from the worst of the tumult down-river. It was unnervingly quiet in the yard, and there was a smell, one that even the inexperienced nostrils of de Quincey and Triumff could recognise. It was the smell of rank sugar, molten and burnt, of caramelised syrup.

There were two lumpy shapes in the yard in front of the entrance steps. De Quincey took them to be piles of rubbish, until he stooped to check.

He started back, a resilience, conditioned by twenty years of gruesome forensic examinations, overwhelmed in one unguarded moment.

The lumps were men. Or they had been men. They had been guild men, drome workers of the Old Union.

Something had melted them, and the remains of their robes were flecking away from the distorted bodies in the night breeze, dry as charred paper.

"They tried to stop him," de Quincey mumbled, bracing himself to act as professionally as possible, even though he knew his voice had a quake in it. "Those metal lumps in their... hands... were weapons. They were protecting the doorway. From the position of the... bodies... you can see–"

"We can see," Triumff said, gripping de Quincey's arm and pulling him away. "Look, maybe you should go back to the river. Cross to Chelsea, alert the Militia. They should know what's going on, in case we don't make it."

De Quincey shook his head.

"If we don't make it, sir," he said, "there'll be nothing any-one can do. Anyway, you might need me."

Triumff nodded, understanding completely, and moved on.

"God knows what for," added de Quincey under his breath.

They went up the steps and in under the entrance arch. The tapers in the hall wall-brackets had burned out, but there was light, a pallid, lambent glow that filtered through the stones all around them. It was a good ten degrees colder in-side than outside. White, sulphurous mist foamed the floor around their ankles.

"Has he staged these creepy effects to put the wind up us?" Triumff asked.

Mother Grundy glared at him.

"He's at work in the Cantrip Chamber," she said. "He's boiling up the power spheres far beyond their operational ca-pacity. This phlogestonic mist is just a by-product of the process: a symptom, and a mild one at that. If he goes on, we'll see worse sights than this."

"Best guess, my lady, what's he trying?" de Quincey wanted to know.

"A meltdown of the Cantrip spheres, Neville? If he Goetically spurs them to melting point, the resultant implosion could leave a vast and smoking crater where the City used to be."

"Oh," said de Quincey, as if this was an interesting thing to know.

"It's called the Ind Syndrome," she continued. "The hypothesis is that if a Cantrip plant like this were to reach overload, it would melt down through the Earth, and eventually explode out of the other side, in India, one presumes."

"Hypothesis, eh? Has it ever, I mean, happened?" de Quincey ventured.

"No, but there was an accident in Wiltshire, recently. It was kept hush-hush, but I learned of it from a local witchlock there. It seems the Church tried to awaken and harness the old power rooted in the stones of the great Henge. Foolish, of course. The Henge power is raw, Druidic energy. It is not compatible with modern processes. It was a disaster, and many died. It could have been worse if they hadn't contained it."

"I heard the rumours," de Quincey nodded. "So it's true? Glory, I knew the Church was desperate for new Magick, but I never thought–"

"It wasn't the Church," said a voice from the shadows.

Triumff whirled, sword ready.

"Step out! Show yourself!" he commanded.

An elderly man in Union robes shuffled into the light. "Put up your sword, sir," he said. "I am Natterjack, of the Drome Union. Vivat Regina. I was hiding in the canteen. I heard your voices."

They stared at him for a moment.

"I've got credentials. Union papers. Hold on, then," he said, and began to rummage in his robes.

"Enough!" said Triumff. "I believe you, fellow. Quickly now, bring us up to speed. What's happening here?"

"Damned if I know," said Natterjack. "I was on a break, waiting for me tea to mash. Next thing, I hear screaming, and smell the smell. You know, the Smell. I came out here and found some of my best men dead as kippers, and the doors to the main chamber shut as tight as a duck's chuff.

"Begging-your-pardons-no-offence, madam," he added for Mother Grundy's benefit.

"Mister Natterjack," she replied, "be assured that I am more than passing conversant with the watertight nature of a duck's fundament. Please go on."

"Well, I tried to get in, and found no joy. Not that I really wanted to get in there, as it was. Then I tried to signal the proper authorities, but no one saw my flare," said Natterjack.

"There's a surprise," said Triumff. "And every witchboard operator in the City's taken the night off."

"Precisely. So it was a right to-do. Then the gentleman came in. He seemed to know his business, and was most keen. I showed him to the Chamber, and then retired to the canteen on his advice. He said I would be safer there, circumstances as given."

"He was lying," said de Quincey.

"What gentleman?" asked Triumff urgently. "What bloody gentleman?"

"An Eye-talian fellow," said Natterjack. "Most proper and polite, he was. Rendered me this lovely speech about the welfare of the Queen and Country, and the Fate of the Free World. And the Unity, I think he mentioned. Yes, certainly he did."

"Where is he now?" asked Mother Grundy.

"At the doors of the Chamber, as I left him," said Natterjack. "I'll show you, shall I?"

Natterjack led them off down the long hallway.

"Just out of interest," said de Quincey as they hurried along, "what did you mean when you said it wasn't the Church?"

"Well, they had no knowledge of the Wiltshire affair. My Union was called in to mop it all up, decontaminate and so on. God's bread, but it was a mess."

"Then who did it?" asked de Quincey.

"That great arse Lord Salisbury," said Natterjack. "He was trying to win favour at Court by igniting the old power. He got a slap on the knuckles and no mistake, but they decided to keep it all shtum."

"Hockrake," murmured Triumff. "He fails in his ambitious little plot and so lends his weight to this conspiracy instead. It all begins to mesh together, doesn't it? In a horrible sort of way."

They had reached the end of the passageway. The doors to the Cantrip Chamber were brand new: vast, interlocking plates of reinforced iron. They had been fused together, melted into one solid sheet.

"We only had them put in the other day," remarked Natterjack bitterly. "Look at them now. Look at them!"

Triumff looked. Strange chalk markings had been inscribed around the seized lock mechanism.

"What's this?" he asked.

"Please do not touch that," said a man emerging from the door of a side chamber with a lamp held aloft. He was a good-looking fellow in his thirties, but he showed the signs of extensive wear and tear. His fashionable clothes were soiled and ruined. He looked as if he had been dragged across Europe behind a refuse cart.

"I am Giuseppe Giuseppo," he announced, bowing low.

"Oh good," said Triumff, his grip on the rapier tight.

"Giuseppe Giuseppo?" said de Quincey. "*The* Giuseppe Giuseppo?"

"I believe so," said Giuseppe, bowing again. "I come from La Spezia, Italy. On urgent business. This business." He gestured towards the doors.

"You know him?" asked Triumff.

"He's the greatest inventor of the age," said de Quincey

with undisguised admiration. "I've read about his work in Scientific Italian. This is an honour indeed, sir!"

De Quincey shook hands with the Italian.

"I'm de Quincey, of the Royal Militia," said de Quincey. "This is Mother Grundy and Sir Rupert Triumff. Natterjack you've met."

"*The* Sir Rupert Triumff?" asked Giuseppe, raising his eyebrows. "The discoverer of Australia?"

"Yes. Yes. Yes," Triumff said, clapping his hand to his brow. "Look, I really hate to be brusque, but the Fate of the Free World and all that? I'm sure we can have a jolly good time getting to know each other over a bottle or ten of musket, later, but that really hinges on there being a later, doesn't it?"

"Indeed," said Giuseppe. "I was attempting to open these doors when you arrived. It is a difficult process. My guidebook is not altogether useful." He produced the Most Important Book In The World from his pocket and tapped its water-stained cover.

"What's wrong with it?" de Quincey asked.

"It fell in a pond. No, I fell in a pond, and it was with me. The ink has run. Certain passages are very indistinct."

"May I?" asked Mother Grundy, holding out her hand.

Giuseppe looked to de Quincey, who nodded meaningfully.

He handed the book to Mother Grundy. She flipped the pages, her eyes widening slightly.

"This is—" she began.

"Yes," said Giuseppe curtly.

Mother Grundy composed herself, and carefully studied the smudged pages in the half-light.

"I see from your chalk inscriptions that you were preparing the Charm of Access."

"Indeed," said Giuseppe, moving around to look over her shoulder at the book. "But as you can see, the notes here are all but washed away. Should it be a Ward of Forgiving? Or a simple Paracelsian sigil? And this arrangement here: is it a runic matrix or a congress of Sephirotic harmonies?"

"Chalk?" said Mother Grundy.

Giuseppe handed her the chalk.

She stepped forward and began to mark out signs on the door next to the ones he had already made.

"An Enochian key! Of course!" Giuseppe said, clapping his hands. "How is it you are versed in Leonardo's Arte, Mistress?"

"I'm not," said Mother Grundy. "I'm versed in Old Miriam's Wicca, for that was my training. The principles are related." She licked her finger and scrubbed out some lines, correcting the inscription.

"There," she said. "Let us withdraw."

They backed away. Smoke began to ooze from the area of the lock, and the iron doors began to shiver like sailcloth in a changeable wind.

"Ready?" asked Mother Grundy. Ready or not...

THE TWENTY-SIXTH CHAPTER.
The End of all these things.

Even in this modern and enlightened year of two thousand and ten, painfully little is really known about the workings of the Arte, or of its relationship to the material world we inhabit. As yet, mankind knows too little of the parameters of the Supernatural to begin to adduce its governing laws, and, furthermore, mankind is still in some doubt as to exactly what is supernatural and what isn't. Though the scientifical knowledge of our race has been furthered and enhanced by the works of Great Men like Newton, Dee, Rutherford, Beronza, Chaney and Hawkinge, mankind still has a tendency to class anything he does not readily understand as part of the machinations of the Invisible World. This may sound difficult to credit, but consider that, until Beronza published his work on the nature of applied gravity, people believed that falling over was caused by malevolent spirits.

Another hindrance to our understanding of the Arte was described by Doctor John Dee, when he remarked that Magick is not only more complex than we imagine, but it is also more complex than we *should* imagine. It is a popularly held axiom that mortal man simply hasn't the breadth of mind to comprehend the profound principles of Magick. To quote Dee's other famous aphorism, "Any sufficiently advanced jinx is likely to baffle the tits off a coypu."

This is not true, well, not entirely. Once in every century or so, an individual comes along who is actually capable of getting his enviable mind around the matter of the Arte. Or if not actually around it, then close enough to draw alongside and exchange pleasantries.

One such man, one such singular man, was Leonardo of Vinci, the often-lauded and seldom-understood progenitor of the Re-Awakening, whose scholarly endeavours broadened our understanding of Magick more than any other, and who made possible the everyday use of the Arte that we rely on today. It was he who first introduced the distinction between the prudent application of Magick, and the wanton abuse of its darker extremes, which we call Goety.

History records Leonardo as a fine, spirited man, tall and lean of limb, often given to flashes of inspiration. He spoke a number of languages, although never more than three at once, and was particularly partial to chicken, be they fried, braised or launched off the local battlements, pedalling furiously in experimental flying machines that looked for all the world like giant sycamore pods, until they hit the ground. Then they looked like messy servings of chicken in a basket. An accomplished artist, sculptor, designer and poker-player, Leonardo wrote many books on the subject of the Arte. As we have previously noted, one of those is now the Most Important Book In The World, and rather hard to come by.

Leonardo's most truly brilliant vision must surely have been his conviction that the Arte was but a natural manifestation of a greater, unfathomed Universe around us. History, who, again, was there at the time, recounts this as having taken place just after the Yule of fourteen eighty-four.

Leonardo was at home, spiritually famished by the ennui that overtakes us all after the great seasonal revelries, and was toying with the various gifts he had been given over the Christmastide period. These were of the usual fare: personalised retort stands and alembics from fellow scholars, and some vulgar paisley-patterned hose from a distant aunt.

Musing distractedly over the garish hose, the Master suddenly noted how the pattern resembled the so-called Sign of Mandelbrot, an emblem of the esoteric Zoroastrian belief that every tiny-most speck in the cosmos acted upon each other in a way that imperceptibly defined the structure and behaviour of our universe as a whole. Many called this Theoretical Chaos, even the Mandelbrotian Zoroastrians, though it is held they had a different connotation for the term.

All at once, and in a state of some excitement, the Master pulled on his new hose, and paraded around, theorising that, contrary to the popularly held belief that Magick was a latent, potential resource waiting for mankind to tap it, the Supernatural was in fact a not-yet-understood aspect of the Natural. He reasoned that the Universe was held together and operated by all its components, and that as Magick was one of those components, it was surely part of that process too. Further, he concluded, the Magick mankind encounters is but a symptom, a sign of some greater, universal machinery that binds the world together, and without which we wouldn't be.

In short, when man dabbles in the Arte, or in Goety, he is playing with the truest, most sublime forces of God's Creation. Once mankind had understood that Magick was not a dark and secret toy, but actually the visible processes of the Universe's great, unseen engine, Leonardo was sure that life in general would become a great deal more comprehensible, not to mention safer.

Shortly thereafter, he caught sight of himself in a mirror, and hurried to remove the hose before shame overcame him utterly. The incisive notion, however, never left him.

I trust my readers will tolerate this digression when I explain that I mention all this now for four reasons, the first being, it is high time someone set the record straight and snapped us out of our blinkered, superstitious attitudes. Secondly, it should reinforce, for us all, the infamy of what the Divine Jaspers is about in the Powerdrome's Cantriptic chamber. Misuse of a dangerous toy is bad enough. Wanton abuse of the mechanism of the Universe is the very darkest shade of evil.

Thirdly, it seemed the moment to do it. You deserved to know these facts, gentle reader, and there may not be time for them later.

Fourthly, and finally, it helps us to understand that when misguided mankind fiddles with the Arte – let's say some ancient, potent aspect of it like the Great Henge near Salisbury – it cannot but help affect the physical nature of the surroundings: bending, warping and refashioning to counterbalance its upset. All of which, I hope, goes some way to explaining the fact that when Uptil and Agnew arrived at the Powerdrome, they did so in the company of a six-foot cat in doublet and breeches.

The fireworks had not abated in the slightest, but Uptil and Agnew didn't notice them. The stonework of the Powerdrome, up whose entrance steps they were running, throbbed with deep-seated power, a vibration that seemed to shudder from the valves of Hell.

The air was dark, and charged with a thick soot that clogged the tongue and throat, and made them both gag. There was a scent to the air too, rich and sickening, and an ozone charge. *Bump-bump, bump-bump* went the stones around them, shaking to a seismic heartbeat.

Uptil was naked, and clutched his come-back so tightly that the bevelled edge bit into his finger-pads. Agnew had discarded his cloak in the thick air, and held a dirk he had been lent by the lighterman whose wherry they had commandeered. Already, the bright blade had been tarnished by the airborne soot.

"This is bad, isn't it?" muttered Uptil as they took the last few steps. Agnew nodded, but was too choked to talk. The entrance hall of the Powerdrome was a long, black cave, lit at the far end by a red, infernal glow. Just like the mouths of fire-breathing dragons are wont to do in fairy stories.

The third member of the trio sprang past them. Having dropped to all fours, he was pounding away in a manner unseemly for one in so finely tailored a pied-à-montaire ruff and cloth-of-gold peascod doublet.

"Wait, my friend! Caution!" called Agnew after the speeding quadruped. The Cat turned and fixed him with glinting yellow-agate eyes, each slit with a slender black-diamond pupil. It hissed something deep and feline back at him.

"Together!" rejoined Agnew as he and Uptil hurried to catch up with their unlikely ally. "In numbers there is strength."

The Cat nodded, a disconcerting mannerism in a cat, however large, and only prowled forward again when they were with him.

Uptil, as we have already recognised, was no expert on cats, but he found himself liking this one. Its eyes were bright and intelligent, its tail swished like a coachman's whip, and its fur was the most exquisite marmalade. For the first time in his noble life, Uptil had yearnings to keep a pet, but when the pet had a head bigger than his, teeth longer than his come-back and a bodyweight in excess of three hundred pounds, just who would end up keeping whom was a moot point.

"Come on," said Agnew, and led them down the grim hall-way towards the hellish glow.

The metal doors of the Cantriptic chamber lay just ahead. They overlapped one another, like the broken wings of a dead bird or the covers of a violently discarded book. They were smoking gently, and seemed limp and flaccid like wet paper.

Beyond them, the inferno burned.

An elderly man, in singed robes, was sprawled, coughing, in the threshold beyond the fallen doors. He looked up as they approached.

"Peace ho!" he challenged, coughing up gobs of viscous spittle. "I am Natterjack of the Union. Don't cross this threshold, friends, I implore thee."

He stopped short as the Cat reached him, and fixed him in a stare, eye to eye.

"Kiss my blind cheeks!" Natterjack observed, his gaze wide in amazement.

Agnew knelt by him.

"We are after Sir Rupert Triumff's party!" he said. "Are they within?"

"God save 'em, they must be!" answered the old man. "When the old dam and the Eye-talian melted down the door, they rushed in there. I followed them, but the smoke... The smoke..."

"Rest there, sir," said Agnew, getting up. "We'll deal with this."

"It wasn't just the smoke, you understand," added Natterjack. The trio paused and looked back at him. The Cat mewed softly.

"The whole world has come apart in there," said Natterjack in an empty, abyssal voice. They didn't ask him what he meant by it. They didn't want to know.

They plunged into the Cantriptic chamber. I just want to remind you here about my digression upon the nature of the Arte. Just don't say I didn't warn you.

They plunged into the Cantriptic chamber. Reality plummeted away.

Space and dimension seemed to have been stretched out by the weird effects of the overloading Cantrips. Perspective and depth were wrenched out to snapping point, and curled around, as if drawn up by Escher, or Ucello on acid. The nearby walls seemed to press down on their faces, while the furthest reach of the vast chamber seemed to lag out a mile or more away, bent through ninety degrees. Every line of architecture was straight and true, and yet the whole was warped beyond the fathoms of mortal eyes. The floor ahead sloped away steeply, yet they sensed no downhill slant as they moved forward. Red fire gouted up at them from the deep distance.

The central columns, marching away into an impossible vanishing point, were painted with relief grotesques in gold leaf. The plastered, chequered floor and the battened ceiling swam around them, like two chess boards about to slap together.

The air was full of howling voices, and none of them were human.

Gripping Uptil tight by the hand, Agnew floundered into the screaming void, the wind licking at his clothes.

"This is… bad, isn't it?" yelled Uptil over the howl.

"It's not getting any better," agreed Agnew.

A figure crouched just ahead of them in the thaumaturgic onslaught. They leaned into the wind, and fought their way to his side.

Agnew grabbed the bewildered man, bellowing into his ear over the roar.

"Sir Rupert! Where is he?"

"Down in that!" answered de Quincey, shielding his eyes against the surge. "God help us, but he's probably dead already!"

"Not Triumff," muttered Agnew confidently, his words torn out of his mouth and lost in the gale.

The cat shook itself and moved on past them, head down, hackles up.

Agnew and Uptil left de Quincey, and fought their way down the impossibly elongated room. The wind tore at them so hard that it was difficult to walk.

They came to Mother Grundy, who stood her ground, beset by the hurricane. She was casting her worst, her most potent and seldom-touched spells into the maelstrom, which ate them like popcorn. By her side, Giuseppe Giuseppo was holding up his little book with one hand to read from it, and had the other outstretched to deliver ferocious Magicks of his own into the storm.

Few things in nature could have withstood a massed assault of such power: the concerted sorcery of La Spezia and Ormsvile Nesbit.

Few things except this.

"It's not enough!" screamed Giuseppe. "Even together, it's not enough!"

"I know," she said.

Ahead of them all, Triumff waded deeper into the blistering blur of the storm's heart, Gull's sword in his hand. Just ahead, through the chaos, he could see Jaspers in the mutated space by the Cantrip altar, simpering at the talisman he clutched in his hands. The great orbs of Cantriptic power on the altar smoked, and glowed with infernal excitement.

Gripping the sword tight, Triumff lunged at Jaspers.

There was suddenly someone in his way. Triumff was facing himself. A smiling Triumff made of black and white light had risen to block Triumff's path.

"What the hell?" Triumff declared, recoiling.

A second black and white Triumff appeared, and then a third. As one, they raised their swords and came for him.

Triumff fought back, dancing on his feet as he tried to keep three swords at bay. All three of his mirror-foes were smiling the same sick smile.

He got under one guard, and performed the unnerving act of killing himself. The smiling black and white Triumff vanished with a pop of bad air.

The other two monochrome visions were still at him. Triumff dodged and fought to keep out of their sword-room. Gull's sword clashed with the phantom blades so fast and furiously that it sounded like someone shaking a sack of cutlery. One sword tip sliced into his thigh. The muscle immediately went cold and distant.

Triumff lashed out, decapitating one of his phantom selves, which vanished like a collapsing mist. Two more black and white Triumff's rose up in its place to meet him.

"Oh, this isn't fair!" Triumff shouted.

As he wheeled and duelled with his other selves, he saw Jaspers rise, crushing the last talisman in his fingers, crumbling out the dust. Jaspers was laughing.

"Triumff!" he bayed. "Late again!"

The Cantriptic cyclone seemed to shift up a gear, and the air around them started to boil and flicker.

With a curse, Triumff impaled one of his phantom selves, and smacked another reeling with a blow from his knuckle-bow. The third and final black and white ghost locked him in a ferocious round of thrust and parry. The sick smile never left its face, not even when he finally ran the blade of Gull's sword through its chest.

The thing popped and fizzled away, but the violence of its disintegration tore Gull's rapier from Triumff's grip.

With no time left to recover it, he leapt at Jaspers anyway.

The Divine, his mouth still twisted in a leer, met his assault with surprising strength. He staggered back only a step or two as Triumff slammed into him, and then resisted Triumff's pressure, gripping his arms and forcing him backwards. Triumff realised that there was no longer anything especially human about the thing he was confronting.

"What are you?" he hissed, straining with every ounce of strength left in him.

"The last thing you'll ever see!" laughed the Divine, and threw Triumff backwards.

Triumff struggled to rise, but Jaspers reached out an open palm, and a wall of pressure pinned Triumff down. He felt the invisible barrier pressing upon him, crushing him into the chequerboard floor, stifling him.

The Cat passed Triumff with a tigerish bound, and hit Jaspers like an alley cat taking a rat. It raked its claws across his torso and face. Jaspers shrieked in pain, his agony lost in the wind. At the same moment, the pressure relaxed, and Triumff was free to move again. He grabbed the Couteau Suisse from his waist.

"A rapier? First time? Just this once?" he pleaded at it as he pressed the trigger.

Jaspers regained his footing and knocked the Cat aside. His robes were claw-torn across his chest and soaked in blood. One stripe of the Cat's claws had put a cut down Jaspers's face so nasty, it had almost hooked out his eye. Venomously, he blasted Magick at the Cat, and sent the animal tumbling across the room.

The Couteau Suisse did not produce a rapier blade as instructed. It instead sprouted a long, sleek whaler's harpoon of bright steel.

"You'll do," he said, hefting it up.

"Jaspers!" he yelled. "Stop this now! Stop this now, damn you!"

"I'm afraid I can't help you!" Jaspers yelled back.

"You already haven't," Triumff replied, and hurled the Couteau Suisse, point first.

Only the basket guard prevented the sharp missile from passing entirely through Jaspers's body. He reeled with the impact, and then turned, slowly, until he was facing the pulsing, blinding altar. He reached up to the weapon embedded in his chest, his hands wet with his own blood.

Then he pitched forward, head first, into the Cantriptic orbs.

Despite the riotous festivities in the City, all of London heard the boom. From one side of the Square Mile to the other, the revellers stopped what they were doing, drink or pipe or taper or skyrocket in hand, and turned to look south-west.

A ring of fire, a doughnut-shaped crown of white-green fire, surged up into the vault of night, mocking the sputtering, sparking fires of the festival. A reverberative boom thumped across the City sky, shaking casements, rattling tiles, echoing along streets and off the vast monuments of St Paul's and the Abbey. The boom echoed on, shaking away into the night, and the Shires beyond London, like the footsteps of a giant out there in the dark.

Those close to the river saw the Powerdrome ablaze with green fire, and cried out the loudest "oooohhh" of the night as one of the great smokestacks leaned and tumbled into the Thames tide.

The great ring of fire overhead dissipated and burned out.

In that single instant, all London sobered up, and knew, with uneasy heart, that something of note had just occurred. Something momentous had just come to an end, but no one was quite sure what.

CHAPTER THE LAST.
Afterwards.

There is money in ignorance.

This fact I have been fortunate to discover since the incidents I have just related for you.

Every soul in London and beyond wanted to know in detail the events of those bloody few days, and few members of the journalistic trade were in such a well-informed position to tell the tale as I, your servant, Wllm Beaver. From dawn on Aftermath Sunday, I began my work, compiling the evidence and the tale for public examination. Of course, in briefer articles, other less-informed reporters have related the events in the broadsheets and pamphlets. This is the first time the entire story has been described within one cover.

Thanks must go to Sir Rupert, ultimately the hero of the hour, who first drew me into this affair, and then, in the tea house on Skitter Lane, suggested I become the custodian of posterity.

So then: a ring of fire that scorched the heavens, a resounding boom that split the sky, a city full of people turning their faces upwards in astonishment. In such a way was it done with. At five and twenty past one o'clock in the morning of Sunday, the fourteenth of May, two thousand and nine, the infernal threat to both Her Majesty and the City of London was overthrown.

Of course, no ending is ever clean. There are other matters, which must be tied up before I lay down my pen.

London was without power for all of Sunday and into Monday, before a Union gang under the command of Natterjack (whose fortitude, stamina and gymnastic fluency with English vulgarity were remarked upon by all) were able to restore a partial supply from a Powerdrome substation at Westminster. Emergency auxiliary stations were being put together on sites across the City. The Powerdrome would be out of commission for at least a year, and the Exchequer coffers would be vexed to afford the rebuilding.

For many days more, a pall of smoke hung over the town, legacy of the boisterous fireworks and the detonation at Battersea. The sun wheezed and blinked down through the rosy smog, and, for a while, people got used to the smell of black-powder and charred sugar.

Around the twenty-ninth, a westerly wind took up, and cleansed the City's air at last, breezing the sky porcelain-blue again, and puffing away the traces of soot. It carried away the last vestiges of Lord Slee's curse, and took with it, out of the Thames estuary and to the sea, a number of ships from the Deptford yards. The *Seagrim*, under the command of Captain Granville Dymoke, was to make haste for Spain, to present a formal report of events to the Escorial. Ambassador Chantain of the Diplomatic School was aboard to make sure the statements and details were unfolded in proper mien, and a detachment of Royal Huscarls was aboard to make sure the noble house of de la Vega didn't quibble about making reparations for the late Regent's part in the affair. The *Great Harriet*, commanded by Commodore Renard, put out for the

Mediterranean, returning a certain resident of La Spezia home with an honour guard. And the *Blameless*...

But I'm getting ahead of myself.

On the Monday morning following the Masque, as an army of household staff attacked the lawns and fields of Richmond with brooms and shoulder-slung litter baskets, Sir Rupert attended the cardinal at the Palace. The tents and marquees were being disassembled and loaded onto ox-carts. Chamber attendants were stripping the Palace walls of bunting. There was a jaunty air to the place: a busy, milling throng of tired, but spirited people.

Sir Rupert left his horse with an ostler in the Privy Yard, and strode along the main pathway towards the great closed tennis-play, which Woolly had converted into his inquest offices.

The workload before the cardinal was immense: the repairs, the political wheeling that would follow the new vacancies at Court, the inquests into how the conspiracy got so far, the thorough review of Church security, the general and Herculean acts of appeasement and public relations that would have to be undertaken to stabilise society at large.

Canvas sheets and matting had been laid down over the play's polished boards, and a score of junior secretaries and curial officers sat at rows of desks, sorting through documents, and sifting information. Every few seconds another courier strode into the chamber, passing a predecessor on the way out, and delivered more reports to the clerical workers. Intelligence was pouring in from all around the countryside, as parish after parish responded to the affair, and thoroughly checked itself over. So far, no further traces of the conspiracy had been found.

England was giving itself a medical, and the workers in the Richmond tennis-play were the cold probe of the stethoscope.

Triumff walked into the hive of industry, nodded to a couple of senior curates who recognised him, and made for the partitioned side-office at the end of play beneath the quarré. He could hear Woolly's voice from within.

The cardinal was at his desk, conversing with four curates and a secretary from the Privy Council. They seemed to be discussing a point of law, which, if carried over, would allow the Crown to seize Salisbury's lands as a penalty for his treason. Salisbury was doomed to meet with the axeman on Wednesday, and Woolly was deciding the fate of his heirs and dependants.

When he saw Triumff enter, Woolly dismissed the clerics, and ushered his guest to a seat.

Sir Rupert sat slowly, as carefully as his mending injuries would allow. Only a small bandage on his right hand gave away his hurt, but Woolly knew that a great deal more bandage wrapped his back, arms and thighs. The impact of Jaspers's body had exploded the Cantriptic orbs, and Triumff had been peppered by crystal shards before the force of the phlogestonic blast had lifted him sheer to the end of the chamber.

"I didn't expect you here so soon. Should you not be resting?"

Triumff shook his head.

"I have the Queen's own physician at my chamber door every quarter-hour," he said, "two of the Guild elders treating me to post-Goetic shock therapy, Agnew concocting every remedy in his damned family herbal, and Doll fussing around me as if I was a newborn babe."

Woolly smiled.

"You deserve no less, Sir Rupert," he said. "You have done the Unity a great service in the last days, at no small risk to yourself."

"This hour has had many heroes, your worship: Gull, de Quincey, the old dam from Suffolk, the Italian fellow…"

Woolly got to his feet, and smoothed his velvet gown.

"Indeed," he said, "and each will be rewarded and celebrated as is his or her due. Lord Gull is to be decorated and made a gift of lands. De Quincey is to be given a stipend and a promotion. Mother Grundy and Giuseppe Giuseppo, both of whom came to our aid unbidden, are to be rewarded with whatever they desire."

"But for them," said Triumff with heartfelt relief, "the Cantrip explosion would have levelled London. Only their Arte contained it and focused it up out of harm's way."

"So it would seem," Woolly said, frowning. "I would dearly love to know how they did that, but it would be churlish and unseemly to interview those who have selflessly aided us." Woolly reached into his desk drawer and produced two sealed envelopes and a small felt pouch.

"Other matters I can attend to now," he said, handing one of the envelopes to Triumff. "Please convey this to your man, Agnew. It is a letter of gratitude and commendation signed by Her Majesty. There is also a bank draft for twenty guineas that he may lavish on himself and your noble savage."

Triumff chuckled and took the envelope. Woolly handed him the second. "It is said, a third man assisted in their part of the affair, a man who perhaps was once of the Service. I will not press you concerning him, for I believe he lives in a clandestine manner. If you ever happen across him, give him this: twenty guineas, and an invitation to approach me once more. The Unity has need of honest, well-trained men in these days."

Woolly slid the pouch across the table. "For your lady, Mistress Taresheet, an item of jewellery from the Queen's jewelbox, which Her Majesty hopes will convey both her appreciation of the performance, and her gratitude for Mistress Taresheet's swift and successful action."

"You don't need to pay us all off, your worship. We did what we did because it mattered."

"And I do the same. Now your reward, Rupert. There will be the usual payments, decorations... but your true reward will be the one you most seek. I will discourage utterly the Court's ambitions on your discovery, Australia. I will ensure that it is left alone, for the reasons you gave."

Rupert looked the cardinal in the eye. There was little need for further speech.

"One last thing you must do for me, however," Woolly added. Triumff frowned, warily.

"To facilitate a swift resumption of public morale, we need a hero, one the people can rally around and be proud of. A PR exercise, really. We need to put a face on this. Of all the heroes in this piece, you are the most suitable candidate, and having been a hero once or twice before, I know you can pull it off."

"That means I'll have to be well behaved for a while, doesn't it?" asked Triumff.

Woolly nodded, and said, "Until they're tired of making up songs about you and wearing your likeness on their doublet fronts."

He paused, and waited for Triumff's reply.

Outside, the sun blazed down across the Richmond Green and the silver river beyond. High up, invisible, a lark was singing. London shone. Even in the Rouncey Mare, there was a brief moment of clearheadedness.

I, your humble servant Wllm Beaver, met Sir Rupert as he walked back through the Privy Gardens to the stables. He was in a good humour. I rose from the bench where I had been sitting scribbling, and fell into step with him. The air was full of the scent of lavender, and someone in the Palace kitchens was whistling a country air.

"William," he said.

"Sir Rupert."

"Doing as I suggested?"

"I am assembling all the facts. Once done, I will compose a fluid piece of heroic prose that will, I trust, do justice to this... this..."

He stopped and turned to me.

"Dog's dinner?" he suggested.

Inspiration had temporarily left me.

"Don't get lost for words now, Beaver," he said. "You've barely started."

"Sorry," I said. "And... one little thing. A question I have," I added.

He signalled that I should ask it.

"The Cat, the creature that your servant Agnew brought to the Powerdrome."

"It perished in the blast."

"That I know, poor thing." I paused. "My question is... what was it?"

"A casualty of greed, a victim of the violation of old Magick. A little time ago, Hockrake tried to rekindle the old power of Stonehenge," said Triumff.

"So I've heard."

"He failed. Magick leaked and twisted things. Things changed their forms. The Union had to clean up the mess."

I waited. I knew he was holding back on something. He was looking absently at the hazy spring sky, toying with the tassels on his gloves.

"Hockrake needed help in his crazed scheme. He faked official papers and persuaded a Churchman to conduct the misguided rite in the belief that it was by order of the Church Office."

He paused for a moment, and then looked at me sharply.

"I warn you, Beaver," he said, "you may not want to know this."

I said nothing.

"The Churchman was caught in the blast," he continued, after what felt like a very long pause. "His body was transformed by the hideous spill of power. In his unnatural new state, he sought revenge on those who had damned him so."

"And?" I asked.

"His name was Jaspers."

I swallowed once. "Jaspers? But then, who…?"

Triumff smiled his roguish smile, and winked.

"Or what? If we're lucky," he said, "we'll never know the answer to that, and if we're really truly lucky, flame and sword will keep it in the grave."

He saluted me, and strode away down the gravel path. As he disappeared from view behind the stable arch, I could hear that he was humming a song about the Guinea Coast.

That was the last time I saw him.

Until the next.

VIVAT REGINA.
FINIS.

ABOUT YOUR AUTHOR.

Dan Abnett is a bestselling writer of combat SF, and comics, foreign and domestic. He has an English degree from Oxford University, and has spent twenty years honing his several crafts. His work on *Torchwood* and *Doctor Who* projects have been particularly well-received, and his novels for Black Library, including the epic *Gaunt's Ghosts* series, are more than a little popular. He has adopted yet another voice to write original fiction for Angry Robot, and is currently working on the military science fiction epic, *Embedded*.

When he's not writing, or attending comic and games-related conventions, he can be found in the kitchen, cooking for his family, or in the ballroom, dancing with his wife. He lives and works in Kent, amongst a large, extended family, and his website is at *www.danabnett.com*

The AUTHOR Reflects Upon the Inception of *Triumff: Her Majesty's Hero*

Sir Rupert Triumff, along with his friends, colleagues and, even, enemies, has been an acquaintance of mine for a surprisingly long time. In fact, I cannot say with any degree of accuracy when I first met him, or under what precise circumstances. I think the chances are, it was right at the end of the 1980s, or the very start of the 1990s, when I was first finding gainful employment as a writer and editor in London. An idea flashed upon me, and I was taken with it.

It's the essence of *Triumff* that's been with me ever since. The actual material of his adventures, though, has metamorphosed and altered over the years.

There is something about his basic milieu that particularly appeals to me as a writer and a creator. As soon as I'd thought of it, I was captivated by its possibilities, and knew that, one way or another, it would be the foundation of a piece of work.

It's possible that I started writing an early draft of what would become the Triumff novel in the late 80s, and that I then adapted part of that text into several episodes' worth of full script for a comic book version that never saw print (although I got as far as collaborating with Simon Coleby, a comic book artist with whom I have worked, with great pleasure, regularly throughout my career). Simon and I certainly tried to get *Triumff* off the ground as a comic project, and he did some character sketches based on my scripts, although neither the scripts nor the sketches remain.

It's equally possible that I first envisioned *Triumff* as a comic, and that I only started to develop it as a novel, adapting the comic scripts I had already written, once I realised that no one wanted to buy an alternate history, magical fantasy, swashbuckling, Elizabethan adventure comic in 1989.

The point is, *Triumff* has been lurking in my brain for a long time, trying to find a way out.

Why has it persisted so? Well, as I have already said, the idea and the setting simply combine so many things that I find particularly appealing (hardly a surprise, seeing as I came up with it), but that doesn't really explain the perseverance of its appeal. I can only conclude that it's one or more of the following reasons:

1. It was an idea that I had at a very particular, formative point in my creative life, and therefore has left an indelible mark.

2. Sir Rupert Triumff is a persistent individual, and he was never going to let me get away that easily.

3. It was simply a good idea that needed to be written, sooner or later.

Whatever the reason, I'm glad it stuck around, and I'm delighted to have this opportunity to finally let it see the light of day. Taking all those old pages of notes, unfinished drafts, scraps and notebooks and half-remembered scenes, and turning them into a coherent novel has felt both like a catharsis and an exorcism, and I feel I've really owed it to the old bugger. I hope you, constant reader, have enjoyed the result of my labour as much as I enjoyed the labouring.

The trouble is, of course, that I've let him out now. I'm not entirely sure that he's ever going to go away again.

Dan Abnett
Maidstone, September, 2009

A ROOM OF THINE OWN

from The Greater City of London Gazette
& Advertizer, *issue of* 10th January, 2010

This week, *the chambers of the celebrated journalist and biographer, Wllm Beaver Esq.*

As you can see, gentle reader, I abide in a loft apartment on Fleet Street. The area suits me just fine given that I am, of course, a person of the press. I am just a few flights up from the street level, and I do enjoy the wonderful, evocative and apparently constant aroma of subcontinental cuisine.

Well, here you have it, lock, estoc and barrel, as they say in the stews. It's an **open-plan** space, so I can both sit and bed, or bed and sit, as is both fancy and fashionable in this modern era. To here, the kitchen area, and to there, the water closet. I have a bathing room cox and box with Pam the Shriver, who lives down the hall from me.

This trinket on the credenza is a dispenser of the dry, tablet confectionary **Pez**, which I acquired when I was working as a fact-checker on the *Doctor Johnston's Dictionary Part-Work* (fifty-two readily affordable weekly instalments). You'll notice that the head is in the shape of Victor Kiam, whose *Rubaiyat* I so treasure.

On this shelf, under the slit window, I keep a copy of a **book** that my neighbour Pam lent me. It's a codex of self-help, that I presume she hopes will help me. It is entitled *Seven Steps to Instant Happinesse!*, though I feel that, if it takes seven steps, it is hardly instant.

Upon here, beside my desk, is an "action figure doll", which was given to me by none other than **Sir Rupert Triumff** himself. As you may know, I am lucky enough to have secured the position of being Sir Rupert's official biographist. I am only just beginning to enfold his multifarious adventures for the publik benefit. This "doll" – though no girl-child's dolly, I insist! – is a finely chiselled mannequin of most exquisite detailing, fashioned for boy's play. It is from the popular "Man of Action" line, and it features the likeness of Lord Gull, complete with kilt, rapier, Stornoway black pudding, and realistic ruff. Sir Rupert suggested to me that it had fifty per cent too many ears for strict accuracy.

I am keen to acquire the "codpiece and doublet play-set" that accompanies this fine scale toy, and I understand there is also a "Stout Cortez" model in the same series, which possesses eagle eyes, presumably for staring at the Pacific with all his men.

For listening enjoyment, I like many things to be placed upon my **wax cylinder**. Currently, I am particularly taken with the works of the young Diseased Rascal, Lady Geegaw, and of course Puce.

Ah, this? Well, yes, it was gifted to me by Lady Mondegreen when I was covering Lord Mandelbrott's set at court. We were having supper at Foccacia in the Rye when she **presented** me with it. It's a bottle of A Scent of Man. I love the smell, but I won't wear it. That's what Sir Rupert wears.

About **town**? Well, tomorrow, it's a toss up between *Look Back in Manga* at the Oh (I hear the eyes and breasts are all too large) or *Hiroshima Monobrow* at the Royal Court. After that, I hope to take in a late gig, possibly the all-girl viol band Undersmile, who are playing at Hobohemia.

Why, yes, I do have a strenuous **beauty regime**. I like to cleanse, facially, with Jojoba's Witness, and then moisturise with Elizabeth In The Forest Of Arden products.

And so to bed... and there's nothing I like better than cuddling up with Rimbaud. Maybe the original, *First Blood*.

yrs,
Wllm Beaver, esq.

THE DOUBLE FALSEHOOD

Your humble author, Wllm Beaver, does not quite know where Sir Rupert's adventures might take him next… but here is one possible start:

THE MIME *of the* ANCIENT MARINER

The sinking winter sun was just shewing across the naked larches at the head of the field, and frost skinned the landscape like settled chalk-dust. Ormsvile Nesbit, a village whose place it was in the general scheme of things to be overlooked, clung to the nap of the Suffolk hill as if it were in danger of slipping off.

This fear was well-founded. Many times in Ormsvile Nesbit's long and lack-lustre past, it had so nearly slipped away into the soil, and become nothing but a ghost etching on the open fields, a feint trace of ploughed-under walls that only those gifted in archaeology or braille could ever have read.

Those threats to the village's welfare had come in many shapes over the years. In the distant pre-Unity age, lost (and slightly embarrassed) Vikings had plundered it twice as they roamed the Suffolk countryside, looking for a coast that they seemed to have mislaid[1]. Then there had been Plague, on what seemed an unfair number of occasions. In 1240, the population of the village

---

1 The bloody career of Olaf Waywardson and his navigator, Tor Cackhand, is well documented in other, better annotated books.

dropped to five, and two of those were geese. Window Tax blighted then, as did Tin Tax and Tax Tax[2]. During the Sixty Years War, army recruiters managed to muster the entire village and march them off to Yaresborough until half a dozen or so of them remembered they had left the supper on. Then the lamentable Leek Famine of 1911 hit them hard. In recent memory, the Great Fire of Ormsvile Nesbit, caused by a nervous heffer called Nettie and a badly positioned tallow lamp, had nearly done the trick.

But always, somehow, it clung on. Such is the tenacity of these tiny, isolated pockets of rural England: the fierce will to survive is bred in the bone.

For the last – well, it would be improper to record exactly how long, that being a lady's prerogative – for the last little while, the village fate has rested in the spindly hands of Mother Grundy.

Mother Grundy. "She's as old as the church weather cock," they say, and the similarity doesn't end there. She is hard, slender, angular, spiky… beaten from whatever precious mettle Ormsvile Nesbit mines up through its genes. And she turns with the wind. Her philosophy – and my! but she has a great deal of that – is to accept the cruel vagaries of life and never fight against them when such a fight is futile. "Turn and bend", "Forgive and forget"… this is the sort of thing she will say. "The willow stands when the oak has blown over." "A dandelion bows before the mower, and springs back up when the surly grass is cut." Honestly, that's the sort of attitude she has. I know the woman. I have her manner well.

However, she deserves no scorn for these sayings nor this philosophy of life. Mother Grundy has seen enough to know that poor folk in a poor village in an impoverished corner of the Realm will only survive if they adapt and roll with the blows. This is, if my Classical schooling has not failed me, called Stoicism. Mother Grundy calls it "the survival of the fittest." Neither I, nor any of her villagers, have any idea where that well-turned phrase comes from.

So, it is Mother Grundy who supervises the village fate. However, she leaves the Village Fete to Mrs Ambussway at number nine, as she "can't do blithering everything."

---

2 Levied by Cardinal Scunge, also called "The Pisstaker".

Mother Grundy is a fixture of the landscape, as permanent as the aforementioned weather cock (lightning permitting) or the long stones at Fulke's Barrow. She personifies the spirit of the village, and the villagers are used to her, reassured by her. They see her striding out across the cold fields, as stark and straight and bare as a long tooth in a beggar's ruined gumline. They turn to her for advice, they hide from her when they have wronged, and they come to her when they need help. She advises. She helps. She also always knows when they've erred.

It's not her job or her duty, or even something she is vocationally drawn to do.

She does it.

That's all. She just does it, because it needs to be done.

The pressing concern on that Michaelmas was not the state of the turkey[3], nor the decoration of the village tree. Luckin Ambussway, four year-old son of Agfnes[4], the eldest daughter of Mrs Ambussway at number nine, was suffering from a milk tooth that simply refused to acknowledge the post-toddler growth of its owner.

By the warming fireside of Mother Grundy's cottage, Luckin Ambussway sat patiently on a milk stool as Mother Grundy finally gave up on her herbal remedies and tied a loop of cotton around the recalcitrant tooth. She was just attaching the other end to the latch of her parlour door, when Fortunate Joseph hurried in out of the biting Michaelmas wind.

---

3 Livy Coolms had already plucked and stuffed it, once Arthur Knite had despatched it with his patent pending "Humane Fowle Killer" (consisting of a sharp hatchet, a blindfold and a crowd of people shouting "To your left! Ahead! Ahead! Now! Ohh! Nearly! Left again! Right! By your elbow!"). The turkey in question ("Blue Gobbler") was a forty-six pound emu of a bird, and would not only do for the entire population of the village, but would provide stock-broth for the flasks of Ormsville Nesbit's shepherd until March.

4 Mrs Ambussway was able to read and write well enough, but Father Coptick, who baptised Agfnes, regularly put the "ill" into "illitterreight". At village coffee mornings, and in step with Mother Grundy's stoic philosophy, Mrs Ambussway pretends the unusual spelling is an aristocratic folly ("The F," she says, "is silent, as in hitting your thumb with a gardening hoe").

Fortunate Joe was the village shepherd, and he had got his name mainly due to the fact that it was he who enjoyed the regular, complimentary flasks of turkey broth right through until March. Joe, not over-blessed in cognitive faculties, had never really been able to reason out why this made him fortunate, or why he suffered from chronic gastro-enteritis each year from late February until early April.

Close on his heels came Less, the miller's son. Joe and Less slewed to a halt in Mother Grundy's parlour, and tried to contain themselves.

"There's a dead man up on Four Acres Paddock," squealed Joe, who was absolutely no good at all at self-containment.

"Shhh! Shhh!" hissed Less. Joe nodded.

"There's a dead man up on Four Acres Paddock," Joe whispered.

There was along pause, broken only by the logs coughing and spitting in the grate. Mother Grundy slowly turned away from Luckin Ambussway's tiny, gaping mouth and stood up.

"A dead man?" she queried, softly.

"All cold and dead. With a frost on him," Fortunate Joe gabbled.

"Shhh!" said Mother Grundy.

"All cold and dead. With a frost on him," Fortunate Joe repeated, quiet as a dormouse.

"I'd better see," murmured Mother Grundy. She patted Luckin Ambussway reassuringly on the head, and took down her shawl form the door peg.

Mother Grundy followed the excited men out into the village yard. Marble-cold, the night closed around them, steaming their breaths. Above, the sky was ludicrously heavy with stars.

"This had better not be another of your fairy stories, Fortunate Joe Clubbley," warned Mother Grundy.

"It isn't, ma'am, I swear. A dead man. Dead. In Four Acres Paddock. And dead."

"Come on," she said.

Fortunate Joe gathered up his crook and beckoned her on. Less the miller's son slammed the cottage door behind them.

"Owww!" came a little, muffled voice from within.

"Well, at least that's done with," said Mother Grundy.

The moon was up, swinging like a bright inn sign from the leafless branches of the black elms. Its bright glare reflected off the hoar frost around them, making the rime glint like diamond chips. Feckless hares, long-limbed and rangy, skittered around the crest of the hill under the lunatic glow.

Fortunate Joe led Mother Grundy and Less up the hard earth slope of the paddock. the ground rang hollow and dead as their pounding feet resonated the ancient rabbit warrens of the hill.

"There!" said Fortunate Joe at length, pointing with his crook. There was a stiff, crumpled shape on the frosty ground beneath the hilltop oak.

"Hmmph," said Mother Grundy, and instructed them both to stay where they were. She strode forward to the foot of the great, old tree.

The man was old and dirty, his face white and pinched. It was impossible to tell where his matted beard ended and the ground-frost began. His clothes were rags, black with grime, caked and swaddled around the bag of bones that was his body and limbs.

Mother Grundy knelt by him and reached out a hand to his cheek.

Stone cold.

She cautiously checked the folds of his matted garb. In one pocket, a knife, blunt and rusty, the hopeless designs of the bored and untalented decorating its scrimshaw handle. In another pocket, a pewter tobacco box, worn smooth by years of use, and a chunky, gold-plated signet ring. On one cuff, a last remaining button, clinging by a twist of thread, gave a clue to the garment's original nature. The button was brass, with the anchor mark of the Admiralty cut into it.

"So you were a mariner..." whispered Mother Grundy as she examined the button.

The corpse's eyes flicked open.

Mother Grundy didn't start or flinch. She adapted to the situation.

"Can you speak?" she asked.

He stared back: wild, bright eyes trapped in a dead face. His jaw moved, but his mouth would not open. It was as if it was frozen shut. Slowly, he shook his head.

She began to turn, to call to the others. "We'll get you to shelter, good fellow, and–"

He shook his head again and beckoned her close. He tapped at his sealed mouth for a moment in frustration, and then, after another shake of the head, held up three knotted fingers.

"Three?" Mother Grundy asked. "Three what? Three… words?"

A nod. One raised finger.

"First word? Two? Two what? Two two? Double?

An eager nod.

"Double then. Second word. Two syllables? First one… mouth? Lips?

He tapped his mouth and then chattered his fingers together stiffly in a biting gesture.

"Bit? Chew? Teeth? Yes? False teeth? False! I see. Double false…"

The old sailor tugged his collar up around his ears.

"False… what? Collar? Hood? Falsehood! Double falsehood!"

Another eager nod. Then he sank back again, fading.

"The third word?" she asked, leaning closer.

The fingers waved again.

"Three syllables. Second syllable… you're shaking your head. No? Is it "no"? Right, something-no-something. First syllable. Sounds like… What's that? Happy? Cheerful?"

The old man hugged himself and tried to look happy. His mouth, frozen, refused to smile.

"Contentment? Joy?"

A nod.

"Sounds like joy-no-something. What rhymes with joy? Boy? Cloy? Roy? Coy? Toy… like toy? Troy?

The eyes shone back at her.

"Troyno-something." There was a long pause. She sensed the desperation in him. The third syllable seemed beyond the capacity of mime. But she had enough. "Are you trying," she said, carefully, "to say 'Troynovant'?"

The eyes closed, relaxed.

"Troynovant," whispered Mother Grundy, to herself. "Troynovant and double falsehood. Why? What are you telling me?"

There was no answer, no movement.

She turned to the waiting men, ten paces behind her across the field.

"Help me here!" she called, urgently.

They made a bed of sacking in the corner by Mother Grundy's inglenook, and Less stoked up the hearth as Mother Grundy covered the stranger with a blanket.

"Will he live?" asked Fortunate Joe.

"I doubt it. Hunger, exposure and ague have all done their worst. And he is neither young nor strong. It is a miracle he has lived this long."

"Why has he come here? What was his message about?" Deep confusion screwed up Less's face into such a frown his forehead looked like a giant walnut. "No one comes to Ormsvile Nesbit unless they once left it. And I don't recognise him."

Mother Grundy arched her eyebrows. "You're not yet two score years, Less. If this ancient mariner ran off to sea, it may have been years before you were born. He may be coming home after a long time."

"But you're old, Mother Grundy," put in Joe. "Don't you recognise him? Hey now, what d'you kick me for, Less?"

"Manners," said Less.

"Right. Right. I didn't mean old as in rude, Mother, begging yours. I just meant–"

"I know what you meant, Joe Clubbley. Unfortunately, I don't recognise him, either. In the morning, I'll ask the senior members of the village. One of them might know him."

Mother Grundy dabbed the dirt from the man's haggard face with a cloth soaked in warm water. The frost matting his beard was melting away.

"Oh God's apples!" she whispered. "That's why he couldn't speak."

It was nearly midnight.

Mother Grundy rubbed her rheumy eyes and stabbed the sulky

fire with the poker. The old man had not stirred, but he was still breathing. Just.

"Who are you, ancient mariner?" she asked softly.

His possessions lay on the kitchen table: the knife, the tobacco tin, the ring. She sat and examined them by the light of the lamp. The tin was full of hard brown leaf, folded into a tight packet, ready to be teased out and thumbed into a pipe. The ring was a milled, Navy-commemoration coin, the type minted and issued to the crews of ships after famous engagements. It had been mounted on a crude finger-loop of brass. She studied the inscription. "Vivat Regina... by the grace of God... Finnisterre... 2003. "So, you're a hero as well as a mystery?"

The knife was a typical mariner's piece, an old clasp-blade whose wooden handle had been removed and replaced by a shank of scrimshaw. The amateur engravings had nearly been worn off by use and sea-salt. There was a four-master, a raging sea, a leviathan sperm whale spouting a geyser into the sky, and gulls. On the reverse side, a badly-spaced inscription: "HMS BLAYMLES" beneath which was the name, "Tobias Frewyr, Marnr."

"Blaymles. Blameless? Hmpph. And Frewyr's not a village name." The fire spat. Mother Grundy searched out her ink-pot, quill and writing paper. "I would know who you are, Tobias Frewyr. I would understand your double falsehood, and would dearly learn what you know of Troynovant. It's been years since I heard that mentioned. And I will know, Tobias, just as I will know who sewed up your mouth."

The sun came up at six and found itself blinded by the snow that had fallen in the night. Fortunate Joe yawned and stepped reluctantly out into the frozen landscape, his crook under his arm as he pulled on his mittens.

There seemed to be no shadows, no features. The snow smoothed everything away into an anonymous white.

"I'll never find the bloody sheep in this," Joe sighed.

A robin darted among the elder bushes in his garden, dislodging snow. Joe tore the corner off the loaf in his pocket and crumbed it out on the white ground. "There you go, Master Redbreast," said Joe with a simple smile.

The grateful robin fluttered down to the feast, and disappeared immediately under an angry, scolding scrum of thrushes, blackbirds and great tits that came out of nowhere.

Joe shrugged and made off up the lane towards the top pastures.

Mother Grundy was waiting for him at her gate.

"Did he die?" Joe asked.

"Not yet. He's sleeping. I… opened his mouth, fed him warm milk."

Joe shuddered, and it wasn't the cold. "Twas inhuman what was done to him."

Mother Grundy produced a sealed letter from her apron pocket and held it out. "I have a job for you, Joe Clubbley. I'll make sure Less looks to your flock for the while."

Joe eyed her doubtfully.

"I can't read, of course," he stated, pre-emptively.

"I want you to go to London and deliver this message," she told him.

Joe sat down hard on the stile. Then he stood up again, opened his mouth, closed it, and finally sat down once more.

"I've never been to that London," he managed at last. "I've never been to Bottom Shallowham. I've never left Ormsvile Nesbit, save as far as the top pastures, and once to Clitherington Heath after a moody ewe. In short, I've never been anywhere."

"In short, you're going. Consider it an education. My travelling days are over, and besides, I must tend to the stranger. In this weather, the post coach will be a week coming if it ever does. You must go, Joe Clubbley, and deliver this letter for me."

Joe looked at the letter.

"I can't read," he reminded her.

"Then remember. Number Seventeen, Amen Street, Soho, London. To be delivered into the hand of Sir Rupert Triumff."

"Triumff," he repeated. He took the letter and handed her his crook. "Right ho. Triumff."

**ANGRY
ROBOT**

Teenage serial killers
Zombie detectives
The grim reaper in love
Howling axes **Vampire
hordes** Dead men's
clones   The Black Hand
Death by cellphone
Gangster shamen
Steampunk swordfights
Sex-crazed bloodsuckers
Murderous gods
Riots **Quests** Discovery
Death

Prepare
to welcome
your new
Robot overlords.

angryrobotbooks.com

> FREE ON MP3 FOR EVERY READER – SEE INSIDE!

> **MOXYLAND**
> **Lauren Beukes**

> "A TECHNICOLOR JAZZY ROLLERCOASTER RIDE
> INTO A DAZZLING ...." – André Brink

SLIGHTS
KAARON WARREN

"Powerful stuff. So powerful, in fact, that my throat
was hurting with my attempts to keep my emotions
under control. I was completely drawn in, totally
immersed. I felt it much of the time."
– Russell Kirkpatrick, bestselling author of
ACROSS THE FACE OF THE WORLD

TIM WAGGONER

Introducing
Matt Richter.
Private Eye.
Zombie.

Nekropolis

"An atmospheric and exciting mystery." – SF Site

"Chris Roberson is a talented storyteller." – Michael Moorcock

CHRIS
ROBERSON

It holds the key to the mysteries of the ages, and everyone wants it.

BOOK OF
SECRETS

ANDY REMIC

KELL'S
LEGEND

BOOK 1 OF THE CLOCKWORK VAMPIRE CHRONICLES

"Remic delivers in the action stakes." – SciFi Now

J. ROBERT
KING

ANGEL
OF
DEATH

"King does everything well – characters,
prose, plot, humour, drama." – Locus